SIMPLY AN ENIGMA

SIMPLY AN ENIGMA

BRITTANY EVANS
CHELSEA LAUREN

REPRESENT
PUBLISHING

Cover Design by Brittany Evans
Cover Art by Sirle Kabanen
Edited by Mountains Wanted Publishing
Formatted by Chelsea Lauren

Dedicated to **her**, *without you this book would have never existed. And to anyone else who has ever felt broken—you are valid. You are whole. You belong. You matter.*

NOTE FROM THE AUTHORS

Simply An Enigma is an **own voice novel** on the subject of asexuality. The thoughts, feelings, and experiences of the asexual characters are a reflection of what the author *has* actually experienced, felt, or thought. It is in no regard a representation for the entire asexual community as everyone has different life experiences.

It should also be noted that our book is not suitable for all audiences. Our book consists of subjects such as sex, foul language, homophobia, slut-shaming, toxic masculinity, forced outing of a lesbian character, and sexual harassment. These topics may be difficult for some readers.

Reader's discretion is advised.

We do not agree with or believe any of the problematic topics discussed in our book. They are all solely used in a fictional sense. What the characters say or believe in this regard are not a mirror of what we believe.

JULIAN

YOU'D THINK I'D BE USED TO IT BY NOW. THE CRUDE JOKES, the pressure, the insincerity, what have you. But nope, here I was again in the same messed-up situation I always seem to be in. After school. Isabella's Coffee shop. In the midst of a teenage battle zone.

"Oh damn," James said, motioning his cup toward a tall brunette who was in line at the cafe.

"Nice ass," Tyler added.

I rolled my eyes. The girl was buying a small latte. She looked over her shoulder and smiled at us. Clearly, she knew we were checking her out. I offered a smile back as if to say, *Hi, sorry my friends are disgusting. I hope you enjoy your latte.*

"She looks easy." James ran his fingers through his over-gelled blond hair in an effort to make it stand up even straighter. "Why don't you go make a move?"

I shook my head. "Seriously, dude?"

"Don't be a pussy now."

"Yeah, bro," Tyler said.

"Hey now," I pointed at Tyler, "don't encourage him."

"Why not?" He smiled, challenging me.

"It's not like we're asking you to sleep with her. Well, not yet anyway." James winked. "Man up and go ask for her number."

"Alright. Fine." I stood from the table, faking confidence.

This wasn't me. I didn't do the whole asking a girl for her number. Hell, I didn't even do *talking* to girls. There wasn't enough self-esteem built up within me for any of that. Yet, here I was, walking away from the table, headed toward the brunette who was sitting with her friends. I was pretty sure she was at least three years older than me and a gazillion times out of my league.

"Go get some!" James yelled from behind me.

Thing is, they weren't always like this. I'd known these two since we were toddlers. Our dads were best friends, so we were best friends. We grew up playing soccer. It wasn't until high school that they turned into jackasses. James used to be the class clown but now was a perverted jock. Tyler used to be the reserved quiet one. Now he was basically James' minion. I, on the other hand, had always been an awkward mess of a human.

"Hey." I smiled at the brunette.

"Hi." She looked up from her cup. Not even a hint of a smile.

Good. This is going great.

Her friends exchanged a look, curious to know if their friend actually knew me.

"So why don't we do ourselves both a favor and you give me your number?" I tried to smile again, this time with my lips pressed too tightly together.

"Seriously?" Her voice was monotone.

"Yes?"

"No."

"Are you sur—"

"Yes."

"Alright. Good chat." I pivoted in place and headed back to my tables.

James leaned back in his chair, the two front legs lifted from the ground in a fit of laughter. Tyler smiled as he took a sip of his coffee.

"Well, that went well," I joked.

"Man," James wiped the tears out of his eyes, "that was brutal."

"Happy?" I sat down. "This is why I knew it was a bad idea."

"No, dude. You just need better practice. Wow," James said between laughs.

"If you keep that up, you'll never get laid," Tyler said.

"You aren't helping." I shook my head, sipping my hot chocolate.

"Oh ho! Look who it is!" James practically jumped with excitement as two girls came in, brushing past our table.

Tyler whistled. "Quinn Kennedy."

Fuck. I ducked my head down. *Not her.*

It wasn't like she had any idea she was essentially a moving target in the eyes of James and Tyler. I really didn't have a reason to hide from her. I'd never spoken two words to her.

It was James and Tyler I should have been running from right then, except I couldn't. They may have been awful, but we'd been friends forever. Or maybe it was because I really just wanted to get through high school alive, and they were my safety net. Either way, I couldn't help but hide from Quinn. For the past month, she had been James and Tyler's top choice for disposing my virginity.

"Well, well, well. Fancy seeing Quinn here. Could it be perhaps—fate?" James smirked at me.

"Mhm, yes. That's what this is, I'm sure." I tried to play it off. "Or is it fate that Paige Brooks is here with her, James?"

"Hey now. It's no secret I have my eyes on Paige. This is about you." He held his cup up, pointing a finger at me. "We see her at Emerald's parties every Friday. Now she shows up at our hangout spot? You're missing ample opportunity to ask her out, dude."

Emerald was the captain of the football team. His real name was Joseph Hantus, but our group of friends created the nickname when he got his ear pierced. He started wearing an awful green earring, and the nickname just sort of stuck.

"And what if I don't want to ask her out?"

"Dude, you want to get laid, don't you?"

I mean, sure. I guess I do? These two sure made it seem like I *should* want to. Except I honestly didn't care. I didn't get the sense that I was missing out on anything in life just because I'd never had sex before. It wasn't something I thought about outside of their harassment. Come to think of it—I didn't think about sex at all. When watching movies with sex scenes I got uncomfortable, and sex jokes, for the most part, went over my head. But I'd always figured that was because I wasn't in the loop of "those who have had intercourse."

"Hey, Paige, Quinn." James waved the girls over as they grabbed their coffees.

"Hey, James." Paige smiled, brushing her brown braid over her shoulder.

She sat on the empty chair beside him. James began bullshitting some conversation about tennis, despite the fact he knew nothing about tennis. Quinn just stood there looking down at me. It wasn't often I saw her with her hair down, her massive red curls falling to her elbows.

I was about to ask *what?* when she pointed at the booth I was sitting in. *Right.* She probably wanted to sit down. I scooted over, closer to Tyler, to give her room, unable to look back at her. She sat down, fiddling with the brim of her cup, seemingly focused on Paige and James' conversation.

Okay, Julian, don't panic here. Yes, Tyler was full on staring at me with this stupid grin on his face like I just pulled the winning hand in a game of poker. *God, why am I short of breath? Nothing is happening. Calm down.*

"Hey," I said to Quinn.

"Hey," she said before instantly turning to face Paige again.

What am I doing? What am I thinking? Like I didn't want to have sex with Quinn. Why did I feel inclined to even start a conversation with her? Was it because James and Tyler expected me to? Or maybe because I knew she was the captain of the girls' soccer team, and I'd seen her play. Her talent bypasses James', our captain, easily. I wanted to ask her how she does it. But then again, I was just a regular defense man. She'd probably take pity on me.

I tugged at the strands of hair that hung in my face. I didn't want to start anything. Quinn was just someone I went to school with. I heard she sleeps around a lot. Even if she did, I didn't care. Made no difference to me what she did and didn't do.

"Should we head to Emerald's now?" Quinn asked, and Paige nodded.

"See ya there." James winked at Paige.

God. The dreaded Emerald's.

QUINN

EVERYONE GATHERED AROUND IN THE DARKENED DEN OF Emerald's house. His house was the place to be. Emerald's parents were from Haiti—having traveled here before Emerald was born to be doctors—so they were loaded. They had a finished den decked out with a wooden bar, flat screen television, leather couches, and a pool table. I hardly remember when the tradition started, but it started with five of us: me, Emerald, Marie, Liza, and Adrian. We became a tight-knit group at the end of sixth grade when the five of us always wanted to be outside playing any type of sport possible (well, minus Marie, who was our cheerleader). Come high school, our group expanded when we met new students on our own respective sports teams. There used to be thirteen of us all together, but in tenth grade, Ian and my ex-friend Liza stopped coming.

Sure, I did enjoy these hangouts. They were all still my friends. But a part of me wondered how many people showed up because it was expected versus those who genuinely wanted to be there. I knew Marie and Emerald were here because they thrived on these gatherings. But there were a few others—myself included—who seemed bored or even bothered by having to come. Julian Raskin was one of them.

Julian seemed different than the rest of us and often was quite reserved. Like, at the cafe earlier, he could barely even say hi. While I've barely spoken to him, I've always been intrigued by him. The day he joined the group in ninth grade with his side-kicks, Tyler Russo, James Clayton, and Ian Kugel, he seemed out of place—the black sheep of the group, you might say. Even after two years, I didn't know who Julian was, whereas I knew everyone else in this group. I even knew Ian better than Julian.

Marie was playing host, as she often did. As Emerald's girl-friend, she had made it her job to ensure every guest was topped off with their drink of choice. We had alcohol—the bar was always stocked. And we had those who drank it, but in all honesty, it wasn't that kind of hangout. People at school assumed we were trashed every weekend, but rarely did it ever get that rowdy. Those who wanted to be invited had a way of creating a scene far more rebellious than we were.

Besides, if I was coming home drunk *every* weekend, my parents wouldn't allow me to go to Emerald's. They knew I was responsible in my choices. My household was, for the most part, a secret-free home. My parents knew who I hung out with and when—even when I was drunk.

As Marie finished circling the crowd, topping off my Dr. Pepper, we started to gather around in more of a circle.

"All right, are we playing truth or dare or spin the bottle?" Marie asked, sitting down in her usual spot right next to me.

I let out a laugh, which only erupted louder by her confused face.

"You're serious?" I tried to stifle my laughs. "What are we? In middle school? We're fucking juniors, for god's sake."

"Quinn." She let out a dramatic sigh, rolling her bright blue eyes. Marie may have been my best friend, but that didn't mean I didn't get annoyed by her antics. "We never do anything fun. So tonight, we are spicing things up."

My eyes scanned the room. All eleven of us were present, no shocker there. One didn't dare miss a Friday night. We often had FIFA and NFL tournaments we took very seriously—losers had to chip in to buy coffee for the champion the following week.

Those tournaments were what I loved about Emerald's, but lately, it seemed as if people were growing disinterested in them —case in point—Marie trying to switch up the night.

I seemed to be the only one who didn't like the change of pace. Well, me and Julian. He wasn't paying attention to what was going on, his eyes looking around the room with an emotionless expression.

"I thought you loved spin the bottle, Q. Weren't you the one in eighth grade who made out with B.O. Brian?" Emerald so happily reminded the group.

Truth was, I *hated* this game.

"Just because I played in middle school, doesn't mean I want to now."

"What? Are we not good enough to kiss?" James laughed.

"What if we combine spin the bottle and truth or dare?" Marie suggested, thankfully turning the topic slightly off-focus. Either option was bad though—so why both?

Emerald dropped an empty Captain Morgan's rum bottle in the middle of the circle. He then pulled Marie closer to him, his broad arms enveloping her petite frame.

"Oh yeah!" Adrian from across the room said, "I did this at another party a few weeks back. So, for example, you would spin the bottle, and the person to your right would decide between truth or dare or kissing the person the bottle landed on. The person up would be able to choose between truth or dare if kissing wasn't chosen. We can have fun with it." He made eye contact with me from across the circle before winking.

I shifted my gaze over to Marie. "I'm getting a beer," I told her, avoiding Adrian's stare.

I was regretting my decision to only have soda tonight. Who actually wanted to play this sober? I opened the fridge and reached for a beer, still in earshot of the group.

"Oh! That sounds awesome," Marie said. "Obviously, boundaries for a kiss, it has to happen from the neck up."

"And if we forfeit?" I heard Julian ask, stopping me dead in my tracks.

"Consider a rumor to be spread about tonight." Adrian smirked, making note to focus on each person in the room before taking a gulp of his beer. His eyes lingered on me as I slowly trekked back to the circle.

The group murmured with excitement. It wasn't that we were mean or that we were out to ruin each other's reputations (well, aside from Adrian); it was usually all fun and games. However, from experience, we knew Adrian wasn't lying. If we didn't follow through on what was asked of us, a rumor would be spread, starting in the locker room during his football practice. For everyone else, it was a simple rumor—something silly like cheating on a test or even cheating on someone they were dating. But for me, my reputation was compromised because of the rumors Adrian spread—or even the overdramatized truth that was no one's business but my own and the person involved.

Julian nodded, but I didn't miss the bob of his Adam's apple before he took a drink from his plastic cup.

How did I always get myself into these situations?

We started with Paige, the tennis team captain, who could pull off wearing a full face of makeup or showcasing her freckles, and all the girls still wanted to be her. We weren't really close, but sometimes, like today, if she needed a ride to Emerald's, I'd pick her up, and we'd always grab tea beforehand. She was sitting to Adrian's left. This way he could show us what it was like to be the person who determined your fate—as if we didn't already know. He started off gently. Paige asked for a truth, and he asked her if she ever would consider dating James. There were oohs and ahhs as she blushed and answered yes, and I knew it would be used against her (or for her) in the coming rounds if it could be.

My eyes flickered across the circle to Julian and James high-fiving, which only deepened Paige's blush. I narrowed my eyes, focusing in on James, catching the wink he gave Paige.

I immediately wanted to shake Paige and ask her what the hell she saw in that douchebag.

I was grateful I was near the end of the circle we had started. I was able to happily block out a majority of it. Nothing worse than a kiss with tongue was suggested—until James was dared to kiss Paige. James being the gentleman he was—went all in, seemingly forgetting we were all there.

"My man!" Adrian lifted his cup and leaned into the circle to toast with James as soon as he separated from Paige. "Gotta appreciate a guy who goes above and beyond!" James' smile grew even bigger.

It was subtle; no one in the group was paying attention, but Julian's eyes rolled at this obnoxious interaction of whose dick was the biggest. He spun the bottle without waiting for the group to be ready. The nose of the bottle pointed toward me. I jumped as I heard Marie's excited glees. My stomach sank as I tried to connect eyes with him. His dark eyes nervously flashed up to meet mine, slightly hidden beneath his shaggy black hair, before looking back down. James sitting next to him had a glimmer in his eyes.

"I want you to make out with Quinn."

Julian finally made eye contact with me, and if I wasn't mistaken, there was an uneasy look in his eyes. I was rarely looked at with apprehension. I never thought twice about Julian in that way, but who was he to think negatively of me?

"W-what?" I muttered. "In front of everyone? We aren't like James."

"Of course!" Marie was grinning from ear to ear. It almost felt like this was rigged. Out of nowhere a couple weeks back, she started talking about how cute Julian and I would be together. "Would you be more comfortable in the closet?"

"Yes," Julian said.

James laughed. "A closet? Dude, you're only getting kissed."

Was he hoping if we were in the closet that we wouldn't actually have to kiss? Could we lie to our friends?

"Or you could forfeit." Adrian grinned, rubbing his hands together, no doubt already thinking of a rumor.

I prayed that Julian wouldn't forfeit. My hope was he paid enough attention to recognize that Adrian treated me differently from everyone else. I couldn't blame him if he didn't. All Julian knew was Adrian—the football jock—that he had morphed into during ninth grade. Julian never knew the guy who was once my best friend—my boyfriend of two years even. If I hardly knew Julian, my best guess was that he only saw me as Quinn Kennedy —the quick, easy lay.

Adrian had taken his personal anger toward me and turned my reputation into a lie. He started a rumor in this room the night we expanded our group fall of Freshman year. The new friends quickly heard that eighth grade Quinn slept with a senior. The following Monday, the rumor spread like wildfire. What was this young girl doing having sex with an older man? What was this girl doing having sex in general?

The original group knew the truth—well, up until I *did* start having sex. Now I wasn't sure what they believed, but it was pointless to try and convince them any differently. For the most part now, the rumor mill held truths about me—but I wasn't here to confirm or deny them. I didn't have the energy.

So why did I stick around? They all became my friend for

one reason or another, and I wasn't a person who easily let people go. I was a sucker for second and third chances because I believed everyone was capable of being better than the day before. And it always seemed like every time I was ready to walk away, there'd be that one great Friday night. It'd remind me of middle school when nothing mattered but having a laugh with friends with no drama or rumors attached.

"No, we won't," I said as Julian's silence continued. I pushed myself up from the floor.

"Just go to the bathroom," Emerald said. "The closets are packed."

"Remember, Quinn, we are just kissing here. Try not to deflower our precious friend just yet," James teased.

JULIAN

OF COURSE.

If there were an award for most likely to have awful things happen to them, I'd be the top contender. Sure, kissing was harmless. Sure, this was just some lame game. Nothing life-threatening. It was the fact that it was *Quinn* the bottle landed on.

Yay ... cue James and Tyler harassing me in three, two, one ....

Tyler and James exchanged a glance, grins plastered across their faces.

James nudged my arm, "Go get her, Tiger."

Mhm. Yep, he did actually say that. I rolled my eyes.

I wish Ian were here. He used to be all the time. He'd find me a way out of this, get Tyler and James off my back. Except, he wasn't, and I was stuck dealing with these two idiots on my own. This was so much more than spin the bottle to them. It was their golden ticket to get me laid. Apparently, I wasn't a real "man" until I did. Because, sure, that's the only thing that distinguishes who is a man and who isn't. Not like trying to be a mature human being qualifies.

I wished the old James and Tyler would come back. I kept hoping they would, and in the times we just hung out, sometimes they were. But James cranked up his douchebag level by a million whenever Adrian was around. I hated that James fed on Adrian's approval and praise. Like it would bring him higher up on the bogus rank of popularity. And I hated that Tyler just went along with it. He was the same as me in that regard, though. Didn't want to get burned, just wanted to survive high school. But he literally just followed James around.

I sighed. I'd forfeit if I could, but—my eyes shifted to James and Tyler. Frankly, Tyler probably would drop it if I said I didn't want to. But James, on the other hand, he harassed me enough as it was. I didn't need to add fuel to the fire. Like I said—it was just kissing. Nothing life-threatening. I would be fine. I hoped.

I stood up, clenching and unclenching my fists. *Remember, just kissing.* But the look on James' face suggested he expected me to do a little more than just that. The lips that would be touching mine were Quinn Kennedy's after all. Quinn was already standing, and I realized how much shorter she was than me. If things weren't awkward enough, I would also tower over her when we kissed, even with my shoulders hunched.

"Well ... shall we?" I smiled, gesturing to the bathroom.

Quinn furrowed her brows. She looked pissed. Like I wanted to be doing this either. She headed to the bathroom without even looking to see if I was following behind.

I closed the door behind us. Honestly, I'm thankful Emerald suggested this instead of a closet. At least there's light in here. And it smelled like lavender as opposed to worn-out shoes. Though, it wasn't much bigger than a closet would have been. There was just enough space for us to stand comfortably without touching one another. Quinn was leaning up against the glass shower in front of me with her arms crossed.

Quinn was pretty, don't get me wrong, but if I had known tonight would lead to this, I would have tried to stay home. I was awkward enough on my own, to begin with; I didn't need anyone throwing me into uncomfortable situations. The only reason I even came was that it was expected of me since I was friends with Tyler and James. It was like a routine I couldn't escape. Even if I had said I was staying in tonight, they would have shown up at my place and dragged me here if they had to.

Quinn was looking up at me, her lips pressed together. What exactly was supposed to happen next? I've kissed girls before, but in the spur of the moment, not because I was demanded to. It was natural in those situations. Here, not so much. Did we talk first? Did we just kiss and leave without a single word exchanged? Or did we stand here in silence long enough to have everyone believe we kissed? What was she thinking? What did she want to actually happen? She *was* known as the "school slut." I heard she lives for this sort of stuff—that in these situations, she'd push me against the wall and start going at it.

We just have to kiss, Julian. That's it. God, what do I do?

I felt awkward just keeping eye contact with her. I shifted my eyes around the room to the flower pot on top of the toilet, to the toothbrush holder on the sink, to the bottles of shampoo I could see through the shower door. Anywhere but her gaze burning through me.

"You have two options." Her voice startled me, bringing my eyes back to her. "One: we lie, or two: we kiss. The question is, how good of a liar are you? Because if anyone finds out, and it gets back to Adrian, you can bet your scrawny ass he'll ruin both of our lives. And that," she started to tie her thick red curls up in a ponytail as her brown eyes pierced my own, "is not something I need."

"Uh ... I," I started to say. I opened my mouth again then closed it.

What the hell. What am I even supposed to say to that? I forced my lips together. I never thought of having to lie. I could picture what would happen if I left this bathroom without kissing

Quinn. I would go back to my spot between James and Tyler. They would exchange looks with me, searching for some verification that I got to second base. I'd give them a cheesy smile. That'd be enough for them to get riled up. But I expected that to be the end of it. Except, knowing them, they wouldn't leave it at that. They would likely talk about this day for eons after.

"What? You don't know how to talk?" Quinn mocked.

So I kissed her. I cupped her face in my hands and shoved my lips at her. They collided with a force that was slightly painful. Our lips moved together completely out of sync. The kiss was sloppy, wet, and uncomfortable. I couldn't even tell which one of us was the bad kisser—or maybe it was both of us. Maybe we were just that incompatible. *It'll be over soon*, I told myself. *It'll all be done in a moment.*

One.

Two.

Three.

I counted in my head.

Four.

Five.

I pulled away, my hands still lingering on her cheeks. She stood straight, her arms still at her sides, her face completely void of emotion. I had no idea if she was pissed off at me or if she secretly enjoyed that. I was also not sure which of those I preferred.

This time it was her turn to fumble. Her mouth opened and closed. As she opened it again, she exhaled loudly. She stepped closer, rising on her tippy toes. Pulling my neck down, she connected our lips again. This time, it was slower. She was in control. She was the guide, and my lips followed her lead. Just as it felt like we could be on the same wavelength, she pulled away, creating space between us.

Holy fuck. Yep, it was just me who was the bad kisser.

"Okay," she nodded. "Just had to make sure you actually *knew* how to kiss. Boy, was that rough."

Before I had a chance to respond, her fingers were knotting through my hair, shaking it slightly. She then bumped me back against the wall, so she could stand in front of the mirror. Quinn tousled her hair, messing up her ponytail. "Have to make it look like we got a little naughty." She winked at me in the mirror.

I let out an awkward laugh. "Well, I guess we should go back then—"

Before I even finished my sentence, Quinn was brushing past me out of the room.

QUINN

THE MOMENT I OPENED THE BATHROOM DOOR, ALL murmuring stopped. Everyone was looking right at me.

Breathe in, Quinn. Do it for Julian.

"You coming, Julian?" I plastered a "cute" smile on my face, looking over my shoulder.

Startled, he was directly behind me. I interlaced our fingers—not even close to being near the same size—and walked us back to the circle.

James and Tyler were grinning like schoolboys with their first crush. Marie's eyes burned a hole through our handholding, so I gave Julian's hand a squeeze, feeling his grow clammy.

"Thanks, Julian." I winked up at him before dropping his hand and walking back over to my spot, a slight pep to my step.

"There's my man!" James exclaimed, clapping Julian on the back when he sat down. "What happened in there?"

Marie nudged me, but my focus remained on them. As did most of the group. They were desperate to know what happened.

"No way in hell you guys just kissed," James taunted. "Just look at her hair."

"Seriously," Tyler said, agreeing with James.

All eyes focused on me as I quickly pushed my hair back with my hands.

Julian half-smiled at this, his hands smoothing down his own hair. "I knew it!" James said. "Second or third base?"

Still smiling, he responded, "Hey, I'm not one to kiss and tell."

I let out a sigh of relief. *Smart.* Not lying but avoiding the truth.

I played the act of needing to undo my hair tie and fix the loose strands. I accentuated what most definitely didn't happen between us as all eyes fell back to Julian.

"How was it?" Marie nudged again, her words luckily in a whisper.

"Julian's great." I smiled, catching a flicker of his eyes, but they couldn't hold my stare. "Tyler's turn." I smirked, changing the topic, hoping he'd get some shitty dare too.

After Tyler, it was Marie and Emerald's turn before mine. All I wanted was to go home.

Tyler spun the bottle, paying no mind as he watched James pressure Julian into giving him more information. Julian held on to his knees while staring at the ceiling, allowing his two friends to make up their own assumptions. He avoided my gaze like it'd make him blind, but without confirming or denying anything, his friends only got more excited.

"Ooh! Tyler got Martin," Adrian exclaimed, stopping all side conversation.

Martin swigged the last of his beer, neck craned, his brown curls tumbling back as he got the last drip. A hint of a smirk was revealed as he placed his bottle on the ground.

Tyler shifted uncomfortably, rubbing his hands across his buzzed hair. It was Julian's turn to grin, sitting up a little.

"Truth or dare, Tyler?"

He cleared his throat, "Truth."

I sat up a little higher myself, eager to witness someone else's awkward moment.

"Would you ever kiss Martin?" Julian asked.

I tried to keep my face straight at the balls Julian had. Tyler's tanned skin turned a deep shade of red, while Martin's pale skin didn't show a hint of shame. Martin Foster was the only gay kid in our group—he wasn't often given any shit, but James and Tyler were known to crack some jokes here and there. Yet, Martin never batted an eye.

"Hell no," Tyler forced out, his entire demeanor changing.

I looked over at Marie, who raised her brow at me. At least I wasn't the only one feeling the tension.

"Why would you even ask me that, dude? I'm not gay!" Tyler said.

Julian held up his hands in defense, but I could see his amusement.

"Emerald, spin. Anyone need a beer?" he asked, standing up from the circle, walking over to the fridge.

With force, he pulled out his own beer, then grabbed one for Adrian, Emerald, and even Martin, who motioned for one, before slamming the fridge.

"Thanks, Ty," Martin winked as Tyler handed him a beer.

Everyone laughed, breaking the tension, except for Tyler, who scoffed, handing out the other beers before sitting back down. Martin was undeniably comfortable with who he was, and despite any criticisms he received, he always brushed it off.

Emerald took a sip of his new beer before spinning the bottle. Tyler took a few sips before asking Emerald to share what most annoyed him about Marie, and because of that, Emerald asked Marie the same question. After Marie answered, the two of them were sharing a kiss and giggling.

Suddenly, Marie was bumping my shoulder, motioning toward the bottle. Even though I had been watching it all happen before me, I wasn't there. I had been watching Julian, who was keeping his eye on Tyler. James and Tyler, however, carried on a conversation as if Julian wasn't there.

Marie nudged me again before I finally spun the bottle. Lo and behold, it landed on Julian. His eyes instantly shot over to meet mine.

"Great," I muttered, only low enough for Marie to shoot me a glance before smirking. This game *was* rigged.

"Yes!" she yelled. "You're doing a dare."

"I'm sorry, what?" I turned toward her with furrowed brows. "I get to choose."

"Well, I'm changing the rules, and everyone agrees with me. We've already all spoken about it." Marie gave me her best grin that I wanted to slap off her face.

"What the hell is going on?"

I looked over at Julian again, but this time, his focus was on the bottle, as if everything *was* the bottle's fault.

"We all want you and Julian to go on a proper date," Marie stated—leaving no room for argument.

"No. We do dares that end tonight." I sat up straight, crossing my arms.

"Well, if that's the case, then you two are free to leave." Emerald flashed his pearly whites, motioning for us to shoo.

"No. This is stupid," I grunted, pushing myself up from the floor.

"What, Quinn? Afraid a date will ruin your rep? Or are all of your sister's college friends keeping you too busy?" Adrian ran his hands over his perfectly styled hair, accessorized with a shit-eating grin.

Chills ran down my spine at his words.

"It's no secret you like 'em older." I narrowed my eyes at him, but he challenged my contact. It's impossible to win against Adrian.

I downed the rest of my beer and walked away to gather my things.

"I don't need this. Believe what you want, Adrian, but you know the truth."

"He has a point, Quinn."

I froze when Marie spoke. Weren't best friends supposed to stand up for one another? With my bag in my hand, I spun on my foot toward her.

"I bet you can't be in a relationship. You don't know how. Honestly, it may be time to learn. Clean up that rep for those scouting you for soccer."

I swallowed her words, avoiding her gaze as I looked around the room to focus on those I considered my friends. My focus landed on Julian. He hadn't spoken a word since my spin landed on him. I expected him to look thrilled; he had the prime opportunity for an easy lay, right? That seems to be all he and his friends talk about. But his eyes were on me, and the look on his face wasn't excitement. It was concern. Concern for me or his own wellbeing? That, I couldn't tell.

"Screw you guys," I mumbled before walking away and up the den stairs.

No one would run after me. No one would apologize. Everyone would continue to play the game or hang out, then continue on their merry way the next day.

ONLY JULIAN and I would be the ones to have our lives changed this weekend by the demanded date. Despite walking out on them, I knew I'd wake up to a message about either the details of the date happening or when the date needed to happen before a rumor was spread. Either way, I didn't like the control they had over my life.

My sister Emma and her boyfriend were home by the time I

got there. Our parents were out with some friends. It was only nine-thirty, and our parents had more of a social life than my sister and I did.

"Hey, Q. What'cha doing home?" Kenny, my sister's boyfriend, asked. He paused the movie they were watching, *Spider-Man: Homecoming*. They both sat up, Kenny's arm adjusting around Emma.

"Everything okay, babe?" Emma asked.

I took a seat in the armchair across from them on the couch and dropped my bag.

"Just usual drama. Wasn't having it tonight, so I left." I shrugged my shoulders before leaning over to grab the popcorn bowl from the coffee table.

"Was Adrian there?" Emma asked.

"Always is." I popped some popcorn into my mouth.

"Why do you let Adrian control you the way he does?" Kenny asked.

Kenny had been dating my sister for just over two years. He was around right after my rep changed but was too new to our family to form any opinions. But now, he was always up to date with everything happening in this family.

Even when I spoke to my sister privately.

I'd hate her for it if I didn't love Kenny so much. And no, not like that. Don't listen to the rumors.

"I'm not being controlled. And it isn't just Adrian who sucks. I don't know. I may just be out-growing my friends." I ate some more popcorn. "Can we just watch this movie? I'm crashing your date." I smiled with kernels in my mouth.

My sister patted the empty space next to her. I jumped off my seat and cuddled into her side.

Kenny started the movie again. And instead of being the slut who went to Alpine High, I was just the girl wishing I was the Liz to Peter Parker.

I WOKE up to a phone call and then a text when I missed it. Marie told me to meet her for coffee in half an hour. After I responded that I'd be there, I checked the other notifications on my phone. I had a text message from a number I didn't know.

> *Hey its Julian. Marie gave me*
> *your number and address.*
> *2pm today. I'm picking you up*
> *OR ELSE. (Adrian told me I had*
> *to put that last part)*

Fuck. There was a part of me that hoped it was all a fun prank. I had hoped that me leaving had actually changed things, and they canceled the dare. But I didn't have that type of luck.

And Julian, well, Julian doesn't deserve to be stood up. I tried to think about what I did know about Julian. Aside from him being quiet, I knew he played defense on the boys' soccer team, and he was friends with James and Tyler. I was also pretty sure James and Tyler were responsible for any dick situation Julian had been in since he joined our group. It seemed unlikely that Julian could be capable of hurting another person.

I dragged myself out of bed after messaging a simple, *okay*, noting that I had about three hours to get coffee and then get ready for my date.

God, I hope this date goes well.

I threw on some jeans and a t-shirt, only taking time to pile my hair into a messy bun before I left my bedroom. On Saturdays, Marie and I often went to our favorite café, Isabella's Coffee, and then we'd hang out the rest of the day. It was usually a refresher from the night before, reminding me of how much I did care for her.

Today would be different though. I knew as much when I walked into the cafe, right on time, and Emerald was sitting next to Marie. He never joined us on Saturday mornings.

I ordered a green tea latte and a warmed croissant before sitting across from them. "What's going on?" I asked.

They barely had a millimeter of space between them in the booth. Marie's hand brushed against Emerald's as she grabbed her half of their shared buttered bagel.

"Nice to see you too, Quinn." Emerald smirked, taking a sip of his black coffee. I kicked him under the table.

"What the hell was that last night?" I ripped off a piece of my croissant and shoved it in my mouth.

"Don't hate us," Marie started, brushing the crumbs off her fingers before she wrapped her manicured hands around her mug. "We've all been kind of talking. And then it was fate when the bottle landed on you."

I laughed as she played the fate card, watching as bits of my croissant landed on the table.

"Look, Quinn, you can't seem to hold a relationship, and Julian, well, he's a bit inexperienced, and his friends want to help him out."

My mouth dropped. "You're whoring me out!" I yelled.

"No, no." Marie's words were slow as she glanced around the cafe before flipping her blonde hair behind her shoulders. "We just think it would be good for you to be in a relationship. Try it out. Clean up that rep."

My stomach dropped, and I sat back from my croissant. Was this her admitting she believed how I lost my virginity? Was she taking Adrian's word over mine?

"It's not my fault I have a rep."

Emerald shifted in his seat, avoiding eye contact. Marie tried to reach for my hand "in comfort" across the table, but I pulled my hands away.

"The group has a bet going." My words just slipped right off her back. "No one thinks you're capable of lasting at least four months in a relationship."

I blinked back to Marie, processing her words.

"Are you fucking kidding me?" If we weren't in public, I would have sacrificed my croissant, so I could throw it at her.

"Relax, Q. This will be good for the both of you," Emerald interjected.

"You love a good challenge. You and I both know that you'll fight to win this, and who knows? Maybe you'll be thanking us in the end."

I hated when Marie decided to know me so well. She was often selective with our friendship, despite knowing me for years. But I was one of the most competitive people I knew.

I looked at the two of them. Both had devious smiles. It was true that I wouldn't back out of this. I refused to fail.

I screeched my chair backward. "I can last six months easily. Just watch."

Grabbing my latte and croissant, I turned away from them, walking out of the cafe.

On the drive home, I only felt slightly bad that I was warping the bet and dragging Julian along with me. They wouldn't win—I wouldn't let them. I knew I didn't need a relationship, but I *never* half-assed a bet. I could make this happen and do so with a smile on my face.

Besides, how bad could Julian be? He had an opportunity to forfeit and let Adrian spread more rumors about me, but he had chosen not to.

It could also be nice to have someone consistent to keep going to. It wasn't that I couldn't keep a relationship like everyone believed. I just got bored easily. I did have a few relationships that lasted about a month—the longest being two months. But I never understood settling down in high school. Why was it frowned upon that I wanted to date around? Flirt, kiss, sleep with different people to really understand who I wanted to be with?

It was difficult to remain with one person in high school, too. I knew in middle school I had a high sex drive. Sure, I didn't know what that meant. I barely understood the logistics of sex. But I had learned through the privacy of my own internet what masturbating was and how I loved doing it. I had also learned the shame in it all too—finding the crevices of the internet and knowing it wasn't something *okay* for a girl to be doing or talking about.

When I felt ready to have sex for the first time, it became abundantly clear that teenagers were all on different levels. Some loved sex; some still hadn't hit puberty; others were waiting for marriage; and others didn't care—when it happened, it happened. But being in a relationship felt like it was so serious, and I had learned fast that if I wanted to have sex, I'd have to be proactive and find people who also wanted to.

Relationships in high school seemed to mean you waited longer for sex—which is cool; I respected that. But it wasn't me. It also was clear that as a girl, double standards were placed on me. If I liked sex, I was a whore. If I didn't like sex, I was a prude. I tried to fall in the middle, tried to remain neutral to the unwanted commentary.

Julian, though, when I really thought about it, might be able to work. So far, he was hard to crack. The puzzle would keep me busy. The most we had ever spoken was yesterday in the bathroom. Would we even be able to carry a conversation today?

When I got home, I took to getting ready. Julian's vague text message was absolutely no help in my decision of what to wear. So, after a shower, I determined casual was the best. Besides, I never dressed to impress anyone—Julian wouldn't be the exception. Dressing in my dark jeans, a V-neck, and tennis shoes, I let my curls dry with just a little product, keeping them free today. With just some mascara, I was ready to go. I grabbed a sweater, just in case, and then found myself waiting in the living room with my parents.

I *never* waited for a boy.

JULIAN

I PULLED UP TO WHAT I BELIEVED TO BE QUINN'S HOUSE. I double-checked Google maps on my phone before I looked up and saw her red hair from the large window at the front of her house; I figured it was the living room. I sat with the engine still running, louder than I knew it should be. It was an old Ford SUV my dad gave me when he got a new car, so it's all I had.

Should I go to the door? Should I wait here? What do people even do for dates? Usually, I just asked a girl to the movies and met her there. But Adrian insisted I pick Quinn up. Not only that, but he told me it couldn't be a typical date. Dinner and a movie weren't enough to fulfill the dare. Not even kidding— Adrian texted me a list of rules for our date:

1. Pick her up
2. Something interesting. No typical dinner or movie.
3. Be a man. Not the awkward thing you are now.
4. Has to be Saturday (the day after the dare).

The list continued. *No promises on that third one, Adrian.*

How did I even wind up in this situation? Why the hell was it

Marie Garca of all people to suggest this? I expected something like that to come from James or Tyler. But Marie? *What?* And to say *everyone* wanted us to go on a date? I didn't get it.

I stayed up all night thinking about it. I knew what Tyler and James expected me to do. They wanted me to take her for a walk or to the park, and when we got tired, suggest going back to my place to *get it on*. But that didn't seem right. I could and would do better than that. They may have wanted me to use this opportunity to get laid, but I didn't want to. Not that I'd tell them that.

It may have taken me all night, but I came up with a date plan. I just hoped Quinn would enjoy it as much as I would. When thinking about a date plan, I realized just how little I even knew about Quinn. All I knew was what I'd heard—and that was nothing but her sex life.

Dammit. Why couldn't Adrian have just thought up the date? I sighed.

What was everyone's obsession with sex? I never understood it. *Is something wrong with me?* Maybe once I'd finally done it, I would see what the big deal was. Except I didn't really care to find out. I never had.

Quinn's face peeked out the window. *Shit.* I probably looked like a pedo just sitting in her driveway staring at her window. I texted her immediately.

Here.

Coming.

A few moments passed before Quinn appeared at the doorway and at my car. She jumped into the passenger side. The second her body was in my car, I was consumed by her scent. She smelled of lavender with a hint of vanilla. It wasn't overpowering, but it masked the cigarette smoke from when my dad used to own my car.

"Hey." I smiled as she buckled her seatbelt.

"Hey." She gave me a quick smile, readjusting her curls as she settled in the seat.

It wasn't until she entered the car that I realized how quiet it was. I turned up the stereo to hear the CD I still had in.

Suddenly, she threw her head back and laughed.

"Problem?" I asked, raising my eyebrows. I looked over quickly before backing out of her driveway. But I caught her amused look.

"*You* listen to heavy metal?"

I pressed my lips together. "What is that supposed to mean? What do you listen to, country or something?"

"No. Well, sometimes." She shook her head and positioned herself in the seat, turning toward me. "But that's not the point. The point is that you, of all people, don't strike me as the heavy metal guy. You seem more like you'd enjoy some emo band or something."

"Emo band? Wow. First of all, it's called pop-punk. Get it right if you're going to insult me." I heard her snort beside me, but I continued anyway, "Secondly, Slayer is amazing. The better question is who *doesn't* like them?" I joked. "Since when do you need to be a certain type of person to enjoy something?"

She was silent for a moment. I could feel her eyes watching me.

"You don't." Her words were soft.

An awkward silence filled the car.

Great. I hope I didn't offend her. I was just trying to joke around. Maybe a change of topic would be better. I racked my brain for something to talk about, but nothing came up.

Come on, Julian, there's gotta be something you two have in common.

"So, uh, when's your next game?" I asked. "Soccer, I mean."

"Tuesday!" she exclaimed, turning toward me. "Against Riverhead. Have you played them yet this season? Fuck, I'm nervous."

"Oh god, yeah. They wrecked us. But I hear their girls' team isn't much to worry about."

"They've got a new captain this year, though. She's rough. But we haven't lost this season, so ... I'm trying to remain hopeful."

I turned onto the highway. "Yeah, but the team has *you* as a captain. You'll be fine." I thought I saw her blush for a moment, but I didn't mean it as a compliment. Well, sort of. There was no doubt Quinn was the best soccer player this century at Alpine High. I bet she'd get loads of scholarships for it. I was just stating cold hard facts.

The houses outside became scarcer until nothing but trees surrounded us.

"Um," she cleared her throat, looking out the window. "What exactly are we doing today?"

"That is for me to know and for you to find out," I teased with a smile.

Another part of Adrian's date rules: it had to be a surprise.

"Julian, can I tell you something?" I could feel her eyes on me.

"Go for it."

"I *hate* surprises." She turned straight in her seat and lifted her feet up to the dash.

The saliva was thick in my mouth. Yet another rule: don't tell Quinn about the rules. This was getting stupid.

"Well, doesn't that suck?" I smirked, hoping my smile would let her know I was just teasing.

I needed to get her talking. Hopefully distracting her would make the trip go by faster. Except I had no idea what to talk about. *Why do I have to be so awful at small talk?*

"You couldn't give me like a hint? Like why we are driving further away from civilization? Or maybe, what exactly needs to be accomplished in order for this date to be satisfied?" She crossed her arms over her chest.

"No, I just want to show you where I bury all my dead bodies," I deadpanned.

I could see her body tense.

"I'm kidding, obviously." I laughed.

"Adrian put you up to this, didn't he?"

I sighed. "Yeah ... he gave me a list of rules to follow."

"Can I give you another rule to follow?"

"I don't think that's how it works but sure."

"Follow Adrian's rules, and you're a dead man. Got it?" She situated herself to turn toward me. "Now, what the hell are we doing?"

I bit my lip. Truthfully, I couldn't tell if she was joking or not.

"Fine." I sighed. "I'm taking you to my favorite spot. According to Adrian, dinner and a movie didn't fit the bill."

"This is a rarity, and I hate to admit it, but Adrian does have a point."

"I guess? But it sure would have been a hell of a lot easier."

"Am I not worth the trouble?" She sat up for this, her feet stomping to the floor mats.

Answering this could go one of two ways: I could tell the truth and admit I was only doing this to get James and Tyler off my back. Or I could go along with making it seem like a real date.

I turned my head to hold her gaze while I spoke. "I don't take just anyone to this spot." My eyes shifted back to the road. "Believe me, you're worth the trouble."

She shifted in her seat, her left hand picking away at her jeans.

"Oh," she mumbled. "Then, I, uh, I can't wait." Quinn flashed her head in my direction, but before I could catch her reaction, she was looking out her passenger side window.

"It should only be a couple more minutes until we're there," I said, turning the car down a dirt road.

The rest of the ride we sat in silence. I kept glancing her way, and her eyes were glued out the window. I couldn't gauge her thoughts or feelings. I wish I knew if she was uncomfortable or if she was actually enjoying herself.

Finally, we arrived, and I parked the car.

"Here," I mumbled before opening my door.

Well, here goes nothing.

QUINN

WE ARRIVED AT THE BASE OF A SMALL MOUNTAIN. I HAD heard about this location before but never made the drive up. The parking lot was deserted, but it seemed like a regularly hiked location. He said this was his favorite spot, and that I was worth showing it to. What did that even mean? We didn't even know each other. So how could I possibly be worth anything to him?

I couldn't help but wonder if it was some more bullshit that Adrian fed to him last night. Maybe he caved on the secret, but he was still playing by Adrian's rules. If so, he'd regret it.

Julian opened and closed the passenger door for me to get out before he grabbed a backpack from his back seat.

"Ready?" he asked, adjusting the bag on his back.

I just nodded.

Julian led the way toward the narrow path we were to follow. A quick glance at the map next to the entrance showed that this place was pretty massive. While we may have both been athletic, I wasn't here to do a strenuous hike. *This is why I hate surprises.*

The trees darkened the path as we walked further in, both in silence, just the crunch of the leaves beneath us. A few squirrels scurried away at our footsteps.

"I discovered this place by accident when I was a kid," Julian broke the silence. "My dad and I were traveling home from visiting family when we stopped to take a leak." Julian cleared his throat. Was he uncomfortable around me? "My dad was taking forever. I mean, really, how long does it take to pee?"

He looked over his shoulder at me, and I just shrugged. How was I supposed to know how long it took a guy to pee?

"So, I got bored and started exploring, 'cause, you know, that's what eight-year-old boys do. And that's when I see this dirt road. It looked different than the highway, so I went down it. And I kept going down. Until—" Julian stopped walking. "Until I got here." He gestured to our destination.

We walked down a short path that opened up to a view of the Hudson River. Honestly, it was breathtaking. The Catskill Mountains were in the distance, and the river looked absolutely still. The changing foliage on the trees filled the valleys below us, only giving way to some homes. It honestly looked like a painting. I suddenly wished I had a place like this to escape to. I rarely ever visited the mountains.

"My dad was pissed that it took him nearly an hour to find me, but I just couldn't leave. I mean, look at it. The moment I got my license, I spent every day trying to find this spot again."

"How long did it take you to find it?" I walked further in. Our path had divided into flat rocks or a grassy patch, depending on where we wanted to stay.

Julian looked up at the sky. "I only found it again about a month ago."

"Oh wow." It didn't tell me much. I had only gotten my license the month beforehand, but I was one of the younger kids in our grade. "It's beautiful." I walked over to the edge, looking down below me. The drop was far. We hadn't climbed all that high, so I was shocked at how different the elevation was. You could see what I imagined to be a few different towns just from this one location.

"Yeah. I come here whenever I need to clear my head."

"I've only properly hiked in the mountains once. I have family upstate, and I went with my cousin over Christmas once. It was freezing, so we didn't last long. But my family doesn't really take trips up north. If it isn't a competitive sport, my family couldn't care less."

He let out a light laugh. "I get that."

I turned to walk back to Julian and saw him opening his backpack. He pulled out a blanket.

Fuck.

I looked between him and the blanket, but he was oblivious to his actions. Instead, he started to unfold it, shaking the blanket until it lay flat on the dirt beside him.

"I was thinking we could sit here and hang out for a bit?"

I swallowed.

While people were quick to harp on me for sleeping around too often, there was never a lack of expectation. If I loved sex, I "apparently" must be ready and willing whenever offered ... right?

Surely, Julian couldn't be one of those guys, right?

When it came to sex, I played by my own rules. I didn't just sleep with others because it was expected of me.

But was having sex a part of the rules Adrian gave Julian? Would I then be responsible for rumors being spread about Julian? Could Adrian even have any dirt to spread on Julian?

"Quinn?"

I shook my head, refocusing back on Julian. His brows were furrowed.

"Is this okay? Uh," he rubbed the back of his neck, "if you don't like this, we can go?"

"Sorry, yeah. Sure. Great."

I plastered a smile on my face and walked over to the blanket. He was already sitting down. I sat beside him, legs crossed, gazing out at the view.

Why couldn't just this once it be about the view before us?

I refused to react negatively to this. *Spin this, Quinn. How could this be great?*

1. Julian seems uncomfortable and seemed weird about his friends talking about his virginity.
2. Julian was cute in a quirky, nerd way, which I kind of totally dig. But I'd *never* tell him that.
3. Would it be so awful to sleep with Julian? Just because he wasn't on my radar that way before didn't mean he couldn't be now.

But did I want to take his virginity? Have that responsibility? All because of a goddamn dare? He deserved better than that. He also seemed like the person who would want to love someone before he had sex. Or maybe Julian wasn't as easy to read as I always assumed.

However, if it were that important to him, he would have chosen to lie about the date, saying he got laid, without us even seeing each other. But here we were, sitting here together. Day 1 of 180 days that I challenged Marie and Emerald.

Shit.

I glanced over at Julian, and he was looking out at the view, his knees bent, his arms and chin resting on top of them. A few strands of hair fell over his eyes. He looked so content. So reserved.

I watched him for a little while longer, grateful he was lost in his trance. He just seemed so unlike the others; I really hoped I was right about that. His features were soft yet defined by his lanky build. It seemed impossible that he'd even hurt a fly. So how could he be friends with James and Tyler? How could he bring me here to lose his virginity? *Why* would he be so desperate to please his friends? Why did anyone care about other people's sex life?

He was an anomaly though. He *did* enjoy heavy metal, but also was sentimental about mountains.

Julian dropped his legs, crossing them at his ankles. This would normally be my moment. I could reach out and place my hand on his thigh. I could slowly move my hand up. It was an easy go-to move to set the mood.

"Julian, I just want you to know we won't be having sex today."

"Wait, what?" He snapped his head to me. "I uh—I didn't even think about that."

"Oh." I cleared my throat. I fiddled with the hair tie on my wrist before running my hands through my curls, getting them ready for a ponytail. "I ... sorry." I pathetically dropped my hands between my legs, avoiding his gaze.

Julian reached for his backpack. "I didn't want to just show you this place. I wanted to show you *why* it's my favorite place."

I swallowed, bringing my knees up against my chest. My mind continued to overanalyze the situation. No one ever denied me, despite their original intention. Yet, he did. That should make me happy, right?

What the hell did you want from him, Quinn?

But it didn't. Because at the end of the day, I was also Quinn, the soccer star. A girl, regardless of the rumors, others wanted to be. So who was he to deny that?

"I-it's not the view?" I looked out at the mountains, trying to refocus.

He had a bag of peanuts in his hand from his bag. "Nope." He smiled and pulled off his mud-stained Vans, then placed one of the peanuts in between his big toe, his sock holding it in place. "Watch this."

In a matter of seconds, a squirrel appeared from the bushes. It approached with caution at first, then scurried to Julian's foot, snatching the peanut right out of it.

"Whoa." My eyes widened. I had never been that close to a squirrel before. They always scurried away so fast. "Where'd you learn to do that?"

"The mafia."

My mouth dropped at his seriousness.

Julian laughed. "You're way too gullible."

Julian's humor was something I had never been exposed to.

"The first time I was here after I rediscovered this place, I was eating peanuts, and a scurry of squirrels just started showing up, stealing them."

"Can I try?" The squirrel had backed up but was eyeing us hesitantly.

"Sure." Julian handed me the bag.

I took off my tennis shoe and tried to replicate his actions. I placed the peanut between my big toe and stuck it out on the blanket.

The squirrel came closer, sniffing out my toes. Right before it grabbed the peanut, I panicked, dropping the peanut and pulling my leg back against my chest.

"Oh, I don't like that." I laughed, squirming as a chill rushed through me.

Julian laughed harder than I've ever heard him before. "You're adorable," he said through his laughs. "Why not just try holding out your hand?"

I shook my head rapidly.

"No, no, no. What if it bites me?!" I wasn't huge on pets, let alone wild animals.

"Don't worry, I'm about eighty percent sure they don't have rabies."

My eyes bugged out. Now was not the time for humor.

"Relax, Quinn, I've done this a million times, and I've never been bitten."

"What about the other twenty percent?" I tilted my head to the side as I kept an eye on the squirrel in my peripheral vision.

"Hold on a second, you have something in your hair." Julian leaned closer to me, brushing my hair behind my ear.

My breath caught in my throat. But before I had a chance to focus on what that meant, the squirrel approached again, taking the peanut close to my leg.

"Told you you wouldn't be bitten." He smiled.

I blinked a few times as he continued to hover in front of me. But his eyes weren't on me; they were watching the damn squirrel.

"But," I cleared my throat, "that's different."

In a normal situation, I would have closed the space between the two of us. We'd already be making out on the blanket. This wasn't normal. Julian wasn't normal. *I* didn't feel normal.

What the *fuck* was happening?

"Nope, it's the same thing," Julian teased.

I reached my hand out, gently cupping his cheek in my hand.

"Julian?" I whispered.

His body tensed. "Yeah?"

"Thank you for this." I leaned in and pressed a kiss to his opposite cheek.

"Whoa, what's that?" Julian pointed to a nearby tree.

"What?" I turned my head as he scooted closer, putting his arm around me. What a juvenile, adorable move.

"Nothing." He smiled.

"Clever move, Raskin. How many girls have you used that on?"

"Exactly two point four."

I held in a laugh, trying to look at him as seriously as I could.

"Uh, did you cut off someone's limbs to make them a half a person?"

"Hey now, that's a very personal question to ask on a first date."

I turned slightly in his arms. "I seriously hope you're joking."

Julian stuck his tongue out. "Guess you'll have to figure that out on your own."

"Julian, you're a mystery." I laughed, rolling my eyes.

He just shrugged with a smile. I turned back toward the view, and he repositioned his arm around me. Despite being on a date initiated by a dare, this was becoming genuine. Maybe it was possible to go out with a guy and not have them be thinking about sex. Maybe it was okay to hang out like this without further expectations.

Honestly, this was refreshing.

His hand rubbed my shoulder, and I leaned into him. I felt him shift, and I looked up at him. He offered me a small smile.

Suddenly, this wasn't something that was forced or demanded of us. It was just me and Julian, alone.

I met his eyes, holding them for a minute before looking down at his lips and back to his eyes. He leaned down, the tips of his hair tickling my forehead. Our lips were nearly touching.

There was rustling in the bushes behind us, but I assumed it was the squirrels. I placed my hand on his cheek, trying to ignore it until there was a voice behind us.

Immediately, I pulled away, separating myself from Julian. Spinning around, I focused my eyes on where I thought the noise was coming from. I saw two figures.

Looking back at Julian, I saw his face had dropped. He moved a few inches away from me. I jumped up and walked toward the bushes before whoever was back there started running away.

"Hey!" I screamed. "Hey! Stop!"

They stopped in their tracks. Turning around, James and Tyler both gave me guilty smiles.

"What the hell is going on?" I yelled, turning around to see Julian standing right behind me.

He towered over me, but that didn't keep his hands from trembling as he held them up.

"Look, Quinn—" he started, and I heard James and Tyler snickering behind me.

I blinked back the unexpected tears that were surfacing. For once, they weren't from humiliation. "This is fucked."

I stormed off, physically brushing past James and Tyler.

"Stop pretending to be a prude, Quinn." James laughed.

"Quinn, wait!" Julian shouted.

I ignored them. I could never win.

When could I just be Quinn?

I took off in a run, going farther down the mountain trail. I didn't care where it led, as long as I wasn't near them. At the end of the day, regardless of who Julian was, he still had douchebag friends. And that would always stand in the way.

The path went for about a mile before another route opened, similar to the one Julian and I were just down. Turning down the path, I saw a family of rocks. I walked over to them before sitting down on the tallest rock. Breathing in, I noticed I had hiked higher up the mountain, but for once, I didn't feel superior to what was below me.

JULIAN

Fuck.

Why the hell were they here? How did they even know about this place? I bet I know— Adrian. Knowing them, I shouldn't be surprised they came here to spy on us, checking to see how far things would go. *Ugh.* Why couldn't I just do something on my own for once? Sure, Adrian gave me a list of rules, and yeah, I followed them out of fear. But I felt something there for a moment. Like it was more than a dare. Then we were blessed with the presence of these two.

I pushed James into Tyler. "What the hell are you two doing here?"

"Just wanted to be around in case you needed any pointers." James smiled.

I massaged my temples. "Well, thanks for your concern, but I'm good."

Tyler stood off to the side, shuffling his feet without commenting. *Come on Tyler, I know you're in there. You must know James is being a douchebag too, right? Why do you just stand there silently following James around? Be your own person, dammit.* Same to James. Everything seems to be about gaining

Adrian's affection. Adrian isn't even here. But if Adrian was the one who told them where we were, it's likely James thought Adrian would get a kick out of them showing up. Why are they like this?

"Besides, we couldn't miss this. Our little Julian finally growing up," James said. "When Adrian told us your plans, we couldn't stay away."

I pinched the top of my nose, trying to steady my breathing. So I was right. Adrian had told them. And, of course, one of the rules was to inform Adrian on what exactly my plans were, location and all.

"So," James placed a hand on my shoulder, "spill. How are things coming along?" He clapped his hand on my shoulder. "No pun intended."

"Good one." Tyler laughed.

I shook my head. Was there even a moment where sex didn't cross their minds?

"Well, I *was* just getting to the part of moving things to second base. But then you two came and ruined the moment." My stomach turned as I tried to keep my hopefully confident-looking smile. *Wow. I guess I'm just like them.* I wasn't planning on having sex with Quinn. But I couldn't let them know that. "Now if you'll excuse me, I'm going to go after Quinn."

James laughed while Tyler forced a smile.

"Sorry, dude. Don't let us interfere," James said.

I brushed past them. I had to fix this. I had to let Quinn know I had nothing to do with them showing up. I had to let her know I didn't bring her here to have sex with her. I wanted a real date. I was sick of the expectations of dating. Small talk over a cup of coffee, hooking up at a party, going to the movies with the intentions of not watching it, "Netflix and chill." All of that was bull-shit in my opinion. I headed down the trail I thought she took.

"Quinn?" I called out. This place was huge, and she'd never

been here before. Without me, she'd get lost. I took a deep breath. I needed to find her.

I made it back down to my car again without running into her. I thought maybe she would head back here and wait for me since I was her ride. But she was nowhere around. I called her name again, though I didn't expect she'd answer, even if she heard me. I hurt her, that much I could tell.

"Quinn," I called out again, "look I'm sorry. Please believe me. I had nothing to do with them showing up." I brushed my hands through my hair. If I couldn't find her, maybe she could hear me?

That's when I noticed footprints in the mud heading off the main path. *Oh no.*

"Quinn?" I yelled, following the footprints.

A few steps in, I slipped and fell. *Wonderful.* The entire side of my jeans and forearm were now covered in mud. I stood, regaining my balance. This date was not going how I wanted it to. I grinded my teeth, trying to brush the excess mud off my clothes.

Fuck Tyler and James.

I continued through the trees, this time holding on to them with each step to avoid slipping again. Eventually, through the green, I could see a splotch of red: Quinn.

"Quinn," I said as I approached her sitting on a rock.

"Go away, Julian," she mumbled, her shoulders caving in.

She wouldn't even look at me. "I'm not going anywhere."

"Please leave. I already called my sister. She's on her way."

I sat down on the dirt beside her. "Then I'll wait with you till she gets here."

"Julian." Her voice rose as she turned toward me, but her anger subsided as she held back a laugh. "What the hell happened?"

"Well, you know, I heard mud baths are supposed to be really good for you, so I decided to give one a try."

She bit her bottom lip, trying to keep herself from laughing, but as I gave her a grin, she let out a laugh.

"How, uh, how ya feeling, then?" She smirked.

"My pores feel revitalized."

She laughed again before looking back out at the view.

I smiled for a moment until I let it drop. "Quinn, look, I'm really sorry."

She frowned, crossing her arms.

I kept my eyes on her even if she wouldn't look at me. I cleared my throat. "I didn't tell them. I'll give you one guess who did though."

"Adrian." She nodded, turning her head toward me. She remained silent for a few moments. I could practically feel the wheels turning in her head.

"Bingo."

"So James and Tyler came to check up on us ... to see if we would have sex."

"Yeah." I shrugged.

"Yet, sex was never on your mind?" She looked at me skeptically.

"No."

"Even though you could have gotten an 'easy lay?' Some would call you a fool, Julian."

"Guess that makes me a fool then." I offered a smile.

Her reaction was slow, but eventually, a smile grew on her lips.

"Hi, I'm Quinn Kennedy, and forget everything you've heard about me. It's nice to meet you."

I laughed. "Uh, Julian Raskin." I shook her hand. "I may not be exactly different, but don't assume I'm like every guy either."

She nodded with a small smile.

"May we start over? Actually get to know each other? No bullshit? No dares? No obnoxious friends?"

"You've got yourself a deal, ma'am."

"I uh ... didn't call my sister, actually."

"Ouch, you lied to me?" I put my hand on my chest. "How could you? You'll have to make it up to me by going with me to get some ice cream."

"Oh, the horror!" Her hand was immediately in front of her mouth. "But I suppose I'll suffer." She winked before hopping off the rock and walking toward the path.

We headed back to my car, and I slid into the driver's side. James and Tyler were nowhere to be found. So today wasn't a total bust after all. I couldn't help but smile as I backed out of the trail. Quinn was definitely not how I expected her to be. She wasn't easy at all. She was a complicated person with walls around her heart the size of mountains. And yet, I wanted to climb over them.

QUINN

Monday morning wasn't how I anticipated it would be. It wasn't the same old Monday. I felt lighter—happier even, despite the frustration I felt about my friends. Julian had changed something.

Saturday was such a whirlwind of emotions that by the time I got home Saturday night, I was exhausted. Julian wasn't who I anticipated him to be. I couldn't figure out how he put up with James and Tyler, but I shouldn't have been surprised. We were part of the same group, and recently, I had been asking myself this same question.

We had driven back to our town for ice cream, so while we ate, we walked through town and ended up at our part of the Hudson River. He was a gentleman the entire rest of the date—opening doors and paying for our ice cream. Even when my ice cream dripped down my chin, he quickly ran to grab me a napkin. But that wasn't what drew me to him. It was his awkwardness and his nerdy stories that kept me interested and laughing. He informed me that I wasn't off the hook for feeding a squirrel, but only because I brought up how nice and different that experience had been—watching him do it, of course. It baffled me that we had known each other for two years, hung out in the same crowd almost every weekend, and played the same sport, yet we only knew rumors of the other.

And at the end of the night, when he drove me home, he only placed a kiss on my cheek before I left. Maybe this would be different.

I had spent the entirety of Sunday with my family, as well as doing school work, happily avoiding the messages blowing up my phone. Only one was from Julian, wishing me a good Sunday.

Now, because I had avoided Marie's messages, she wouldn't shut up in U.S. History class. We were supposed to be working on essays—individually—but she wasn't getting the hint.

"Come on, tell me something! Anything! You two must have slept together. You've been smiling all day!" Marie whispered.

"No, I haven't. Besides, am I not allowed to be happy?"

"No. You have a massive game tomorrow; you should be worrying like crazy. You guys can't lose this one."

"Don't remind me," I grumbled. "Way to bring down the mood, Marie." I shifted, writing a sentence down on my paper.

She just smirked and wrote something down on her paper as the teacher eyed us.

"Look, you've never held out before. If you don't tell anyone what happened, Adrian is going to spread a rumor."

"As far as I'm aware, sex wasn't a part of the deal. We went on a date."

"And ... do you remember our deal?"

"Yes, Marie. I never said it was bad." The bell rang as soon as I finished my sentence.

I threw all my books together and darted out of the classroom. Why couldn't anything ever be normal? Why couldn't Julian and I just be left alone?

Marie wasn't in my next class, so she couldn't follow me as I sped to my locker to exchange my books. Weaving in and out of the crowds, I made it there in record time. I turned the dial and unlocked it, tossing the books I didn't need inside. As soon as I closed the door, I was trapped against my locker by two arms. Before I even turned, I could smell Adrian's awful Axe cologne.

"Looks like I'm going to be able to spread a nice little rumor about you," he whispered against my ear, causing me to let out a shiver.

I turned around, pressing myself into the locker, creating as much space between us as I could. The lock was digging into my back.

"What are you talking about, Adrian? Julian and I went out."

"Two little birdies told me that you ran away from him, which means you failed to complete the dare."

"Two little birdies left before the date was finished." I tried to push past him, but his arms were rock solid. "Besides, Adrian, isn't it about time you start to focus on your own life instead of mine? What happened afterward with me and Julian is none of your business."

"Kennedy, Dunn! Get to class!" My head whipped toward my homeroom teacher, who was sticking his head out of his classroom.

I nodded over and smiled.

"We aren't done here, Q," Adrian whispered, and I avoided his glance.

"Will do, Mr. Ram," I called out.

Smirking, I ducked under Adrian's arm and pushed past him as I jogged to class, hoping I made it before the bell rang.

By the time I got to soccer practice, my mood had significantly dropped. Adrian kept eyeing me at lunchtime. Marie and Emerald kept nudging me for information, which followed through to Spanish class. It was satisfying to tell them to leave me alone in another language, but they didn't catch on in Spanish either.

With the drop in my mood, the stress of the soccer game started to catch up to me. My team was counting on me to lead an easy win. But it would be anything but easy, according to our coach. And this was only reiterated as she hounded us on the field after school.

I was distracted and frustrated. Liza, whom I still saw at soccer, kept ignoring me, passing to others, despite me always being open. And I couldn't get what her deal was. We stopped being friends a year ago—why now the sudden upset?

While it was nice to be able to take some aggression out on the soccer ball (when I did have it), I either kept kicking the ball too hard or missing it entirely. Everything suddenly seemed to start piling up, and soccer was *always* my stress relief. But today it wasn't working.

It was infuriating to be roped into a dare, to complete the dare, and then not be believed. At least when Adrian talked about me, he was doing so on his own, working off my own decisions. But to play their petty game and still be fucked over? When did it all end? When was I able to live in peace?

Downing the rest of my water at the end of practice, I started packing up my bag.

"I know what happened over the weekend," Liza said behind me. Startled, I dropped my water bottle. "Don't you dare hurt Julian. Or you'll have me and Ian to deal with." She left before I had the courage to turn and face her.

She jogged away, fixing her dirty blonde hair into a new ponytail as she met up with a boy I didn't recognize.

I groaned. I didn't fucking need this. I picked up my water bottle and shoved it into my bag before throwing it over my shoulder.

My coach was immediately behind me as I spun to leave the

field. A lecture came about how I needed to compartmentalize what was going on in my life, that I needed to get rest, and maybe even get some more practicing in tonight. I was far from my A game. Definitely not captain material, which only meant we had even less of a chance of winning. With that, she left me alone.

As I walked with my head down, kicking the grass with my cleats, I heard his laugh in the distance. Looking around, I saw Julian on the opposite field, where the boys often practiced their soccer. He was surrounded by James, Tyler, a guy I didn't recognize, and their goalie, Ian. James and Tyler were kicking the balls at Ian for him to defend.

Walking closer, I saw him listening to the one guy I didn't know, but he was jumping side to side, kicking his soccer ball between his feet. Every once in a while, he let out a full-on laugh, one that had graced my presence a few times on Saturday, leaving my heart skipping a beat and my stomach fluttering.

Being only a few feet away from him now, I noticed my body was reacting in the exact same way. I didn't do love. I didn't do dating. Who was Julian, and why was he making me feel like this?

My anger was already subsiding, and he had no idea I was near him. His happiness was in no direct relation to my mood. It only made me want to feel angrier, but instead, I awkwardly stood there, watching them, wondering how the hell I made it to the other side of the soccer field and not my car.

He accidentally tapped his soccer ball too hard, and it rolled out from between his feet. He jogged out of the circle to chase after it, but on his way back with the ball, he caught my eye.

I awkwardly held up my hand and gave him a measly smile.

This was a mistake. What excuse did I have to just be standing here and watching him?

Julian waved back, returning my smile. He turned to his

friends and kicked the ball back to them before facing me again. "What's up?" he called.

"Hi," I mumbled before clearing my throat and closing the short distance between us. "So, uh, you remember how I said I was nervous about tomorrow's game?" Julian nodded, looking back at his friends, who were now looking at us. "Um, well ..."

Fuck, Quinn. Get it together.

"I kind of had a real shit practice and was ... well, wondering if you wanted to practice together for a bit?" I alternated my footing, avoiding the looks of his friends.

I felt so stupid. I was Quinn Kennedy. When I had crushes, I acted on them ... confidently. So why was Julian now ruining that? Him, of all people.

Julian raised his eyebrows. "You want *me?*" He laughed. "Aren't you the captain? I'm pretty sure you're better than me." He was smiling as he shook his head. "But yeah, sure, I'll help you out. We've just been fooling around with the ball anyway."

I gave him a small smile. I couldn't receive his compliment. I sure didn't feel like a captain.

"Thank you." I nodded toward the field I came from, definitely not in the mood for James and Tyler to get involved. "Wanna go over there?"

"Sure, just give me a sec."

I watched as he jogged back to his friends and said his goodbyes. The suggestive looks James and Tyler both expressed to Julian weren't lost on me. Eventually, he grabbed his bag and walked back over.

We were silent the whole walk to the girls' field where I wanted to practice. How did one talk after you'd gone on a date that wasn't your idea, but you actually liked it?

Once at the field, I dropped my bag and dug my soccer ball out of it. He placed his next to mine, reaching into his bag for his water. Taking a few sips, he returned it before standing up beside me.

"So, uh, I suck." I laughed. "I couldn't seem to get anything right today. My coach even took me aside, telling me I wasn't ready for tomorrow's game."

Julian's eyes widened. "Wow. That's rough."

We took to playing one on one, with a focus on Julian being the goalie, keeping the game to one side of the field. He kept getting the ball as I fumbled and cursed each time I lost it. I could even see James and Tyler off in the distance. I wasn't sure they were even looking our way, but just the sight of them was weighing on me.

I just wanted to be alone ... with Julian. It was taking everything in me to not comment about them. I stuck to mumbling under my breath, but it only heightened the anger.

Julian had backed up toward the goal, waiting and giving me a chance to try and score. I took this as the prime opportunity to finally get my aggression out. Drawing my foot back, I put everything into kicking the ball. Instead, I slipped and found myself crashing in the grass, my tailbone breaking the fall and then the back of my head. As both throbbed, I looked to see if I made the goal. The ball barely moved. Julian looked like he was holding in a laugh.

I groaned, gripping the grass between my fingers, arching my back from the ground.

"Are you okay?" Julian was next to me in an instant.

I was fine. I wasn't really physically injured. Just my goddamn ego.

"Fine." I pushed myself into a seated position. "I just need to try again."

My vision blurred, but I blinked rapidly. I ran both of my hands over the flyaways my curls were producing. Sweat held them down against my scalp, and the slight pressure helped my head.

"Okay, superstar, let's take a timeout." Julian sat beside me, his shoulder brushing against mine. "Too much practice and you won't even give the other team a fair chance." I rolled my eyes, looking out at the field. "But seriously, you don't want to wear yourself out before tomorrow."

I looked up at him. He hadn't moved away; his body shifted my way as he offered a small smile. I hated that butterflies started to flutter as his eyes softened. I cleared my throat, blinking away from him. Suddenly, he wasn't the boy I was interested in. There was no time for that. He had become my competition, and I was determined to win.

"Just a little longer." I jumped up, trying to remain eager, despite my tailbone aching. Julian looked like he wanted to argue, but I shot him a glare, and he shut his mouth as he stood. I acted quickly and kicked the ball, making a perfect goal. "See? I'm brilliant!" I forced a laugh, only becoming genuine when Julian shook his head at me.

"Whoa, whoa, whoa. That wasn't even fair. I wasn't in position!"

"Tough shit." I grinned, running to grab the ball to try again.

"Sure, you little cheater," Julian teased. "I won't let you get one in that easy again."

"We'll see about that," I said, putting on my game face.

I did end up getting a proper goal in, with Julian on his A game. It only helped boost my ego, and my force of trying to steal the ball away from him became rougher as I imagined being up against the captain of tomorrow's team.

After I tried to kick the ball away from Julian, he sent it flying behind me. Instead of getting to it, we both tripped. A searing pain shot through my ankle, and before I could reposition myself,

Julian fell toward me. We both landed into the grass with an "oof."

There was no cutesy, romantic "we looked into each other's eyes and kissed" moment. I shoved him off of me, grateful for his boney build, and sat up quickly, examining my ankle. With just a gentle touch, I was wincing in pain.

"Goddammit!" I screamed, punching the grass with both hands. My eyes brimmed with tears, but I refused to cry. I never cried in front of anyone but my family. I sure as hell wouldn't start now. I pressed my fingertips up against my eyelids, leaning my head back, willing the tears to disappear.

Julian was silent for longer than I would have liked. "Shit," he said under his breath.

I looked down at my ankle again and saw it was beginning to swell. Tears fell when I bent my head

"Fuck," I muttered. "Fuck, Julian! What am I going to do?" I wiped my face furiously before looking over at him.

Julian looked as panicked as I felt. He leaned down and scooped me into his arms. "For one, you aren't going to walk on it." I latched on to his neck as he began to raise me off the ground.

"What are you doi—"

"Taking you to a bench so you can at least sit."

I succumbed to the pain and leaned my head on his shoulder as he carried me over to the bench on the sidelines. The walk wasn't long enough, and soon he was sitting me upright against the cold metal.

"I need to play tomorrow," I whispered.

"And you will. But for now, you really do need to rest." Julian let my leg rest on his lap. "It won't be a hundred percent tomorrow, but it doesn't look that bad either."

I nodded, looking down at his hand that rested on my shin. "I'm sorry."

"I should be the one apologizing. I'm the reason we tripped."

"No, no. I'm sorry about all of it. It's just a rough day, and I was trying to take it out with soccer, and well, on you, not intentionally."

"Ah I see, I'm just your personal punching bag." He smiled.

I kicked his leg with my left foot, smirking.

"Exactlyyy," I drew out. "I'm glad you understand your place now."

Julian's body shook as he let out a laugh. If possible, he was able to ease my discomfort. I wanted more of that infectious sound, but I wasn't a naturally funny person.

"I should uh, maybe ... probably call my mom. See if she can pick me up." I wasn't ready to leave, but I was sure that caring for me wasn't on his list of things to do for the night.

"Okay. Did you want me to wait with you till she comes?"

"Do you mind?" I gave him an uneasy smile.

I still wasn't sure where we stood and what was asking too much. We weren't officially dating, nor were we even *really* friends.

"Sure." He shrugged. "I don't mind."

"Thank you." I smiled, searching for my bag.

Julian was lifting my leg and standing up before I could even ask. He jogged over to our soccer bags and brought them back to us.

I then called my mother, explaining the situation, and she said she was on her way.

"Do you mind if we head down to the parking lot? We can wait there?" I suggested.

"Sounds good." Julian kneeled in front of me with his back to me. "Hop on. I know I look super buff, but I don't think I can carry you the entire way there."

I slid our bags over my shoulder, resting them on my back before climbing onto Julian's back.

He stood up with some difficulty, and I wrapped my hands

around his neck tightly. We took off slowly down to the parking lot.

"Hey, Julian? Can I ask you something?"

He just nodded his head, his breathing growing heavy.

"I know we only really hung out because of a dare, and we need to talk about that, but, first, do you, uh, do you think you may be interested in hanging out again, without anyone controlling us?"

Julian was silent for a few moments. "Sure," he said softly. "I don't see why not." I nodded into his shoulder.

Neither of us said anything else the rest of the walk. Even when we sat there waiting for my mom to pick me up, we didn't say anything. I thought maybe I should have asked him if he truly was okay with hanging out, but I was too afraid of his answer.

JULIAN

THE MOMENT QUINN'S MOM'S CAR WAS OUT OF SIGHT, I jogged back to where Tyler, James, Ian, our other defenseman Carter, and I were all practicing earlier.

Wow, Quinn asked me for help. She was full of surprises. Being scared of squirrels, enjoying the mountain view, asking for help when she really didn't need it. Again and again, I was learning new things about her. Here I was all this time avoiding her because I had heard rumors from James and Tyler that she was easy, that she's slept with nearly every guy in our grade and then some. How she prefers older guys, but when it comes down to it, she'd sleep with anyone. It always gave me this vibe to stay away, like if she was so easy, she must also be a horrible person. Dirty and devoid of any real emotions. But Quinn wasn't like that at all. She was a separate entity from the rumors. Like the rumors were a completely different Quinn Kennedy than the one I just helped practice soccer.

It was intriguing. It made me want more. More time with her. More knowledge of who she was. To get to know the real her. Maybe, just maybe, she was assumed to be "easy" because of the number of times she'd been screwed over? I didn't know how or why the things said about her even came up. But I was determined to pull back the layers of the rumors and learn the truth.

Ian and Carter had already left the field. Tyler and James were still standing around waiting for me, on their phones having long given up on anything soccer-related.

"Dude, what the hell?" James asked as he saw me approach.

"Yeah, are you and Quinn a couple now or something? We've been waiting around for forty minutes for you. I thought you were just going to use her to get laid?"

The comment from Tyler took me back. It wasn't like him to add on to anything James said. He usually just agreed. Did he really have the same mindset as James?

"Sorry. She seemed desperate for help."

"You gotta learn to say no sometimes, bro." James shook his head at me. He was right. I struggled to say no to anyone when they asked me to do something. It led to a lot of people trying to walk all over me and use me for stuff. But Quinn was different. I couldn't reject that look in her eyes. She trusted me. I just had to help her out.

I shrugged. "Yeah, you're right."

James slung his arm over my shoulder despite being two inches shorter than me. "But seriously, dude, what *is* the deal with you and Quinn?"

"She's not my girlfriend if that's what you're asking." I brushed his arm off of me.

"Then what's the point of hanging around her?" We began walking toward our cars.

"Oh, I have a plan, trust me," I winked.

God, I hated myself. I hated this need to fit into their stupid mindset. Quinn was a person. No one should be spoken about like that. But still, these guys were my friends. *Ugh.*

"Oh! Easing her into bed, are you?" James laughed, slapping me on the back. I smiled at his praise.

"Why waste the time though? Quinn's legs are basically an open door," Tyler added softly. I couldn't help but notice the smile that formed on Tyler's face as James laughed and said,

"Seriously."

My smile faltered. I wanted to throw up. How could they talk about Quinn like that? Or *anyone* for that matter? All these two ever thought about or cared about was sex. Girls were just objects for them to put their dicks in. I grinded my teeth and shrugged.

James elbowed Tyler in the arm. "I bet you Quinn will end up *begging* Julian for sex."

Tyler laughed, thrilled at the attention James was giving him.

"Julian, you are a genius. Quinn's so easy, she'll go crazy if Julian is hard to get. Why don't we make a bet to see how long Quinn will last?" James added.

Oh god, no. My mind replayed Quinn's words from earlier: "Do you, uh, do you think you may be interested in hanging out again, without anyone controlling us?" *I'm sorry, Quinn. I'm sorry my friends are awful. I'm not using you for sex. I don't even want to have sex with you, period.*

"I bet she won't even last three months," Tyler predicted.

"Wow, you're generous. I give it three weeks," James said. "What do you think, Julian?"

I shook my head with a grin. "I don't think it'd be fair if I contributed to this bet."

"Agreed." James said, "Okay, whoever is the closest pays for the other person's lunch for a month."

"Deal." Tyler and James shook hands. *Could they be more immature?*

James backed out of the parking lot first, window down and music blaring as he headbanged to the beat. As his car was screeching out of the parking lot, I changed CDs in mine. Tyler waved as he backed out and left, and soon I was on the road too.

As I entered my house, I hung my keys on a small hook just

inside the door before kicking off my cleats. Shrugging my soccer bag off my shoulder, I let it land on the floor by the door. My dad was sitting in his usual spot on the living room couch reading one of the *Game Of Thrones* books—his guilty pleasure. Aside from the glasses he wore too low on his nose and the gray patches of hair, I looked exactly like my dad. Dark wavy hair. Tall, lanky build that was the definition of scrawny. Large brown eyes with deep bags under them. Nothing about my appearance resembled my mother, who had straight blonde hair and was only five foot two.

"Hey," I said to my dad as I walked through the hallway behind the living room couch, headed to the kitchen.

"Your mother called," my dad said without looking up from his book.

I stopped cold in my tracks. My dad and I were sort of close. For the most part, we just did our own thing, though we did have a relationship more like friends than father and son. I didn't tell him everything, mind you, but I was at least comfortable talking to him. But whenever my mother came up in conversation, my dad became a different person. He suddenly lost his charm, his humor, and his ability to treat me like another adult. Instead, he would become this stern, strict father type as if talking about my mother was worth getting grounded over. I don't know the whole story. And I wasn't about to ask. I don't know if my mom cheated or if she was just the one who asked for a divorce, but I do know my father never forgave her.

"I'll call her after," I said, entering the kitchen to retrieve my container of leftovers from last night's dinner. Mashed potatoes and turkey with carrots. I heated it up in the microwave and then plopped myself beside my dad to eat.

My mom and dad got divorced when I was only five. She moved for her job, making her a whole whopping eight hours away, so I never got to see her. Her busy job also prevented me from talking to her much either. She remarried some guy named David I've only met twice, and they had a daughter of their own, Alyssa. I wouldn't call her my sister. She was, in my opinion, just my mom's daughter. Same went with my stepdad. He was just the guy my mom was married to. It wasn't that I was bitter toward my mom or hated her; I just felt distant from her in more ways than one. No matter what I did, I never felt I could close the gap in our relationship.

"You're home later than usual," my dad noted, still refusing to take his eyes off his book.

I shrugged, despite knowing he wouldn't notice. "I helped a classmate with her soccer practice."

"Her?" My dad finally looked up from his book with his eyebrows raised at me. I rolled my eyes at his sense of humor.

"Yes, Dad. A girl. Those things exist, you know."

"I see," he said, returning his gaze to the book.

"You're ridiculous." I knew why he was suspicious. I never had a girl over before, nor do I speak about girls pretty much *at all*. So any mention of the opposite gender always spikes my dad's curiosity.

After I ate, I went upstairs to my room. I called my mom, and we talked for a total of ten minutes. It was a whole lot of how is school? —good. How's soccer? —good. How are things at home? —good. Then she went on about a cruise she and David went on a couple of weeks ago to the Caribbean.

When I got off the phone, I pulled open my laptop to do my homework with my phone sitting on my bed beside me. I stared at the computer longer than I got any words of this essay down. Occasionally, I wandered onto social media with the intent of remaining productive. After about an hour, I gave up and closed my laptop. It wasn't due for another week, so I didn't have to worry about it yet.

I laid down on my bed and stared at the ceiling. My mind

kept bouncing back from my conversation with Quinn and my conversation with Tyler and James. I didn't want to hang out with Quinn just to have sex with her. I didn't want to use her like that. And I regretted what I said to Tyler and James, but I just wanted them off my back.

I raised my phone above my head and stared at my home screen. Quinn did say she wanted to hang out again. And now I had to, or Tyler and James would think I was lying.

I texted Quinn.

> *Hey. I helped you with soccer,*
> *now it's your turn. Help me with*
> *my chemistry homework tomorrow*
> *after school?*

God, I should have at least asked her how her foot was first. Especially since she had a big game the next day. I rested my hand holding my phone on my forehead. I hated this. I liked Quinn. A lot. I enjoyed the time we spent together and wanted to see her more. But I didn't *want* to have sex with her. But why? Was something wrong with me? I rubbed my eyes. How come every other guy treated sex like the ultimate goal in life? Like sex equaled happiness? Why was I the only one who seemed to think differently? It wasn't that I was repulsed by sex or anything. It didn't gross me out. I masturbated just like the next guy. But the actual act of sex just didn't interest me. I sighed. Maybe I should have sex with Quinn. Maybe that would fix my thinking.

My phone buzzed.

> *Can't. Our game is away.*

I thought about my response. I could text something witty, but it might come off rude through a text. Man, I felt lame for even asking her. I didn't even know if she's in Chemistry. We didn't have any of the same classes.

> *Kk. But you owe me.*
> **tongue out, winky face**

After a moment I sent another one.

> *Good luck tomorrow. You're*
> *going to be great.*

> *When do you have lunch?*

> 12:30.

I couldn't help but feel surprised. I expected that to be the end of the conversation. I didn't anticipate her making an effort to see me.

> *I have study hall. Meet me at*
> *Isabella's Coffee off campus, and*
> *I'll be happy to help. BUT, don't*
> *you DARE tell James or Tyler,*
> *or I'm out.*

> *It's a date!*

> *Oooh, a date? Does that mean*
> *you're buying my iced tea?*

> *I guess it does!*
> **tongue out, winky face**

Thank you again for today.
Night, Julian!

Night.

I put my phone down on my bedside table and laid on my side. James and Tyler were going to be pretty upset when they *both* lost the bet.

QUINN

It was a total piece of shit. Completely unfair. The ref didn't call two fouls that should have aided in us, at least, *sort of*, winning. But it was their turf. We didn't have a say.

The moment the bus door closed for us to head back home, our coach started the lecture. About how we were so much better than that. How we made our team look pathetic. How I failed as a captain, *especially* because I was injured.

I never told my coach I was injured. I walked as normally as I could all day and then pushed through the game. But now it was throbbing. More swollen than at its worst yesterday, but I already pushed this far, I could push a bit further.

After our lecture, making sure we all felt more like shit than we already did, our coach sat down, and we made our hour journey back into town.

Most of the team had found their own seats—taking advantage of the free time. Some were starting homework, others popped in headphones, and a few were talking in the front of the bus.

I had noticed Liza sat alone in the seat in front of mine. She was still giving me the cold shoulder, aiding in a goal lost tonight.

But I was hoping to catch her before she placed her own earbuds in.

I eyed the coach and the bus driver and took my chance to hop in the seat next to her.

"Hi," I said softly.

She turned her head, looking at me with her dull green eyes.

"Hi," she responded before looking down at her lap, where she started to untangle her earbuds.

"Hey, can we talk?" I placed my hand on her arm. She didn't respond. "Look, you weren't even there this weekend; why are you pissed?"

She turned her head, making direct eye contact with me. "Because I care about people, Quinn."

"What the fuck is that supposed to mean?" I crossed my arms.

She sighed, closing her hand around her earbuds.

"Lately, I just don't know who you are anymore. I've become close with Ian after we were fed up with the group. And Ian is friends with Julian; therefore, you're on my turf again. Don't fuck over Julian like you did with me."

We sat in silence for a few minutes. We hadn't ever spoken about what happened. I had avoided her at all costs. It happened right at the end of soccer season last year, and by the time we started back up this season, we were able to just pretend we weren't ever friends.

"I'm sorry, you know, about everything." I closed my eyes, leaning my head back against the seat. "I'm a bitch sometimes. Well, I suppose most of the time lately. I just, there are a lot of complicated things about me. One is, it's difficult to be in a relationship. But also ..." I looked down at my hands, hoping Liza would understand what I wasn't saying. "Look, I know I'm not perfect." I sighed. "And neither were we, and I think we are better friends. But the problem is, we haven't been that since. I miss us as friends."

"A lot happened in the time we were with each other, Quinn. I know it wasn't long. But I trusted you; I came out to you ... you, you fucking initiated our relationship, Quinn. I don't get it; I still question what happened. Why you thought we'd work when you've always been with guys ... but I believed you. I wanted to believe in us. But god, Quinn, you—"

"I know," I said softly, picking at the skin on my hand. She didn't have to say it; she didn't have to relive it in her head.

She cleared her throat, shifting toward me a little.

"Do you like Julian, or are you playing him to make Adrian happy?"

I tried to shake off her change in topic. Focusing on what she asked. "I like Julian." There was no use lying to her. Really, I needed to stop lying to myself. "It was a bet. But, he's really sweet and unlike anyone I've been with. And you know what?"

"What?" She gave me a small smile, but it was a smile.

"He didn't even expect to get laid. We, like, went on a proper date."

"Sounds just like him." Her smile remained intact, growing just the slightest.

Did Liza know Julian?

Liza let out a laugh. God, I had missed hearing her laugh.

"I think Julian will be good for you," Liza said.

My eyes widened. "Excuse me? Why? Because I apparently can't *hold* a relationship?"

"No!" she exclaimed. "No, Quinn. You know I don't judge you for what you enjoy. I just think lately it seems as if you're falling into this image Adrian has created. You're forgetting who you really are. You used to have control. You knew what you wanted despite what others thought. A year ago, you wouldn't have given a shit about this dare."

I sat there silently, finding immense interest in my soccer shorts.

"I know about the bet Marie, Emerald, and Adrian have set. I understand the consequences and why they matter to you. But try to have this relationship organically, okay? Julian's a good guy when Tweedle Dee and Tweedle Dumb aren't around him. When he's with Ian, he seems more authentic. He doesn't deserve to be fucked over."

I swallowed and looked up at her. She spoke from experience, but I knew her saying I'd fuck Julian over was just her clarifying that I did, indeed, fuck her over.

We sat in silence the rest of the ride. I couldn't tell if it was a mutual understanding, or if I had ruined things further. But I didn't want to open my mouth to make it worse. Liza put one earbud in and turned her music on, but conveniently left one earbud out.

With a small smile, I reached for my bag in the seat behind me and took out my phone as Liza stared out the window.

She spoke the truth that no one wanted to say to my face—and always had since we became best friends in grade school. I truly didn't want to screw Julian over, and despite the bet, I actually wanted to try dating him. I just wasn't sure what he really wanted.

I mean, he had asked me for help on his homework, which I had done earlier during study hall. We met at the café, where he was already sitting with the iced green tea latte he promised me. He called it a date, but he didn't seem to be struggling at all—with few questions on the work and quickly understanding my explanations when he did ask.

So, I decided to act on my instincts. Liza told me I lost my control, and the competitive person I was wanted to prove her wrong.

I texted Julian.

So, we got destroyed. Coach is
pissed. I'm in pain. And, well,
I was thinking there may
be only one cure.

Yikes, that sounds rough.
But what's this magic
remedy you speak of?

You, me, and a pint of ice
cream. Half hour, my place.

I'll be there!

You're the best. Also, pressure's
on for the ice cream flavor. Makes
or breaks the evening. Have fun
smiley face

I couldn't keep the smile off my face. I kept checking the time, wishing it would go faster. Also, hoping my mother would approve. She'd never met Julian. And it was a school night.

"Julian?" Liza questioned. I just nodded my head and looked back to check the time. Three minutes had passed.

"Promise to treat him well?"

"Promise," I whispered, catching her eye.

WE FINALLY ARRIVED at the school grounds, and with one last lecture and a demand to show up better at practice tomorrow, we were set free.

Despite my mother's protests, I told her I was driving my car home today—it had stayed at the school the night before because I was in too much pain to drive. I drove home as fast as I could, ignoring the stop signs and the pain in my driving foot. I only had a few minutes to check with my mom if Julian was cleared.

I limped into the house with a record of five minutes to spare.

"Mom! Dad!" I yelled once I closed the door.

It was near eight at night, and the house was dark and quiet. My sister's car was gone, but my parents were both home.

"Hi, sweetie!" My dad grinned, walking down the hall. "How'd the game go?"

"Miserable. Look, is Mom around?"

He closed the space between us and pulled me into a hug. "I'm sorry, pumpkin. She's in the shower, what's up?"

"Um, well, my friend Julian is coming over with ice cream; is it cool?" He pulled me back a little, amusement in his eyes. "We'll stay on the couch and hang out. I'm just not feeling so great."

"Sure, but not too late, okay?" He looked down at my ankle. "Oh, bug, go change and then sit down. I'll get you some ice." He kissed the top of my head, and I limped off to my bedroom to quickly change.

Unfortunately, I didn't make it out of my bedroom before Julian knocked on the door. My dad was already walking to greet him before I could make my presence known, so I decided to tiptoe down the hall and listen in. They always say the parent conversations really show whether or not they are a good guy, right?

"You must be Julian!" my father greeted.

"Yes, sir, nice to meet you. I'm told Quinn is expecting me?" I smiled at his tone.

"Yes, she's getting changed. She just got home. Are you the gentleman who helped her out yesterday?" I saw the two of them walk into the living room. Julian had a plastic bag in his hand that looked like more than one ice cream.

"Yours truly." Julian smiled.

"Thank you." My father gestured with his hand for Julian to follow and led him into the kitchen. "I really appreciate it. Quinn just doesn't know when to stop sometimes. I'll get you some bowls."

I heard my father clanking around with the dishes before I made myself known.

"Hey, Julian," I greeted.

"Hey," he nodded, "special delivery." He held up the bag in his hand. "I couldn't decide on just one, so I brought two." He pulled the two containers out of the bag. "One Cookies and Creme. The other Heavenly Hash."

"Ooh!" I exclaimed, walking over and examining the two containers. "I shall inform you that neither is a favorite; *however,* you get points for two options. And a point for teaching me something. Where the *hell* did Heavenly Hash come from? I've never heard of it before."

Julian's eyes widened. "You've never heard of Heavenly Hash before?! It's only the most heavenly ice cream flavor there is! It's vanilla and chocolate with almonds and chocolate chips."

"Julian, my dear friend," I placed a hand on his shoulder, "don't you know that nuts are too healthy for ice cream?"

"That's nuts." He smirked. "So tell me about this awful game you had."

"Ugh! Hold up, we need ice cream first." I winked, leaning up on my left foot and pressing a kiss to his cheek before I started opening the containers. "Dad, shoo!" I said as he hovered near the pantry, trying to pretend he was busy, but he ignored me.

I grabbed the ice cream scoop, took a scoop of each and placed them both into our bowls.

When I was finished, I threw the containers in the freezer, then handed a bowl to Julian. I led us over to the couch.

"Quinn, elevate your foot, I've got some ice," I heard my father say from behind me.

I did as he asked, not wanting to be as far from Julian as I was. I leaned up against one end of the couch, and he sat at the end of my feet, helping put a few pillows under my foot. My dad then rested an ice pack on it.

"Thanks, Dad. Go hang out with Mom now." I gave him a cheeky smile, and he saluted before leaving the room.

I took a big bite of the Heavenly Hash ice cream and grinned. "Okay, you got me," I mumbled with ice cream still in my mouth. "This is great."

"Told ya so."

"So, basically, the refs suck. Oh, and my coach is pissed that I'm injured. She went off on us twice on the way back. But can we talk about something different? I want to just be done."

"Sure," Julian leaned closer to me, "did you know a group of crows is called a murder? Who came up with that? Who was the person who decided 'hey, see this all black terrifying birds? ... You wanna know what I call a group of them?'" Julian shook his head.

I let out a loud laugh, throwing my head back. "Julian, where the hell do you come up with this stuff?"

"Come up with it?" He feigned shock. "That was a cold hard fact!"

"But how do you know this?" I asked, scooping another bite of ice cream.

"Google is a wonderful thing." He smiled. "But don't ask me why or how I googled that. If you do, I'd have to kill you." He sucked on his spoon, giving me a wink.

"So what other random, wonderful facts do you know? Educate me, Mr. Raskin."

"Well, human saliva has a boiling temp three times that of

regular water." Julian paused. "I'm starting to think I have way too much free time on my hands."

"You're cute." I smiled, poking his leg with my left foot. "Keep going; I'm intrigued."

"Well, there was one time at lunch where I looked up a hundred cat facts for fun. Did you know cats sleep seventy percent of their lives? Like, wow, I wish."

"Oh Julian, we need to get you a hobby." I chuckled. "But I agree, sleeping that often would be great!"

Julian laughed. "Yeah, I should probably get myself one of those."

"Stick with me, and I can dumb you down a bit."

"I will forever be in your debt," he chuckled. "By the way, thanks for helping me with my homework today. I appreciate it."

I watched his face to see if there was any hint of a lie. "You know what I think?"

"What?"

"You're actually a great Chem student and just needed an excuse to see me." I smirked, poking his side again.

Julian blushed, taken aback. He took a moment to regain his composure. *Yes, spot on.*

"Oh yeah? That's a pretty big assumption you're making there," he teased.

I giggled, and I hated myself for the noise that escaped. Leaning forward, I narrowed my eyes, trying to keep a straight face. "Lying to me already, Julian?"

His face went serious. "No."

"Good." I grinned. "Then I think it's adorable that you don't know how to just ask to hang out with me."

Julian remained silent, but I caught his blush. Deciding to let him off the hook, I grabbed the remote from the coffee table.

"Movie?" I suggested. Before he could answer, I was already clicking on my Netflix profile. "Any ideas?"

"Not a one."

"You're useless, Julian." I flipped through a few movies and put on *The Mask*. An oldie but a goodie.

We watched the movie silently, but I couldn't focus. It didn't help that I had seen this movie a thousand times. It was my go-to when I was bored. But here I had Julian Raskin sitting right next to me, and I could barely get myself to open up to him.

I couldn't be his friend if I couldn't figure out if there was something more. For some reason, it felt like it was both or none in our situation. And to quote Liza, I couldn't "screw him over."

Our ice cream bowls had been discarded on the coffee table, and Julian seemed hooked on what was happening in the movie.

"I like you," I blurted, trying not to slide down on the couch, but instead, I looked over at him.

Don't look away, Quinn. Be confident. Be in control.

His head snapped in my direction, shock plastered all over his face. "What?"

"I like you?" I repeated, more hesitantly this time.

It had been a year since I'd had feelings for someone like this. And I wasn't sure I was happy it was happening again.

Julian blushed, unable to make eye contact with me.

"I like you too," he mumbled.

"Really?" I leaned forward again with a smile on my face. "Like, like-like or like as a friend?" I felt childish for asking, but with the way our relationship started, I needed to be sure before I made a fool of myself.

Julian laughed. "I haven't heard that line since elementary school," he took a moment to calm his laughter, "but yes, you dork. Like-like."

I felt my body grow warm, and I instantly sat up. I moved my left leg underneath of me and let my right foot hit the floor, the ice pack falling beside it. I ignored the pain that rushed through my foot and focused on Julian. *He like-liked me.*

"This isn't a prank, right? No dare you've been requested to fill? Julian Raskin actually likes me?"

I wasn't sure why I was putting him on such a high pedestal. It wasn't like he was the sought-after boy in our grade. Or captain of anything. Or even ... what was he even great at? I supposed I'd find out.

But maybe that was it. Maybe he was special to me because he was different. Nothing wrong with that, right?

"So ..." Julian took a moment to collect his thoughts, "does this make you my girlfriend?"

I blinked a few times, the nerves in my stomach starting to get the best of me. "Oh, um," I stuttered. Could I actually be someone's girlfriend again?

"'Cause if it does, I think this calls for a proper date. A do-over that James and Tyler *won't* know about."

I felt a blush rise to my cheeks. "I, uh, I don't know how to be, uh," I cleared my throat, the word foreign to my lips, "a girlfriend." I looked down at my gym shorts, picking at a loose string.

Julian leaned over and kissed my forehead. "Just be you."

I looked up at him and really, truly saw him. Julian Raskin, the teenage boy he wanted me to see, and not the way high school portrayed him to be. We played along with the game, but it was the one game where we didn't belong.

"Okay," I whispered. "I, uh, I'd love to be your girlfriend." I reached down on the couch and took his hand in mine. "But if I'm bad at this, will you let me know?"

"Of course, I'll send up a smoke signal to let the world know."

I pushed his shoulder and let out a laugh.

"I'm serious!" I exclaimed. "I really don't want to fuck this up."

"Yeah ... I feel the same way." Julian's voice was soft.

I nodded and gave him a small smile. He was a genuine person. Unlike the rest of the guys I'd met, making the risk of screwing up even higher. If I had assumptions about Julian, I could only imagine what he assumed I was like.

I moved over on the couch, so I was sitting next to him, our shoulders touching. "C-can I?" I asked, resting my head on his shoulder before he responded.

I never needed to be properly comforted by someone who wasn't a part of my family before, but something was telling me Julian would bring something new to my life.

"Of course." He kissed the top of my forehead again after putting his arm around me.

I adjusted myself, cuddling into his side.

We were both silent for a while, returning to the movie that had been long forgotten. It was nearing the time where my parents were due to kick Julian out. We still both had school in the morning, and I hadn't even touched my homework for the night.

"Julian? Can you do me a favor?"

"Depends," he said into my hair.

"Can you tell James and Tyler to tell Adrian that we fulfilled our dare? He cornered me yesterday and threatened to spread a rumor."

"Yeah. I can do that."

"Promise?"

"I promise." He held out his pinky.

I connected my pinky with his, bringing our hands up to kiss them. He replicated my movements, leaning toward our hands. My breath caught in my throat at his proximity. Julian's eyes danced around me before he kissed his hand. Swallowing, I blinked a few times before I followed suit.

"S-sealed with a kiss," I breathed as he left my bubble.

We managed to finish *The Mask* before both of my parents came out of their room. The moment my father caught us cuddling, he crossed his arms. He gave his fake macho impression of wanting to kick Julian's ass—which my mother and I knew was a joke; Julian was up and off the couch in a second.

"Thank you for having me, Mr. and Mrs. Kennedy."

I laughed, looking over at both of my parents. My father wouldn't correct him, but my mother was already making her way over to him.

"It's lovely to officially meet you, Julian. Please call me Lydia." My mother pulled him into an awkward hug. "Thank you for taking care of Quinn yesterday," she glanced down at our empty bowls, "and so it seems today." She smiled.

"A bowl of ice cream and you two are dating now?" my father asked.

"Well, there's a lot of magic in that Heavenly Hash, Dad. Maybe you should have some, and it'll help your romance with Mom." I raised a brow, and my mom started to laugh.

"She's got a point, sweetheart."

My father just scowled playfully. "I've got enough game, thank you two very much." He wrapped his arm around my mother's shoulders and kissed her temple.

I rolled my eyes, but honestly, I loved them and this.

"Julian, let me walk you out." I stood up, with Julian's assistance.

"Goodnight, sir and Mrs. Lydia." He held up a hand, and then the two of us walked out the front door.

I wasn't an idiot. I knew my father's shadow was directly behind me. I limped my way to Julian's car, trying to get as far from his shadow as possible. He opened his car door and climbed in.

"So, I, uh, I'll see you at school tomorrow? Boyfriend?" I smirked, leaning on his open car window.

"See you then, girlfriend." He smirked back.

Julian leaned over and placed a kiss on my cheek before he started his car.

I walked back into my house, a smile on my face. My parents were both sitting on the couch, where Julian and I had just sat.

"So, boyfriend, huh?" My mom smiled, patting the empty space next to her. I plopped down and rested my head on her shoulder.

"I guess so." I tried to hold back a grin, but I honestly couldn't. Of course, I hoped for a kiss. And I could have kissed him first, but for once, I wanted someone else to make the first move.

I hated that this started because of a bet. I wanted to rid that negativity. But I was going into this with all of my true feelings. Fuck Marie, Emerald, and Adrian.

"Tell us about him," my father asked, flipping through the channels on the television.

"Well, I don't know much about him, aside from the most important: he's not like anyone I know. And right now, that's all that matters. I'm gonna go do some homework."

"Okay, dear. We love you." My mom kissed the top of my head.

"I love you both." I stood up and hobbled my way to my bedroom.

As I got ready for bed, I made the decision to just go to sleep instead of doing my homework. Not the smartest decision, but every great student could fail at some point, right?

Instead, I let the memory of Julian's embrace ease me to sleep.

JULIAN

Quinn Kennedy was my girlfriend. I couldn't even wrap my head around it. She was actually my girlfriend. A laugh erupted out of me just thinking about it, my stomach encased with butterflies. I've gone on dates before, but I never really had a *girlfriend*. Just small talk with girls I thought were cute, only for us to eventually stop talking altogether. But now I had an actual real girlfriend. *Like what?* And Quinn, of all people. She was funny and independent, and damn was she hot. But not in the *man, I want to have sex* with her kind of way. But more a *damn, you're so cool; I admire you* way.

After yesterday I was shaking with excitement to go to school with the chance of seeing her. Just being able to see her face sent chills down my body. My heart skipped a beat every time I heard my phone vibrate, hoping it was her. This was so crazy. I couldn't get over it. And fuck the rumors. I planned to erase them all— show the school who the real Quinn was. The funny, witty girl I was getting to know, not the easy lay everyone made her out to be.

There was just one thing still tugging at me. I liked Quinn a lot. I thought she was beautiful, yes. Beautiful like Christmas lights or flowers. But her appearance or personality didn't make me horny or want sex. You were supposed to want sex when you were in a relationship with someone, right?

What. The. Hell. Was. Wrong. With. Me?

It was the day after I had gone to Quinn's and met her parents—which I'd never experienced with anyone before. I had texted her good morning before I left for school, but she never responded. Heck, I hadn't even seen her yet today, and it was almost lunch. My eyes caught sight of every person I passed by in the halls, hoping we'd cross paths. But we didn't. It made me really wish we shared at least one class together. Where could she be? Did she change her mind and not want to be together after all? I tried to shake the nervous feelings off.

Tyler and James were hanging out by my locker waiting for me. I swallowed the moment I saw them. I knew I had to tell them. It wasn't that I wanted to date Quinn in secret. Hell, I wanted to scream it in the middle of the halls for everyone to hear. I just didn't want to have to deal with these two. Their pestering me to have sex would only intensify the moment they learned I actually made things official.

"Yo, you never answered any of my texts last night; where the hell were you?" James asked me as I approached.

I shrugged. "At Quinn's."

They exchanged a glance. "Did you get her in bed?" James wrapped his arm around me.

"Not yet." I shrugged James' hand off me.

"The bet's still on then." Tyler smiled, looking at James, awaiting his reaction.

"Damn, hurry up, Raskin. I can't afford Tyler's lunch every day." James laughed while Tyler's smile grew.

I let out a fake laugh, unsure how to respond. The bet was stupid. It only made me more nervous about having sex. I knew it'd likely happen eventually. But I didn't want the *when* to be dictated by anyone. "Speaking of which, though ... Quinn and I are a thing now."

"Wait, *now* she's your girlfriend? You just said the other day —" James started to say.

"Yes, she's my girlfriend, so you two need to stop talking about her like a sex object and more like an actual human being. In fact, you shouldn't be using words like *whore* or *slut* to describe anyone."

Whoa. I held my breath. Did that actually come out of my mouth? *Fuck.* But seriously. How can anyone be as disgusting as they were? I never went into this just wanting to lose my V-card. When I was dared to date Quinn, I wanted to show her what a proper date should look like (despite the rules I had to follow). It just so happened I caught feelings along the way. Dare or no dare, my feelings were real. Except I didn't mean to say that. *Fuck. Act cool and confident. That's how you survive high school. Fuck, Julian. Fuck.*

James lifted up his arms in a truce. "Whoa, chill. We get it. But our bet's still on." They high-fived each other.

I let out a breath of relief. "Whatever. Do what you want, but do me a favor, will you? Vouch for me with Adrian? Tell him the date was the real deal and that we're a couple now."

"Why does he matter?" Tyler asked.

"He threatened to start a rumor if we didn't, and I just want to end this school year in peace."

"Sure you aren't just asking us for your *girlfriend*?" James teased.

The way James said girlfriend made my blood boil. It was like the word was empty. Like Quinn was just some asset to have without any real value. My jaw started to ache from clenching it.

"Guys, just help me out, will you?" I asked.

Tyler nodded. "Yeah, dude, sure. Though we doubt Adrian would be much of a threat. He has nothing on you. Even if he did make a rumor about it, there's nothing he could come up with that would be believable." It was moments like these that reminded me of the old Tyler. He knew when to take someone seriously.

"Quinn, on the other hand, now that would be interesting," James said.

"Okay, I'm ready to change the subject," I said, and the conversation switched to our thoughts on our soccer game tomorrow—anything to get these two to stop talking like that.

AT LUNCH, I eyed Ian sitting toward the back of the cafeteria with Liza and their friend I didn't know. I had been so preoccupied with Quinn, I hadn't seen much of Ian outside of soccer lately. He was a real friend, unlike the two idiots I couldn't seem to get away from. Tyler and James *were* my friends; they just annoyed the hell out of me when it came to sex. Ian, on the other hand, was nothing like them. He was the one person I could actually confide in about things without the fear of judgment.

It had almost been a year since we stopped hanging around him. I still talked to him and hung out with him at soccer and sometimes on the weekend, although Tyler and James protested. Before, the four of us were inseparable. Then, one weekend we were supposed to hang out at Tyler's. Neither James or I could make it, but I heard Ian still went. Come Monday morning, Tyler announced that Ian was a lying scumbag and stole from him and that we shouldn't associate ourselves with someone like that.

I didn't know if I should believe him or not. It didn't seem like something Ian would do. He was the most trustworthy person I knew. But it was also out of character for Tyler to get so upset. It was something I expected from James, who tried to dictate what we did and didn't do. But Tyler? It was hard not to take it seriously, so I went along with it. The only times James and Tyler acknowledged Ian were when we practiced soccer together. I was grateful, though, that there were no hard feelings between me and Ian and that we were still able to be friends as if nothing happened.

James and Tyler paid for their food. I brought my own lunch, and we turned toward the door of the cafeteria. As we got to the door to head to our usual lunch spot in front of our lockers, I stopped.

"I just have to piss. I'll be right back," I said, and they nodded.

I made my way to the back of the cafeteria where Ian was sitting. I knew I couldn't spend the entire lunch with him without those two becoming suspicious, but I needed to tell someone about Quinn who wouldn't expect me just to sleep with her.

I put my paper bag on the table, and Liza slid over for me to sit, Ian across from me. He had his finger set on the line he was reading in his textbook and adjusted his glasses. If it weren't for his glasses, people would mistake us for each other. We've thought of switching shirts, seats and me wearing his glasses in class to see if the teacher would notice.

Ian was the most reserved out of our friends, the least likely to drink alcohol or do any drugs. And probably the only one who actually studied for tests. I've known Ian since middle school. He was the type of person who got along with every group: the jocks, the nerds, etc. He fit into them all seamlessly. He used to be what balanced out our small group. He wasn't afraid of putting James in his place when his jokes went too far. He got Tyler out of his shell. And his social skills made up for my lack of them.

"Hey, long time no see," Ian said, and I pulled out my sandwich.

"Yeah, no kidding. It's been what? Forty years?" Ian laughed. "I thought you guys ate your lunch in the science room; what brings you to the land of teenage angst?"

"Looking for you, actually." Ian closed his book and propped his chin on the back of his hands.

"Me?" I asked, raising my brows.

Liza turned to me. "How are things with Quinn?"

"What are you talk-"

"She told me she likes you." Liza smiled. "She and I are friends."

I swallowed. I didn't know Liza and Quinn talked, let alone were friends. When I had seen Ian in the cafeteria, my first thought was that I wanted to tell him about Quinn. That she and I were a couple, and I didn't think I'd ever been this happy in my life. Except I didn't feel comfortable enough to say that here. It wasn't because of Liza. I liked her and trusted her. I've hung out with her and Ian together before.

It was because of the third party sitting at the table. A guy sitting next to Ian, a little too close to him. Their arms were touching. You don't sit comfortably next to someone like that. I knew Ian was gay. But this guy I didn't know, was he his boyfriend? Was that a rude thing to ask? Either way, I had no idea who the hell he was and was not about to spill my heart out in front of him.

Ian must have been able to see my discomfort because the next words out of his mouth were, "This is Connor, my new boyfriend, by the way."

"Hey." I nodded.

"Hi," Connor said.

I looked from Connor to Ian and back to Connor. It didn't feel like the right time to talk about Quinn. So instead, I asked Connor about himself. Asked him what classes he was in and how he and Ian got together. No one asked why I ate lunch with them today, or if there was something I wanted. I felt like I belonged, like me eating with them was an everyday occasion, which I was happy about. I didn't want them to feel like I was using them, because they really were my friends.

God, I should hang out with these guys instead of the two jerks I called friends. But it wasn't that simple. I couldn't just ditch James and Tyler. Despite their asshole tendencies, they were still my friends.

By the time the end of school came around, I was dying to see Quinn. I still hadn't gotten any texts from her, and I was really starting to freak out. I didn't see her anywhere at school, even when I asked to use the bathroom just so I could purposely pass by one of her classrooms to see if she was there. Nothing. Was she even at school today? I wanted to text her again. Ask her how her ankle was or something. But a double text ... did that seem desperate? I didn't want to come off as clingy and scare her away.

On my way to practice, I stopped by the soccer field where I knew the girls' team was having a practice. I looked around, but Quinn wasn't there either. It was unlike Quinn to miss a practice. Worry flooded my insides. *Is she okay?* I knew she hurt her ankle, but was it really that bad?

"Hey," Ian called after me. "You seemed off at lunch. Is everything okay?"

We walked to the soccer field together. "No. Actually, I really wanted to talk to you. I just didn't feel comfortable with Connor."

"You should have told me. We could have gone somewhere else to talk in private." Man, was I grateful for Ian. He never got angry. He always understood my thoughts and feelings and was empathetic toward them. He never made me feel stupid for anything I did or said. He could read me like an open book. I wish everyone was more like him.

"Yeah, but I figured I could just wait till soccer today." Ian nodded at my words. "So Quinn and I are a couple now," I said, getting right to the point.

"Whoa. You never even told me you had feelings for her. Last I knew, you guys went on a date from that dare. When did this happen?"

I laughed, scratching the back of my head. I did text him after Emerald's to tell him I had been coaxed into kissing *the* Quinn Kennedy and now had to go on a date with her. It made me wish he still went to the parties so he could have been there experiencing the social humiliation with me. "Last night. After our date, I don't know ... I really like her, Ian."

"I'm happy for you." Ian smiled.

"Except I feel like something is wrong with me."

"Oh?" Ian raised his eyebrows. "What's wrong?"

"Well, Tyler and James are always pressuring me to lose my virginity."

"And they are idiots who can't even get laid themselves," Ian commented.

I chuckled. "Yeah. But sex doesn't even cross my mind."

I could feel Ian's eyes on me, but I couldn't bear to look. We were almost at the soccer field, where everyone was waiting. I really thought something was wrong with me. Maybe I had some sort of hormonal imbalance or something medical like that. Maybe I was born without the part of my brain that desired sex.

"So? Relationships aren't just about sex."

I almost stopped dead in my tracks. He was right, of course. I never really thought of it like that. *Yes. Relationships don't just have to be about sex.* A smile crept onto my face as hope flooded inside me. "Yeah. You're right."

Before we could say anything else, we arrived at the field and started practice. *Relationships aren't just about sex,* I repeated in my mind. At least, I liked to think so, anyway. Except I knew Quinn liked sex. Which was fine. She wasn't the "whore" everyone claimed she was, but I couldn't escape sex entirely. She'd want to eventually.

I couldn't prevent the uneasy feeling in my stomach all practice. Something about this whole thing didn't feel right. Like sex would be the end of us. It took everything in me to stop my eyes from watering. I needed to see Quinn.

QUINN

I was under very strict instructions that I wouldn't be headed to school. I'd remain in bed with my foot elevated. There were no arguments from me—especially because I never did complete my homework. I had been wanting to play hooky anyway. I did sometimes but never on days with soccer practice. And today, I had practice.

After my coach had a fit yesterday, I didn't care to see her. So when my mom came to deliver me ice and lift my foot this morning, I ended up going back to bed.

That was until my sister woke me up, telling me she was in charge. "Make sure Quinn doesn't waste the day," she mimicked our mom's voice.

Naturally, that meant we'd waste away in front of the television for a bit; she'd go get some lattes and bagels, and we would gossip before we settled down to do work. At least, that's what happened on days she wasn't in school, which seemed few and far between lately.

Today was my lucky day.

By the time she got me to the couch, I saw she already made the coffee run. Her iced latte was condensing on the coffee table, soaking the bag with the bagels, while my hot green tea latte sat next to it. I hated coffee, but for some reason, everyone else in my home loved it.

Emma flipped on the television, finding reruns of *Friends*, and then turned toward me.

"You've been up this long, and you're already holding out on me?" she asked, handing me my drink.

I choked on a laugh.

"I've been awake for approximately four minutes. What haven't I told you?"

"You're not single?" She wiggled her eyebrows suggestively before she picked up the bagel bag and threw me my wrapped bagel.

A blush rose to my cheeks. Julian had messaged me "Good morning" with a smiley face, but I had fallen back to sleep before responding. I lifted my phone and found his message, reading it again before looking back at my sister.

"Julian and I made it official last night."

"Girl!!" she exclaimed, opening up her breakfast. "I'm shocked! But first, where the hell did he come from? I don't ever remember a Julian?"

"He's quiet. And kind. And really handsome in an absolutely quirky way. But he respects me."

"So basically, he isn't a part of the group?" I swatted at my sister, and she ducked fast. "What? Your friends are assholes!"

She wasn't wrong, but not all of them were assholes. It just seemed like the ones who stuck around were. But Liza? And even Ian? They weren't. Getting to know Julian, I was even more baffled as to why he stuck around and didn't follow them in leaving, especially if they were friends.

"Liza isn't," I said softly.

"No ..." Her words were slow. "No, Liza is not. But she still hurt you."

I shook my head. "No, Emma, I'm the one who broke up with her."

She blinked a few times. I was almost certain she was reeling through our conversations. It was the one and only time I lied to my sister, saying Liza didn't trust our relationship and ended up cheating on me.

Emma knew about us. It wasn't something I could or even wanted to lie about it. Especially because I was confused as to why I even felt romantic feelings for Liza. I identified as straight, but that only became crystal clear when I ruined things between us.

"What happened?" Emma finally asked. I shook my head and plastered a smile on my face.

"Topic change: yes, I'm dating Julian. Yes, we are official. Yes, he's special." My smile turned genuine as I continued, "Yes, he's a part of the friends group, and no, he isn't an asshole. Actually, he was a gentleman with Mom and Dad last night."

"Dad told me! He was still up when I got home from Kenny's. Said he was polite and even took care of you. But that he was an ass who held his daughter too close." She laughed, and I choked on the bagel I was eating.

My dad knew I had lost my virginity. So the fact that he was afraid of us cuddling was cute. *Of course*, I didn't actively tell my Dad. I'm not that honest. But he fell victim to a loud exclamation Emma made when I told her.

I turned to the television, trying to pay attention to whatever ridiculous thing Joey was trying to do in this episode. We carried on eating our bagels and drinking our lattes before I looked over at her again.

"Sis?" I stared.

She glanced over before seeing the worry on my face. Muting the sound, she turned her entire body toward me.

"How do I be a girlfriend?"

She frowned and placed a hand on my knee. It made me feel small. Made me feel like there was more than just two years between us. We were both so different that it often felt like we were the same age with how we excelled in certain things. I was talented in sports, and she was talented in music and art. While she had been on the basketball team, her sports career ended when she started college, whereas I was banking on a soccer scholarship. We both excelled in school, but my sister had always either been absolutely single or in a relationship. Kenny was her first everything. It took her quite some time to get over the fact that one, I lost my virginity only a few months after she did. And two, I didn't want a boyfriend. It wasn't until she got to college this year that she truly understood that I was just exercising my sexual freedom.

"It'll come natural to you, babe. There's a reason Julian is interested. He likes you for who you are, right here and now. Don't change because you think there's some other, better way of doing it. Remain active and present. And if you get bored, either try and talk to him or go your separate ways before you venture off. Relationships are about trust and commitment. That's my only fear for you. Can you be happy with just him?"

I thought back to when he said sex wasn't on his mind. And then again to last night. We never even kissed, just pecks on the forehead or cheek. Could I do slower-paced? Would I be able to hold out for him?

"He's a virgin," I whispered.

Her face went slightly off-kilter. She had been too at my age, though.

"Quinn, I love you, but please don't hurt this poor boy."

I nodded. That was my fear too.

THE REST OF THE DAY, my sister and I hung out in front of the television, *Friends* still playing in the background as we did our respective schoolwork. Every so often, I would check my phone, hoping Julian would check in with me—noticing I wasn't in school. But that was unrealistic because we rarely crossed paths.

I also never answered his morning text, but I didn't really know what to say. How do you text a boyfriend? Often, my messages with guys were just times and dates. No follow-up, no questions beforehand. *Of course*, I knew how to text, but only in regard to my close friends. But a boy I was having feelings for?

I wanted to see what kind of boyfriend Julian would be, and I was stubborn enough to believe how often he texted me was an indication.

I had a few messages from Marie throughout the day, first realizing I wasn't in school to then messaging me any tiny piece of gossip I might be missing—somehow never questioning me on my new relationship status. Was Julian embarrassed by me? I half-expected Marie to be blowing up my phone the moment she heard ... but maybe he hadn't actually told anyone? Nerves started festering in the pit of my stomach. Was this a bad idea? Did he actually like me? Or did he just go along with what I asked? Did he feel pressured?

I *hated* this feeling. I never let anyone make me feel this way. Why was I letting Julian get into my head? How could one boy change everything? Julian seemed like he'd stand up for himself—right? If he didn't like me, he'd say so. *And* he was the one who asked if I was his girlfriend. I was just talking about dating. And he was the one who put a label on it.

Liza even texted me—after soccer practice—to tell me Coach was livid that I didn't show. Was a simple conversation on the bus enough to mend us?

But the school hours came and went all without a single word from Julian.

Were we even dating?

"If you don't text him right now, I'm going to do it for you." I jumped at my sister's voice. It's like she could read my mind. "You've been obsessing over your phone all day. Don't play those stupid games, Quinn. You fucking hate them. If you're willing to date this boy, I assure you he hates them too. You two *just* got together; don't ruin it over a damn text that may or may not have come in."

I looked over at her, and she was ready to snatch my phone away. With a roll of my eyes, I sighed and went to compose a message to Julian. But I couldn't stop the nagging in my mind.

My question was met with a knock at the door.

Before I could even comprehend that his SUV was outside, my sister was up and at the door.

JULIAN

WHILE I STOOD ON THE STEPS TO QUINN'S HOUSE, I wondered if maybe I should have called first. It also occurred to me that maybe I should have brought flowers or ice cream for her. Except, the moment soccer was over, I couldn't get here fast enough.

The door swung open, and a girl who looked *almost* identical to Quinn answered, a smile forming on her lips. The only difference between the two was Quinn had fiery-red, curly hair, and this girl had pin-straight dark brown hair.

"Why, hello!" she greeted, opening the door wider, gesturing for me to enter with her arm. "I'm Emma, Quinn's older sister; you must be Julian!"

"Um, yes. Is Quinn home?" God, this was beginning to feel like a terrible idea. Who just shows up at someone's house uninvited? But I needed to see Quinn, to make sure she was okay. My brain wouldn't let me think of a more logical way to go about it.

"Yes, she's just inside." I looked over at the couch where we had sat the night before to see Quinn with her foot still elevated.

I entered with no idea why I was here or what to say to her. I just needed to see her. But if I said that, it would sound desperate. I realized I could have just texted her. Or I could have asked Marie for her notes and homework for the day. It would have given me a reason to stop by. Instead, here I was with nothing to offer. *Dammit, Julian, think things through more.*

Quinn was looking at me expectantly as I approached the couch.

"Hey." I smiled. "And if you look to the left, you'll see a Quinn Kennedy. An elusive creature who missed school today." Quinn laughed.

"Please save her; she's been moping here for the past few hours because she doesn't know how to send you a message." Emma laughed.

Quinn shot her a death glare—one I knew I never wanted to be on the receiving end of.

"Shove it, Emma. Come on, Julian." Quinn started packing up her books and then stood up from the couch. "Let's go to my room." She started walking down the hallway.

"Allow me," I said, grabbing Quinn's books and offering my arm as a crutch.

"Thank you," she said, smiling.

I couldn't stop my brain from wondering what was going through her head. Was she okay with this? Was it weird that I was here? She seemed fine with it. I swallowed, trying to not let my thoughts consume me.

Quinn walked us in and looked around as if she were seeing her own room for the first time. Her walls were a silvery gray. One entire wall was dedicated to photographs; from a distance, they ranged from silly photos of her friends to seemingly professional photography, all in black and white. She stepped away from my hold and sat down on her bed in the middle of the room, looking up at me.

"I, uh, welcome." She laughed, looking down at her hands. "I barely bring anyone in here. Sorry, this is weird." Quinn ran her hands over her curls, tightening the ponytail they were in.

Her room was messier than I would have imagined. I always thought girls were the neat ones, but compared to my own room, hers was a disaster. Clothes were in heaps on the floor. The top of her dresser was hidden under hair ties and used post-it notes of to-do lists—ninety percent of them said "clean" underlined multiple times. Even her dresser drawers weren't properly closed.

"It's very tidy. I see organization is important to you."

Her cheeks grew red, but she blinked away her nerves and raised her eyebrow. I was glad to see, though, that I wasn't the only one who was nervous.

"Well, you see, Julian, there is this thing called letting someone know you're coming over. Maybe I would have cleaned for you." A hint of a smile appeared on her lips.

"My apologies for caring about you." She looked away from me. "I was worried when I realized you weren't at school today." I now wished even more that I had something to say like, *Oh I thought I'd bring your homework for you.* Or something like that. So I guess the truth would have to do.

"When did you realize I was missing?" Her tone seemed off—defensive even, but I couldn't figure out what I had done wrong.

"When the police filed a missing person report and hung posters all around the school. They even had milk cartons with your face on them." She rolled her eyes, letting out a soft laugh. "No, I stopped by the soccer field on my way to practice and saw you were M.I.A." I was going to say, "Pretty much first thing in the morning." But that seemed a little too stalkerish.

She nodded. "My coach was apparently pissed. But mother's orders this morning." Quinn then smiled. "Though I had contemplated playing hooky last night." She patted the comforter next to where she was sitting. "I promise I won't try and sleep with you." She winked.

"Thanks for the reassurance." I laughed as I sat down next to her. My laugh sounded forced, and I hope she didn't notice. Why did she have to say that? Was it that obvious the fear crossed my mind?

"Have you told anyone?" she asked, reaching over and taking my hand in hers.

Her phone dinged behind us. *So her phone was working.*

Quinn reached for it with her free hand before muttering under her breath.

"You two are off the hook, but not for long, I imagine. I'm always watching, Quinn." She read her message out loud, imitating who I could only imagine was Adrian.

"To answer your question—yes. Yes, I did." I paused. "I didn't go around handing out our wedding invitations if that's what you're asking." She glared at me for my joke. I shrugged. "I only told Tyler, James, and Ian."

"I'm impressed it hasn't made its way through the rumor mill yet."

To be honest, I was shocked too. Nothing ever traveled slowly.

"I haven't heard from Marie or Emerald." As if on cue, her phone kept alerting her of new messages coming in. She placed it on silent before tossing it gently across the room. "But Ian?" she continued, scrunching her brows. "Do you see him often still?"

"Yeah. He's probably my best friend." I looked down at our hands on my thigh.

"I'm not here to control you, but that makes me really happy." She squeezed my hand, and I looked over to see her smiling. "Liza loves him. But what do you see in James and Tyler?"

I let out a laugh. "Convenience? Honestly, if I didn't see them so much between school and soccer, I probably wouldn't be friends with them.

"I get that. It's similar to me and Marie. I mean, we've been friends since grade school, but high school has changed us. Honestly, I'm better friends with my sister than anyone in school." She climbed off the bed, letting my hand go. Quinn closed her bedroom door, and before I had a chance to question what that might mean, she continued talking, "Do you have siblings?"

She climbed back onto her bed, but this time sitting up against the headboard, her legs stretched out long. I joined her, our shoulders touching. I stretched my legs out, my feet extending at least a foot longer than hers.

"Sort of. I mean, I have a half-sister I've never met," I responded once comfortable.

"You've never met her?" Her eyes bugged out.

"Yeah. My parents got divorced when I was pretty young, and my mom remarried and had a daughter. But since my mom lives out of town, I never see her."

"That's so sad," Quinn said.

I shrugged. "Meh. Not really. The whole thing has made me closer to my dad at least."

"I can't imagine not having both parents. They've been my solid rocks through everything. I'm happy you have your dad, though. He never remarried?"

"No. I think he's still heartbroken over my mom, to be honest. I don't think he's even gone on any dates since they split." I didn't like talking about this. It didn't feel like my business to talk about their personal life.

Quinn looked over at me and then slid down on the bed, so her head was on her pillow.

"Come here." Her words were soft as she opened her arms. I laid down next to her, and she wrapped her arms tightly around me. I nestled my head in the crook of her neck, her curls clouding my face.

"Sorry to make the mood somber." I gave a fake chuckle into her hair.

She shook her head and kissed my cheek. "No apologies necessary. I wanna know this stuff. I promise you can trust me."

Before I let my brain think about it, I lifted my chin and kissed her. I held her there, our lips moving in perfect rhythm. This is how it starts, isn't it? Sex, I mean. I tried to convince my brain to just let it happen, to not think about it. I tried to convince one of my body parts to let it happen. I put one of my hands on her lower back to hold her close to me, my other hand cupping the back of her head.

We hadn't kissed since the night of the dare. But this kiss was real. And it felt so good. I didn't want anything more than this. I wanted to savor this moment. I wanted to kiss her till our lips went numb and then cuddle and laugh together afterward. But that isn't what's supposed to happen, right?

I pulled her closer and moved my hand down from her hair and onto her waist, tracing her curves along the way. This felt so good. I couldn't understand why people took it any further than this.

In an instant, Quinn removed her lips from mine, and she sat up, looking down at me. "We haven't eaten yet. Are you hungry?" She looked away from me.

I sat up. "Yeah a little," I answered, unsure of what just happened.

Did she not want sex after all? Relief washed over me. If she was the heartless robot who only cared about sex like people thought she was, she definitely would have pounced on that opportunity. But she didn't. She let us just kiss. Maybe I have nothing to worry about after all.

A smile formed on my lips. *Quinn, you amaze me.*

WE WENT to an arcade that had just opened up downtown called Game On. The inside was huge. Classic pinball games and other vintage games like Pac-man lined the walls. In the middle of the wide-open space were more modern games like air hockey, Dance Dance Revolution and a giant version of Connect Four. To the far side of the arcade was a bar where we ordered a slice of pizza and fries (well, Quinn ordered four slices of pizza and a large fry for herself.)

Once we finished eating, I bought us tokens to play some games with my allowance.

"What do you want to do first?" I asked.

She glanced around the arcade, a devilish grin appearing. "Definitely air hockey. I'm about to kick your ass."

"Hold up. I'll have you know I used to play hockey as a kid. I'm basically a pro."

"We'll see about that." She winked before heading toward the table.

I followed, inserting two tokens into the coin slot. It started up, a yellow puck clinking into a slot on my side. I hit it with force, the puck bouncing off the sides with speed, only to quickly spring back to my side.

"Can't win if I don't let you touch it." I stuck out my tongue.

She didn't even laugh; her eyes narrowed in on the puck, game face on. I hit the puck again, ready to have it hit off the walls and into her goal. But Quinn slammed her striker onto the puck, stopping it dead in its tracks. She looked up at me, an evil grin plastered on her face. *Oh god. I'm in for it.* She hit the puck, and before I even had the time to react I heard it clink into my goal slot.

"Damn," I said as the scoreboard changed to 1-0. "Didn't realize I was playing with an NHL star."

"Told you I'd kick your ass. 'Bout time you start to take me seriously, Raskin."

"The game isn't over yet." I dropped the puck onto the table, making a fast hit and getting a goal.

She shook her shoulders before taking the puck out. Placing the puck on the table, she leaned down, calculating her aim before looking up and making eye contact with me.

"You're going down." She hit the puck; it slammed the wall on my side before bouncing back to her. With another hard strike, the puck bounced up and toppled off the table.

"Man overboard!" I reached down to pick the puck up, laughing.

"Fuck." She laughed but quickly covered her mouth. "Let's pretend that didn't happen. Doesn't count." She drummed on the table. "Quick, quick, quick! We're gonna lose time."

"Aaah." I rushed to put the puck back on the table, hitting it only for Quinn to rebound it back to me and into my goal.

"YES!" she shouted, hopping around on her good foot as she did a little dance. "You're gonna lose, sucker."

"Not if I can help it." Before she put her striker back down, I had hit the puck into her goal. I grinned, showing off my teeth. "We're neck and neck now."

She stuck her tongue out, placing the puck back on the table. Suddenly, her eyes diverted.

"Oh, hey! Isn't that Ian and Liza?"

I looked over my shoulder before hearing the clink of a goal and the table shutting down. I snapped my head back at her. "Wow. Cheating? Too scared I'd beat you fair and square?"

She placed her hand over her heart. "How dare you accuse me of such a thing. We made no rules." She grinned, walking around the table. "But I do believe you owe me a milkshake."

"What? *Me*? Sorry, lady, but I don't buy cheaters anything." I smiled, looking over at the claw machine nearby. "However, I'm going to be cheesy and try to win you something." I pointed to the machine before jogging over to it. "Which one will it be?"

"What's your favorite animal?"

I looked through the glass. "Hmm. Definitely giraffes. Just imagine never struggling to reach the top shelf again with a neck like that."

She laughed, rolling her eyes before focusing in on the stuffed animals. Her hands fell flat against the glass.

"Do you think you can actually win?"

"Pft. You're speaking to Julian Raskin here. I am the ultimate master at claw machines."

"That is one thing I'll never try to compete with you on. Show me your moves."

The rest of our tokens later and Quinn standing beside the machine trying to direct me, I finally managed to get the large giraffe plush from the machine. I pulled it from the prize hole and lifted it over my head triumphantly.

"Ah-ha! Told you I was the master." I handed it to Quinn, the stuffed animal nearly the size of her head.

Her smile grew as she looked over the giraffe, hugging it against her.

"Thank you." Her eyes met mine. "No one has ever won something for me before."

Her tone was soft and genuine, and I could feel my cheeks growing warm.

Wow. It was so strange how you could think you know someone just by seeing them around, just by hearing things about them from others. But then, when you are actually with them, outside school walls, outside of the pressure and judgments of anyone, you really see them. You see different parts of them. People will surprise you. Intrigue you. There are so many layers to a person, and rumors and gossip are just the outside layers. A crusty fake layer over who the person really is. First impressions are wrong. Rumors are wrong.

I found myself shaking my head. Sure, we started from a dare.

Truthfully, I probably would have never given myself the chance to actually get to know her. Because that's the thing with rumors. They make you believe you know what someone is like. But they were wrong. People are more complex than that. There is so much more to a person than what lies on the surface.

I couldn't wipe the smile off my face. Here I was with Quinn, a girl I thought I knew, yet every time we were together, I just kept learning new things about her. She was competitive and headstrong but had a soft side to her too.

"Earth to Julian," I heard her giggle as her hand came in front of my face. "Let's go get ice cream down the street."

"Didn't you just eat?" I teased.

Her eyes widened. "What's your point?"

"I'm too afraid to argue with you without getting my head chopped off." I smiled. "Let's go."

"One day you'll learn, Julian. There's *always* room for ice cream." She linked her free arm with mine.

QUINN

THE FOLLOWING MORNING I WAS ON CLOUD NINE. NOT ONLY had I fallen asleep replaying the night with Julian, but I woke up to a goodnight message. Clearly, I had passed out before our conversation ended. When I rolled over to reply to him, the giraffe hit my back. I pulled the stuffed animal into my arms, reading his message.

> *Hey. I had a wonderful*
> *evening with you *smiley face**
> *Have a good day! Take good*
> *care of Steve! (yes, I named the*
> *giraffe, don't judge me.)*

I took a picture of me cuddling Steve before attaching it to a text message.

> *Good morning!*
> *We hope you have a*
> *wonderful day too.*

I couldn't shake the smile from my face all morning as I got ready and ate breakfast. Luckily, my parents just exchanged a glance and didn't question me.

It was so simple, so easy to be with Julian. Never would I have imagined that we could get along as well as we do. Yeah, he was still an awkward guy, but in an adorable and funny way. And I liked to believe I was catching on to his nerdy sense of humor.

The disappointment came when I entered the school hallways and remembered that Julian and I didn't share classes, nor did I know what classes he had or at what times. All I knew about was his lunch period, but I couldn't possibly skip study hall every day without getting caught.

Before I made it to my locker, Marie was sprinting down the hall to meet me there.

"Thank *god*," she breathed. "Don't ever leave me alone again."

I rolled my eyes, but I smiled as I turned the dial on my locker. She may not be the friend I wished she still was from back in middle school, the girl I could turn to with no drama, but she was still a good friend when she wanted to be. And it felt nice to be wanted—needed even.

"I was injured. Mom's orders." Opening the door, I started exchanging my books for what I needed.

Emerald slid up behind Marie, wrapping his arms around her waist. He even went as far as placing a kiss on her neck. The two were disgusting ... but I couldn't hide my smile.

"Good morning, beautiful ladies." He flashed his pearl-white teeth.

I slammed my locker shut and threw my bag on my shoulder.

"Morning, Emerald." From behind him, I caught a glimpse of Julian.

I wanted to brush them both aside and run over to him, but I forced myself to slow down. Just a couple of days and I was already losing my cool.

"Should we head off campus today at lunch?" Emerald asked.

Marie answered him, then started telling me something about yesterday, but my line of vision was directed to Julian, who smiled wide when he caught my eyes.

"Quinn? Are you even listening to me?" Her words broke through before I was instantly distracted again.

Julian was directly in front of me. I stumbled back a step, running into the locker. I heard Marie's voice speaking, but I couldn't comprehend her words.

"Good mor—" His lips crashed into my own, grasping my cheek in his palm, caressing my skin with his thumb.

I kissed him back, standing on my tippy toes, wrapping my hands around his neck, breathing him in. God, his scent was delightful—just a hint of citrus and cinnamon. I wanted to get him alone, nuzzle my nose in the crevice of his neck, and nibble away at his skin.

School, Quinn. School.

Where the hell were all of these emotions coming from?

He pulled away, moments too soon, but he leaned his forehead against mine. I could still feel his warm breath on my wet lips, only making me want to get him alone.

Julian would *never* be boring.

"Good morning," I breathed.

"Indeed it is." He smiled, pecking my lips once more.

I could feel the cold air brush between us as he took a step back. He seamlessly interlaced our fingers. As my eyes watched his movements, his wide grin greeted Marie and Emerald.

"Well, hello."

"God, this is perfect!" Marie exclaimed, swatting me excitedly on the arm. Her eyes flicked back and forth between me and my interlaced hand. "I knew this was a genius idea!"

"Now, calm down," I started, holding up my hands. "We just started dating."

"Oh no, Q," Emerald said. "This is all going according to plan." I hated the shivers that coursed through my body at his words. I looked up at Julian, who seemed equally worried.

We were still goddamn puppets to them.

"We all knew you'd be perfect together. It's just you two who didn't know," Marie explained.

"Come on, Marie." Emerald took her hand. "Let's leave the lovebirds be; the bell is about to ring." Emerald winked over at Julian, and I felt his hand tense in mine.

With that, Emerald led them down the hall, but not before Marie gestured that we had *so* much to talk about.

The warning bell rang, letting us know we had two minutes to get to our respective classrooms.

"Wanna grab dinner after your game?" I suggested, turning toward him.

I'd be able to catch the second half of his game after my own practice. Luckily, it was a home game.

"Of course. I'll meet you outside the gym? After I shower?"

"Perfect." I smiled. "Good luck this afternoon!"

Standing on my tippy toes, I kissed his smiling lips before the two of us took off in opposite directions, both of us late as the bell rang out.

QUINN

THERE WERE MULTIPLE REASONS I DIDN'T CARE FOR relationships in the past, and one of them was losing my own free time. At least if I hooked up with someone, it was a minor thing in my life. But relationships took time and work—all of which were easy with Julian—however, it did sometimes take energy to remember that I needed to be a constant presence in someone's life. I couldn't simply be selfish anymore.

But let me clarify: that wasn't a bad thing. It was just a new thing.

Julian and I both tried to get out of the Friday get together, hoping two forces instead of one would be strong enough. Last week had returned to our normal Friday night hangout—Martin and Emerald were neck and neck in a FIFA championship— Martin winning free lunch for the week. This Friday, Julian and I wanted to spend time with just the two of us. But we were roped in.

So, we found ourselves back in the den, surrounded by this mishmash group of people—but tonight, unlike other nights, more of us were drinking than not. Julian and I included. Julian and I sat curled up on the couch, trying to remove ourselves from the group as much as we could.

There wasn't even a debate when Emerald handed me a whiskey and coke and Julian a beer upon entry.

An hour in and people were already getting a little out of control. It was a party that would end with more people sleeping on the floor than driving home. It was interesting to see from the perspective that I was in. Sure, I often spent most Fridays looking out at the group, but it seemed that Julian's presence in my life heightened the ridiculousness of it all.

We all partnered off into smaller groups, yet somehow, we all needed to be here together. Marie and Paige were gossiping as Emerald joined James and Tyler tonight—no doubt coming up with some conniving plan. Adrian was flirting with a few of the other girls in our group, yet every so often, I caught his eyes on me.

"Where's Martin? Have you seen Martin?" Julian whispered to me. I laughed, noticing Martin across the room wearing a camouflage hoodie.

"Undercover F.B.I. Quick! Hide your drink," I whispered, leaning closer to him, shielding our plastic cups between our torsos.

Julian eyed over my shoulder.

"He's suspicious. Act natural!" I giggled and pressed my lips against his, the first natural reaction I could think of.

I could feel Julian's smile through the kiss before he broke it with a laugh.

"The F.B.I. is after you, and the first thing you do is kiss me?"

"If I'm committing a felony, I might as well go all in," I answered with a wink.

Drinks were continually poured, and mine and Julian's cups were refilled, though we were only starting our third cup when others were on their fourth or fifth.

I felt happy, giddy even, thinking I could handle Friday nights if I could spend them just like this. The alcohol made me feel brave, and I leaned up to kiss Julian. Despite cuddling most of the night, I didn't act on any other PDA. I didn't want to draw attention to us. But fuck everyone else. If I was going to be in a relationship, I was going to do it the way I wanted to.

He returned my kiss, and I drank in the way his beer tasted on his lips. I only drank beer if it was the only thing available, but fuck would I devour it if it tasted this way. I wanted to be alone with him. I wanted to be back in my bed wrapped up in his arms, away from the commotion. Julian and I had yet to even come close to sleeping with each other—while unspoken, we were both taking things slowly. Honestly, it was far slower than I anticipated, and the alcohol was only heightening my urges.

My hands found his hair, and I gripped his locks, pulling him closer to me as I leaned back against the end of the couch. Julian's hand found my waist, gripping it as he began to hover over me— his own alcohol beginning to get the best of him. I breathed in, arching closer to him, desperate to have more. I had to remind myself we couldn't go further—not here. This shouldn't have been more than a simple kiss.

"This would be a new one, Quinn."

I shivered as the words connected in my mind. His laughter floated through the room, and I instantly shoved Julian off me. Connecting eyes with Adrian, I saw how intoxicated he already was.

"Taking someone's precious virginity in public? How desperate must a girl be?" He stood up, wobbling a little as he took a few steps toward me.

Julian took my hand in his, and I gripped it hard as I felt myself beginning to shake.

"What is with you, Quinn? Why do you search for the

virgins? Taking something meaningful to them, only to walk away right after?"

"I don't do that." My voice was grave. I was amazed I even was able to speak.

"Just shut up, Adrian," Julian said.

My heart raced, glad Julian would defend me. And yet ....

Don't let him have control, Quinn.

"No?" He laughed. "Hmm, shall we go through your history? Maybe it would be good for Julian to be educated on the whore he's dating."

I started to get up, but Julian pulled me back.

"He's not worth it," Julian whispered in my ear.

For a second, the sound of his voice was pulling me back into our bliss. But the engraved smirk on Adrian's face caused me to dig my fingernails into the palm of Julian's hand. His intake of breath only softened my fingertips slightly.

"Let's see, you sure as hell didn't start with me—as you should have. But maybe that's where the fascination comes from? From the fact that an older guy took your v-card at thirteen?"

"You know that isn't true." I tried to be reasonable, but drunk Adrian was never reasonable.

"Let's see ..." He took a sip of his drink. "Well, there was that tenth-grader over the summer. Alex, was he? Poor guy thought you liked him. I bet you didn't know that he's a family friend. Or that he trusts me with his problems."

My heart skipped a beat. Alex wasn't a lie. We just had a miscommunication. But ... but what had he told Adrian?

I swallowed the onset of tears. I refused to be weak in front of them. Why did he even care?

"Rob in ninth grade was bragging you took his v-card a week after Alex and immediately afterward slept with his friend."

"That's bullshit," I started.

Truth was, it wasn't immediately afterward. There were a

few days between. Honestly, I had been interested in Rob's next-door neighbor, Garrett. He was a senior, and I had my eyes on him for quite some time. So maybe I used Rob to get to Garrett. But it didn't happen within the same day. And that rumor was starting to spread before Garrett and I even slept together.

A few people in the group were egging him on now as if we weren't all supposed to be on the same team. We now had everyone's undivided attention. Why was I becoming the victim? Why did everyone hate on me for enjoying sex? Why wasn't I allowed to do exactly what Adrian, James, Tyler, and all the other guys did on a daily, weekly, and monthly basis?

"Adrian." Julian's voice startled me. He stood, placing a hand firmly on Adrian's chest to stop him from coming closer. I had forgotten Julian was even there. "Back off."

"Oh, Julian." Adrian laughed, brushing Julian's hand off. "You see, we aren't done here. I'm doing this for you, man." Adrian winked at me and swallowed the rest of his drink. "It's real sweet here that Quinn claims she's a changed woman. But those three people? That happened the last three weeks of the summer. Shall we continue?"

Emerald walked up behind Adrian and placed his hands on his shoulders.

"Come on, Adrian. Let's go outside. I think you've proved your point."

My eyes shot up to Emerald, who was avoiding my gaze. He was only my friend when convenient.

"He's proved his point?" I spat. "What fucking point?" I screamed, standing up and walking mere inches from Adrian's face. Emerald let go of Adrian and backed up with his hands held high.

Emerald just shook his head and laughed, walking back to Marie. I could barely focus on her in the background with Adrian breathing heavily in front of me.

"Alright, folks, let's continue. Now everyone, remember Liza?" Adrian's eyes challenged mine, the one secret Adrian promised to bring to his goddamn grave. Adrian was a lot of things—many I hated—but at the end of the day, I still trusted him.

There was a deafening silence. It was as if time stopped.

"Adrian," I whispered in warning. His eyes danced with revenge. "Please." There was a flicker of recognition before he broke our eye contact and took a step back. For a brief moment, I had my friend back, the one I truly believed would take my secret to the grave.

How could I have been so foolish?

"Let's gather round for story time, kids." Adrian looked around the room, beckoning everyone closer, but no one moved an inch—some weren't even looking toward us.

I'm sorry, Liza.

"It was November of tenth grade. Quinn was up to her usual antics: sleeping around without an emotion in sight. That's when she claimed her next victim, Liza Reynolds. Yep, you heard me correctly. Quinn got bored of guys and moved on to Liza. The sweet innocent closeted lesbian."

There were a few gasps and rustling as everyone started talking amongst themselves.

"Adrian," I tried again. What happened to the kind, compassionate boy I dated? The kid who always did his best to make sure I was happy? The kid I could count on? It was silly of me to keep hoping a miracle would happen. But I had to try for Liza. "Anything, anything but this. This isn't about her, and you know it."

"You see here, boys and girls, Quinn thinks she has a heart." *Where was* his *goddamn heart?* "She thinks she's doing the right thing. But, in reality, Quinn Kennedy only wants two things: control and sex. She'll do whatever it takes to achieve them."

My hands shook as I balled them into fists. I couldn't seem to find my voice anymore.

Julian's hands came to rest on my shoulders, his thumbs massaging into my neck. I hated the way I wanted to shrug him off, the way my body wanted to violently shove him away.

He isn't the enemy, Quinn.

"Adrian." Julian's voice deepened, and I shivered at its intensity.

Any normal person would be concerned by Julian's warning. But Adrian? He didn't even acknowledge Julian existed, his eyes narrowing in on my own.

"In this case, Liza was the poor victim. But what makes it worse? Liza trusted Quinn with all of her secrets. And what did Quinn do after she took Liza's virginity? Within just a few hours, she ended their relationship, told me all of Liza's secrets, and was moaning underneath me—not once, not twice, but three times."

Julian's hands fell from my shoulders, and the act alone destroyed me far worse than anything Adrian could say. But Adrian was the cause of this. The reason for all the negativity in my life.

I wanted to double over with the pseudo stabbings I was receiving. There was a part of me that believed real stab wounds would hurt far less than betrayal from all sides.

Without another thought, my fist drew back, and I punched Adrian directly in the mouth. There was a collection of screams— one belonging to Adrian as he stumbled back.

Adrian wiped the saliva off his lips. He was about to speak again.

Not good enough, Quinn.

I gripped his baggy shirt, pulling him closer to me as I took another shot at him. Someone's hands were on my arms, trying to pull me away, but I shoved my elbow back, connecting against someone's cheek. Adrian was my one and only target, and I'd be damned if anyone stopped me.

"You're dead to me, Adrian," I growled.

He tried to swing back at me, but his aim was off, as he only grazed my cheek. His failed attempt only made me more determined. His feet shuffled him backward, people moving out of his way until he ran into a wall.

Cornering him, I gripped the collar of his shirt.

"I'm done playing your stupid little games. You can't control me anymore."

His eyes rolled, and I pulled his body down, kneeing him directly in the stomach. Without giving him the chance to stand, I took advantage of his angle and connected my knee directly into his face before letting him go.

He let out a groan, and I watched as his blood trickled down my knee. He fumbled as he stood, holding the wall for support. His mouth opened, and blood trailed down his chin. In a gut reaction, I slapped him across the face. I wanted to beat the living shit out of him, but I couldn't be that person.

"Once a whore, always a whore," Adrian snickered. "Even without me, your wicked ways will spread—just like your legs." Blood and saliva spit out with each word, sinking into the carpet and his t-shirt.

I glared into his dilated eyes. One arm drawn back with a calculated swing, I aimed directly for his nose. Hit precisely on target, he covered his face and fell to the floor, cursing under his breath.

Before anyone came to his rescue—if they even would—I bolted up the den staircase and out the front door.

I looked around, spotting Julian's SUV down the road. I cursed under my breath, wishing I had my own car so I could just drive away. It didn't matter if it was after my driving curfew or that I'd been drinking. All I wanted to do was get out of here, but there was no way in hell I could walk home.

Jogging to his car, I tried to open the door, but it was locked.

"Fuck you, Julian!" I groaned, jiggling the door handle a few more times before I slapped the car, turned around and slid down the passenger side door.

Hugging my knees to my chest, I shuddered as the wind blew. It was the third week in October, and the temperature was starting to drop. I hugged my arms around my chest.

I could still feel the way Julian's hands fell from my shoulders —the emptiness and the loneliness that consumed me in one small—but game-changing reaction.

I *was* heartless.

I *was* a bitch.

I *was* the greatest asshole there ever was.

Adrian *was* right.

My hand throbbed in pain as I gripped my biceps tighter. Removing my right hand, I saw it was already swelling red and crusting in blood.

I had never punched someone before, but god had I always imagined the way I'd kick Adrian's ass. I scared myself with how far I wish I had gone. One more drink in me, and I probably wouldn't have had the self-control to stop.

But what absolutely shitty friends to just watch all that transpire without anyone stepping in. *Especially* the fighting. It was all pure entertainment to them.

I looked up at the sky and hated the millions of stars that shined brightly down on me. Julian and I were hoping to stargaze tonight—it was one of the clearest nights in weeks—if we had gotten out of Emerald's. Now it was like they were taunting me.

I moved so I could lie down in the grass beside Julian's car. Wrapping my arms around myself again, I watched the motionless stars. Where was the joy in this? Why had I even suggested it to Julian earlier in the day? If anything, this made me feel more insignificant. Who the hell was I, and why did I matter?

I hated that my defenses had been down in there. I hated that I got lost in my happiness with Julian and wasn't on my A game. I used to have control and power. I used to be strong. But something broke down the line. I was feeding into the lies, accepting them as true, and I wasn't even certain who I was anymore.

"FUCK YOU!" I screamed at the top of my lungs, knotting my curls around my fingers as I pulled my hair from my scalp.

When my lungs ran out of air, I gasped and let out the tears that had begun to nestle in my forehead, emerging in a headache. I couldn't even be bothered to wipe them away, just letting gravity do its job as they slid into my ears.

Julian's head came into my vision as he stood above me. "Fancy seeing you here."

I wiped the tears from my eyes. I was afraid to look up at him. "How'd you find me?" I mumbled. I didn't think I was visible from Emerald's home.

"I think you're forgetting whose car you're lying beside." I could hear Julian's smile in his words. "Besides, your red hair gives you away."

I couldn't understand why he was here. Why he was smiling. Why was he talking to me?

"Go away," I groaned, sitting up but pivoting so my back was to him.

"And if I don't?"

I stood up and started walking down the street.

"Ah, yes, I do agree it's a lovely night for a walk." I could hear his footsteps behind me.

I crossed my arms tightly against my chest and quickened my pace. "Just go home, Julian."

"Can't. I've been drinking. So looks like I'm walking too."

I stopped abruptly, turning on one foot, finding slight satisfaction in his shocked expression. He was quick to stop as well, his arms tight against his body with his hands in his pockets from the cold.

"Stop the goddamn charade, Julian. You've learned the truth. I'm a heartless bitch who is only here to steal your virginity. Stop acting like you care. Stop acting like you don't want to run for the hills but can't because you're a goddamn gentleman."

"Only if you stop acting like you know me." He shook his head. "You have this tough act up, and you're using it against me. Pretending like you know what I'm thinking. What I'm *feeling*. But you don't know anything, Quinn. I'm not just all about sex. I actually care about you."

I looked up, trying to keep my tears at bay, but I was seconds from breaking down again. I needed to get away. But honestly, I was terrified. This area wasn't safe enough to walk in the dark, especially while intoxicated.

"Why would I believe you?" I swallowed, rubbing my eyes. "What makes you so different from all the rest of them?"

Julian let out a breath. "I'm still here, aren't I?"

I choked on my breath. A few tears escaped, trailing down my cheeks. I looked over at him, trying to maintain eye contact. Trying to convince myself it was true. He *was* here. But god, I couldn't forget the way it felt when he had momentarily abandoned me in there.

And it wasn't fair. I knew that. Everyone else had done far worse. But the truth was, I held him to a higher standard.

"Well, now is your time to walk away. Full permission. No hard feelings. Get the whore outta your life. Save your rep. Save your friendships. Find yourself a sweet and innocent girl."

"Have you not been hearing what I'm saying? I want *you*, dammit." Julian looked up at the sky, and that's when I noticed he was crying too. "Fuck, Quinn. You're stubborn as hell. You don't listen to anything but your own thoughts. But you have more passion in you than your body can contain. You're literally exploding with it. You have this fire in you. No one can tell you not to do something. And even if they did, you'd do it anyway."

"I've discovered so many things about you on my own, Quinn. You know the one thing I haven't found? The girl the rumors say you are. So why are you so convinced I'll walk away? Why do you believe I want an out?" His voice wavering, Julian took a deep breath. "I had heard the rumors, and I'm here anyway. So what is it you want? Am I not good enough for you? Because I'm at a loss, Quinn. I don't know how to make you see me for me and not this perception you've created."

My legs trembled as I tried to mend the cracks he was making. I forced myself to look into his eyes, to really see the boy who stood before me. The one who was laying his heart out. He was still standing here. *Fuck, he was still fighting for me.*

The walls crumbled faster than I could manage, and my legs gave out. I fell on the pavement, drawing my knees up to my chest, and started to sob. I hated myself more now in this moment than I ever had.

Pull yourself together, Quinn. This is how you'll lose him.

I couldn't concentrate on anything but breathing. But even that was difficult. I could feel myself beginning to hyperventilate. I gripped my knees tighter and buried my head into my chest. Maybe I could become invisible.

I could feel him near me, his hand on my back before he pulled me into his arms. His actions only caused me to cry harder as he held me tightly, resting his cheek on the top of my head.

I could hear his heartbeat, slightly elevated, but it comforted me. It beat in a rhythm, unlike my own restless heartbeat. He placed kisses on my head periodically, his hand rubbing up and down my arm.

He's not disappearing, Quinn. He's here. He's real. He's

*honest. Give him a chance. No one else would hold you while you
covered them in snot and tears.*

My tears were slowing. My breathing was starting to regulate
as hiccups appeared. I buried my head further into him and
gripped my arms around him. I had one final thing to say, one
thing that could make him walk away. Now that he fought for me,
I wanted to remain in his arms. But that wouldn't be fair.

"J-Julian?" I hiccuped. I took one arm off him and wiped my
snot away.

"Yes?" His voice was soft.

"What Adrian said tonight?" I sniffed before pressing a kiss to
his chest. What if he did leave me after this? "They weren't r-
rumors. Well," I swallowed. *Don't lie, Quinn.* "There was a
couple of days between Rob and Garrett, but that's not important. That's not the point. The point is, why the hell does my sex
life matter to anyone other than me?"

His grip tightened on me. "It doesn't. Or at least it shouldn't."

"I'm not apologizing for who I am or what I like. But god, I
fucking hate how awful they make me feel," I groaned, rubbing
my eyes. "The only thing I apologize for is how I treated Liza,
and how he now outed her. She doesn't deserve that." I blinked
rapidly. "And fuck, we were just becoming friends again. How
will she ever trust me? Forgive me, even?"

Julian remained silent, his hand just rubbing my back. I
couldn't stop the thoughts from spiraling about what would
happen Monday morning. I was certain Liza would know by the
end of tonight; someone in the group would make sure she
found out.

I pulled my head away from Julian's chest a few minutes later
and looked up at him. I most definitely didn't deserve him. Nor
did he deserve to be brought into the mess of my life.

"J-Julian?" I whispered.

"Mhm?"

"I'm sorry for this." I took a deep breath.

Julian's brows knit together, but his hand came to the back of my head and directed it to his chest. His arm tightened around me as he pressed a kiss to the top of my head.

I felt another sob try to rumble through my system. I hiccuped, and my chest vibrated with my uneven breathing. Julian readjusted us, guiding me off the rough pavement and onto his lap. The pressure of his hold had me breathing through the sob, only a few tears escaping.

"Let's get out of here. Let me call my dad to take us home," Julian whispered, resting his head on my own.

I shook my head. "I don't want to meet your father like this."

"Do you want me to call your parents?"

"No ..."

"Uber?" he offered.

"Okay." I started to unravel out of his hold, but before I could get too far, his hands cupped my cheeks, and he kissed my forehead.

I used my shirt sleeve to wipe my snot, letting out a pathetic laugh.

"I look and feel disgusting." I looked down at his shirt. With the little amount of light we had from a street lamp, I could see it was soaking wet. "I'm sorry." I gave him a measly smile.

JULIAN

It wasn't five seconds into the Uber that Quinn was fast asleep. Her body was leaned up against the door, her head resting on the window. She looked so peaceful. A complete switch from how she acted at the party. I didn't know how to feel after everything that happened. The night started out so perfect. It made me think if every night at Emerald's were like that, I would go every week in a heartbeat. But then Adrian had to be Adrian, and the whole night went to shit.

My blood boiled at Adrian's words, but I chose to sit back. Quinn didn't want a knight in shining armor to step in for her rescue. She was no damsel in distress. It was one of the things I admired about her. She didn't need anyone else to fight her own battles.

My jaw clenched as the streetlights flashed through the car like strobe lights as we drove past. Society was so messed up. If you're a virgin like me, you're pressured to have sex even if you don't want to. If you enjoy sex and have had it with more than one person like Quinn, you're considered a whore.

So where the hell was the middle spectrum? Why was sex such a big deal? No, why were your own sexual relations a big deal to other people? Isn't that something that should be private? Only shared between you and the one you're having sex with? I didn't get it. No one should be ashamed to say no to sex. No one should be ashamed to say yes to sex.

Why was it that women were labeled whore or slut for having too much sex? Hell, I'd heard girls called that who hadn't even had sex before. Why was it such a crime for them to like sex? Yet, men catcalled women like their bodies didn't even belong to them. It was so messed up. We were all on autopilot, having been programmed to think that way—that it was okay to call woman these derogatory terms when it wasn't. Words like "slut" and "whore" dehumanized woman .... The worst part was that it's so ingrained in our society that so many people are unaware of the hurt, fear, and isolation it created. Just like everyone at the party.

Everyone there was part of the problem. Even I had been a part of the problem, not properly standing up for women. No one defended Quinn or stood up for her. They just watched. I only sat back because I knew it'd hurt her pride if I stepped in at all. I did follow her after she left so she knew she wasn't alone. I wanted to comfort her and make her feel better. She needed someone who cared. But she also shouldn't need a man to stand up for her to make people listen. Women don't need men period.

I hit my forehead against the window of the car.

I also couldn't help the uneasy feeling in the pit of my stomach. Quinn *confirmed* some of the rumors I'd heard. She admitted to sleeping around. Which doesn't make her a bad person but ... I felt lied to. If those rumors were true, what else was? So they weren't just rumors like I thought they were, but was that a bad thing?

I got together with Quinn knowing the rumors could be true, and while we never spoke of them, there had to be some truth to them. But the Quinn I saw tonight and the Quinn I was dating seemed like two entirely different people. Was Quinn even who I thought she was? I thought she proved the rumors wrong. But now ... I didn't know what to think.

What kind of person did that make Quinn? Was it even okay to be with someone like that? *Someone like that.* God, what kind of person did it make me knowing I shouldn't judge Quinn for what she enjoys, yet I kept finding myself doing just that?

Although ... my dad told me once that the first thought that goes through your head is what you have been conditioned to think by society or how you were raised, but what you think next defines who you are.

It took about fifteen minutes to reach Quinn's place. I thanked the driver before scooting out of the car and to Quinn's side. She was still fast asleep and didn't even stir when I opened her door. The lights were still on inside her house. What did I do? Her parents were up. Quinn's fist was covered in dry blood, and my hands were shaking.

I gently shook Quinn's shoulder. "Quinn, you're home."

She moaned in response.

Great. This was probably going to look awful to her parents. What would I even say to them? *Hey, uh sorry your daughter got into a fight—not with me—but she's okay. You should see the guy she hit.* I sighed and reached over her to undo her seatbelt.

"Seriously, Quinn. Wake up." She didn't respond. I swallowed, looking back at the house. Her dad's shadow was in the window.

"One second," I told the driver. I skipped up to Quinn's porch and knocked on the door. Just as my knuckles made contact, the door swung open, and her father looked down at me.

"Um. Hi, sir," I said, trying to shake off my nerves.

What did this look like? A guy bringing home their drunken daughter late at night. God, I hoped they knew she was just at Emerald's and not my place or something. I didn't know her parents well enough to predict how they'd react, especially since

Quinn was basically unconscious. And not to mention the state her hand was in. Her father just stood there waiting for me to say more.

"Um, I'm just dropping Quinn off..." What else did I even say? Should I explain how the night went or let Quinn do that tomorrow? "She's asleep. May I carry her inside?"

Her father nodded skeptically. I tried to offer a smile before I turned and jogged back to the car.

"Thanks for waiting," I said to the driver as I scooped Quinn up in my arms. A soft murmur escaped her mouth as I kicked the door closed behind me.

"Is she okay?" Lydia, Quinn's mom asked as I reached the door. They both backed away, allowing me to enter. I inhaled, trying to push back the feeling of nausea from nerves.

God, this looked bad. So bad.

"Look at her hand." Her father's voice was stern as he narrowed his eyes at me.

"I assure you I had nothing to do with that. But the guy who did got what was coming to him." My voice shook with a half-smile, trying to lighten the mood. "I think she's okay though. Just asleep." I sidestepped him in order to head to her bedroom.

"A fight?" Her father raised his voice over the sound of my heart racing.

Quinn, how the hell are you such a deep sleeper? I wondered.

"Dan ... let him be," Lydia said, then whispered something else I couldn't hear as I made my way down the hall.

After a game of "try not to hit the walls with any of Quinn's limbs," I made it to her bedroom. I eased her onto the bed, sliding my arms out from under her and brushing her hair off her face to kiss her forehead. I sat there for a moment watching her sleep, the easy movements of her chest rising and lowering with each breath.

As I made my way back down the hall, her parents were waiting for me as I had expected.

"Thank you for bringing her home," her mother said.

I nodded, still trying to ease my breathing. "Of course. Um, do you mind if I stay here for a couple minutes while I call my dad to pick me up?" I asked, knowing very well the Uber would be long gone by now.

"It's so late. Why don't you just stay here for the night? We can get you some blankets and pillows for the couch." Her mom smiled at me, but I couldn't help but notice the glare Quinn's father shot her.

"I really don't want to be a burden to you," I said, trying to smile. Well, at least they seemed to believe I wasn't the cause of what happened.

"Nonsense. You brought our daughter home safe and sound. It's the least we could do. I doubt your father would appreciate being woken up at this hour anyway."

She was right. My dad would be pissed and would give me a lecture on this is why he gave me a car to begin with. He had no idea I ever drank, so I couldn't even use that as an excuse. "Thank you," I mumbled.

I sat on the couch on my phone as Lydia went down the hall to grab me a blanket and pillow. Scrolling through social media, I saw pictures from the party. Most were group photos of people holding their drinks. The girls with their arms around each other, the guys holding up their red cups and giving the finger. Some were filtered to be black and white with cheesy song lyrics attached beneath them. I wasn't in any of them, but there were a couple with Quinn beside Marie.

It looked like our regular Friday nights—except one photo stopped me cold. It was one Adrian had posted of Quinn and me curled up on the couch. The caption read, "The slut is at it again." I threw my phone beside me on the couch, resisting the urge to leave a comment. I knew it wouldn't do any good. If anything, it would only make things worse. My heart hurt knowing Quinn would likely see the photo in the morning.

"Here you are," Lydia said, handing me a comforter and pillow.

"Thank you." I smiled.

"Let's hope you don't make a habit of this," her father warned.

"Of course not, sir."

"Oh, leave him alone, Dan." Lydia swatted at her husband. "Goodnight, Julian. And thanks again."

I spread the blanket out over me as Quinn's parents left the room. I held on to my phone thinking of the photo, thinking of the night that just happened, until sleep overcame me.

MY EYES OPENED NOT LONG after the sun began to peek into her living room. I laid there on the couch for a while, just listening to the still quiet of the house. Clearly, I was the only one awake. I hardly ever slept well when I drank, though, so I wasn't surprised. I checked my phone. I had a text from my dad reminding me about helping him clean the house today. I had a few text messages from James and Tyler asking if I was free to practice later with our big playoff game coming up on Tuesday. Neither of them asked why I had left the party early or where I even went. They didn't care. I stretched my body across the couch before sitting up. I wanted to thank Quinn's parents again for letting me stay over, but I also had things to do today.

I dialed my dad's cell number. Quinn's house was way too far to walk home, not to mention I still needed to get my car back. After a couple rings, he picked up.

"Julian?" he asked, confused. He probably didn't even notice I hadn't come home last night.

"Hey, can you pick me up?"

"Uh, where's your car?"

"Funny you should ask that."

"Julian."

"I really just need a ride to my car. Please."

I could hear my dad sigh, giving up on finding out details. "Fine. Where are you?"

I gave him Quinn's address without actually telling him whose house I was at. He told me he would be there in ten minutes and to watch for him before he hung up.

Just as I was putting on my shoes, Lydia appeared in the living room. "Oh, you don't want to stay till Quinn wakes up?"

"No, sorry. I have things to get done today." I felt bad. I should probably talk to Quinn about what happened. But I wasn't sure what to say or how to make things better. "Thank you again, though," I said as I headed out the door.

"Nice house," my dad commented as I jumped into his truck. "Whose is it?"

"A friend's."

"A girl?"

"Dad, stop. Yes, a girl. But nothing happened. I brought her home with an Uber, and her parents let me sleep on their couch since it was so late."

"An Uber? Why didn't you just drive?"

I sighed. I guess I should just tell the truth. My brain wasn't quick enough to think of a believable excuse.

"I had a couple beers last night. Sorry for being responsible."

My dad was silent for a moment like he was contemplating giving me a lecture but decided against it. "Well, I'm glad you at least didn't drink and drive. So where's your car?"

"At Joseph's," I said. It felt weird calling Emerald by his real name, but I knew my dad would have no idea who I was talking about if I didn't.

He nodded. We drove the rest of the way in silence. It made me wish I had parents like Quinn's. A secret-free home. I wanted to tell my dad about everything that happened last night, how shitty I felt, and how I didn't understand anything. That I hated rumors and how the world seemed so messed up. Why I felt like I was the only human alive who didn't care about sex. Except I couldn't. It's not that we weren't close or that we had a bad relationship or anything. It just felt like something I was better off keeping to myself.

QUINN

My memory was fuzzy when my eyes opened. My mouth was dry, and my hand throbbed. I wasn't hungover, that much was clear. But I could barely remember getting into my bed.

I blinked a few times, rubbing the sleep out of my eyes before I caught sight of my giraffe.

Julian. Of course. He must have brought me home.

I reached for my phone to thank him, but it buzzed in my hand. Liza's phone number showed up—but not her name, as I had deleted her contact information last year. However, her number was one I had memorized.

> *Hey, you free today?*
> *Want to get some practice*
> *in before playoffs start?*

Playoffs started this week, and we were in no shape to win. Had she not found out what happened last night? Was it possible that despite Adrian blabbing, people had kept it within the walls of Emerald's den?

I clicked out of the message, afraid to answer too soon. It was only ten in the morning; there was still time for the word to spread. But closing out of the message was the worst thing I could have done. Twelve notifications appeared on my iMessage. I had numerous notifications for Instagram. And a few voicemails. None of the messages were from Julian.

Had we ended on bad terms? Despite him saying he'd be there?

Marie:

What the hell was that?
Quinn! You can't ignore this.

How could you not tell me?

I don't care that Liza's a lesbian.
But you fucking slept with Adrian!?
And Liza??

That's low, Quinn.
Real fucking low.

Are you bi?

Adrian:

Go to hell. You're a
fucking basket-case.

Emerald:

I'm sorry, Quinn. Adrian
wasn't proving any point.
There was no point to prove.
You know I don't think of you

*that way. At least, I hope
you know that.*

*Please answer Marie.
She's flipping out.*

Quinn?

Paige:
*Hi Quinn, I hope you're
okay. We should have been
better. Emerald tried to talk
Adrian down. I think everything
is okay. If you need anything,
let me know.*

Martin:
*About time someone put him
in his place. I hope you're okay,
Quinn. Sorry for not standing
up with you.*

I clicked out of my messages without responding to a single one. Taking a deep breath in, I opened up my Instagram. Checking my notifications, I saw I was tagged in a few photos from last night; most of the other tags were people commenting on the photos. Marie and I were in a few under her own account. Some with Paige. Emerald had even photobombed us a few times.

But the photo getting the most comments was one under Adrian's account, a photo of me and Julian cuddling on the couch. If I had been given this photo under other circumstances, I would have printed and framed it. It appeared to be taken earlier in the night when Julian and I were fooling around talking about Martin and the F.B.I.

My eyes flickered down to the caption: "The slut is at it again."

I wanted to scream, throw my phone across the room and never use it again. I hated that I needed it. I hated that social media even existed. As if it wasn't bad enough to walk the halls with Adrian and people judging me for my choices. I now had it filtering into the privacy of my own bedroom, the entire football team feeling like they have the freedom to speak on my behalf.

There was a knock on my door right as I had almost convinced myself to just shatter my phone. Before I had a chance to respond, my door opened.

"Quinn?" My mom peeked her head in, smiling when she saw I was awake.

I stuffed my phone under my covers and sat up.

"Hi, what's up?" I curled my hands underneath my comforter.

"Can we talk about last night?" She sat down slowly on my bed before placing her hand on mine under the blanket.

"Sure, what about?"

"Care to explain who you got in a fight with last night?" I shifted myself further up on the bed, moving my hands away from hers.

"I didn't."

"Quinn," she sighed, "there's no point in lying. We know you were drinking. Julian brought you home, tucked you in, and spent the night. He also mentioned that the guy had it coming. How else do you explain a bloody hand and that comment, dear?"

Wait. What?

"Is Julian still here?"

That would explain him not messaging me. Not that he needed to or was expected to always check in on me. But his track record showed that he would. Besides, since we started dating, he hadn't missed one good morning text.

"No, he left a few hours ago. Something about needing to do stuff today?"

"Did he say anything before he left?"

"To tell you? No, dear. Did something happen between you two?"

I shook my head. I could feel how close my phone was to me and how I just wanted to contact him and see what was going on. Something felt off. This didn't seem like normal behavior for him.

But how should I know his behavior in a situation neither of us could fathom?

"Okay, then why were you fighting someone?"

I shook my head again, throwing off my blankets and getting out of bed.

"All you need to know is that they deserved it," I said as I started rummaging through my drawers. "And I stood up for myself." Pulling out shorts and a t-shirt, I turned toward my mom again. "I gotta go; I have to practice for playoffs. My team is waiting."

At the word "team," she stood off the bed, nodding slowly as she walked to my bedroom door.

"We'll continue this lat—" I closed the door and rushed back to my phone.

I texted Liza.

I'll be at the school in 20.

If she still didn't know, I could take advantage of the prime opportunity to pretend my soccer ball was Adrian's face.

JULIAN

DESPITE PRACTICING UNTIL OUR BODIES GAVE OUT FROM exhaustion, I still didn't feel ready for the game come Tuesday. James, as the captain, ordered us to come an hour early to get one final practice in. When I got there, everyone was already taking laps around the field.

I texted Quinn.

> *Game soon, text you later.*
> **kissy face**

I hadn't seen Quinn the rest of weekend, blaming it on getting ready for the playoffs. We texted here and there but didn't have any real conversations. I wondered how she was feeling about Friday night. Did it change anything about us? Should it change anything about us? I didn't hear anything at school Monday or even today about last Friday, so maybe we were in the clear. At least for now.

We also hadn't really talked about having sex yet, a topic I was grateful to avoid. I knew it would have to come up eventually, but for now, I soaked up all the time I could when it wasn't an issue. But should we talk about the rumors? I wanted to know what was real and what wasn't. I didn't want to build a relationship on assumptions, false accusations, or lies. Except, I had no idea how to bring it up without the potential of upsetting her. I didn't want her to think I believed the gossip spread about her. Yet, she admitted to some of it being true. *Ugh. Why was this so confusing and hard?*

As practice ended, the other team began to show up for the game. I was already exhausted, and the game hadn't even started yet. Sitting on the grass on the sidelines, I laid down, propping my torso up with my elbows. Ian jogged over to me, grabbing his water bottle from his bag and squirting some into his mouth.

"Ready?" he asked, clicking the spout of his water bottle down.

"I wish." I let my bag fall to the ground.

"Everything alright?" Ian sat beside me. The other team started dropping their bags on the other side of the field.

"Am I that much of an open book?" I laughed.

"Very. So, what's up?"

I shook my head. "Just ... I don't know what's real anymore. Rumors, I mean."

"Is this about Quinn?"

"Okay, seriously, get out of my head."

Ian laughed. "Sorry. So what exactly is bothering you?"

"Quinn basically said the rumors of her liking sex were true."

"Uh, Julian, do you not know Quinn? What do you expect?"

"Okay, ouch."

"So she likes sex. Big deal. The rumors are just an overdramatized version of that. Girls are allowed to like sex too, you know."

"I know ..." Still, I felt betrayed in a sense. I didn't understand this weird feeling I had.

"So what's the issue then?"

I sat up, looking over at him. "Nothing, I guess."

Ian stood up, smiling down at me. "It's also okay for sex not to be a big deal."

My body stiffened as he read my thoughts.

"Well, the game's about to start, so I better get into position." Ian jogged onto the field toward our net. I watched as the game started, not my turn yet on the field.

"RASKIN, ON," my coach said to me for the first sub.

I hustled onto the field to take my usual left defense spot. As the ball was coming toward me, I ran at it, my head entirely in the game. Until I caught sight of him in the corner of my eye.

Adrian had come to watch the game. He was sitting on the metal stands with a few of his friends from the football team, joking and laughing together, hardly paying attention to the actual game. But then our eyes locked, and he gave me a sly smile.

Fuck. I forgot that most of the school would be here to watch our game. Nerves washed over me. In the stands, I also noticed Marie and Emerald sitting side by side cuddled into each other. Even Quinn and Liza were here. They were sitting beside each other, still in their soccer uniforms, laughing together. They must have come here right from their own practice. Quinn gave me a smile, and I tried to give one back, hoping Adrian wouldn't cause any issues here.

We needed to win this game to move on to the next round, and I couldn't afford any distractions. It made me grateful that my dad had to work and was unable to make it.

I missed the ball, and the other player darted past me straight for our net. They kicked hard, and I felt helpless. I, standing there, watching.

"What the hell, dude?" James said as he ran past me, trying to catch up with the other player.

They made their shot, and I winced. Luckily, Ian made the

save. All the players ran back, waiting for Ian to kick the ball. Ian shifted his gaze at me for a moment, worry in his eyes. I offered him a smile to ensure him I was fine. And with that, he kicked the ball back onto the field.

The ball soared over my head toward Tyler who was playing forward. I watched the ball, trying to predict the next moves of the game so I would be ready if it made its way back toward our net. Tyler dodged around a player and passed the ball to James, who carried it up the rest of the field.

I waited near the centerline, prepared in case it came my way as the ball stayed in the other team's zone.

"Did you hear about Liza?" I could hear Adrian's voice.

My body tensed. *Oh god.* I thought Friday had been long forgotten about. I turned my head to look at Ian, but his eyes were glued to Adrian and his friends. He heard it too.

Looking back to the stands, Liza's eyes were also on Adrian. I could see Quinn shift uncomfortably in her seat before she stood up and walked down from the bleachers.

"That she's a lesbian?" one of Adrian's friends asked.

"Not just that, but she slept with Quinn." Adrian smiled.

"Poor Julian. Does he even realize he's dating a whore?"

Quinn must have still been able to hear Adrian's words because she was now running away from the field. I wanted to run after her, but I was stuck in this game. Again, the ball passed by me, and before I even noticed, the other team got a goal. Ian was also too distracted to stay in the game.

"What the fuck?" James shouted as we got into position for a kickoff. "You better get your shit together, Raskin, or you're going to cost us our game."

I tried. I really did try. The rest of the game I kept my eyes on the field and not the stands, but I couldn't shut my ears off. I heard the whispers flow through the crowd like a breeze, reaching everyone who was here. We lost. 4-0.

James pushed me as I headed back to my soccer bag. "Consider this loss your fault."

"He's right, Raskin." My coach's voice stung. "If you don't bring your A-game Monday, I'm going to have to bench you."

"Yes, Coach," I said, slinging my bag over my shoulder.

I didn't even care about the game anymore. I just wanted to make sure Quinn was alright. As I turned to head toward my car, I realized Ian hadn't come to grab his bag yet. Most of the crowd had left already, Liza included. But Adrian was still here with Ian standing in front of him.

Oh no.

I hurried over to them with Ian's bag in hand.

"Would it kill you not to be an asshole for one goddamn second?" Ian shouted.

"Would it kill you to mind your own goddamn business?"

"Ian, let's go. Nothing we say will help." I grabbed Ian's shoulder, moving him away.

"Hey now, boys, this is a public place." Adrian smirked.

Ian turned, his fist clenched and jaw tight, shrugging my hand off him.

"Seriously, let's just go." I pulled Ian away, and he finally gave up throwing his bag on his shoulder, following me.

"Julian, first off, something should be said. This isn't okay. Quinn hurting Liza was wrong. Adrian using those words isn't okay. But y*ou* should be standing up for your own girlfriend."

I stopped walking, but Ian kept going without looking back. "What are you saying?"

My brain didn't process Quinn admitting to sleeping with Liza, which meant not only did she sleep around with guys, but she had also slept with a girl before. It was like I pushed that information out of my brain. That I chose not to think anything of it. Quinn was straight as far as I knew, but her admitting that also outed Liza in a cruel manner. This was only feeling more complicated. But he was right. I should have been over there as well, standing up for Quinn being called those things.

Finally, Ian stopped and turned to look at me. Adrian and his group were far behind us now. "I'm saying that these things shouldn't just be pushed aside. I don't care if what I say won't change the way Adrian acts. But I am worse than he is if I stay quiet about it." He sighed. "Let's just go. I'm tired of all this drama."

I nodded as we headed back to our cars. I was going to Quinn's. I was planning to head there straight from the game, except Ian's words kept playing on repeat in my head. The rumors flooding along with it. Ian stood up for Quinn when I couldn't.

Ugh. Why couldn't I have gone up to Adrian the moment the game was over? Or even right after the words left his mouth? I sucked at being a person. I couldn't even defend my own girl-friend. My fucking best friend did it for me. Even when Quinn had hurt Liza, Ian still stood up for her.

Slamming my palm onto my steering wheel, I turned left instead and headed home.

QUINN
JULIAN'S CHAMPIONSHIP GAME #2

"QUINN! LIZA! GET OVER HERE!" OUR COACH SHOUTED.

We had just been dismissed from practice—one that ran late, leaving little to no time to watch Julian's final game just across the field.

The two of us jogged over to her. I tried catching Liza's glance. I knew all too well what Coach was about to say, but it was Liza who needed to cut the shit.

"What's going on between you two?" Coach greeted us.

I pleaded with my eyes for Coach to drop the subject, to just accept that whatever was happening could be fixed on our terms. But she ignored me, focusing on Liza. I was already on thin ice.

"We'll be better, Coach. I apologize," Liza said softly before standing up straight and looking her in the eyes.

"Your entire team is counting on you two—two of our strongest players. Don't fail them. Don't fail me. And please don't fail yourselves." Coach looked between the two of us before she shooed us away with her hand. "Go! Get some rest and sort this out."

We both gathered our things in silence. There was an ice wall that only seemed to get thicker as the days passed. I wasn't sure this was something we could sort out before tomorrow.

But I wanted to. I needed to.

"Li—" She wouldn't even let me say her full name before she brushed past me and jogged over to the boy's game.

I tried to catch up. I rounded the bleachers on the side she went, but Ian's boyfriend and Nile, Liza's younger brother, sat on either side of her. With a look in my direction, I knew better than to make a scene and force myself in. So I walked to the other side, where there was one place available on the first row. According to my phone, there should only be a minute or two left of the game. Julian's team was up by two, but the opposing team had possession and seemed determined to fight until the end.

I couldn't focus on the game, though. Liza and I had been so great together the night after Emerald's. We were both so on point with our practicing that we ended our session having no doubt we'd be champions. I had come home on such a high that it barely bothered me that Julian was being distant. I was starting to get my best friend back, something I never let myself think about.

But then, Adrian and his big fucking mouth had to not only spread a secret but to do it during the busiest time in soccer. It's like he *wanted* us to lose everything. If we lost our next two games, I'd lose my position as captain, and I could be sure to kiss some of my scholarships goodbye.

I had tried talking to Liza. I tried catching her before or after class, after soccer practices, and I even tried to go to her house after school twice.

Each day only seemed to get worse. Liza grew angrier, refusing to pass the ball to me when necessary. She'd take every opportunity to trip or run her shoulder into me when we'd scrimmage on opposing teams. But at least on the field, she acknowledged I existed. Off of the field, it was like I was invisible. I wasn't even worth a glance.

The whistle blew, ending the championship game. Snapping to, I watched as Julian's entire team ran and jumped on Ian, celebrating their win, ending the boys' soccer season on a high for the year. Under other circumstances, I would have run to the field and pulled Julian into a kiss, congratulating him. *Under other circumstances*, he wouldn't be surrounded by people who hated me.

We made eye contact for a moment, and I waved excitedly, hoping to make it known it was cool for him to celebrate for a bit. Then I left the bleachers, heading toward the gym.

Often, I'd go straight home and shower there, but I wanted to take Julian out. So after sending a quick text to him telling him to meet me outside the gym after his shower, I then took a quick one of my own.

I was only waiting outside for a few minutes before Julian and the rest of his team started to file out of the gym. James and Tyler clapped him on the shoulder before saying goodbye. Ian glanced over my way before directing his attention to Julian. They shared a few words before Julian headed over to me.

"Hey, champion!" I met him halfway, throwing my arms around him. "Great game!" He wrapped his arms around me tightly.

We had barely seen each other all week. We were both thrust into extended soccer practices and mid-semester tests.

"Thank you, beautiful."

I smiled, leaning back and pecking his lips.

"I hate to say that I missed almost all of it. But can I buy you a milkshake?" I asked, dropping my arms.

"Ow, my heart," he teased, putting his hand on his chest. "I think the only cure for this broken heart would be, in fact, a milkshake." He smiled.

I laughed, shaking my head at him before interlacing our fingers. "Come on, drama queen."

We made the short walk off campus and down the street, walking to the cafe that had the best milkshakes.

After we both ordered, we took our number and headed to a free table.

"So what now, champion? What is Julian Raskin going to do with all his free time now that soccer's over?"

"Be a professional hermit who forgets what the sun looks like." He paused. "Oh and go for milkshakes with pretty girls." My stomach fluttered as he smiled.

"And who are these pretty girls you speak of?" I knew he was talking about just me, but the thought of losing him to someone else, especially with everything happening, wasn't something I liked to imagine.

It crossed my mind a few times since he brought me back home from Emerald's. The first time was when I woke up, and my mom told me he spent the night but left early. That was the first time I felt the sinking feeling in more than just my stomach, but an aching in my muscles. I was falling for Julian. He wasn't someone I wanted to lose. I was done trying to pretend that I was above being in a relationship. I was done claiming this was a dare, and I'd end things when the six months were finished. What I felt for Julian was more real than anything I'd experienced.

He put a finger to his lips. "That information is classified."

I rolled my eyes as the milkshakes were delivered. Cookies and cream for Julian and chocolate peanut butter for myself.

"Well, just remember, I'm the best company." I winked before scooping up some whipped cream and holding it up for a toast. "To Julian and his kickass soccer skills!"

"Cheers." We clanked spoons.

Just as I was about to take another mouthful, Julian bopped my nose with his spoon, covering it in whipped cream.

He laughed before shoving his spoon in his mouth. "Sorry, I couldn't resist."

"Julian!" I laughed, sticking my tongue out to catch the dripping whipped cream. I then scooped some off of my milkshake with my finger. When he looked down to get more on his spoon, I leaned over and slid the whipped cream down his nose.

He flinched away, letting his mouth hang open over-dramatically. "Excuse me, ma'am, but we are in a public place." He smiled, grabbing a napkin to wipe his nose.

"That's never stopped me before," I teased before wiping my nose off as well.

He laughed. "So how's soccer going for you, anyway?"

My shoulders tensed as I twirled the straw in my milkshake. "Stressful, but fine." I shrugged, looking down and taking a long sip of my milkshake. "So the weather's sure nice today."

"Wait, wait, wait. Don't go changing the subject on me. Stressful? How so?"

I sighed. I didn't want the tension to come between us too.

"I don't want to talk about it, Julian. You're already in a weird position. It's fine. I'm just trying to focus on winning."

He raised his eyebrows when I said "weird position." We hadn't spoken about it, but I wasn't an idiot. I knew Ian supported Liza, and well, James and Tyler were assholes in general.

But his face grew serious. "Well, if you need to talk, I am here. But I understand."

"Just support me where you can, okay? And maybe we can grab dinner after my final game? Regardless of the outcome?"

"Okay. It's a date."

We finished off our milkshakes, catching each other up on our days and what the rest of the week looked like before we walked back to our own cars in the student parking lot.

Quinn's Championship Game #1

HALLOWEEN WAS SPENT with early morning practice scheduled by me with a few girls from the team—Liza excluded. Then there was a day full of tests. By the time our first championship game started, I was exhausted. Liza and I had already gotten our first warning of the day from our coach during our afternoon practice, saying we needed to act more like teammates instead of enemies.

Julian was on the bleachers before the start of the game since he was finished with his season. The game started off on a positive note before steadily declining. Liza passed the ball continuously to another player when I was the one open—the opposing team was not oblivious to the tension. After her anger caused the other team to score, she was benched for the rest of the game.

Taking advantage of my own chance to shine, I turned the team around, ending our game 4-2.

Once back in the locker rooms, our coach stalled Liza and me from showering.

"If you two pull any of this on Thursday's game, you'll both be benched, immediately. Liza, you're lucky Quinn stepped up and saved the game." Liza directly looked at me for the first time in over a week, but it was only to shoot daggers at me. "Figure it out or cost yourselves a championship and your title, Quinn."

She let us go, both of us grabbing our belongings and heading in opposite directions—skipping the showers all together.

Quinn's Championship Game #2

BY THURSDAY, I was running on little to no energy. We practiced longer and harder on Wednesday. I even recruited Julian for a bit after practice before he had to go study. All throughout school on Thursday, Adrian kept making snide remarks. Not about anything in particular, but he was constantly a smartass toward me and even Liza. Marie kept trying to get me to explain to her what the hell was going on, and why I had slept with Liza. No one understood.

Fuck, I barely understood. That's why I was in this goddamn situation.

I tried to corner Liza before our last practice, but Ian was in the hallway and called her name, telling her he needed her for something important. At practice, we were placed on opposite sides of the field, but I knew that wouldn't last long. It was almost impossible for us not to have to work together.

When it was game time, the bleachers were filled. Julian was sitting with his soccer team, while Marie and Emerald sat with the rest of the group. Even my parents, sister, and Kenny were in the crowd.

With one last warning, we were all sent onto the field. We started out okay. The opposing team was the toughest team yet, so there wasn't any time to waste on drama. Liza and I had to remain focused.

"I'm open," I called to Liza. But she looked ahead, determined to get through on her own.

"Move, *dyke*," an opposing teammate said before kicking the ball out from Liza's feet and to another teammate.

"I said I was open," I yelled at her.

"You seem to be open to a lot of things." Liza darted past me toward the ball.

"What the hell does that mean?" I screamed, running to catch up to her.

We couldn't afford to make any more mistakes. As soon as I caught up to her, I had the opportunity to get the ball. I'd be damned if I let her get it.

I sidestepped in front of her, hitting my shoulder against hers before taking possession of the ball. Liza stumbled, losing her balance.

The opposing teams' coach shouted at the ref, but I could barely hear her.

Right before halftime, we had the perfect opportunity for Liza to pass me the ball. Once again, I was open and had the perfect shot, but instead, she tried to make it herself, costing us yet another goal.

"Liza, Quinn! Get on the bench; you two are done!" our coach yelled as soon as the whistle blew.

"Coach!" I yelled, jogging back. "Please. Please." I skidded to a stop in front of her. I had to play. I couldn't lose this.

"It won't happen again, Coach!" Liza panted, coming up right next to me.

"Sit!" she yelled and pointed to the bench. "Now!" She then turned her back on us and focused her attention on the rest of the team.

"Good job. Thanks for ruining everything," I mumbled, side-stepping her and walking to the bench.

"This isn't my fault!" Liza yelled, reaching out for my arm.

I spun toward her, watching as her arm fell pathetically at her side.

"Now you want to talk?" I took a few steps toward where she stood only inches away. "Now? In the middle of this fucking game? I tried, Liza! This is *all* your fault."

"Girls! Bench! Now!" Our coach was fuming as she approached us, leaving the team who was now watching our every move.

"Maybe if you weren't such a bitch, we wouldn't be in this situation!" Liza screamed, pushing me backward. "But how could I be so stupid? Quinn Kennedy was and always will be a whore."

I stumbled on my feet, my breath catching as I tried to steady myself. Liza never, I mean *never*, spoke like that. What had I done?

Liza crossed her arms, lifting her brow in a "now what?"

expression that had me stepping forward, hands out to push her back before our coach pulled me away.

"Let go of me!" I yelled, trying to scramble out of her arms.

"Quinn, you need to calm down." Coach tightened her grip.

"Bitch fight, bitch fight!" I heard from the bleachers.

"Fuck you, Liza!" I spit before Coach tried to turn me away. I struggled again, harder this time, managing to get out of her grip.

"Fuck you, Adrian!" I screamed across the field where he was the only one left chanting. The rest of the crowd sat there in shock. I avoided Julian's side; I didn't want to see the disappointment on his face.

"Fuck all of you!"

I grabbed my water bottle and ran off the field, ignoring Coach yelling that I wasn't allowed to leave the field until the game was over.

I WAS BARELY EVEN OUT of the shower, still wrapped in a towel before my mother was banging on my bedroom door.

"Quinn, get dressed and come to the table. Your father and I need to speak with you."

I had beelined it home and immediately jumped in the shower—staying there until the water ran cold, trying to avoid this conversation altogether.

No one had followed me, though. Everyone just let me leave.

Throwing on a pair of sweats, I joined my parents at the table, where they had three mugs of tea. They had been talking amongst themselves until I walked in.

"Quinn," my father sighed. I pulled my mug closer to me, holding it tightly. "I don't even know where to begin."

Nerves bubbled in the pit of my stomach, and I looked down at the tea bag floating in the hot water. I gripped the bag, spinning it around the mug.

"I don't even recognize you anymore."

"Dan—" My mother spoke softly.

"No, Lydia." I looked up briefly to catch him taking her hand off his arm. "Her behavior is absolutely unacceptable."

I sank in my seat, bringing my mug to the edge of the table, refusing to look up from its gold-dotted rim.

"First off, you're grounded." My eyes shot up, and I sat straight, spilling some of the tea on the table. I had never been grounded before.

"W-what? Mom, that's—"

"Your father and I have already discussed it. You're changing, Quinn, and not in a good way."

"You also need to end things with Julian," my father said.

I squinted my eyes shut, removing my hands from my mug and massaging my hot fingertips over my eyelids. My eyes had burned from the moment I left the soccer field, but, of course, they would choose *this* moment to tear up.

"D-dad," I started, desperately trying to force the tears away. "None of this is Julian's fault."

"None of this happened before Julian."

I opened my eyes, blinking them to adjust to the blur. "Please don't make me end things with him. I promise you, he's the only good thing I have left."

"Quinn, honey." My mom's hand came to rest on my arm. "You need to explain to us what is going on. You've never kept secrets before. How are we supposed to know that Julian isn't responsible if he's the only new addition in your life?"

I shook my head, brushing the tears that fell with my free hand. "I can't talk about it."

"Then we'll be sitting here until you do." My dad positioned himself so he was more comfortable.

"Please don't make me talk about it." I leaned against my

chair, tilting my head back to try and stop the tears. "I'm already humiliated enough as it is."

"What is going on with you and Liza?"

I choked on my breath, watching my parents as my vision continued to blur, leaving them as only shadows.

"You two haven't been close since last year. What's going on now? What happened then?" My father's voice softened.

I blinked rapidly, taking both of my hands to rub away the tears.

"Why did you get into a fist fight a couple weeks ago? Why was Adrian Dunn taunting you? Why did Liza call you ... that word?"

My mother put her hand on my father's arm again, trying to slow down his questioning. They thought we lived in a secret-free home. They knew what they needed—more than most teenagers told their parents—they just didn't know my label at school. Or that those friends they thought cared for me, in fact, didn't. It was easy for them to believe what they wanted to when they rarely saw any of my friends at our house.

"If I don't tell you, what happens?" I didn't miss the concerned look my mom shot my dad. I never spoke to them like this.

"You'll be grounded until Christmas; you won't be going on our ski trip; you won't be dating Julian, and you'll be helping your mother and I more around the house, no arguments."

"And if I do tell you?"

"You'll be grounded until Thanksgiving, and if you can prove Julian is a good influence, you can keep him around," my mother offered before my father could interject.

I took a few sips of my tea, quickly running over the pros and cons of both situations. My parents wouldn't be proud of me either way. I was a bigger disappointment than they could have imagined.

"Can we lock it in right now, that despite what I tell you and what you might think of me, that I'll only be grounded for three weeks? I promise I'll be honest."

They exchanged a look before my mother nodded and reached for my hand.

And so, I started from the beginning.

JULIAN

You okay?

I TEXTED QUINN AFTER I GOT HOME FROM HER GAME. MY phone sat beside me while I studied for my final midterm, my eyes constantly shifting to the black screen. Most of the evening was spent hitting my pen against my textbook waiting for a response from Quinn. Nothing. All night there was silence on her end. I considered texting her again, but if she really wasn't okay, she probably wanted the space. I sighed, closing my book and giving up for the night.

THE NEXT DAY I didn't see her around school either. Which I expected, not sharing any classes together. But I even walked past her locker, and she was still nowhere to be found.

Hey?

I texted her again. She blew her championship game. It was painful to watch, so I could only imagine how she was feeling.

But that wasn't a reason to just completely blow me off, right? Even if she was upset. I had intended to actually properly talk when we were out for milkshakes. Ask her about Liza ... about everything, really. But she seemed behind a closed door, unwilling to let me in. Still, my heart raced when I felt my phone vibrate in my jeans. I couldn't pull my phone out of my pocket fast enough to check it.

> *Sorry, grounded till*
> *Thanksgiving. Can't text. Phone*
> *only for emergencies at school.*
> *My parents are pissed about*
> *the game. *eye roll face**

She texted. She answered. *Thank god,* I thought. So she wasn't just blowing me off. I kept typing and deleting a response. I had too many questions to ask. How was she? Why was she grounded? Was she still captain? Was she going to Emerald's Halloween party tonight? I guess she wouldn't be if she was grounded. I stood there in the hallway at a loss about what to say. I wanted to see her, actually talk to her. I settled on:

> *Ouch. That bad?*
> **sad face**

She never responded. But at least I was able to go through the rest of my day happy that Quinn was at least alive.

After school was Emerald's Halloween party. It was definitely one of the few times a year when everyone was likely to get hammered. It was a costume party, and I had originally planned to pull the whole "wear a flannel shirt and claim to be a lumberjack" act. Except after last Friday, I had no desire to go. I usually never wanted to go. Despite occasionally having fun playing

FIFA, I wouldn't mind a night at home. Thankfully for me, James and Tyler both hated Halloween. They claimed dressing up was for little kids. So instead of their usual pestering to get me to Emerald's, they agreed when I invited them over to play video games.

James showed up first, bringing his Xbox because my Playstation wasn't good enough for him. My dad was out at work as usual, so we had the living room to ourselves. As James was hooking his Xbox up to the T.V., Tyler showed up, his arms full of bags of chips and a case of beer. Tyler's family was the only one of the three of us that always had alcohol handy.

We situated ourselves on the couch, each grabbing a controller to start our night of *Call of Duty* when there was a third knock on the door. My heart sank. I invited him, but I didn't think he'd actually come. Maybe he didn't realize James and Tyler were here too.

"Dude, please tell me you did not invite Quinn," James said. "I thought this was going to be a bros night."

"I didn't. And it is," I said, getting up to answer the door, stepping over all the bags of chips.

Ian was standing on my porch. A smile on his face quickly vanished when he saw Tyler and James behind me.

"Dude, no," Tyler said, standing up.

"I can go—" Ian started to say.

"No, stay," I said, allowing Ian inside. "What's the problem? We used to hang out all the time." I sat back down on the couch, grabbing my controller to unpause the game.

Ian lurked by the door like he was still unsure if he should leave or not. I wasn't one to face conflict, always avoiding it if I could. And like I mentioned, I didn't think Ian would actually show. But he did. So I guessed now was as good of a time as any to face why we don't hang out with him anymore. Fuck all these goddamn rules. Fuck these two. Fuck rumors. Ian was my friend, and I should still be allowed to invite him over.

"I told you you shouldn't keep hanging out with this *fag*. He'll brainwash you," Tyler said, refusing to sit back on the couch as if it were lava, his voice rising with each word.

James sat there, watching Tyler with concern.

"Brainwash me to do what exactly? Are you that uncomfortable with your own sexuality that you're worried about hanging out with someone who is?"

Could it be a coincidence that Tyler wanted to stop hanging out with Ian shortly after he came out?

Tyler let out a laugh, pacing the room. "This is bullshit. Are you forgetting he fucking *stole* from me?"

James dropped his controller, giving up on the game. "Seriously, dude, what the fuck? Why'd you invite him?"

"I'm just trying to understand the issue here," I said, eyes on the game, moving my character around the screen.

"You know ... I can still go," Ian said from the doorway.

"Yeah, get out of here, faggot!" Tyler opened a beer, swinging the bottle to shoo Ian away.

"No, Ian is welcome here, just like you both are. Please tell me what exactly it was that Ian stole." It was my turn to put my controller down.

Clearly, there was no being civil here. Why couldn't these two just grow a pair and let Ian play with us?

"Tyler, let's just play." James' eyes shot from Tyler to me and back.

"No! Fuck."

All I could do was shake my head. "For once, I actually want you to listen to James."

"Fuck you, Julian," Tyler spat.

It looked like he was trying to blink back tears, and suddenly there was a sinking feeling in my stomach. This was a bad idea. But I still didn't understand why Ian caused Tyler to be so riled up. What exactly happened between them? Sure, I was the one who initially invited Ian into our group in middle school. But he and Tyler seemed to get along and might have even been better friends than Ian and me.

James must have noticed too because he was on his feet and by Tyler's side in an instant. "Let's go, Ty."

Tyler grinded his teeth before darting toward the door, brushing past Ian.

James collected his Xbox before following Tyler to put on their shoes. It was odd seeing James follow Tyler around, James being the usual leader of our group. I wasn't sure if I should protest. I didn't know what else to say. That didn't go at all as I had hoped, and I still felt like I didn't have any answers.

"Sorry," James said before shutting the door behind them.

"Thanks for the warning," Ian said.

"Sorry, I wasn't sure if you'd come. Wanna still play? Be a shame to let all these chips go to waste."

"Of course, I came." Ian shrugged off his coat and slung it over the couch before sitting beside me.

We started a game of *Crash* on my PlayStation, indulging in the munchies Tyler and James left behind.

"So, what *did* you steal?" I asked.

"Nothing."

"So why does Tyler think you did?"

Ian shrugged. "A misunderstanding, I guess."

I nodded, although I still didn't quite understand. However, a part of me felt like I shouldn't push for more.

"How're things with Quinn?" His question shocked me. Last we properly talked, Ian was pissed at Quinn for hurting Liza. Him caring about things with her didn't seem likely. Not to mention the guilt I felt pretending everything was fine with her after what Ian had said.

"Good, I think."

"You think?"

"Well," I leaned back onto the couch, letting the controller rest between my thighs, "I haven't really talked to her about what happened at Emerald's. Or about the rumors. Or about Liza." I sighed. "I don't know if I even should."

Ian paused the game, putting his controller on the coffee table before turning to look at me. "Look, Liza is more my friend than Quinn is. I can't speak about any of the other rumors with Quinn, but the one with Liza is real. For once, Adrian didn't make it up or over dramatize it."

"But—what does that mean? Like for Quinn? For me?"

Who the hell was Quinn, honestly? I wanted to scream out of frustration. I didn't know anything. I didn't know what was right or wrong, what was truth or lies. It still bothered me, but I didn't know if it should.

"I don't know, Julian. And it's really not my place to say."

I didn't respond. I knew it was something I had to figure out on my own. So instead, we continued our game with nothing but small talk the rest of the night.

THE NEXT MORNING, I decided to text James and Tyler.

Sorry about last night, we cool?

To which they both responded:

We cool.

I may not have gotten the answers I was hoping for, but I also didn't want to toss my friendships out the window for it, either.

By the time Sunday came along, not seeing Quinn was killing me. My stomach dropped even more as I scrolled through social media, seeing pictures from Emerald's on Friday night. Marie and Emerald were dressed up as Minnie and Mickey Mouse. It made me almost wish I had been able to go with Quinn to dress up together as something cheesy like that.

That's when the thought hit me. I wanted past all the high school drama. I wanted past all the rumors. I wanted to trust Quinn and figure out who she really was. A smile formed on my lips as I jumped out of bed.

It was already three o'clock in the afternoon. I wasted the entire day doing nothing but sitting around on my phone. But it was still early enough that *they* wouldn't be mad, right?

I rummaged in my closet for an old tote box from when I was a kid with costumes from past Halloweens; most wouldn't even fit my arm now. Once I found what I was looking for, I threw it in a plastic bag and headed downstairs to the living room. From the shelf beside our T.V., I pulled out my three favorite horror films and stuffed them in the bag before heading out the door. I made a stop at the grocery store, picking up a huge box of assorted mini chocolates.

Finally, I pulled up to her house. Her parents' car was in the driveway along with her sister's. I sat in her driveway for a moment, taking deep breaths to prepare myself. This could make or break things with her parents, making them hate me even more. She's grounded. I should respect that. But I couldn't even talk to Quinn. It was like she disappeared off the radar.

One. Two. Three. I counted in my head before stepping out of my car.

It only took one knock on her door before her father answered. I swallowed.

Breathe, Julian, you got this. What's the worst that can

happen? All he can do is just say no. Sure, that'll hurt your pride a little, but it's not the worst thing in the world.

"Hello, sir."

"Julian."

"It has come to my attention that your daughter, Quinn, has been grounded. I assure you, I respect any reasoning behind this. However, because of this, she has missed the wondrous holiday that is Halloween. I cannot let her be denied the joys of her youth, sir. So, since she had to miss Halloween, I have brought the holiday to her instead." I let out a deep breath after my speech, hoping my sense of humor was enough to win him over.

He seemed to be holding in a laugh. His arms had crossed at some point during my speech, but he was leaning against the doorway. I had been too focused to realize how relaxed he was.

"Well, then, Julian," Mr. Kennedy smiled, "after all that work, I'm not sure I could deny your request. Under three conditions."

"Anything, sir."

"One: you continue to respect and be a good influence on my daughter. Two: you must hang out in the living room. Three: have fun."

"Yes, sir. Thank you, sir."

I brushed past her dad to see Quinn already standing in the living room, eavesdropping on our conversation.

"That was quite a speech, Mr. Raskin. What did I do to deserve it?" She lifted her brow, a small smile on her face.

I smiled at her and reached into my bag, handing her a pair of cat ears. "Here, wear these."

Quinn burst out laughing. "No, absolutely not."

I took out a pair of dog ears and put them on my head. "Oh, come on, don't spoil the fun."

Her face grew serious. "Are you a dog or a cat person?"

"Cats, actually." I walked over to her, placing the ears on her head before sneaking a kiss. "Now you sit here," I said, motioning to the couch as I made my way to her DVD player.

"Yes, sir." She saluted before hopping onto the couch.

I put in *Friday The 13th* before I turned around, spilling the contents of the assorted chocolate onto her coffee table. Discarding the box in her recycling, I found my spot beside Quinn, wrapping my arm around her.

"Quinn Kennedy, I bring you: Halloween." I swept my arm out in front of me.

She tucked her feet underneath her body, curling into my side.

"Thank you, Julian," she said softly, looking up at me. Her hand came to rest on my cheek. "This is exactly what I needed."

"I would have used any excuse to see you." I smiled.

She leaned up and pecked my lips before resting her head on my shoulder. "How was the Halloween Party? It's one of my favorite days at Emerald's."

"Uh, yeah, I didn't go."

She pulled back from my arms. "How the hell did you manage that one?"

"Well, truthfully, I wanted a break from Adrian, and luckily James and Tyler hate Halloween, so they came over for a game night."

"Oh." She nodded before curling back into me. "How was that?"

"Good until Ian showed up."

"Was he invited? Or did he crash?"

"Oh no, I invited him. Just Tyler freaked out about it."

She leaned out of my arms and grabbed two chocolates, tossing one at me.

"So spill the beans," she started as she unwrapped the chocolate. "What the hell happened to you guys?"

"To be honest with you—no idea. Tyler claims Ian stole from

him. Ian says he didn't. But Tyler won't even say what exactly Ian stole, to begin with."

She groaned, rolling her eyes. "Why does everything have to be so difficult?"

"I second that."

"So did it become Emerald's 2.0?"

"Oh yeah. Though short-lived. James and Tyler ended up bailing, so Ian and I just played together."

"So, nothing is resolved? And there's still some secret?" She sighed. "Can you promise me something right now?"

"Depends," I teased. She nudged me before I smiled. "Of course."

"Can we not be as complicated and frustrating as our friends?"

"Hm, okay. Then I have a question."

She turned so she was facing me. "Go for it."

"What all is true about you? Like what's the deal with Liza?" I turned my head away, unable to make eye contact with her. I needed the truth, even if it hurt.

"Oh," she breathed, distancing herself a bit from me. "What you've heard about Liza is true." I saw her shoulders shrug from the corner of my eyes. She grabbed a pillow from the couch and hugged it against her.

"Yeah, I got that from that Friday."

"Then what are you asking me?" She was becoming defensive, her walls going back up. I didn't know what to ask to be let back in. I didn't know the right things to say. Yet I still felt like we hadn't made any progress with this conversation.

"I want to hear what happened. From you. Not from Adrian. Not Ian. Not from any rumor. But you. I want to know you, Quinn, every part of you."

I gave her space and waited patiently while her mouth opened and closed a few times. Her grip tightened on the pillow.

"Liza and I," she sighed, dropping her eye contact. "We grew up together, inseparable. Closer than Marie and I ever have been. She knew absolutely everything about me. Last year, almost to the date, I went over to Liza's house to bitch about some boy who had mistreated me. But Liza had other plans. Before I could even say my part, she told me she needed to confide in me, and that's when she came out to me.

"She was scared and nervous. Fearful of what others would think. Of how her parents would react. How the group would react. All of it. And it pained me to see my best friend so distraught. I wanted to do everything in my power to protect her. To love her. To care for her. So I did what I knew I could do: I held her, and we cried together on her bed. I told her I would always be there for her; I'd keep her secret until she was ready, and that I'd protect her."

Quinn squinted her eyes shut, pulling her knees up, squishing the pillow between her.

"I—" She choked. "I kept kissing her head and her temple in comfort and got caught up in the actions, and I kissed her on the lips. But it wasn't just a kiss of pity or comfort. Yes, it started that way, but it became far more than that. I loved Liza as a friend. But suddenly, it felt like there could have been so much more. Why couldn't I be that person for her, you know?"

All I did was nod. I had never seen Quinn like this before, laying her heart open like this.

"So, one thing led to another. All of a sudden, we had this new element to our relationship. We didn't really define it. Or speak of it. And it was all kept in secret. My parents didn't even know." She paused, looking over the couch to reassure her parents were in their room and out of earshot. "But because we had always been inseparable, and then there's the messed-up gender rule of closed doors, we got away with sleepovers and kissing in our bedrooms. And I loved her. I *do* love her." Quinn rubbed her eyes, leaving her cheeks wet with tears.

"It was great, really. We worked well together, but there was a massive piece missing: I love sex. And that wasn't the issue, but I don't like sex with women. Unfortunately, Liza fell victim to that experiment.

"What Adrian, or Ian, or Liza won't tell you is that Liza asked me, begged me, really, to sleep with her. She wanted her first time to be with me. And I thought, well, I loved her so much romantically, surely it would be sexually too. But it wasn't. I panicked. I was stupid and immature. I ended things almost immediately. Without thinking, and I clearly wasn't, as I went to Adrian's."

I pulled her into my chest. "It's okay," I said, rubbing her back. I nestled my head into her hair. "I don't judge you for any of it."

She pulled out of my arms.

"Julian," she took a deep breath, "I don't want to lie to you." Quinn pinched between her brows. "I didn't hold out on Adrian. I went to him in distress, immediately spilled Liza's secret, and he comforted me into bed. I had refused to sleep with Adrian up until that point. And I don't know why I did it, why it was him, but it's not what Liza deserved."

I just looked at her, unsure of what to say. "Okay," I said to fill the space.

I understood things with Liza—I think. I could see why Ian was angry at Quinn being Liza's friend. I could see why Liza was hurt. But Quinn was hurting too. I wanted to hug her and suck all the pain out of her. But there was still one thing tugging at me.

"What about all the other guys?"

"What do you mean?" Her arms crossed, and she made space between us.

"Why does everyone think you're ..." I couldn't bring myself to say the word.

"I'm not going to apologize for liking sex if that's what you're asking me to do."

My head snapped in her direction. "No. No. That's not what I meant. Um. I just," I paused, trying to collect my thoughts. "Is sex just meaningless to you?"

"No, definitely not."

"Okay." I grabbed a chocolate from the coffee table, playing with its wrapper. "So what is it, then?"

She watched me, untangling her arms. "Sex can be meaningless. Sex with Adrian? Meaningless. But sex to me can also be fun; it's a stress reliever. It's this weird bizarre act of vulnerability that can somehow be shared between two random people sometimes. It's also a need for me. Whether that need is fulfilled through sex or masturbation, it doesn't often matter. And I'm not ashamed of how much I love it."

I nodded, trying to smile at her confidence, at her honesty. But I struggled too. Sex was a big deal to her. But it wasn't to me …. A need. A need for some reason I didn't have. Was it because I was a virgin? And maybe after the first time, it would become a need?

"Does it bother you that we haven't had sex yet?"

Quinn moved back over to me and took my hand. "No. At first? Yes, because I thought it was all you were after. I enjoy sleeping around, but I don't like when it becomes an expectation. I'm not a sex object. But when I started to get to know you? It felt like this would be different. Have I thought about it? Yes. Have I wanted it to happen? Of course. But I don't want to mess things up with you, Julian. For once, I'm trying to think before I act."

"Okay," I said, hoping she wouldn't ask me the same thing.

Frankly, this month with Quinn had been pure bliss without the pressure of sex latched on to it. I wasn't ready to give that up yet. I didn't want to move forward to that part of our relationship. I didn't know if I ever would.

Don't think about it, Julian. Your mind will change once you have sex. Don't worry about it.

"Does it bother you that you're with the girl who seems to give it out to anyone, and you haven't gotten laid?"

I let out a laugh I tried to hold in. "Not even a little bit."

She leaned up and kissed my cheek. "Then Julian, we are on your timeline. When you're ready, I'll be here."

"Okay." I pulled her back to me, kissing her on the lips this time. At least she didn't expect sex out of me. Not yet anyway ....

QUINN

I HAD AN APPOINTMENT WITH MY COACH BRIGHT AND EARLY Monday morning. A family emergency had our coach out last Friday, which left me off the hook—temporarily. But an email came in with a mandatory appointment before homeroom. She mentioned she had already spoken to Liza and that this was a private appointment.

No one told me what happened after the game. Well, Marie and Emerald had tried on Friday, but I walked away from them. I didn't want to know what happened. Liza and I blew it, costing us the championship. They played with two players down; the ref almost needed to kick the spectators out of the bleachers because of the disruption. But that's all I knew. My parents didn't even fill me in, just enough to let me know Liza's parents were angry—of course, they had been in the crowd too. Our overly passionate sport's families were the reason we were star players. They wouldn't miss a massive game, but it would have been better if they didn't care.

When I walked into my coach's office, she put down the paperwork she was doing and gestured for me to sit before even saying anything.

"Coach, I'm—" I started.

I was thankful she held up a hand to stop me because I wasn't sure what I was going to say. Yes, I was sorry. Sorry I messed up the game. Sorry I fucked Liza over. But not sorry for being angry and frustrated that Liza couldn't be a team player.

"Quinn," she sighed, taking her reading glasses off, "you've always been my best player. You're a smart student, one heck of a captain, and you've always been ready to help out your other teammates. Stay late or practice early if someone needed extra help. I've been going insane this weekend trying to figure out what happened. Is everything okay? I checked with your teachers, and they said your grades have been good. Is there something going on at home? Are students harassing you? It started that day you hurt your ankle. You were miserable at practice. Are you and Liza fighting over a boy?"

What?

I blinked, taking a few breaths to think. I had prepared myself for a lecture.

"You already talked to Liza, right?"

"Yes, after the game. She stayed until the end." She tilted her head slightly, raising her brow. My discipline was on its way. "I am here to listen to your side of the story, Quinn."

"Everything is fine. I'm sorry for embarrassing you, Coach. I was out of line, and I'm embarrassed and disappointed in myself. It won't happen again." Simple was best, right? The less I said to everyone, the better.

She rubbed the bridge of her nose as she let out a sigh.

"Quinn," she started, and I shook my head. "Okay," she rustled her papers, stacking them neatly, "then Quinn, I regret to inform you that you'll be suspended from the first game of next season, and you won't be eligible for the position of Captain."

"I understand." Despite telling myself this outcome numerous times over the weekend, it still didn't stop the train from barging through my chest, full force. I knew the rules and the consequences. I'd known the handbook like the back of my hand since middle school. I had always promised myself that nothing would get in the way of being the best player I could be. "Thank you. Is that all?"

"Yes, Quinn. You're dismissed." I stood up quickly, rushing toward the door. "But my door is always open if you need anything."

I nodded, but I couldn't turn around. I needed to move forward and on. Keep my head down and push through on my own. The group was starting to cost me what was most important.

There was always that fear of what would happen if I walked away from the group. If I cut those ties. What would my status in school look like? As a Captain? As an envied soccer player? As *Quinn Kennedy*? I had always believed there were so many positives to having "the group." But I never took the time to step back and realize I was actually harming myself.

LATER THAT DAY, I started trying to speak with Liza. I wanted to apologize for what I had done and try to explain to her what I had told Julian. Maybe if she could hear everything, we could start over?

I had made a deal with my parents—I was not going to talk to her Friday because I wasn't calm enough. I wasn't ready for a house call yet on the weekend because that felt like cornering her. I convinced them that school—with bystanders present—was the safest. It'd keep us both in line. Of course, they argued that our biggest soccer game didn't even keep us in line, but they gave me a week at school. If by then we hadn't spoken, I was to go to her house and apologize not only to her but her entire family.

But my plan was poorly thought out. Liza was always

surrounded. Whether it was Ian or Nile, they were her escorts when they could be—and when they weren't, Liza was out of sight before I could spot her.

It crossed my mind a few times that it wasn't even worth it anymore. That she wouldn't listen to a damn thing I said anyway, so why even try? But I had dear 'ol Julian reminding me every day after school that it was important, that Liza needed to hear my side, and not just what Adrian had said.

Since soccer was finished and I was grounded, Julian and I chose to spend our after-school period together either in the library or across the street at the coffee shop doing our homework. My parents weren't opposed as long as I could show them progress of getting work done and I was home no later than 3:30 p.m.

It had become my only saving grace of going into school every day and my only time spent with Julian. Even though he was allowed over on Sunday, he wasn't allowed over on weekdays.

Being grounded sucked.

I was told I couldn't see Julian outside of school until things were sorted with Liza. And that's how I ended up outside her door at nine in the morning on a Saturday.

I knocked, and her parents dismissed me, saying she was asleep.

I came back an hour later with her favorite coffee and bagel; Nile answered the door, didn't respond, yet took the offering.

I sat outside her house in my car, reading a book for English class, waiting another hour before I knocked again. Her parents asked me to leave this time.

So I respected their wishes and drove down the street with a view of their home, but in a place where I knew for a fact that they couldn't see my car.

It was late afternoon by the time her parents left the house.

Barely even giving them time to turn the corner, I hopped out of my car and ran down the street, knocking on their front door again.

This time I was ignored. Maybe they had all left the house? Did I miss Nile and Liza getting into the car? I peeked in the living room window and saw Nile in the kitchen. Within seconds, he was closing the curtains and still ignoring my knocks.

But I continued to knock because this needed to be resolved. I needed to explain myself.

Finally, the door swung open. I stumbled back as Nile forced his way out onto the porch and shut the door behind him.

"Quinn, you need to get the hell out of here. Give it up. You fucked up; pay the consequences. Liza does not want to see or speak to you. Stop harassing us. Stop trying to find her in school. Ignore her in the classes you share. If she chooses to forgive you—to listen to whatever bullshit excuse you may have come up with this time—then that's on her. But I am asking you now, giving you a chance to leave on your own terms. Please don't make me call the police."

The police? What the fuck was happening?

"Nile, I'm—" I rushed as he started to open the door. But he turned toward me again.

"No, Quinn. You don't understand. If you cared, if you were sorry, if you loved Liza in any way, then you would have thought twice about what you did. You wouldn't have done it. *Any* of it. But you don't care. All you care about is yourself. It's about fucking time it bit you in the ass. You can't get away with everything, Quinn. You've finally been put in your place. I'm just sorry my sister had to be involved. So please, remove yourself from our fucking doorstep, or I'll call the police."

He slipped through the door before I had a chance to argue, slamming it behind him. He reappeared in the living room window, tapping for my attention, holding his phone up.

My feet carried me off of their property and down the block before I could even register what happened.

Needless to say, I wasn't allowed to see Julian. If anything, my parents were even angrier that I harassed Liza's family. My parents proceeded to call up Liza's parents and apologize on my behalf, promising that I'd never act like that again.

The number of times that promise had been given in a week's time was one too many.

I was told to keep my head down, do my schoolwork, come home immediately, and do my chores. If I managed to not get into trouble or cause any inconveniences, then I might be able to see Julian over Thanksgiving break.

One and a half weeks later

My mother and I were in the kitchen, starting to prep the turkey. Usually, this was my father's job, but he decided it was one last punishment for me before being set free today.

"Quinn, honey, why don't you invite Julian and his father over for desserts later? We're already having Kenny's parents here for dessert. It'd be nice to get to know Julian's father."

I paused what I was doing and turned to face her. She was just finishing up the stuffing before we placed it in the turkey.

"But I've never met his dad; wouldn't that be weird?"

"Absolutely not. I think it'd be a nice gesture. Besides, you've been begging to see Julian." I sent her a glare. I had not been *begging* to see him. That was overdramatic. "Finish up the turkey, and then you're free. Invite them and insist they don't need to bring a thing—we have plenty."

I nodded but tried to figure out a way I could possibly get out of asking them. For one, it was the morning of. You didn't invite people the morning of Thanksgiving. Wouldn't that seem like we had forgotten to invite them earlier? And two, did I really want to put Julian and his dad through the torture of our big family gatherings?

My mom finished the stuffing before I had a good excuse. Together we closed the turkey up and put it in the oven before she was shooing me away.

My dad was there to take over my place, my cell phone in his hand.

"I guess your punishment is over now. Did you learn your lesson?"

"Yes, Dad." I rolled my eyes, reaching for my phone. He tightened his grip on it.

"No more fist fights? No more screaming fits? No more parties at Joseph's?"

"I promise. Well, I promise to the first two." We watched each other—seeing who would break first.

"Fine," he conceded. "But—"

"But if something ever happens again, then I'll be grounded," I groaned. "I understand. I do."

With a nod, he pulled me into a hug, kissed the top of my head, and finally handed over my cell phone.

Before I even made it down the hallway to my bedroom, I dialed Julian's number.

"And to what do I owe this pleasure, Quinn Kennedy?" he answered the phone.

"Happy Thanksgiving!" I grinned as if he could see me.

He laughed. "Happy Thanksgiving."

I walked into my bedroom and shut the door before I hopped up onto my bed.

"So, what are your plans for the day? Because I, for one, freaking love this holiday."

"Basically, what I'm doing right now—a whole lot of nothing. You?"

"Excuse me?!" I exclaimed. "You're not prepping dinner or watching the parade? Or eating before you eat too much?"

"Hm. Nope. My dad and I basically just have the football game playing in the background while we eat T.V. dinners."

I almost dropped the phone as he spoke. Who the hell has T.V. dinners on the greatest food holiday of all time?

"Nope. Unacceptable. I won't have it." I shook my head as I stood up as if he'd see my own distress. "I expect you and your father at my house this afternoon. 2 p.m. sharp. Unless you'd love to grace me with your presence earlier."

"Uh. But," he paused, "is your family aware of this?"

"Of course!" It was only a small white lie ... I mean, the more the merrier, right? That's what my mom was alluding to. He didn't seem convinced, but he agreed to my invite.

"QUINN, I need you to get started on the sweet potato casserole!"

After I had informed my mom that we would be having two more guests, I was required to run out to the store and pick up more food because, of course, she claimed we just didn't have enough.

But from the moment I walked in with the food, I was being ordered around as if we were feeding people of higher importance than us. I didn't understand the big deal. But better to do as she said than argue.

So I got to cooking, mashing, and then placing marshmallows over the mashed sweet potatoes, and it was good to go in the oven. Despite our extra two guests and a delayed start to the rest of the food, we were running seemingly on time—if you forgot about my mom's frazzled hair and lovely food combination on her apron.

At two on the dot, our doorbell rang, causing my mother to scream that she wasn't ready from the bedroom.

I peeped out the window, catching a glimpse of Julian straightening his shirt. I opened the door seconds later to reveal Julian and his seemingly older twin.

"Hey," Julian greeted me with a smile. "Quinn, this is my dad—"

"Tom." He nodded at me as they entered my house.

"Nice to meet you! I'm Quinn." I smiled, offering my hand after I closed the door behind them. "Thank you for coming."

"So this is the girl you're always talking about." Tom looked over at Julian.

"*Always* is a bit of an exaggeration, Father." Julian shrugged off his coat. "Don't listen to him. He just wants to embarrass me," Julian said to me.

"No need to be embarrassed, Julian, Quinn's been begging us to see you."

Of course, she'd make her entrance now.

I shook my head at Julian, trying to debunk my mom's words. But I couldn't stop my face from heating up.

My mom came up behind me, placing her hands on my shoulders. Not even two minutes in, and this was going to be miserable for both me and Julian.

The oven sounded, breaking up our introductions as my mom motioned for Julian and Tom to settle themselves. Tom followed my mom into the kitchen, greeting my dad on the way.

"I apologize in advance for whatever may happen today. Kennedys are serious about Thanksgiving." I laughed, trying to make it seem like it wasn't true.

Before Julian answered me, the front door swung open.

"Happy Thanksgiving!" Emma greeted, Kenny in tow with some dishes. "Julian!" Emma exclaimed, smirking over at me. "What a lovely surprise. Babe, this is Julian, Quinn's boyfriend."

"Hey, man!" Kenny nodded, lifting the food in his hands as his greeting. "I've heard a ton about you. Nice to finally meet you."

"Nice to meet you too." Julian smiled.

We all filtered into the kitchen, Julian offering to grab a dish off of Kenny's pile. By the time we were there, my mom was setting the table, and my dad was taking the casseroles out of the oven.

"Please, please sit!" My mom started placing everything on the table, including wine and water pitchers.

"I hope you're hungry." I nudged Julian's side, motioning over to a seat for him.

"Starved." He scooted his chair closer to the table. "It all looks delicious, Mrs. Lydia."

My mother blushed as she took her own seat across from him. "Eat as much as you want, dear. I'm so thrilled you two are here!"

Dinner went as it usually did on Thanksgiving—mostly loud as everyone spoke over each other. Everyone always had the most "important" news to share. But I hadn't felt this much pure joy on this holiday since I was a kid. I kept looking back from Julian to his dad, to my parents, and Emma and Kenny. I couldn't seem to keep the smile off my face. I have never had a boy over during any holiday before. I hoped Julian would be around for many more.

I placed my hand softly on Julian's thigh to get his attention. He looked over at me, the smile on his face melting my heart.

"Thank you for coming," I whispered, squeezing his thigh a little. "It means a lot to me."

"Thank you for the invite. This really beats T.V. dinners."

I laughed and nodded. "My mom is a pretty great chef if I do say so myself. Just wait until you try her pumpkin pie."

Julian's eyes lit up, and he placed his hand on top of mine.

Dinner suddenly couldn't finish fast enough. While I had already eaten my second helping, I often went in for a third of the best dish. But having Julian here, after not properly seeing him in weeks, made me greedy for all the time I could have with him.

Eventually, the plates were cleared, and the food was covered for later. And when the adults—Emma and Kenny included—went to watch the football game, I pulled Julian down the hallway instead.

I partially closed the bedroom door behind us and pulled Julian into a hug.

"Hi," I whispered, kissing his chest, where my lips naturally fell.

"Hello, beautiful," he breathed in my ear.

I leaned up on my tippy toes, and he met me halfway, connecting our lips. It had been far too long since we last kissed.

"You didn't want to watch football, right?" I questioned, pulling away only enough to drag him over to my bed.

"Not even in the slightest."

I smiled, hopping up on my bed, moving up so my back was against the headboard. "Then come join me!"

His smile seemed hesitant before he sat next to me.

"I've missed you." I kissed his shoulder.

"I've missed you too. It's too quiet without you around," he teased.

"You may regret saying that," I laughed, "because now I'm a free woman, and you won't be able to get rid of me that easily."

"Well, the peace and quiet was nice while it lasted." He let out an overdramatic sigh.

I leaned back and punched his shoulder softly. "Harsh!" I tried to frown, holding back a laugh. He let his head fall back and laughed, the kind of full-bodied laugh I loved.

"Admit it, you didn't know what to do without me." I smirked, poking him in the chest.

"I was lost. It was like I was stranded at sea with no sense of direction. No one to guide me home." He put his hand on his heart and looked off into the distance, trying to make his eyes close to crying.

I placed my hand on his cheek, guiding it in my direction. "Well, then, shall I save you?"

"What's this? A beautiful mermaid has come to my rescue?" He smiled.

"A strong," I leaned in to kiss him. "Warrior," I whispered. "Mermaid," I mumbled, pressing my lips firmly against his.

I pushed my body onto him until his gave out, lying against my bed. Straddling him, I continued to kiss him, unable to stop. I just wanted more of him. I needed him. All of him. But he put his hands on my shoulders, breaking our kiss.

"What's wrong?" I breathed.

"Nothing, just—everyone's here ..."

I shrugged. "Football is on. I doubt they even know we left." I ran my hand down his side, slipping my fingers underneath his shirt. I leaned in to kiss him.

He turned his head to dodge my kisses. "Seriously, Quinn. I don't know if this is a good idea right now."

I sat back on his thighs. "Is it you who doesn't want to fool around, or are you that paranoid about everyone?"

"No, no. That's not the problem; it's just that—" He sighed. "I've never done this before. I figured our first time would be a little more private."

"Fooling around doesn't mean we need to have sex. I don't want your first time to be around others either."

He was silent for a moment, his brows knit together. "Okay."

"Have you ..." If he hadn't had sex, how far had he ever gone? I quickly tried to remember all the times we had spoken of sex, and not surprisingly, they all were about me. Had I never asked Julian about his previous experiences? "How far have you gone?"

He looked away, unable to meet my eyes. "This is embarrassing. Can we just do and not talk?"

I furrowed my brows, sliding off his thighs, so I was lying beside him. "Why is it embarrassing?"

He propped himself up with his elbows. "Look, I've never had a real girlfriend before you. I've gone on dates, but I haven't really done anything besides kiss a girl. And here you are with all this experience—and—it's just embarrassing, okay?"

"Hey," I whispered, caressing his cheek with my hand. "It's okay. There's absolutely nothing to be embarrassed about. I don't think any less of you."

He wouldn't look at me. I wish I could tell what he was thinking. What he was feeling. "Let's just drop it. Please?"

I pulled him into a hug, pressing a kiss to his neck. "You tell me what's too much then, okay?"

"Okay."

I pecked the same place on his neck a few times before I trailed the kisses up and over his jawline. Once I connected our lips again, my hand slipped back underneath his shirt, pushing my body tightly up against his own. I tangled my leg around his, making sure we were as close as we could be—our breathing almost in sync—before I focused more on what our lips were doing. What *he* was doing. And where this could lead.

Julian pulled away again, his breath short. "Okay."

Okay? What?

"Okay?" I fumbled.

I hated that I needed so much more from him. This was an entirely new element for me. Even the guys I'd been with who had less experience were rarely ever honest about it. Was he just nervous? Intimidated? Did I try to push forward and make him more comfortable?

"Are you not enjoying this? We could try something different? This is just one way of fooling around."

"No. This is fine."

I nodded, trying to brush away the nonchalance. We were teenagers; shouldn't we both be thriving off the idea of getting caught by our parents?

I went to kiss him again, but before I could, my mother called for us, saying it was time for dessert.

JULIAN
CHRISTMAS BREAK

IT WAS LIKE A SWITCH WAS FLIPPED. EVER SINCE Thanksgiving, I had been struggling to keep Quinn off of me. Luckily, her parents were home for the most part, and we never hung out at my place, giving us very little time to actually be *alone* together. I missed when I could just kiss her and know nothing else would come of it. Now every time our lips met, I was on edge, hyperaware of the speed of her breathing and where her hands are. We had *sort of* done things. But it was just weird and awkward. At least for me. I didn't understand her. She said we were on "my timeline," but it didn't feel like that at all. I guess, in her defense, if we were truly on my timeline, we probably wouldn't ever end up having sex.

It was the first day of Christmas break, and tomorrow I would be traveling out of town with my dad to visit my uncle for Christmas. I wouldn't be back till the day before school started up again.

I never saw my mom for Christmas. She would just call me Christmas morning, wishing me a Merry Christmas, asking me what I got (she always sent me a gift card in the mail), and then she'd talk about what she got Alyssa and David.

I parked in Quinn's driveway, my breath forming clouds in front of me. We agreed on not getting each other gifts since neither of us had a job. But I still wanted to do something with her—have our own little mini Christmas together. As far as she knew, I was just taking her to get some hot cocoa.

"Merry early Christmas," she wished me with a smile as she hopped into my passenger side.

"Happy early Christmas. However, I hate to inform you that this is actually a kidnapping, and I will not be taking you for cocoa."

Quinn gasped, trying to play along, but let out a laugh. "So where are you taking your hostage?"

"You'll see." I smirked.

She groaned. "You know how I feel about surprises, Julian."

"You'll love this one. I swear."

I drove downtown to city hall where an event called "The Festival of Trees" was being held. Outside the pathway was lined with real pine trees decorated in multi-colored lights.

"So pretty," Quinn commented.

"You've seen nothing yet."

We reached the door, and I paid for two tickets to enter. Christmas music flooded our ears the moment we stepped inside. The entire building was bursting with Christmas trees in every direction. A small path intersected between them, crowded with people gawking at the beautiful displays. Each tree had a different theme, companies having decorated and donated them.

One tree put together by a local candy store was pink and filled with lollipops and toffee ornaments. Another done by a toy store made a black tree look like Mickey Mouse with Mickey ears as the topper, his face made out of construction paper and even the yellow shoes sitting on the bottom branches with toys scattered beneath it. A jewelry store took a white tree and dangled silver tinsel on it. It actually had real jewelry amongst the tinsel hanging from the branches. A classic green tree was filled with canned foods and boxes of mac and cheese by a grocery store. There was even a tree literally made out of beer and wine bottles by a liquor store.

Clipboards sat on small podiums beside each tree where people could bid to buy the tree and everything on it. All the money they collected was dispersed between the local food banks in the county, helping feed families over the holidays.

"This is amazing! I've always heard about this festival, but I can't believe I've never gone," Quinn said.

"It's so magical. It's like Christmas threw up everywhere."

"Literally." She laughed. "But it makes me so happy. It's just so beautiful."

"Yeah," I said, looking at her.

Quinn was beautiful. Regardless of all the trees, she was still the prettiest thing here. Her red curls shone under all the Christmas lights. The freckles sprinkled across her face accented her brown eyes, eyes filled with wonder and fire. My heart fluttered. I just wanted to care for her and make her happy.

"So, favorite Christmas memory! Three, two, one ... go!" she exclaimed.

"I'd have to go with the time I accidentally started a fire and ruined Christmas."

Quinn spit out a laugh. "You started a fire? How?"

"Well, when I was a kid, I was obsessed with helping out around the house. When I was ten, I insisted on making something for Christmas dinner. So my dad allowed me to make simple mac and cheese because you'd think even a ten-year-old is capable of that. Oh no. I got distracted by a Christmas movie on T.V. while the noodles were boiling and thus beginning the fire. Thus ruining Christmas."

"Oh my god." Quinn held her stomach as she laughed. "That's hilarious."

"My dad didn't think so. He won't let me live it down." I laughed. "So what about you? Your favorite Christmas memory?"

"My first family ski vacation. I had practiced a few times here and there when we would visit our family upstate, but this was like the first legit trip. Resort, week-long ski passes, unlimited hot cocoa. I was like eight, and my sister was ten. We didn't get much for Christmas that year because of it. But it's okay because my sister had ruined Santa for me a few months previously, and skiing definitely made up for it. And now we do a big vacation like that every other year or so."

"Wow, that's amazing." It almost made me wish I was able to spend a day or two with her on her ski trip this Christmas.

After we made our rounds through the labyrinth of trees, we decided to take a short stroll outside despite the cold. All the shops downtown were decorated in tons of Christmas lights, while Christmas music still filled the air. We did eventually stop at a cafe to grab our original planned cocoa when we both got tired of the cold.

"So," she grinned, wrapping her arms around my waist, looking up at me, "my parents are at a Christmas party tonight ... I was thinking," her fingers trailed up my back, "we could go back to my place?" Her hands brushed across my ribs, running up my chest and interlacing behind my neck.

Standing on her tippy toes, her lips hovered by my ear as she whispered, "Maybe we could fool around?" With a kiss on my cheek, she dropped to her feet and looked up, batting her lashes.

The shittiest part of this whole situation was it started out being about sex. Tyler and James wanted this set up so I could quickly and easily get laid. At first I was going to go along with it to get them off my back. But—I couldn't. I didn't have the capacity in me to just have meaningless sex with someone. I also felt like I wanted to prove a point that not all guys were just about sex. So I gave Quinn a real first date with no sex attached. Except

I liked her, which was the start of this disaster. Because how could I go on happy with Quinn, when at the end of the day, she herself *was* about sex? She said so herself that she loved sex. If it was going to happen, today would be it. So again, it was about sex. But this time it wasn't for Tyler or James. Maybe it wasn't even for Quinn. But for me. If I just had sex, I would get over my lack of interest, *right?*

"Okay." I smiled at her as we headed back to my car.

I took a deep breath. Why the hell was I so nervous? If Tyler and James could see the mess I was right now, they'd hit me across the head and tell me I have gold at my feet, gold being sex, of course.

I've jerked off before. What guy hasn't? But I could never get into porn. It honestly just didn't appeal to me. I only ever thought about sex around Tyler and James because they talked about it all the goddamn time. Even then I usually just blocked out what they were saying. It wasn't until Quinn came along that sex seemed to be all I could think about. But I wasn't thinking about *wanting* sex. More so, I felt anxiety over whether or not it was going to happen.

God, something was definitely wrong with me. I just wanted to get this over with.

"WANNA WATCH A MOVIE?" She climbed on the couch after we got to her place.

"Sure, what were you thinking?"

She shrugged but reached for the remote and turned on the television to Netflix. The first suggested movie was *Pitch Perfect*.

"Ooh! I love this movie," Quinn said, clicking.

She leaned back into the couch and onto me, my arm wrapped around her shoulders. Her fingers trailed up and down my thigh. In return, I rubbed my thumb against her upper arm where my hand was comfortably resting. Quinn's hand started to move further up my thigh each time her fingers trailed back and forth. The closer her fingers got, the more my body stiffened. At first, I thought she was just trying to show affection but now ... her fingers accidentally touched me. I gasped instinctively.

"Is this okay?" she asked.

"Yeah," I said as calmly as possible.

Although my mind didn't seem to know what to think or feel, my body sure did. My pants grew tighter as Quinn kept going.

Her focus left the television, and she turned toward me slightly. Quinn's hand hovered over me before she rubbed atop my jeans, her eyes dancing up to meet mine.

I pushed the back of her neck, so our lips collided, avoiding her eyes. A part of me wished it could just be kissing. I enjoyed kissing; I wanted to kiss her more than doing anything else. Why did it have to lead to sex?

Her hands grasped my cheeks, her body quick to straddle me. I was thankful to know that my body worked, but why wouldn't my brain follow through?

My mind kept bouncing back to the movie, listening to the lines more than I was aware of what was happening to me. It was like there was two of me. There was the physical being here with Quinn, reacting and following her movements. But then there was the me inside my head who felt detached from my body, in another dimension.

Quinn's lips left mine as she kissed along my jawline, inching her way to my neck. My eyes opened, looking down at her and swallowing. She kissed her way to my collarbone before making her way back up and to my ear. Her teeth nibbled on my earlobe.

"Shall we go to my room?" she whispered.

I nodded. I knew this was going to happen. I didn't know why I thought anything else could happen.

Quinn pulled away, trying to meet my eyes.

"You sure you want to do this? I don't want to pressure you."

"No, it's fine. I want to." I smiled.

I did want to; I wasn't lying. But I also didn't .... What the hell was wrong with me? Why couldn't my stupid brain be all in this?

I stood up, lifting her from under her arms to bring her to her feet before walking her into the wall. Pushing my body against hers, I kissed her hard, demanding my brain to shut up. Demanding every part of me to want this. What she was doing felt nice. And yet ....

She moaned against my lips and kicked away from the wall, trying to pull me down the hall while not breaking the kiss. I followed her lead, trying to match her passion, pulling her hips into mine, stopping us for a moment to get more of her lips. She smiled as her hands started to play with the bottom of my shirt. Quinn inched her fingers underneath, grazing my stomach. Instinctively, I sucked in at the feeling of her touch.

She broke the kiss, giving me a wink before she pulled me into her bedroom by my shirt, directing me in front of her bed. She gripped my arms, forcing me to sit down.

"Arms up." She giggled, lifting her own arms up for show.

I listened, lifting my arms while my brain tried to think of all the movies I'd seen and how it was done. I thought of the moment in *The Notebook* where he sees her in the rain, and it's like a spark goes off between them, where they are so consumed by passion, they can't think of anything but having sex with each other. That was how it should be, right? So caught up in the moment, there was nothing else but each other. Except here I was thinking about goddamn scenes in a movie instead of being in the present.

She gripped the bottom of my shirt and lifted it over my head. With a step back, her eyes trailed over my body, a smile forming.

"Well, this isn't fair. It's your turn." I smiled back.

"Will you do the honor?" She stepped forward, lifting her arms.

Grazing my fingers along the edge of her sweater, I began to pull it over her torso. My breath caught in my throat the moment I had her shirt off. She had on a maroon lace bra, one that looked like it may have been too small.

Quinn smiled at me, but not her usual smile. This smile was lustful and eager. I could hear my heart beating in my ears. Quinn was beautiful. But the word sexy wouldn't enter my brain to describe her. Yet here she was half-naked in front of me. Shouldn't that make her sexy? I tried thinking of a time before when I thought someone was sexy, but nothing came to my mind. I pulled her on top of me, laying us both down on the bed.

Quinn sat up, her legs straddling me as she positioned herself ever so delicately atop the tent in my pants. She circled her hips, pressing further down. Her eyes glazed, and her tongue flicked over her lips, wetting them. Quinn's hands came to my sides, trailing up and down my bare skin, and a shiver escaped me. She giggled before leaning down and pressing her wet lips over my heart and up my collarbone. Her mouth licked and nibbled all the way back up to my ear, her hot breath causing another shiver.

I wanted to want this. I wanted to want this so bad. I wanted it how Quinn wanted it. Like some natural instinct. Where was the part of my brain that is supposed to consume my thoughts with sex? Why wasn't my brain engulfed in the moment, in desire? At least my body was following through with what was happening. So why couldn't my brain just do the same?

"Don't be nervous. First times are highly overrated. It'll be weird and awkward. Ask questions and say no. Tell me what does and doesn't feel good, and I'll do the same, okay? No one is here but you and me, so don't be embarrassed to say something silly."

"Okay," I choked out.

Sure, nervous, that's what it must be. I'm just nervous. I evened my breathing. *Calm down, Julian, you're fine. Everything is fine. This is normal. You are normal.*

IT WASN'T AS LONG as I had always pictured sex to be. Afterward, I stared up at the ceiling with nothing but a thin blanket over me. Quinn's head was nestled on my chest quietly sleeping with my arm wrapped around her.

Well, it happened. My virginity lost forever. My lip twitched thinking about it. There was a part of me that believed losing my virginity would change everything. That afterward I'd feel somehow different. I'd understand how sex was the grand prize Tyler and James made it out to be. I'd no longer feel uncomfortable with sex scenes in movies. I'd be able to join in on sex jokes. But more than anything, I thought I'd actually want sex. Except here I was, lying here beside someone I deeply cared about, and I still felt no desire to have sex with her. Even as it was happening, my mind didn't care for it. I kept hoping that at some point my mind would take a turn, and I'd start enjoying it, but nothing happened.

I didn't understand. I really liked Quinn. I thought she was beautiful. I wanted to be with her, and I was happy she was my first. Yet ... something was off. Something wasn't right. But this wasn't something I could talk to Quinn about. It would just upset her. She might get mad and feel like she pressured me to have sex with her, which wasn't true at all. I wanted to. I wanted to for her. But I also couldn't talk to either Tyler or James about it. They'd probably just laugh at me, make jokes about it.

I looked around at Quinn's room, so unfamiliar compared to my own. On her dresser, I could see a photo of us together. She was giving the peace sign in the photo while I was sticking my tongue out, arm wrapped around her. It was shortly after our first date. We had Ian take the photo for us after we made things official. It was before everything started to take a shit. Before the fight at Emerald's. Before I learned the rumors about Quinn were true.

What was wrong with me? Was I ... could I be? I kept staring at the photo, thinking of Ian. Ian ....

I reached for my phone, careful not to move too much to wake Quinn. I pulled open my contacts and started typing a new text.

Can we talk?

QUINN

A SMILE WAS ALREADY ON MY LIPS BEFORE I OPENED MY eyes, remembering scenes from the night before. I couldn't keep the smile from forming wider or the tingling sensation that ran through my bloodstream at the thought of his name, his face, and his body. The way his hands felt on me the night before, how tentative, and nervous, and gentle he was.

How *loving*.

It wasn't picture perfect. There were hiccups and questions. We spoke more than I ever had during sex. Hands and limbs got tangled awkwardly. "I'm sorry" and "Is this okay?" were said plenty. But to me, it was perfect. *He* was perfect.

I held the giraffe close to my chest, breathing in the air around me. He didn't sleep over, but my sheets and the giraffe smelled of him—more so now than they had a few days prior. All of this was brand new. I'd be lying if I said I hated the way I felt.

The cage was open, and now I just wanted him even more. They say sex changes things, but I used to never believe it. I could sleep with any random person, and it wouldn't change the way I saw them the next day. It didn't make me fall in love or pine after them. But with Liza, it changed everything—for the worse. And with Julian? Well, with Julian, I ....

My phone vibrated beside me.

Good morning, beautiful.

I felt the blush rise to my cheeks, and despite being alone in my room, I buried my head under my sheets and giggled. If one simple message could make me want to explode into a giggling mess, this path to love would be a painful, exciting, and an exhausting journey.

And let's be clear, I wasn't sure if I was okay with it.

My door swung open.

"Good morning!" my sister exclaimed, jumping on my bed before I had the chance to pull the sheet down. "Get your butt up and ready; it's skiing time!"

"Morning!" I smiled, sitting up. I briefly eyed my phone, wanting to message Julian back instantly. But what would I even say?

Her eyes danced across my face, a glimmer suddenly shining in them. "Holy shit, it happened!"

I looked down, pulling the sheets up to my nose, trying to hide the blush that I feared would become permanent.

"Oh my god," she laughed, "and it was good too."

"Emma!" I laughed, swatting her arm. "Stop."

She shook her head and jumped under the covers next to me. "Details, girl!"

I shook my head and tried to climb out of the bed. "We have to go."

"Oh no, no, no." Pulling me back, she tickled my sides. I let out a squeal, roaring with laughter, as I jerked away from her, but she pinned me down until I called mercy.

"Okay, okay!" I panted, chuckling. I rescued the giraffe from the tangled sheets between us. She gave me a knowing look as she eyed the stuffed animal. Sitting up in front of her, I fixed my now messy hair into a bun.

"He's changed you, Quinn." Suddenly serious, she sat up straight and looked over at my bedside table where there was a picture of the two of us. It was a selfie I had taken over Thanksgiving break during our first snowfall. I was kissing his cheek, and he was smiling at the camera.

I could only nod, a smile forming.

I struggled with the idea of change. I didn't think a person could change someone per se. But I believed a person could ignite *a* change. But was that okay? Did I even need to change who I was before?

"Stop the wheels, babe. You're going to exhaust yourself." My eyes left the photo and found Emma's. "It's a good change, a fun change. You're still Quinn, the headstrong badass. My favorite sister—"

"Your only sister." I rolled my eyes.

"*Not* the point. The point being, you aren't losing yourself by falling for him. You shouldn't be. And if you start to, we can fix it. But don't ruin this by thinking you could ruin it, okay?"

"I really am falling for him," I whispered, looking down at the giraffe.

I was never someone who cared for stuffed animals. Even as a child, people would give them to me as presents, and I'd leave them in the corner to go build something or play a sport. But this wasn't about the stuffed animal. This was about having a piece of Julian with me. And it certainly would be traveling upstate with me this week.

And *that* feeling terrified me.

JULIAN

CHRISTMAS WAS THE SAME AS USUAL. I WENT TO MY uncle's where we had dinner with him, my aunt, and two cousins. My one cousin was a year older than me, and the other, a year younger. When our parents hung out drinking coffee in the living room, the three of us were in the basement playing video games. We stayed at their place until New Year's Day, my dad getting their guest room while I was stuck on the couch. I didn't get to see Quinn at all during the break after the Festival of Trees. Though we did make it a point to FaceTime each other Christmas Day before dinner. But other than that, we had settled for a text here and there.

The day back from Christmas break, I was determined to approach Ian. He had gone to Florida for the holidays with his family, preventing me from getting a proper chance to talk to him. He offered to talk through text or phone, but it felt better to express my thoughts to him in person.

While in line at the cafeteria, I spotted him at a back table studying, Liza and Connor not yet there. Perfect. I had a chance to catch him alone. I nodded at James and Tyler before I headed over.

Eyes focused on Ian, my brain repeated what I would say to him. "Ian, I think I might be gay." Over and over. My breathing quickened with my steps. Passing each table. *I think I might be gay. Am I gay? What do you think?* Over and over. Step after step. *I slept with Quinn, but I still don't think about sex. I must be gay, right?* He wouldn't judge me. He'd give me advice. He would know for sure if I was or not. Finally, I was standing in front of his table. I inhaled, ready to let the words out. But my mouth went dry.

Ian looked up from his textbook. "Oh, hey, what's up?"

"Hey," I choked out.

Fuck. Come on, Julian, you got this. This is Ian we are talking about. He wouldn't think anything of it. He wouldn't make a big deal about it. Except, what if I'm not gay? What if it's something else? I've never felt any attraction to guys before. But I haven't with girls either ....

"So ... are you going to sit down?" Ian furrowed his brows as I continued to stand and stare at him.

I let out an awkward laugh. "Sorry, no. I just wanted to know how your trip was?"

Maybe it was best not to bring it up to Ian. At least not yet. Not till I knew for sure. I couldn't rely on him for an answer. This was something I had to figure out on my own.

"Oh. It was good. The usual. My family can never decide on what activities to do together, and my sister always gets her way."

I nodded. "Still, at least you got away from the cold weather."

"Yeah, that's about the only good thing about it." He laughed.

"Well, I should get going. James and Tyler are waiting for me."

"Sure thing."

I smiled and turned to leave just as Ian asked, "Wait, Julian?"

"Yeah?" I peered over my shoulder.

"You okay? Wasn't there something you wanted to talk about?"

"No." I shook my head, hoping to convince him. "I'm fine." I forced a smile before I turned and left the cafeteria.

A WEEK LATER, I found myself in front of my locker where Tyler and James were waiting for me. It was our go-to hangout spot after we grabbed food in the cafeteria. I watched as the occasional student walked by our mostly deserted hallway. Tyler sat beside where I stood, against the lockers, pulling his sandwich free of plastic wrap. James was leaning against the wall across from us, determined to get the last drop out of his juice box. I threw an M&M into my mouth.

Quinn and I had sex a total of four times already. Four. Times. Every goddamn time we hung out since Christmas, it had happened. It was like our relationship had become all about sex. Truthfully, we only had actual intercourse twice. The other two times were more so attempts that resulted in me just pleasuring her in other ways. But still. It all fell under sex to me. Maybe it was weird that I was counting. But I couldn't help it. How many times did someone need to have sex with someone before they started enjoying it? Was there some sort of cut-off line where you were supposed to give up? My lip twitched.

The problem was I liked Quinn. A lot. I thought I was maybe even falling in love with her. Sure, sex felt nice, I guessed. But it was almost like getting a massage when you aren't actually sore. Or eating when you aren't hungry. And it wasn't like she was forcing me to have sex with her. It was more like I felt obligated to, like I should do it for her.

But I didn't want to have sex. All I wanted was to cuddle and occasionally make out. Just kissing. That was what I enjoyed. So much so, I fantasized about kissing Quinn. Every time I saw her, I wanted to kiss her. But that desire was also linked with fear. Because when we kiss, her hands eventually start to wander toward my leg. And I'd think: *this is fine. I'm okay with this too.* Because it was still just kissing. But then her hand would move too far, and soon she would start taking off my clothes. And my brain would stiffen while my body followed along with the movements. Because now I had let it go too far. I had to keep going, or it would upset her.

It was like a light switch. Most people were dimmers, slowly turning on and off. Mine was like a switch. The light suddenly flicked off, and my brain stopped enjoying it.

My body allowed for the actions while my brain started to wander, thinking about the most random shit. Like if I needed to pick up any groceries on my way home, or if I remembered to lock my car. Or sometimes I would have to hold in laughter because I was listening to the T.V. in the background. Then it would be over, and I'd think, *I just wanted to kiss.*

I'd googled hormonal disorders and reasons for low libido about a dozen times, rereading the same articles over and over again. Wishing for an answer. Something to make me feel normal. But nothing worked. I didn't seem to have anything medically wrong with me. I could still get hard. I still got urges. I still masturbated. What was missing then? Which led me back to Ian … could he help?

Even from the first time with Quinn, I wondered how I was supposed to feel afterward. Before her, I had thought maybe my lack of desire was because of my ignorance. If I had known what sex was like, I thought I would want it more and be more influenced by it like James and Tyler. Sometimes I had felt like if I wasn't a virgin, I would be a lot more inclined to have sex and want it more. But then I did have sex, and I was still confused.

I thought maybe my lack of desire for sex could have just

been that I hadn't found the right person yet. But I knew Quinn *was* the right person. And yet ....

I also never really had any sort of *crush* growing up. When all my friends started pointing out girls they thought were hot and deleting their browser history so their parents wouldn't know what they'd been doing, I was still just me. It's almost like I skipped over that part of puberty. *What the hell was wrong with me?* Even with Quinn, I wouldn't call it a crush more so than a friendship where I wanted to kiss and cuddle her.

I'd been wondering how Ian knew he was gay. And if I was too. But I also thought Quinn is pretty. *Could I be bisexual?* I bit my lip. *I don't know.*

What the hell was my deal?

"So Paige and I hooked up," James said, pulling me away from my thoughts.

"Fucking finally, man!" Tyler exclaimed, hitting James on the back.

"How'd that happen?" I asked.

"Well, you see here, Julian, I took my penis—" James started, raising his index finger and making a circle with his other hand. "And I—"

"Okay, you can stop; I get it." I held up my hands in defense. Even talking about sex made me uncomfortable. "I just mean, what took so long?"

"Well, I got her number that night she said she liked me, but she's been playing one hell of a game with me." He rolled his eyes. "But damn," he laughed, clasping his hands behind his head, "she was well worth the wait."

"Congrats, boy. What about you, Julian? Have you finally gotten some yet?" Tyler asked.

James laughed. "Seriously. You two must be having sex all the time."

I shrugged. "I don't kiss and tell."

"Oh, come on, nothing's a secret with Quinn," James teased, punching my arm. "Besides, dude, you're our best friend. Spill it."

I just shook my head.

"Wait, so everyone's getting laid but me?" Tyler asked. "What the hell, guys?"

"It's not our fault you aren't as smooth with the ladies," James said.

"Hah. Yeah sure. Whatever," Tyler scoffed.

I almost wished I was in Tyler's position ....

QUINN

I FOUND MYSELF AT MARIE'S HOUSE AFTER SCHOOL, something I didn't think I had done all year. Ever since Christmas, she had been trying to rekindle our friendship. The two of us hung out a couple times when I came back from my ski trip and Julian was still away.

Neither of us knew when we started to lose each other—or why she decided to bet against me—but I found myself unable to say no over Christmas break. But since then, we barely had time to hang out between school, studying, and finding time for our boyfriends. Julian and I even found ourselves seeing less of each other as the pressures of high school started to settle in—our alone time becoming study sessions. Not even study sessions in my home, which ironically had my parents more on edge about whether I was studying or acting out.

This is the year that counts, Quinn, my father repeatedly said. Along with: *If you aren't planning a full-ride with soccer, you need to ace this year.*

If only they knew that Julian and I were, in fact, studying more than fooling around—much to my disappointment.

My parents still weren't over the blow-up at soccer. They still expected me to miraculously be able to speak with Liza one day. And while I had only gone to Emerald's four out of the thirteen parties thrown since the end of October, they made sure to tell me each time how much they hated it.

Marie and I were both doing our nails, sitting on her carpet, listening to a playlist she created of all the popular songs so far this school year. Most were awful—I hated Top 40 hits, but it somehow felt like we were falling back to our early high school days.

"So how are things with you and Julian?" she asked, moving on to her second coat of lilac nail polish.

We had successfully avoided the topic of Julian, both knowing there was still this bet hovering over us. Julian and I had made it to almost four months together. I hated that there was still a part of me repeating "only two more months" in my head. Two more months and then what? Would I break up with him? No. Absolutely not. But would it still be a pure relationship? What would I have done before this bet? Julian and I would have had the dare, awkwardly kissed, and probably would have gone on our merry way for the rest of the school year. Maybe we would have casually waved each time we saw each other. But now we were dating. And we were serious.

"We are good," I commented, focusing on getting the nail polish just right. I had pride in my ability to almost never get polish on my skin.

"But ...," she trailed off, forcing me to look over at her. "Have you two?" Her voice sounded hopeful, but I couldn't decide if it was for the gossip outside of this room or for genuine interest in my life.

I remained silent, studying her for a moment.

She sighed, capping the nail polish. "I'm sorry things have been weird, Q. I'm sorry you haven't been able to trust me—that I haven't supported you. Haven't let you live your life the way you want. I promise you, whatever happens in this room will not ever get out."

I sincerely wanted to believe her half-assed apology. A part of me needed to know she didn't *really* think I was a *whore*. That I didn't need a relationship. I wanted my best friend back. I was more desperate for that friendship than I'd like to admit. With things feeling like they were crumbling with Julian, it was becoming apparent I had no one in my circle.

High school was hard enough as it is; the last thing anyone wanted was to walk the halls alone.

"Have things changed with you and Emerald?" I wasn't avoiding her question. I just needed more information before I could continue.

"Definitely." The smile that floated flawlessly onto her pale skin was my answer. They weren't in the same position as me and Julian.

In an instant, her eyes connected with mine, and her smile dropped.

"Oh shit. He's not good, is he?"

"It's not—" I sighed. I closed the nail polish and blew on my nails.

The truth was, Julian was amazing at what he did. It was more what he *didn't* do that was the issue.

"Quinn, what's going on?" Marie lowered the music and picked up the mess from doing our nails. "I promise you I'm not turning into Adrian; you really can trust me."

"We slept together over break."

Fuck. I shouldn't have said a damn thing. But Marie was different from Julian's friends, right? She *was* my best friend, right?

"And he was great—it was great. And I ... I've never felt that change you've always warned me about. Which, by the way, wasn't okay considering you just lost yours." I raised a brow at her and watched as her face spotted pink.

Despite all her comments on my sex life, she and Emerald just had sex for the first time over break as well, even though they'd been together for two years.

"But with Julian? Everything changed. In a good way, for me."

"Julian didn't enjoy sex with *The Quinn Kennedy*?"

This was a mistake. The feigned shock on her face was enough for me to know she wasn't going to change.

"Sorry, sorry, sorry!" She held her hands up, shaking her head. "I'm just confused."

"Me too," I groaned, forcing myself to stand.

I blew on my fingernails again before shaking my hands out. I took to pacing the small amount of free space Marie had. She wasn't a messy person; almost everything was placed perfectly, but the size of her bed was far too large for the small room.

"We've only had sex twice. And fuck, I'm trying to be patient." My mouth was on a goddamn roll. Where was this coming from? "But suddenly we're never alone, and on the rare occasions we have been, he gets all weird and strange, focusing his attention on pleasuring me. Like, I can't do anything for him or it stops. Like, he suddenly has to leave or suddenly his mind is too focused on an exam, and we need to study again."

"Will it make you feel better to know Emerald and I have only slept together twice, and we've had plenty of alone time?"

I stopped my pacing, looking down at her. "Because something is wrong?"

She shook her head and laughed. Standing up, Marie walked over to her bed and jumped onto it. Her pillows fell out of place.

"It's just what is natural for the two of us. Things have been great. Emerald and I have only gotten closer—so much so, college discussions terrify me." She sighed, looking down at her hands.

Her eyes slowly reached mine again. "You love sex, Quinn. And I get it; it's great. But despite what you may think, not everyone's having it, and not everyone has it often. I felt weird after losing my virginity even though I know I love Emerald. There was still a weird transition period. Have you given that to Julian?"

I never answered her question, but it kept spiraling in my mind for the next two hours while we caught up. I had forgotten what it was even like to lose your virginity. And even how that affects everyone differently. But guys were *supposed* to love sex, right? Julian should be the one asking for it. I should be the one turning Julian down, right?

Goddamn society. I hated these double standards. I hated being considered a whore for liking sex. I hated that I couldn't be treated like Adrian and the rest of them. But if I love sex just as much as society tells me guys do ... was it possible guys might not be thinking about sex all day like I assumed?

EVER SINCE I left Marie's house a few days ago, I couldn't get our conversation about me and Julian out of my head. It didn't help, either, that I had barely seen Julian. He had gone to Emerald's this past Friday and left early, claiming he had a study session on Saturday morning. I understood we were all under a lot of stress. These regent exams were important for our college applications, but there had to be some give and take.

So, I decided that I was going to kidnap him for a change, and we were going to take a break away from all textbooks. I missed him at his locker, so I jogged down to the student parking lot, hoping he hadn't left yet. By the time I got there, he was saying goodbye to James and Tyler. I waited for them to walk away before I headed over to Julian's car.

"Julian! Wait!"

He turned around, keys in hand. "Hey, what's up?"

I closed the distance between us, taking the keys out of his hand. "You and I are going to get some milkshakes and relax."

He reached for his keys, but I pulled my hand back, smirking at him. "Quinn, I really can't. I have to study."

"Nope. Not allowed. You, sir, have studied far too much. So much so, you'll actually damage your brain. Now let me cure you."

"I don't think that's possible. But okay, fine." He snatched his keys from me while my guard was off. "Ah-ha! Got 'em." He stuck out his tongue.

"Then I guess you're driving." I grinned, walking over to the passenger side door and climbing in.

He tossed his belongings in the back seat before getting in the driver's side, and then we were off.

To try and ease his mind before we got shakes, I asked him about which exams he had left, and he rambled on about his Health exam that apparently was supposed to have trick questions. He wouldn't listen to me when I told him it was the simplest state exam I had taken, and that was ninth grade.

After our milkshakes were ordered and he had a few sips, his guard finally started to come down. "Did you know when milkshakes first came into existence they were actually an alcoholic beverage? Then, one day, some Walgreens employee thought, you know what would be good? If I added two scoops of ice cream to this malted milk. And thus, the milkshakes we know and love today were born."

My mouth dropped. "Walgreens? As in, like, the drugstore?"

"Yes, ma'am."

"Wow, that's crazy. Who would have thought?" I took a sip of my milkshake. "That employee was definitely a genius. See, now your brain won't rot because you're having a milkshake!"

"So this brain freeze is just a sign that it's working, right?"

"Absolutely!" I giggled. "I've missed this. I feel like we haven't hung out in forever."

"Me too."

"Is it possible to push off studying for a few more hours? We could watch a movie? Just hang out?"

His face twitched, and he spun his straw in his glass.

"I don't know. I really should study. I can't solely rely on the power of this milkshake."

I felt my heart drop. No one I knew was spending this much time studying for their exams. It didn't make any sense. I shouldn't have to beg for my boyfriend's attention.

"Please? Just one movie. That's it, and you can be free to go. You need a break."

Julian smiled. "I promise once exams are done I'm all yours."

I sat back in the booth, scraping the condensation off my glass with my thumb. The two of us used to be so good, despite me never imagining we would work out. So why did things suddenly change in the past month? Shouldn't things have gotten better since we had sex?

"What's going on, Julian?"

"Nothing." I met his eyes for a brief moment before he looked down at the table.

"Bullshit. Things have been off between us for weeks. Don't tell me it's just me."

"I've just been busy with exams."

"It's been weird since before exams. Now I think you're just hiding behind them. I'm sorry, Julian, but there's no way in hell you need multiple days or even hours to study for this Health exam. Did I do something?"

"No ...," he sighed, and I could have sworn his eyes were glossy. "It's just that—I miss hanging out like this. Spending actual time together. Every time we've hung out alone since

Christmas, it feels like we've had sex. It makes me feel like our relationship is *just* about sex."

I sat up straight on the edge of the cushion, gripping the milk-shake glass.

"So instead of standing up for yourself and saying 'no, I don't want to do this,' you turned into a coward and started avoiding me?"

He let his back lean against the booth, his fingers rubbing the bottom of his glass. "Yeah. I know it's dumb. It just felt easier? I guess. I don't know. I didn't want to upset you."

"Upset me? I shouldn't have to tell you this, but my life doesn't revolve around sex. How the hell am I supposed to know you don't want to do something if you don't tell me?"

"Hi, I'm Julian, and I've never been in a real relationship before, so I don't know what I'm doing, but I suck at it." He offered a weak smile before he let it drop. "I don't know what else to say besides I'm sorry."

Was he serious? What kind of excuse was that? I didn't know what I was doing either, but at least I could be honest.

"It's called being a decent person, Julian. You don't need to have a relationship in order to know you should be honest."

"Have you met my friends? I'm not used to being in a situation where I can be honest and not get humiliated for it."

I groaned, falling back against the seat, massaging my eyelids with my palms.

"But have you met me, Julian?" I let out a sigh before looking at him across the table.

"Old habits are hard to break," he mumbled.

"Well, then let's start now. Be honest with me. Are you saying no to a movie because you think I'm going to want to sleep with you or because you actually have to study?"

What kind of person needs to ask their partner that? It wasn't like I controlled him, or I was forceful. He had every right to say no. Even if I did try to force it, he should say no. The only indication I ever had that he might not be enjoying himself was because he couldn't get hard. Why proceed to make sure it was good for me if you're not into it at all?

"I'm worried you want to sleep with me."

I made eye contact with him. He tried to look down, but his eyes slowly met mine again.

The entire situation was so bizarre that, despite being upset, I actually wanted to laugh. What guy was worried a girl wanted to sleep with him? Shouldn't he be over the moon that he was getting some? It was usually the girls who said no because the guys were horny *too* often.

"Worried is not often an adjective used to describe having sex with your girlfriend."

He shrugged, dropping his eyes. "I guess so. Look, it isn't you. You haven't done anything wrong. I just feel this pressure that I'm supposed to think about sex all the time. That I'm supposed to want sex like an animal. But I just don't."

Huh?

"And it makes me feel like something is wrong with me."

Could it be that something was? I mean, every guy I'd encountered could always keep pace with me, or at least, they claimed they could. And most of our group acted like they all wanted it often.

"Oh." I leaned over and took a sip of my melted milkshake.

On the other hand—Emerald *just* lost his virginity with Marie. But James, Tyler, Adrian ... Martin even, they all had had sex and with multiple people. And all the goddamn movies, music, television shows, they all talked about sex too.

I mean, we even learned about it in health class. It was like every two seconds or something sex crosses a guy's mind, right? But was it possible sex didn't cross every guy's mind all the time?

Sex didn't cross all girls' minds as often as it did mine, so it was possible, right?

I leaned over the table and took his hand in mine.

"Um, okay," I started. "First off," I gave him a playful glare, trying to mentally shake off my overthinking.

Figure this out with him, Quinn. Joke, make him laugh, lighten the mood.

"It isn't nice to compare someone's sex life to an animal's libido." I tilted my head, but my words were lost on him. So instead, I squeezed his hand. "Second, I doubt anything's wrong with you. We're all different, right?" I offered him a small smile. "But, if something is wrong, we are in this together, okay?"

He forced a smile back. "Yeah."

"So, how about no sex until you initiate? Just a movie and hanging out. Do you think your studies can be pushed off for a bit so I can spend time with my boyfriend?"

"Okay." He smiled.

JULIAN

After our last exams, James, Tyler and I took to our usual hang out spot at Isabella's Coffee before we ventured to Emerald's. We sat at a two-person table beside the window, and James pulled over another chair. Our preferred lounge chairs were taken up by a group of girls studying. I don't actually like coffee, so I got a white hot chocolate while James got a black coffee and Tyler, a coffee with extra cream and sugar.

"So." James cleared his throat. His focus was on the girls studying. "I think we need a plan." He smirked while focusing back on me and Tyler.

I raised my brows. "And that would be?"

"A plan to get Tyler laid." James' eyes lit up as he sipped his coffee.

I paused mid-drink to glance over at Tyler. For once I wasn't the focal point of James' harassment. Tyler just smiled at James, taking a sip of his own drink to avoid answering.

"Alright. So what's the plan?" I smiled, slightly thrilled and ashamed of my excitement to harass someone else besides myself.

"The plan is," James settled back in his chair and interlaced his fingers behind his head, "we either invite all three of those girls to Emerald's tonight and decide who the lucky girl will be, then pawn the other two off. Or, we figure out our target here and now, and Tyler doesn't come to Emerald's."

"I'm just going to say right now, you can't pay me to sleep with the blonde. She's ugly as shit," Tyler said between sips, avoiding eye contact with either of us.

I inhaled at his comment. I would never call a girl ugly, but I couldn't help but feel like Tyler was using it as a mask.

"Okay, so that leaves two choices." I smirked.

"We could always give the blonde to Adrian. He always talks about getting laid, but is he really?" James tilted his head in suspicion.

"Deal," Tyler said, but his response lacked any confidence.

"The one with the glasses is cute, could have something kinky up her sleeve." He nudged Tyler's arm. "And if she doesn't, you could show her a thing or two."

"I doubt she could handle the *Ty Machine*," Tyler said rolling his shoulders back.

"If you want to get laid, I suggest you never say "Ty Machine" ever again," I said.

"Shh, Julian." James waved his hand in my direction. "You just maybe, probably didn't lose your virginity. Some girls are into that shit."

"Shut up, James." I leaned back in my chair.

"Well, have you?" James crossed his arms. "Have you been holding out on us?"

I fell silent. Do I tell them to get them off my back and risk upsetting Quinn with the possibility of everyone in the world finding out in two milliseconds? Or do I keep my mouth shut and play it off? Since Quinn and I talked over milkshakes, I did go to her house for a movie and nothing sexual happened. In fact, she hasn't even tried all week. It feels like things have finally gone back to normal.

I finally settled on: "I've gotten more action than Tyler ever has."

"I will have you know I have fucked plenty of girls," Tyler said, pointing at me.

"You both need to get fucked more. Jeez." James rolled his eyes. "I know for a fact that Tyler has never lied about it. But what's your deal, Julian? You're with Quinn Kennedy. Either you two have fucked, or there's something wrong with you. Which is it?"

"We have," I let out, my tone flat before I took the last swig of my hot chocolate. "If I remember correctly, this plan was about Tyler?"

"Oh no," James shook his head, smiling, "we have time for Tyler. You, on the other hand, was it awful? What a terrible way to celebrate losing your virginity."

"Just drop it, James. It isn't a big deal."

"Either way, it looks like I won the bet." Tyler grinned, obviously pleased with the change of subject. "I'll have two slices of pizza, a soda, and a large fry for lunch for the next month. Thank you."

"Fuck," James said.

I had forgotten about their stupid bet. *Whatever.* At least that's done with.

James looked over at me, about to say something else, but stopped as one of the girls stood up. "One sec," he rushed before standing up and walking over to her.

I exchanged a look with Tyler before we got up and followed. By the time we got there, James already had introduced himself to all three.

"Julian! Tyler! Meet Kate, Brianna, and Courtney." He turned to us, smirking. "Courtney and Kate are sisters. Brianna is the best friend." I nodded at them while Tyler said hi. "I was just going to tell them about the fantastic party we are going to later."

His attention directed back to them. "Plenty of people, plenty of booze, and plenty of opportunities to get lucky." He winked.

The girls giggled, and in a matter of minutes, we were all up and in our cars on our way to Emerald's.

THE MOMENT WE ARRIVED, I hurried inside, leaving James and Tyler behind with their new friends, in search of Quinn. She was already there chatting with Marie.

"Hey," I kissed her on the cheek as I approached her, "please save me from the idiots I call friends."

"What happened now?" She rolled her eyes, patting the cushion next to her.

"James brought three extra guests for Tyler to get laid."

Her eyes bugged out, glancing behind me. "He's a pig. And the girls willingly came?"

"Somehow. I don't know how he does it."

"Do you want a drink, Julian?" Marie chimed in. I had forgotten she was even there.

"Beer, please." I smiled as she got up and skipped to the mini fridge.

Quinn leaned in and kissed me on the lips. "How was the rest of your day?"

"The usual. Better now, though." I smiled at her.

"We still on for tomorrow?" she asked, resting her hand on my thigh.

I swallowed and hoped she didn't notice. Sure, I had told her my concerns about our relationship becoming about sex. And I felt absolute happiness when we were together and nothing happened. However, it was the weekend. Her parents were usually busy on the weekends. Time alone together ... perfect opportunity for sex to happen. And I'd have no excuses to avoid it.

Okay, wow, Julian, grow up and talk about how you feel with her. It went well last time, didn't it? But just because we would be alone didn't mean we *had* to have sex.

"Absolutely."

The night went by like normal. Some people drank—more than they should and everyone chatted while a movie played in the background. I was thankful we weren't playing any dumb truth or dare games tonight and that everything was casual. I was happy off in my little corner with Quinn giving her occasional kisses and focusing most of my attention on her. Marie and Emerald were with us most of the night as well, the four of us chatting together. I had no idea where Tyler or James went or the girls they brought. And I couldn't care less. This was one of the rare occasions where I actually found myself enjoying Emerald's and not wondering when it was acceptable to leave.

That was until James stood up on the coffee table, arms raised above his head, rum and coke in hand.

"Ladies and gents! I have an announcement!" he began, slurring his words. His eyes searched the room for Adrian. The moment the two locked eyes, James raised his glass higher, his smile growing with Adrian's.

"Dear god," I mumbled to myself. *Please, James, get off that fucking table.*

"This isn't gonna be good." Quinn laughed, burying her face in my chest.

I tried to laugh into her hair, but my body could barely move.

"I'd love for you all to look over at my buddy, Julian, and his girl, Quinn." His cup pointed directly at the two of us. I pressed my back against the couch.

Fuck, fuck, fuck. Don't say what I think you're going to say, James.

Quinn dug her fingers into my side as everyone turned their heads toward us.

"I'm sure most of you know that our precious Julian was a virgin before he got with Quinn."

Quinn let go of me, stepping out of our bubble. I looked over at her, but she wouldn't look back. I wanted to say *come here, don't listen to him.* But everyone was watching and listening. There was no escape.

"Well, tonight I want us to raise a glass and toast to Julian! He's one of us now. Thank you, Quinn."

My lip twitched. I felt stunned. *What should I even say? What should I even do?* Quinn still wouldn't look at me.

Fuck.

"To Julian!" James shouted while there was a collective cheer and plastic cups splashing against each other, most less enthusiastic than him.

"Julian!" I heard Adrian shout.

No, no, no. I needed to get out of here before things got worse.

He rushed up to me and Quinn—whose face was flushed.

"If it isn't the greatest couple in the room." He smirked, placing one hand on my arm and the other on Quinn, trying to force us together.

Quinn tried to shrug off his arm.

"Congratulations, my man!" Adrian slapped my arm. "You've got a feisty one. But one hell of a good lay!"

Any form of words seemed to have fled from my mind. I couldn't speak. I just stood there in disbelief at the turn tonight took. I could practically feel the rage fuming out of Quinn right now. Sorry wouldn't be enough. I went against her trust. But I just wanted the guys to leave me alone.

God, why was I so stupid? I should have known not to trust them with anything. The world felt like it was spinning. I couldn't tell if it was the booze or not, but nothing felt real.

"Quinn—" I started to say, ignoring Adrian. "Listen, I didn't want to tell him—"

She pushed Adrian's arm away, glaring at me while she did so.

"Save it." Her words were sharp. It felt like my heart dropped to my stomach. "I'm so fucking done with all of you being the same." Quinn then pushed past Adrian, ignoring Marie's pleas for her to stop.

I couldn't do anything but watch as she stormed out of the room. My eyes stung, and my head was pounding. *No. Dammit. Why?* Why did my friends have to be the biggest idiots alive? I couldn't lose her over this. I refused to lose her over this.

"No worries, my friend. Just pull out your dick, and you'll have her moaning underneath of you in no time. She gets off on this shit." Adrian punched my shoulder, laughing.

I turned my head and stared at him. A cocky grin was plastered across his face. Before I could think about it, I had already punched him. I shook my hand, trying to relieve the pain. *Fuck, I hated this guy.*

He rubbed his cheek, standing back up.

"Holy fuck." He laughed before throwing a punch back at me, getting me right in the eye. "Don't you fucking touch me, man. I was just trying to help you out."

I clenched and unclenched my fist, then threw another punch at him, desperate to teach him how much of an asshole he was. Like I could drill it in him with each punch. I ignored the pain in my face that was now throbbing. I remembered hitting Adrian across the face and him hitting me back. But I didn't know how I ended up on the floor, him on top of me, smashing his fist into my face over and over again. I felt something warm trickle down my face. Blood?

This wasn't how it was supposed to happen. I tried to throw more punches, but Adrian grabbed ahold of my wrists, pinning them to the ground while he screamed something at me. I couldn't make out the words; my ears were ringing, and black splotches dotted my vision.

"Dude, calm down; you're drunk." I could hear Tyler's voice, his arms under Adrian's.

I looked up at Adrian, blood spilling from his nose. Marie hurried over with tissues, kneeling beside me, patting my face. James was still standing on the coffee table chugging his drink, oblivious to what was going on around him. Emerald grabbed Adrian from Tyler, escorting him away from the scene. Everyone else was watching us in silence. Their eyes didn't show concern but rather excitement for the gossip they now had to share come Monday morning.

God, I hated these people.

I pulled away from Marie, standing up. "I'm going home," I said, turning to head out the door. My head was pounding. I needed out of here. *Now.*

"Let me drive; I didn't drink anything," Tyler said, following behind me.

"What about your easy lay? Isn't that what life's all about?" I asked, shocked at the volume of my voice.

"That's not important right now," Tyler said calmly, his voice low. But it only made me want to scream.

"Yeah, sure it isn't. Sex. It's fucking everywhere. Movies. Books. Music. It's shoved in our faces. It's the grand prize of life. There's no escape from it. Society forces it down our throats. If you aren't having it, you're worthless. Oh, but don't have too much of it, 'cause then you're a whore. You aren't worth anything but the amount of sex you have." I waved my hands in the air as I shook my head. "Can't somebody actually *feel* something? What is love, anyway? Can't a guy actually care for someone without it having to be about sex?"

"Let's go, buddy." Tyler pushed on my shoulder, and that's when I realized I was crying.

Fuck. I've lost the one person I actually care about. And now I'm the center of their gossip. I never wanted this. I never wanted things to be this way. I swallowed, trying to stop the tears from drenching my cheeks.

"Put your damn phone away," Tyler called behind him. "Leave the guy alone."

"Fuck," I mumbled as Tyler ushered me outside and helped me into my car. "What about those girls?" I asked, my tears slowing down.

"Forget it. James talks a big game, but I could never actually follow through with it."

I didn't respond. I just stared out my window the whole ride home watching the street lights go by, wondering how the hell things wound up to be such shit.

QUINN

THE VIDEO REPLAYED OVER AND OVER AGAIN FROM MY phone lying beside me. I had watched it a few times before dropping my phone and closing my eyes again. I dug my fingers into my eyelids, wondering how the hell to get out of this mess, this vicious circle of high school.

Marie had sent me close to a hundred text messages plus this video to wake up to. I had shut my phone off as soon as I left the party but stupidly decided to turn it on this morning. However, if anyone wanted to make a real apology, they could do so at my doorstep. But until then, I wasn't leaving this bedroom.

I couldn't seem to turn off the video though. Adrian beat the shit out of Julian. I *hated* that I felt a small satisfaction in the first punch Adrian threw. I felt the tears behind my lids as I tried to press them away. Why did Marie have to get Julian talking in it? I didn't *want* to feel for him. It'd be far easier if he *was* like one of the guys.

But no. He was Julian Raskin, the one-of-a-kind guy, who makes stupid mistakes and then immediately regrets them. Not only that, but goddamn tears fell from his eyes.

"Shut up!" I yelled, picking my phone up and throwing it across the room. It hit the giraffe I had discarded the night before.

The video restarted, just as my doorbell rang.

I waited, hoping my parents or sister were home. But after three rings, I pulled myself out of bed, dragging my feet as I walked to the front door.

What could possibly be so important this early? Julian and I had plans today, but I was hoping he wouldn't show.

One glance out the window, and I regretted getting up. Julian's SUV sat out front.

So much for that.

I brushed my tears away and pulled my curls into a messy bun before opening the door. I leaned against the doorframe but didn't offer a greeting.

"Hey," Julian said, straight-faced.

He looked awful, like he hadn't slept. His hair was messier than usual, and bruises were forming under his eyes. He was still wearing the same clothes as yesterday.

"Hi." I crossed my arms over my chest. I hated that I just wanted to pull him into a hug and make sure he was okay.

He was the one who messed up, Quinn.

He massaged his eyelids—wincing as he did—before taking a deep breath. "I'm so sorry," he finally choked up, holding back a sob. "James just kept harassing me. You don't know how awful those two can be. I didn't know how to avoid it any longer. The easiest solution to get them to leave me alone seemed to be to just tell them."

I sighed, pushing away from the door frame, and motioned for him to follow me. I walked us back to my bedroom where I immediately climbed back into bed, pulling the covers up over me as I sat back against the headboard.

Julian's voice was still playing on my phone. *Fuck.*

He stared at my phone on the floor, his skin growing pale.

"Should I go?" he mumbled. He stood there almost like a hollow being. He was a mess.

I shook my head and twisted my hands beneath my comforter, bringing them up under my chin. "Can you just turn it off?"

He nodded as he went over to the phone, turning the video off, and placing my phone on my dresser.

I took a breath as silence finally consumed my room. I don't know how many times the video played, but more than enough times to have the sound of Adrian's punches ingrained in my mind.

"How is your face?" I asked pathetically.

Julian scoffed and shook his head.

"Well?" I pressed.

I was afraid if we spoke about anything else right now, permanent damage could happen.

He forced a smile. "Just peachy."

"Can I say something?" I swallowed, sinking further into my bed.

"Sure," he said, sitting at the end of my bed.

"My entire high school career has seemed to revolve around who I sleep with, when, where, and how often. Whether true or not, it's haunted me, but I've tried to shrug it off. It isn't anyone's fucking business, except the person I am sleeping with. But I can't just shrug this off, Julian. Not when you casually dropped our sex life into a conversation to jackasses like it wasn't a big deal. Because, in case it wasn't clear, sex with you is a really fucking big deal to me." I blinked back the tears that were resurfacing. "Was it too much to ask for it to be private?"

"I'm sorry," he mumbled. "I was wrong. I'm sorry. I shouldn't have told them."

I wanted to shake his shoulders and ask him if he knew who his friends were, if he had any inkling of an idea that this would happen. Because I could have told him it would have. As their best friend, he should have known better.

I hated this. This hot and cold. This sex and no sex. He can't avoid me because he's worried we are going to have sex and then blab to his friends about us doing it, when we weren't, in fact, *doing* it. I wanted to groan, or scream, or punch my fists into the mattress. Anything to release all the pent-up frustration.

"I'm tired, Julian." I exhaled, giving up. I took a breath, trying to focus my mind. "I'm just exhausted by all this bullshit."

He nodded.

I pulled part of my blankets down, scooting over on my bed, making a space for him. He tentatively climbed up under the covers next to me.

"Can we just ..." I sighed, running my hands over my face. "Thankyouforstandingupforme," I rushed out. "But can we please avoid another situation where someone needs to get the shit kicked outta them?"

Julian let out a laugh. "Agreed."

"Good, now let's hide under these covers and never come out because, frankly, high school fucking sucks." I tugged him down with me.

He wrapped his arms around me, burying his head in my neck. I could feel his frame relax against me. I hated how angry all of this could make me. How I couldn't separate Julian from the rest of them when just his touch alone made me certain he was different from everyone else.

"Quinn, I'm falling for you," he whispered.

I leaned back, and his arms loosened a little. He lifted his head, holding my eye contact. I didn't know what to say. Was it too soon to tell him I thought I actually loved him? But, how could we be falling for each other if all it seemed like we were doing lately was walking on a thin wire?

"What?" I breathed.

Why did it feel impossible that he could feel similar to me?

He was silent for a moment; he must have known I heard him. "I said I'm falling for you."

I held him closer and kissed his neck, more out of comfort than anything. To ease him. To ease me. To settle the racing thoughts in my head. If I said what I wanted to say, it would change things. But for the better, right? Would he then be more comfortable? Would we then be the couple I wished we could be?

"I think I might be falling in love," I whispered, my lips meeting his skin with each word. His breath hitched, and he shivered as I continued a path up his neck until I caught my lips with his own.

"Can we?" I whispered against his lips. He nodded.

It started out like every other time, where we were loving and caring, possibly even more so. I pushed away the doubts of him actually wanting it. But I couldn't get my mind to shut off. It was a movie reel of incidents on repeat. It wasn't just the lack of times Julian and I have had sex, it was the fear of a relationship in general. I had spoken these words before. I had messed it all up. But we were different, right?

I was losing control. The fear of losing him, fear of fucking it up like I did with Liza, fear of not getting over these petty arguments—all of it was weighing me down.

I was on top of him, face buried in his neck, trying to hide the tears that started to brim. It was fucking happening *again*.

I don't get it. He tells me he's falling for me; he said he was ready. We haven't slept together in a couple weeks. I've respected his boundaries since our conversation at the beginning of the week. So why were we in the same situation we've fallen into numerous times?

One time? Sure, it happens. It's happened with other guys

before. But three out of five attempts? Surely it was personal now.

"Julian," I faked a moan, trying my hardest to hide my actual frustration. He smiled before linking our lips together.

I reached between us, trying to take things into my own hands--literally *and* figuratively. But nothing seemed to help. This may have been the only time in which I praised myself for my reputation. I *knew* I was good. I *knew* exactly what to do in these situations. But why wasn't it working?

"Julian." I sighed, pulling my head away to look him in the eyes. "Everything okay?"

"Yeah," he said, trying to smile. "I don't know what *his* problem is."

"Am I doing something wrong? I don't understand why it keeps happening. If something isn't working, it's okay. I just," I breathed, "I just need you to tell me."

"Sorry. I'm just struggling to relax after last night." He offered a smile. "Perhaps if I try something else, it'll help things along?" He winked, sliding his fingers down my stomach.

I breathed in, trying to keep my eyes from closing as his fingers slid further down.

"N-no," I stuttered, pushing myself off of him. Julian froze. "You keep coming up with some bullshit excuse. I don't want to just fool around with you, Julian. It's been weeks since we've had sex!"

"I don't know what to tell you." His voice was soft. "It's not like I exactly have *control* over it. It doesn't get hard on demand."

"From my experience, more often than not it can." Julian didn't answer me. "I'm confused, Julian. Do you even want to sleep with me ... ever? Because it sure as hell feels like I'm not worth it to you."

I sat up, looking down at him. His silence was about to send me over the edge. I could already feel my hands beginning to shake. Why isn't he standing up for himself?

"What the hell is going on, Julian?" My voice wavered as I swallowed nerves. I was trying to keep my anger at bay.

He shrugged.

"Are you kidding me?" My voice was louder than anticipated, but I played it off as planned while Julian furrowed his brows and shifted next to me.

I pulled the blankets up over me, crossing my arms to hold them up. "I'm not stupid, Julian. I know something is up. I just thought you'd have the decency to talk to your girlfriend, especially after our goddamn conversation. *Especially* after telling me you're falling for me."

"I—" he started to say before he closed his mouth. "I'm sorry."

"So you're admitting that there's a problem? And you're still going to remain silent?"

"No." He shook his head. "I don't know what's wrong, okay? I don't know what my problem is."

"I ... I think you should go."

"Wait. What?" Julian pressed his lips together. "Are you breaking up with me?"

"No. Of course not." I sighed. "I fucking love you," I groaned, shoving my palms against my eyelids. "I just don't know what to do, Julian. You tell me you're falling for me, yet you still can't have sex with me. You're hiding something, and I can't for the life of me figure it out. You're friends with assholes ..." I exhaled. "I'm sorry, but I need to protect myself if you can't give me any fucking answers."

Julian's eyes went wide, brimming with tears. He snapped his head away from me and got up, collecting his clothes before quickly putting them back on. I could have sworn I heard him mumble *everyone just wants sex* as he was buttoning up his shirt.

I wanted to take it back. I wanted to calm myself, but I

couldn't. I wanted to tell him it wasn't all about sex. Because it wasn't ... but was it?

"Bye, Quinn," he mumbled as he left the room without looking back.

I watched as he left, hoping maybe he'd turn around. Maybe he'd fight for us. Maybe he'd tell me I was being stupid, that I didn't know what I was talking about. That he'd give a damn. He said he was falling in love. Falling in love isn't walking away after a fight. Falling in love isn't hiding something from your partner ... isn't lying back silently.

I stood, trying to urge myself to follow his footsteps, but then he slammed the front door. I swiped all of my belongings off my dresser, watching as a picture frame of us crashed, before I dropped on the floor, pulling the comforter with me.

Fuck Julian. Fuck Adrian. Fuck James and Tyler.

Suddenly Marie and Emerald popped into my head.

They were right. I'm not girlfriend material. I don't do relationships and feelings. I'm there for sex, and the rest is too complicated.

It's always the goddamn same.

Fuck you, Quinn.

You're not better than anyone else.

JULIAN

I had woken up this morning to a text from Tyler asking how I was and if I wanted to come over later and game. I wasn't going to. Especially after the morning I had. I didn't know what to say to Quinn. I didn't understand why I felt the way I did or how to stop it.

After I left her house, I circled her block five times before I finally turned, heading to the highway to my favorite spot. I considered going back, apologizing to her. Yet ... should I? Did I really do anything wrong? I went over there to apologize for last night, to say I'm sorry for not having gone after her when she left the party and beg her to forgive me for telling James we'd slept together. Except, just like everyone else, all she wanted was sex. I should have figured as much.

Tears welled up as I laid on the grass staring up at the sky. Even my favorite place now felt tainted with the memory of being here with Quinn.

I still hadn't talked to Ian. We'd hung out a few times since Christmas break, and he never brought up my text to him and neither did I. I didn't know how to bring it up, and I was still undecided if I even wanted to. There had to be another reason I felt this way ... right? I just didn't understand myself.

Other than Tyler's text, I ignored my phone and the multiple notifications I had. I wasn't ready to face the embarrassment that would follow me for crying in front of everyone, let alone getting the shit beat out of me by Adrian. I didn't fight people. That wasn't my thing.

Sure, I hated Adrian's guts for how he treated women like objects. But to actually hit him? And now I was pretty sure I had a black eye to pay for it. How the hell did I get in this position? How did my life go from being simple, keeping to myself, just following James and Tyler around, to the chaos it is now?

Fuck, fuck, fuck.

Maybe I should go to Tyler's. He seemed to be the only one last night who actually *cared* about me as a person. Others only cared to see where things would go so they could gossip about it. Tyler actually made sure I made it home safely. He even told everyone to leave me alone. Besides, playing a few games would help get my mind off things. Reluctantly, I sat up and headed back to my car before I went to Tyler's.

When I got there, Tyler's driveway was empty. No sign of his parents or even James. I knocked on the door. Tyler's black lab, Bentley, barked the moment my knuckles made sound. Within moments, Tyler answered the door, holding his dog back. His face was first confused but instantly switched to delight.

"Hey," he smiled, "I didn't think you'd show."

I shrugged. "I guess I should have answered your text."

"No worries. Come in."

I took off my shoes and patted his dog before I followed him through the hallway and into his kitchen.

His kitchen was massive, all black cupboards with a matching counter. Everything new and modern. It was an open concept room, the living room cutting through half of the space. He had his phone hooked up to the T.V. playing an Eminem song I didn't recognize. His dog had followed us, settling beside the glass door in the middle of the room that led to a deck outside.

"Is James coming?" I asked.

"No, I didn't invite him. No big deal." Tyler shrugged and opened his fridge. "Drink?"

"Yes, please." Tyler slid a beer over the counter for me.

I twisted the tab off, the beer hissing as I did. He didn't invite James. That *was* a big deal. For the past three years, Tyler's life has revolved around James and his approval. We *never* hung out just the two of us. Could it be because of how James treated me last night? Was Tyler finally coming around and becoming his own person?

"Where are your parents?" I asked.

Tyler leaned up against the fridge, opening up his own beer. "They went into the city to see some Broadway show. Made a mini trip out of it, so they won't be home till tomorrow." I nodded, taking a sip. "So last night was fun." Tyler smiled.

"Oh, a blast." I rolled my eyes.

"How's Quinn?"

I shrugged. "Who knows, honestly? I went to her place this morning to apologize, and I don't know. It didn't go well."

"She still pissed?"

"I think so, yeah." I stared down at my beer, rubbing my thumbs against the condensation on the bottle.

A silence settled between us, and I didn't know what to say. Tyler wasn't the person I went to about my problems. He wasn't good at dealing with other people's emotions. It made him awkward and stumble on his words. It was no surprise that he didn't have a girlfriend. If someone told him they were sad, he'd hesitantly pat them on the back while he half-heartedly said, "It's okay." No, Ian was the one I went to when I needed to talk or wanted advice. I should have gone over to his place instead. I sighed. *Oh well, I was here now.* Besides, I was here to try and forget my problems, not throw them all out in the open.

"So I believe you promised me some gaming?" I said, raising my brows, attempting to break the silence. Tyler looked up at me with a shimmer in his eyes.

"Yeah, I have the new *Call of Duty* game downstairs in my room if you want to check it out."

"Great." I smiled, following him down the stairs to the basement.

We crossed through his laundry room that had another living room area before we reached his room. His room felt like the smallest room of the house. It was dark without any windows; a few random posters were hung on the wall. His only furniture was his bed and a dresser that his T.V. sat on top of. I sat at the edge of his queen-sized bed while he knelt to grab the game out of a pile on the floor. He put the disc in, then sat beside me, handing me a controller.

We didn't talk other than to yell at the T.V. or to high-five each other for a kill. It felt like every five minutes Tyler was pausing the game to run upstairs to grab us another beer. How many had I had now? Four? Five? I couldn't remember. Everything was becoming fuzzy, but I was at the point of a good drunk. Not quite at the *I'm going to be sick, pass out, or blackout* stage. But at the stage where everything seemed hilarious. I couldn't remember the last time I laughed so much.

It felt like old times. Like, here I was with one of the guys I had grown up with as friends. We weren't pretending to be someone else to impress anyone. In this moment, we were just enjoying each other's company.

Through our broken laughter, Tyler asked, "So what's your deal with Quinn, anyway? Why is not talking about having sex with her such a big deal? Are you gay or something?"

I went silent trying to process his question. Did I even hear him correctly? Had I blabbed that I thought my lack of desire to have sex with Quinn was because I thought I might be gay? But I didn't actually *know* if I was. I didn't know how I could tell if I was or not.

I looked at him, our eyes meeting. We stared at each other for a moment like that, his eyes flicking down to my lips then back to my gaze. I leaned forward, but he backed away.

Fuck. I thought at first, *what am I doing?* But then Tyler leaned back in, clasping our lips together. I reached for his neck, and he pushed himself on top of me, forcing me back against the bed, his lips hungry for more. He tasted like beer; that was all I remembered. The skin around my mouth burned from where the stubble on his face rubbed against me.

Everything else happened in flashes. Tyler pulling away from me to take off his shirt, revealing the hint of abs he was working on. More kissing. Me on my stomach, clothes long discarded. The shadow of Tyler's hands opening a condom. Sensation. Pain. Moans. Blackness.

WHEN MY EYES SHOT OPEN, I had a moment of panic, forgetting where I was. My heart raced as I sat up, instantly regretting the sudden movement. I fell back onto the bed, holding my head, quickly remembering I was still at Tyler's. He was sleeping beside me, his body pressed up against the wall as if there was a magnetic force keeping him as far away from me as possible. His back was facing me, but he was still undressed, making all the memories of last night come back to me. I jumped off the bed, still in pain. Blood splattered where I had been lying.

Scooping my clothes up and throwing them back on, I kept my eyes glued on Tyler. He didn't acknowledge if he heard me, but his body looked too tense to be asleep. Without saying a word, I turned and hurried out of his house.

It felt like the walls were closing in on me. Like gravity was pushing on my chest so hard I couldn't breathe as I sat in my car. I replayed the night in my head, trying to piece together the parts I couldn't quite remember.

Oh my god. Oh. My. Fucking. God.

I massaged my eyelids before I pulled out of the driveway. *Fuck.* I tried squeezing the steering wheel to stop my hands from shaking. I was an idiot. Tyler was my friend. Why did it even cross my mind to .... Tears were streaming down my face. *Fuck, fuck, fuck.*

But the thing was ... I still didn't feel like I understood why I wasn't into sex. I wasn't even into it last night. I was just drunk. I thought maybe ... maybe that was the answer. But it wasn't. I slammed my hand against the steering wheel before I pulled over. I didn't want to go home, or even go to my favorite spot, but this was at least far enough away from Tyler's house.

Why did I have to do that? I wished I could go and take it all back. How was I supposed to show my face at school now? How was I ever supposed to talk to Tyler again? And what the hell even happened? How the hell did that even happen? Did Tyler enjoy it? Did he want to do it again? Did *I* want to do it again?

A laugh erupted out of me. Just when I thought my life was a mess, I went and made it a disaster.

What was I supposed to do now? And Quinn ... should I tell her? Not that any good would come out of her knowing. Because I still didn't have an explanation. I cheated on her. The thought made my stomach turn. How could I even do that to her? Before, I could have played it off as questioning my sexuality. But now ... now I have no fucking clue. I don't fit into the box of straight or gay. So what the hell am I? Should I try having sex with a guy again just in case? No. No matter how many times I'd done stuff with Quinn, I hadn't been into it, so how would it be any different with a guy?

I didn't understand what my problem was. All I knew was that I didn't care to have sex. Why was my brain wired this way? I wished I could just be fucking normal. Why did sex have to be such a big deal anyway? But sex was a big deal. It definitely was to Quinn. I started sobbing, unable to hold back. How did I expect anyone to love me if I couldn't love them that way?

The clock on my dash said it was ten in the morning. I had gone twenty-four hours without talking to Quinn or anyone other than Tyler. I turned on my phone finally. The moment it was loaded it began to explode with notifications from missed calls and text messages, some from my dad and James. But most of them were from Quinn. She sent me a text message late last night, and I tightened my lips. I put my car back in drive and headed to her place.

QUINN

I REMAINED IN A HEAP ON MY FLOOR AFTER JULIAN AND I fought until I heard the garage door opening. My parents were home, and the last thing I needed was to be found naked and distraught. Too many questions and not enough satisfying answers.

In an instant, I was up and running to the bathroom, turning the water on in the shower all before I knew they turned off the car.

A game plan needed to be made.

1. Shower and fine-tune my acting skills.
2. Admit and believe I was an asshole.
3. Acknowledge that while Julian made some mistakes, he couldn't be faulted—on almost all accounts. (His silence not included. That I *could* be upset about.)
4. Apologize, grovel, and try to understand.
5. Don't fuck up again. It's really not that difficult. (Or shouldn't be.)

The shower helped clear my head. My mind was simple in

that way. As long as I made a plan, I was able to follow through and find the motivation to act on it. So by the time I had to make my presence known to my family, my acting skills didn't need to be superb. Because Julian and I would be fine by the end of the night.

"Stranger!" I heard Emma yell before she ran out from the kitchen and pulled me into her arms.

Normally, I would have laughed and tried to push her off of me, pretending to be annoyed, but maybe there were cracks in my facade. I let her wrap her arms around me tightly. I could feel her playfulness melt away as she rested her cheek against the side of my head.

"I've missed you," I said softly.

She had gone away with Kenny for their winter break from college after our family ski trip, and when they got back, she spent a majority of her time over at his place. The only explanation was that they were busy with school, and I had been too.

"I've missed you too. I'm sorry I haven't been around often. We actually have some exciting news."

She pulled out of the hug, and I stumbled slightly. I didn't realize how much I trusted her to hold me up.

Kenny then rounded the corner as Emma and I walked further into the living room. My parents were sitting on the couch, coffees in hand. I glanced around at everyone and then over to the kitchen island—noting that they had at least brought me home breakfast—even though it was mid-afternoon.

"Where did you all go this morning, and why wasn't I invited?"

"Sweetie," my mother started as I grabbed my breakfast and brought it over to the couch. Maybe if I was invited this morning, I could have cooled down enough before I spoke to Julian. "You always come home late from Joseph's on Fridays, so we already made plans assuming you'd sleep in."

"But I was home before you two even attempted to go to bed last night."

"True," she nodded, "but you often aren't. Besides, it wasn't a big deal. We just went apartment searching."

My brows narrowed as I shot looks over at Emma and Kenny.

"For you two?"

Emma nodded excitedly.

"Yeah, we think it's time to move out. So I recruited Mom and Dad for help. We genuinely didn't think you'd have fun."

My heart sank at the idea of now never seeing my sister. If she couldn't stop in long enough to say hi when she was just a couple of blocks away at Kenny's house, would she ever stop in after she moved out?

"Right." I faked a smile, putting my tea up to my lips. "You're right. Thank you for letting me sleep in. I needed it."

For the next hour, Emma and Kenny told me about all the different complexes they had gone to this morning and how they were almost certain on one. Closer to their school, further from us. The entire time I tried not to think about the fact that if I lost Julian and now my sister, I'd have lost everyone I cared for.

Back to the game plan, Quinn. My mind kicked back in gear. Truth be told, I didn't care about what was great and what wasn't, especially not this morning. I needed to get on the road and learn how to apologize.

Eventually, I excused myself and was almost out the door, but not before my family decided we were going to have game night and told me to invite Julian. After promising them something I couldn't be certain of, I left the house.

Once in my car, I finally looked at my phone. I had a message from Marie this morning, checking in. But only one message after her massive play-by-play. And definitely nothing from Julian.

I tried to bite the bullet and called his phone without over-thinking it. It immediately went to voicemail—the act alone making me frustrated and want to forget about my plan. But instead, I powered through.

Every few minutes, I tried his number again, hoping by some chance he'd want to contact his other friends. But there was no answer by the time I reached his house. I only knew of his home, I had never been to it before. For some reason, he never cared to have me over here, insisting it was nicer at my house. And while I could agree that the outside of my house was indeed nicer, that wasn't an excuse to keep me away, either.

A car was in the driveway, but it wasn't Julian's. But maybe his dad would have some answers.

Knocking on the door, Julian's dad answered, a smile forming.

"Quinn, this is a pleasant surprise."

"Uh, hi, Mr. Raskin, does Julian happen to be home?"

He nodded, opening the door further. "I think he's still asleep, would you like me to wake him?"

I looked behind me, thinking I might have missed his car. Had he come home and gone back to bed?

When I turned back, I saw Julian's father looking too. Confusion consumed his face.

"I could have sworn he was still here."

"Oh, um," *Think, Quinn, think.* "Yeah, we spent the morning together, and then I had to go do something. Maybe he left really early? But, uh, I was wondering where he could be now."

"I'm not entirely sure. Maybe with James and Tyler? Have you tried calling him?"

Just the sound of their names made me ill. But it was clear I wasn't going to get an answer here. And even more obvious that Julian had a far different relationship with his father than I had with my parents.

"Oh, yes, of course! He did mention them. Silly me." My laugh almost sounded realistic. "Thank you! Sorry for wasting your time." I rushed off before he could question anymore and got back into my car.

It wasn't until I started driving that I realized I had no idea where James or Tyler lived. Julian still didn't have his phone on. I didn't even have an inkling of an idea of what neighborhood to drive to. And there was no way I'd be contacting Marie or Emerald for either address. I knew it would result in an interrogation as to why I needed their address and why I couldn't ask my boyfriend. It was crucial that Marie and Emerald didn't find out about this fight.

After driving around aimlessly, hoping by some miracle I'd pass his car, it finally hit me. Julian was most likely at his spot.

So I took the drive a half hour out, praying to the universe that this would be it. We'd have a moment to talk with no one around, and hopefully, neither of us would end up off the cliff.

The drive was calming. I had rehearsed what I would say to him. It would go smooth. I would actually listen. I'd hear him out. There had to be a reason for this. If he was falling in love, we wouldn't be having these issues. Yet, was that even the truth?

Be comfortable. Make a safe space. He's obviously hiding something. But he made it crystal clear that I wasn't a person he could talk to about it.

I was ready, and almost even excited to mend things—believing I had it all figured out. Up until the point that his car wasn't in the parking lot of the mountain. I still didn't believe it though. So, I climbed and climbed up until the point that it grew dark. As I was traveling back down, I used my phone's flashlight, hoping that there wouldn't be any animal—or humans lurking.

On the drive back, I constantly hit redial on Julian's number. I was starting to get nervous that something had actually happened to him. I had clearly stated that we weren't breaking up. We both just needed space. So that would mean that we'd resolve this by the end of the night, right?

With one last drive by his house—no cars in the driveway this time—I messaged my mom, telling her I got sick and that I'd opt out of game night. By the time I got home, my mother had ginger ale and crackers sitting by my bedside table and a bowl just in case I got sick. She made sure I was tucked into bed before she joined the family.

Before I let sleep—because I was indeed sick to my stomach and exhausted—consume me, I sent Julian an apology.

> *Hey you, I'm sorry. I'm really*
> *sorry about what happened today.*
> *And I apologize, but also don't, for*
> *the phone calls you'll have missed.*
> *Please call me or come over when*
> *you get this. I don't care the time. I*
> *just want to talk to you. Apologize in*
> *person. I was being a shitty girlfriend ...*
> *and person. And you deserve better.*
> *I hope you're safe. Still hopelessly*
> *falling for you.*

I felt pathetic and ridiculous. I immediately wanted to write that I loved him. But maybe that wasn't the case. Because how do you treat someone as poorly as I did if you love them?

I had wanted to keep my phone on loud, just in case Julian messaged me, but a few hours into me sleeping, Marie started calling and texting me, so I had to turn my phone off.

I did what I could for Julian. If he was ready to talk, he'd come to me.

THE NEXT MORNING, I woke up early, not able to get much sleep. I heard a knock on the door and realized my parents were once again not home. I climbed out of bed, throwing my hair up, and headed toward the living room, still in my pjs. When I answered the door, my heart stopped. Julian was standing there disheveled.

"Julian," I breathed, "come in."

He shook his head. "No, it's okay."

I stepped out onto the porch with him. His eyes were swollen and bloodshot. "My parents aren't home or anything—" I started to say before he cut me off.

"I think we should break up." My hand caught the door-frame, steadying my legs.

"W-what?" I dug my fingers into the wood.

What the hell was happening? What was he saying? No, no, no.

"That's all I wanted to say." He turned around, heading toward his car.

I watched him walk down the cement path before the words registered in my head.

What. The.

My head grew heavy, and I forced myself to take a breath—despite feeling like my lungs were in overdrive.

"Julian!" I screamed, running down the steps after him. His shoulders straightened at my voice, but he didn't turn around. "Julian! What the hell?!" I forced out. I could barely catch my breath.

He opened his door and climbed in before connecting his eyes with mine—only for an instant. But that second stopped me dead in my tracks.

I couldn't breathe. Gasping, I doubled over at the sound of his car door shutting. His tires screeched as he pulled away from the curb. Swaying forward, I stumbled and fell on my knees.

He never sped. It wasn't like him, despite being angry or frustrated. But it was clear why when seconds later Emma's arms wrapped tightly around my frame.

I choked on a breath, desperate for a sliver of air. Tears wouldn't come; my eyes were dry, even after squeezing them shut. I start to hyperventilate, needing some release. Some escape from my body.

I gasped, leaning over Emma's shoulder, dry heaving. Even my body had stopped cooperating—forcing the toxins back down into my body instead of out.

What had I done? Why was I such a bitch? An asshole?

You can never change, Quinn.

I DON'T REMEMBER GETTING to my bed or even how long it could have been. My sister was lying next to me when I woke up, watching a movie on my laptop. My head was heavy, and my mouth was dry. I felt like I had a massive hangover. The only time in the world that I wished this *was* a drunken hangover.

I loved him.

Fuck. I loved him.

Loved? No. *Love.* Present tense.

How could I love him if I was missing something? *Was* I missing something, or was it all in my head? Had I been so eager to find a reason? Had any of the fight been valid on my end?

I frantically searched for my phone, rolling from side to side before my sister grabbed my right arm.

"First, relax. Second, he didn't text or call. Third, I think it'd do you good to be away from your phone."

"Where is it, Emma?" I sat up and immediately regretted it.

It was getting dark outside, and I hadn't had a single thing to eat all day.

"Give him space. You can figure it all out tomorrow."

"I don't even think it's valid!" I screamed before shutting my mouth quickly.

Emma nodded, reaching out and pulling me into a crushing hug.

"I know, babe. But if you're meant to work it out, it can wait until tomorrow. I promise you."

Her hands ran through my curls as she buried her head in my mane, lulling me back to sleep.

I woke at various hours of the night only to find my sister hadn't moved from my bed. She wasn't holding me close—as I was cocooned in my comforter—but she never left my side.

Come morning, my mother woke us both up, announcing breakfast on the table. I barely even climbed out of bed before I was given permission to spend the day at home—after I tried to eat.

And that was when reality set in.

I was given a mental health day, but everyone else had to return to their lives.

Starving when I saw the eggs and toast in the kitchen, I finally ate for the first time in over twenty-four hours. I refused to partake in any morning conversation aside from thanking my mother for breakfast. Eventually, my sister had to leave for college, and my parents had to go to work.

Under strict instruction to call anyone at a moment's notice, I was kissed goodbye and left to my own devices.

Immediately, I ransacked my room in search of my cell phone. *Maybe,* just maybe Julian regretted his words and felt too embarrassed to apologize in person. Maybe I missed a ton of text messages asking me to forgive him for being ridiculous. Maybe I heard him wrong ... maybe, just ...

No one had contacted me.

JULIAN

When I got home from Quinn's, my dad had already left for work as I had suspected. I wondered if he even noticed I was gone for almost the entirety of the weekend. For some goddamn reason, that only made me feel worse.

Like, here I was an absolute wreck, and no one fucking cares. No one around to ask me how I am, to be worried or concerned. I knew I shouldn't be angry at my dad. He was working; it wasn't his fault. But the longer I stayed in the house, the worse it got. I laid down in my bed only to bunch the sheets up in my fists, jaw tight.

Fuck everyone. I didn't even last an hour before I was out the door again.

I went back to my spot, hoping, praying, desperately wanting it to bring the peace it used to, unlike yesterday. Anything to escape reality. The familiar smell of pine filling my lungs was enough to ease my breathing at least. But there was still this pain in the dead center of my chest that just wouldn't go away. It felt as though there was a metal ball right between my lungs, expanding by the second. It hurt to breathe.

I sat on the hood of my car with no energy to venture

anywhere else. Before, this spot could clear my head in an instant. Why wasn't it working now? It was like a puzzle with a piece missing, but the box was empty. Why the hell was I hurting, anyway? I shouldn't have been. I didn't deserve to be. I was the one who fucked up my friendship with Tyler. I was the one who cheated on Quinn. I was the one who broke up with her. So why the hell did I feel so goddamn broken?

Maybe if Tyler had acknowledged me, we could have talked about it. That I was just curious, that I thought maybe that was the solution to my problem. I was wrong, of course. So fucking wrong. Which didn't make it okay. But Tyler, where the hell did he even stand with this? I should have just told Quinn. Told her I'm a fucking mess, and I don't know who I am and that it'd be better not to bring her down with me. But the moment I was given the opportunity to speak my feelings, my throat grew tight, unable to form the words. If I had just been open with both of them maybe ... maybe things wouldn't be so messy.

Fuck, why was life so complicated?

I decided to try going for a walk anyway. The farther away from my car I was, I figured the farther away I would be from anything that reminded me of reality. This place used to keep me in the present. It always felt like I was finally breathing when I was here, that anything in the future could wait, that the past wasn't important, and the present was all there was. Me, here. Nothing else. But my brain was too loud. Like I wasn't actually here after all, but rather in some virtual reality where all my emotions were standing in front of me demanding attention, shouting things at me I couldn't fix.

I stared at my feet, the dirt path with an occasional rock being my only view. Images of the last forty-eight hours were on replay. It'd be easier to just never go to school again. To never face a single other person from that place. To avoid all my problems completely. But they wouldn't go away, I knew that. I just wished this pain would, at least. Or to have that peace this place brought me again.

Why didn't anything feel like healing? Not breaking up with Quinn. Not ignoring my phone. Not even here. Nothing I did had been the medicine for my pain. I wished I could just go back to before. Before the dare with Quinn. Back to when everything seemed simple. Back before any of this pain.

I woke up Monday morning to the phone ringing. I slumped downstairs to check the caller ID and saw it was past nine o'clock. The school was calling wondering where I was. I ignored the phone, though. It was just one more problem to deal with. But there was no way in hell I was showing my face there. I knew I would have to eventually, but for today, I was hiding from everyone.

Just as I was about to head back up to my room, I caught sight of my dad out of the corner of my eye. I jumped, having assumed he'd be at work like always. Except today, he was sitting in his recliner in the living room drinking his coffee while working on a Sudoku book. He didn't look up from his book to acknowledge me or the phone. His eyes were glued to the paper, peering down his nose through his glasses.

I hoped he hadn't noticed me as I headed to my bedroom. I couldn't even face my father. I didn't have any energy left in me to talk about what happened. I just wanted everything to settle, be forgotten, and move on. I wanted to go back to the way things were before this weekend, back to even before Quinn. Just as my feet reached the stairs, my father spoke.

"Sick?" I could hear in his voice that he was really asking why I wasn't going to school today. And why I hadn't told him in advance.

"Yeah," I lied. But I might as well have been. Sick of life.

"Quinn came looking for you Saturday." I snapped my head around to look at him. He had finally put his book down, his eyes on me.

"When?" I spoke without thinking better of it. Saturday? Was it after I left her place? Was it when I was already at Tyler's?

He shrugged. "Early afternoon, I'd say." He paused, waiting for me to comment, but I had nothing to say. "I really like Quinn. She seems like a smart girl."

I nodded. "She is." I knew he was waiting for my explanation, but I wasn't sure I was ready to give it. "She seemed really worried about you. Everything alright?"

"Yeah," I lied again, this time trying to blink back tears.

God, how many times was I going to cry this week?

My father leaned forward in his chair, seeing right through me. "Your face." He pointed to his own eye. My jaw tightened. Despite the pain, I hadn't looked in the mirror to actually see the damage Adrian had done. "Sit."

Reluctantly, I sat in front of him, leaning back with my hands gripping my knees.

"Son, you look rough." He gave me a half smile.

"Gee, thanks." I rolled my eyes.

"What's going on with you? You know you can tell me anything, right?"

My lip twitched. That was true. Since my mom left, my dad and I were close. He was my Ian before, well, Ian. Except I didn't feel like this was something I could discuss with him. No way in hell could I talk to my dad about my sex life, or lack of, or desire for lack thereof.

What did I even say? I was coaxed into dating this girl deemed a "slut," but turns out, she was amazing. I fell in love with her only to not want to have sex with her. So I must not love her then, I guess. So I must be gay then, I guess. So I slept with one of my best friends. But I didn't like having sex with a guy either. Except I still cheated on said girl. Only to be filled with so much guilt and disgust for myself that I ended things with the one person who made me feel alive. All because I couldn't give her the love she needed.

Before I even got a word out, the tears were pouring down my face.

My dad was beside me in an instant, with his arm around my shoulders. "Shh, it's okay," he whispered.

"I don't know what's wrong with me," I choked out.

"There's nothing wrong with you." He rubbed my arm.

I sniffed. Although I didn't believe him, I felt better hearing it from him. "Dad, I ruined my life."

"I highly doubt that."

I shook my head. "I've messed up a lot of things this weekend. I messed up so bad. I don't think I can fix any of it." I couldn't look up at him. My eyes stayed on my hands, blurry from tears.

"Take a deep breath. Just focus on yourself today. Take one thing at a time. You can make it through this." His voice was calm and soothing. My chest felt a sense of release. The air felt cleaner and easier.

I nodded, wiping my nose on the back of my hand. "Thanks."

He rubbed my back once more before he allowed me to get up and go to my room. I knew that didn't fix things. I knew that didn't make anything go away. But it at least made me feel better, got me to stop crying and keep my mind on other things for the rest of the day.

I went through the day constantly checking the clock, thinking about where I would be each hour had I gone to school. I wondered if Quinn was at school. I wondered if Tyler was. I wondered if Tyler said anything to James about what happened Saturday. I doubted he would. He couldn't even face me the next day. I wondered if the video Marie recorded had made its rounds through the entire school yet. *God, I wish I never had to go back.*

When four-thirty in the afternoon came, there was a knock on the door.

"Ian's here," I heard my dad call from downstairs.

I waited in my room with my bedroom door open, knowing Ian would come straight here. The moment I saw him in my doorway, the tears almost started again.

"You okay?" he asked, sitting beside me on my bed.

"No," I admitted.

"I saw the video."

I nodded. "I broke up with Quinn."

He was silent for a moment, and I couldn't look up at his face. I couldn't bear to see his reaction. "Why? What happened? You two seemed to be doing great."

I tried to speak, but the moment I opened my mouth, I was overcome with tears. He waited patiently, watching me with empathy until I could regain my composure. He didn't try to touch me or comfort me. He gave me the space he knew I wanted —needed.

"I slept with Tyler," I choked out.

Ian's eyes grew wide. "What?"

"How did you know you were gay?" I asked, unable to explain my actions.

"The fact that when I looked at guys I felt attraction, but when I looked at girls, I didn't," he said softly, remaining patient with me. "And then I had sex with Tyler, and I knew for sure."

My eyes grew wide this time. "Wait, what?"

He laughed. "Yeah. I guess what I stole was his pride." He let out a breath. "We were fake wrestling with each other, and one thing led to another." He went silent. "Shit happens. I figured myself out even if Tyler hasn't."

I nodded, unsure what to make of what Ian was telling me. So that was why Tyler was so against hanging out with Ian. Not because he stole something. Not because Tyler's homophobic.

But because he, himself, has his own sexuality he needs to face. But at the same time, it all made sense why they seemed closer than the rest of us.

"Did you guys date—did you have feelings for each other?"

"I did. But I think Tyler saw me more as a distraction for how he felt."

"What?" I furrowed my brows, trying to understand. This was all news to me. This had all happened without my knowledge.

"It isn't my place to say. That's Tyler's business, not mine." Ian offered a smile, and I nodded. "I didn't know you were questioning your sexuality," he said, changing the topic back to me.

I laughed. "It's more like questioning who the fuck I am."

"What's going on, Julian? What brought this on?" His eyes were trained on me.

Here I was, finally talking to the one person I had wanted to talk to about all this, and I couldn't get the right words out. A part of me wished we had spoken sooner. That I accepted his offer to chat via phone, text, or mentioned something in the cafeteria that day. Maybe that would have stopped me from sleeping with Tyler. Maybe that would have prevented me from ruining everything.

"I don't know." I shook my head. "I don't like sex. Not with Quinn. Not with Tyler. Not with anyone. That's all I know. But I feel like I have to. Like something is wrong with me because I don't."

"You don't have to like anything," Ian said, and it only made me start crying again. "I'm just trying to understand, Julian. So you don't like sex, but you cheated on Quinn with Tyler? I just don't understand how that happened."

I shrugged. "I figured if I didn't like having sex with a woman, then I must be gay or something." I wiped my tears. "But I don't know anymore. Sorry if that sounds dumb or whatever."

"Wanna hang out Thursday after school?" Ian leaned back onto his hands, his face serious.

"Wait. Aren't Thursdays when you go to that LGBT+ group?"

A smile crept onto Ian's face. "Yes."

"You're asking me to go with you?"

He shrugged. "It was just an idea. You don't have to. But it might help."

I knew very little about the LGBT+ group. All I knew was they were in charge of organizing a lot of the events that happened like pep rallies and formals. I also knew a bunch of them went together to the pride parade every year. But other than that, I knew nothing.

"Okay. Sure," I said, uncertain if I'd actually go or not. It didn't seem like my crowd.

"See you at school tomorrow then?" He offered me a smile.

"God." I rubbed my face. Just thinking about everything I had to face tomorrow made me feel nauseated. "Yeah, unfortunately."

"Don't worry. This won't last forever. Things will clear up eventually."

"I hope you're right about that." I tried to smile as I walked Ian to the door.

I knew I couldn't hide from everything forever. No matter how much I wished to.

QUINN

Everyone had seen the video of Julian by the time I made it to school Tuesday morning. But because we both apparently fell off the face of the Earth over the weekend, everyone assumed Julian and I had made up—even further from the truth, that we had spent the day together on Monday. He also hadn't gone to school.

I *wished* that was my weekend. A weekend where we were so madly in love that we couldn't be bothered to attend school. I wasn't going to be the one to ruin that rumor. Because debunking it meant I lost the bet.

The goddamn bet I never wanted to be a part of.

I vomited in the bathroom after lunch when Marie told me how happy she was that we worked things out because it'd be a real shame if I couldn't even manage to hold a boyfriend for one more week.

I wanted a life where Julian and I were able to exist in each other's worlds solely on the basis of our own happiness. Not tied down by high school bullshit.

Let me be clear though—bet or no bet—my feelings for Julian

were real. Despite how much I cared for him, don't be fooled, I borderline hated him now.

There was a good and bad thing in regard to me and Julian never having classes together. The good thing: we didn't have to have the awkward, uncomfortable moments in a small classroom, and I didn't need to worry about running into him. The bad: when I was actively trying to seek him out, the boy was a chameleon.

I had found him a total of three times. Once was in class when I was on my lunch. That time, he didn't see me, so I had a few seconds to acknowledge that he arguably looked far worse than I did. The second time, we made eye contact before he bolted—in what I knew was the wrong direction for his seventh period class. And the last time was right before we both went to our respective cars. That time was the most painful—but I wasn't sure for whom.

We weren't the only two heading to our cars after school; we were separated from each other by all the other students rushing off campus. What caught me completely off guard, though, was that Tyler and James were completely ignoring Julian, who walked with his head down, shoulders hunched. I understood Julian being mad at James ... but what happened between Tyler and Julian?

I hadn't decided if I was proud of myself for trying to understand that Julian was going through something I couldn't understand. Or if I should just be heartbroken that he was an asshole about the entire thing.

But there was a massive piece missing to this puzzle. It couldn't possibly be just about this weekend. It had to be more deeply rooted—whether on the basis of our relationship or something I wasn't even involved in.

WEDNESDAY CARRIED on very much the same. That was until lunchtime when Marie bounded over to the table where I sat alone. She had given me my space most of the morning—mainly because I was "ruining her vibe." But the smirk on her face as she sat before me, told me everything I needed to know: *I didn't want to know.*

"A little birdy told me that you've been lying to me."

The slight raise of my brow even seemed like too much effort.

"You're excited about this, why?" I picked away at the sandwich my mother forced into my hand this morning. I appreciated her for trying, but I hadn't eaten much since breakfast Monday morning.

Marie swayed her hand in front of her face, telling me she wasn't concerned with the lie. "You and Julian aren't dating."

"Wow," I mocked shock, "thank you for letting me know."

"Which means, you've lost the bet."

I let out an audible sigh, dropping my sandwich and looking directly at her. "Are you serious? I'm six days shy!" Marie shrugged with a smirk. "Can we drop all this bullshit?" Marie straightened her posture—her face barely losing its amusement.

"It's the stipulations of the bet. We're just looking out for you."

"Right." I gave a curt nod and collected my belongings. "Then be sure to send Adrian my way. I can't wait to see what fucked up thing he can do to my reputation now. At this point, it doesn't even matter."

Before she could answer, I walked out of the cafeteria, spending my remaining lunch period outside. If I wasn't already on a very short string with my parents, I would have skipped the rest of the day.

As I WALKED out of the school at the end of the day, Adrian

caught my attention. He didn't say a word but motioned with two fingers that he had his eye on me before running off down the hall to meet Emerald, who was waiting.

How the hell was I going to get through the rest of this school year with his bullshit?

Walking with my head down, trying to avoid everyone, I didn't realize Garrett was leaning against my car door until my eyes caught sight of his damn red Nikes.

"Hey, Quinn." His words were gentle. They hinted at the smile I knew I'd see once I lifted my head.

And of course, there it was. His dimples were so deep and his grin wide, I couldn't help but offer him a smile. With just one grin, he was able to weaken my senses.

"Garrett," I greeted, adjusting my shoulders upright.

My palms grew clammy, and I could feel my pits moisten against my sweater underneath my winter jacket.

"I heard about you and Julian. You okay?"

I swallowed, trying not to let my smile falter. He was still paying attention to me?

He towered over me, but not like Julian. He was relaxed, his hands casually in his pockets as he leaned back. His build was bigger than Julian's—more confident too—but he wasn't buff. Nor was he athletic.

"I'm okay." I nodded, gesturing to my car. "Uh, I was just trying to leave."

"Cool, right. Of course." He moved away from my door as I unlocked it, but he swooped in and opened the car door. "Listen, uh, do you want to get some food?"

I smiled at his nervous stature. It was different when I slept with him over the summer. He was a challenge for me. And even when we did slightly let our guards down, the competition for dominance was intense. But now? Now he seemed nervous. He was still out of my league, so what changed?

"I'm not looking for a boyfriend."

"Good." His voice deepened as he stood straight. My hand gripped my car handle. "Because that's not why I came here."

I fumbled, trying to open the door. *Act natural. Be cool, Quinn.* I leaned in my car and placed my belongings on the passenger seat.

I, Quinn Kennedy, didn't need a boyfriend. I could do whatever the fuck I pleased, whenever I wanted.

Turning toward him, I placed my hand on his jacket, squeezing his bicep. "Great. I'll meet you at your place," I offered with a wink.

He cleared his throat and tried to hide the blush spotting through his tanned skin. Garrett leaned in, placing a kiss on my jawline before he sauntered off to his car.

JULIAN

I DRAGGED MYSELF TO SCHOOL TUESDAY MORNING, grateful I didn't share any of my classes with Quinn. I couldn't help but avoid her. I knew it wasn't fair. I owed her some sort of explanation. But I didn't have one. I loved her. How could I go up to her and tell her I broke up with her because I love her? She deserved someone who could love her in a way I couldn't.

When I got to my locker in the morning, James and Tyler were waiting for me like they usually did. I wanted to sigh with relief—some normality in the chaos that happened over the week-end. Except my stomach filled with nerves. This couldn't go well. Not only did I avoid James since Friday and Tyler since Saturday, but I threw my friendship with Tyler out the window. I could tell from the end of the hallway that they were pissed at me.

"Hey," I said as I approached, trying to act casual as if nothing was wrong.

Tyler was leaning up against the lockers with his arms crossed, his eyes trained on his feet, refusing to acknowledge me.

James shook his head. "What the fuck was Friday, dude?"

"It was February first," I tried to joke.

"Cut the bullshit. All I've ever tried to do is look out for you, and you fucking repay me by humiliating me and Adrian?" Of course, he had to add Adrian. It was always about their stupid pride. It was always about getting someone's approval.

"I—" I shut my mouth. "I'm sorry?"

"You should be! We specifically chose Quinn because she's a slut. This was never supposed to be a situation where you turned on your best friends."

I laughed under my breath. "Quinn's treated me more like a friend than either of you ever have. And excuse me, but she isn't a slut. What even determines who's a slut, anyway?"

Screw it. I was tired of playing one of James' pawns. I didn't need his friendship. Why should I keep friendships that are only hurting me? I was sick of the bullshit. I just wanted to be me.

"I can't believe she's fucking brainwashed you." James laughed. "I'm done trying to help you, Julian. You've only ever weighed us down anyway."

"Whatever." I shook my head.

There really was no getting through to him. I was exhausted. I just wanted this to be done.

"That's it?" He laughed. "After everything, you're too pathetic to put up a damn fight for us?"

I looked over to Tyler, who hadn't said a word since I got here. But he wouldn't look up at me. "I'm sorry, but you made a very opinionated remark on someone you don't really know, so I'm just asking, "says who?" Who the hell created this rule book on what someone is and isn't? Why not, for once, you learn to think for yourself? Maybe then you'll be a decent person. You know, James, maybe you're the pathetic one. Ever think of that?"

"Do yourself a favor and go fuck yourself. Maybe the next girl won't be so ashamed for everyone to know she's slept with you." James stepped away from the lockers. "Let's go, Tyler. We're done here."

James headed down the hall; Tyler waited until he was out of earshot before he pushed himself off the lockers. He stopped for a moment before turning to look at me. His eyes were glossy, but his lips were pressed together tightly. I wanted to tell him I knew he also slept with Ian. I wanted to tell him I was sorry. I wanted to let him know if he needed someone to talk to, I was willing to listen. But I was also pissed he could still go along with James. That he still just followed him around and let him say those things. So instead, we stood there in silence as if we were trying to communicate through telepathy.

"I won't tell anyone about Saturday," I finally said.

"Thank you," he whispered before turning to follow James.

Well, at least that was two problems faced and I guess dealt with. There were still two problems left: Quinn and my sexuality. I wanted to deal with the second one before I took on the first. I wanted to be able to go to Quinn with an explanation. One that was genuine and sincere.

QUINN

THE PAIN OF BEING HUNGRY STARTED TO OUTWEIGH THE loneliness that was settling in. I wasn't actively trying not to eat. It's just that when there wasn't food around, my body was starving. The moment food was in front of me, I was sick to my stomach. But I carried on because that was what was expected of me. I didn't have a choice in the matter. I had to be in school; there weren't many ways around it.

Thursday, I grew more anxious, though. Not only had I woken with the memories at Garrett's the night before, but each day that passed without saying a word to Julian was one more day separated—unmended, broken. They all worked the goddamn same; no synonym could make it better.

Nor could sleeping with Garrett and pretending Julian didn't exist. *Despite* how good it was. *Despite* how much I missed sex, my mind still focused heavily on Julian, even in the moment.

I deliberately cut classes in order to see Julian. I made excuses to leave class a few minutes early to stand and wait for him outside his classroom. Or I was late to the beginning of class because I was trying to catch him. Each time, six in total before school let out, he walked away. He ignored my motions. I wasn't an idiot. I wasn't about to shout his name—embarrass both of us. But his actions confirmed that he saw me each and every time. Whether he'd slip into a classroom or strike up a conversation with the person next to him, it was obvious he had no interest in speaking with me.

At the end of the day, we crossed paths organically—so much so, it startled me. I wasn't prepared to see him. I was about to say something. He wasn't running, but his eyes began to narrow.

"Quinn!"

I jumped, goosebumps rising underneath my layers. I didn't turn around. My eyes remained focused on Julian. His eyes darkened, looking no doubt at Garrett before glaring my way. As soon as I opened my mouth, he darted toward the student parking lot.

What right did he have to be angry with me? *He* ended things.

Garrett's hand touched my lower back.

"Your place?" I suggested, turning toward him with a smirk.

"Absolutely." He winked before wrapping his arm around my shoulder, directing us to the parking lot.

GARRETT HELD his phone above his face, typing a message. We had only finished having sex literally two minutes beforehand. During, his phone kept vibrating on his bedside table.

"You should come party with us sometime." He glanced my way before responding to another message.

I pulled the sheet up further and turned toward him. "Where at?"

"Andrew and Kyle, the senior twins, are having a birthday party soon. Invitation only, but you'll be my plus one."

"Sounds fun."

Garrett then threw his phone back on his table and wrapped

his arms around me. He nuzzled his head into my neck, nibbling on the raw skin he had heavily focused on just moments before.

"How about another round?" I answered him with a kiss, trying to redirect his thoughts.

I've only ever had a hickey once, and that was before I realized how awful they were to hide. But somehow, I let Garrett continue. Was it a punishment of sorts?

It wasn't the same. And it seemed I kept trying to convince myself of that.

Actually, it was vastly different. His touch was stronger, more in control, more dominant. *Not bad* per se. But *not* Julian. In fact, Garrett was great to have sex with. He had been the first time, and he was even better this second time. He did want to pleasure me. It wasn't all about him like many guys tended to be. But he wasn't gentle, caring ... dare I say, passionate. He didn't make me feel like I was the only one he wanted to be with.

I spent so much time when Julian was pleasuring me focusing on the fact that he wasn't giving me what I thought I wanted. Yet, he had been letting me experience something I never had before. Yes, it didn't make sense as to why he didn't want to have sex with me, but why couldn't I have been more patient? More understanding? Was it really because it was all new to him? Was it okay for sex to not be on a guy's mind all day every day?

Garrett redirected my attention as I involuntarily moaned.

This wasn't about Julian. It couldn't be. Julian didn't want me. This was why I didn't do relationships. Goddamn feelings got in the way of everything. And what was it all for?

It was bullshit.

I refocused, flipping us so I was straddling him, and vowed that today would be the first day I went back to who I was. The new me didn't suit me.

JULIAN

THE REST OF MY MONTH WAS HELL. I THOUGHT NOT BEING friends with Tyler and James would ultimately be a good thing, but I never considered how alone I would feel. Sure, I had the opportunity to be myself, unafraid of any thoughts or feelings I had. Free of their judgment. Free of their constant peer pressure, not just about sex, but doing anything stupid and reckless. I was free to make my own decisions. It felt liberating, like I was finally able to breathe.

Yes, my reputation was absolutely shot, but that wasn't the end of the world to me. I was still the same person. I didn't act any different. I just was alone instead of with two other people.

Thankfully, Ian tried to spend as much time with me as possible. Though I was grateful, I felt guilty he was neglecting Connor to be around me. I knew people would whisper, make up stories, add false details to the incident that happened at Emerald's. Question and assume why I was no longer around Tyler and James. But again, I just shrugged it off.

I was thankful soccer was over, which made avoiding Tyler and James easy. Though I did dread how next season would go.

Oh, well, high school isn't forever. This won't be forever. I kept reminding myself.

Eventually, Ian started inviting Liza to hang out with us, and we became a group of three. I laughed with them. I could be myself with them. Why did I waste most of high school around a couple of assholes just because it felt safer? Felt like what I had to do? Looking back, it all seemed so idiotic. I missed out on having real friends this whole time.

Ian kept asking me to go to the LGBT+ group. Still, I wasn't sure if it would help or not. I learned Liza started going shortly after Adrian outed her to the entire school. She insisted it helped her feel less alone, and that was a feeling I was desperate for.

I went through school without actively avoiding Quinn. I went my usual routes to all my classes, sat in my usual spot at lunch, thinking *if I see her, then I see her.* Except there were times she purposely sought me out. Each time I turned the other way, hoping she wouldn't realize it was intentional. It hurt.

There was a pain in my chest every time I saw her that made it hard to breathe. I didn't know what to say to her. I was an ass. But, I didn't know who I was. I didn't see how we could work things out if I couldn't give her something she needed. She loved sex. I didn't. I couldn't figure out a solution to that. Besides, she could easily do better than me anyway.

She'd already proven that hanging around some guy named Garrett. I didn't know if they were dating. Fuck, I didn't know what the hell *was* between them. But it sure as hell looked like they were a thing the way they acted around each other at school, him always leaning closer to her while she giggled at everything he said. And who was she kidding, trying to hide those obvious hickeys on her neck by wearing chokers or her hair to one side?

Ugh, fuck, Julian, you shouldn't care. You were the one who broke up with Quinn, remember? Except I thought Quinn would care. At least enough to hold off for a while before bouncing onto the next guy. I shouldn't be surprised ... she did have a reputation, and this must have been the way she got it. But it made me want to throw up. It made me feel betrayed and lied to. Did she ever actually care about me at all? Was it always about sex? I always believed our relationship was more than that. It was for me, at least.

AFTER A FEW WEEKS of Ian and Liza trying to convince me to go to the LGBT+ group, I worked up the courage and went. I shockingly learned Ian ran and organized the group. How the hell was I best friends with this kid, and I didn't know he fucking ran an entire club at school? I knew he went, but also *ran* it? Some friend I was. Though Ian found my shock pretty hilarious when he told me.

I had to come alone because Ian had to stop at the library to print stuff out beforehand. They got together after school every Thursday in the drama room. Despite having taken drama in ninth grade, I had never actually been inside the room before because class was always held in the auditorium.

Chairs were set up sporadically instead of the circle I had originally expected. The walls were hand-painted with scenes from different plays the school had put on in the past. One of *Beauty and the Beast*, *Guys and Dolls*, *Into the Woods*, and even an old, chipped painting of *Grease*. Props and old set pieces were pushed up against the walls to make room for everyone. Half the room was occupied by racks packed with different costumes. Although the room had so much extra stuff inside, it still had a ton of space for everyone without feeling claustrophobic. It was bigger than any of the other classrooms in the school.

In the middle of the room, a table was set up with a fruit tray and a platter of baked goods. On the floor beside the table was a cooler, and I saw a few people take soda cans out of the pool of ice.

A couple students had put up some posters around the room. They had rainbow-painted backgrounds with the letters LGBT+ written in bold black letters on them. I never really thought about the acronym for the community before. L for lesbian, G for gay, B for bisexual, T for transgender. But then there was the plus. I stared at the plus as if it'd miraculously tell me what that involved. What was included in this plus sign? I knew so little about such a large community, it made me feel ashamed to even be here.

Martin waved to me as he came in, sitting on the opposite side of the room talking to a guy I didn't know. I learned Martin was one of the first people to ever attend these meetings. It shocked me to know a guy who seemed so comfortable with himself, who was a part of that shitty group of friends, would also attend something like this. I guess there were multiple layers to a person after all.

"Hey." Liza sat down beside me.

"Hey." I smiled at her, grateful to have someone to sit beside.

It felt natural and normal to be around Liza now, even without Ian. I could sit here and carry a conversation comfortably without needing Ian's presence.

"What are you doing tomorrow night?"

"Same thing as always—nothing."

She laughed. "Well, wanna leave your house for once and come to a movie with Ian and me?"

"Sounds good to me."

Ian finally entered, waving to us as he made his way to the center of the room. He turned to acknowledge the crowd.

"Welcome again. So this week, I thought we'd talk about a sexuality called Asexual." He gestured to a girl who was sitting on the other side of me. Her crazy blonde curls were tied back in a ponytail, and her face dimpled when she smiled. "Claire here was the first asexual of our group. She's been open for a year now." The crowd clapped, and one guy even whistled.

I awkwardly clapped beside her. *Asexual? What was that?* Ian's eyes met mine, and he gave me a smile I could only counter with confusion. Obviously, there was more to that plus sign than I thought there was.

"Since asexual is a relatively unknown term in our society, I figured this would be the perfect opportunity to spread some information on what asexuality is."

Although Ian had papers in his hand to refer to, he spoke to everyone with eye contact. He seemed so professional, so confident. I could only wish I possessed those features.

"I haven't seen you here before," the girl Ian introduced as Claire whispered to me.

Her blue eyes were huge, almost bulging out of her face as she spoke, getting increasingly more enthusiastic with each word. She reminded me of a dog that got excited the moment it saw a treat.

I nodded with a weak smile. I wasn't ready to mingle. I was just here to check things out. I felt like an outcast here, like going to a church without being religious.

"I'm just here for the free snacks. What brings you here?" She winked while Ian handed out papers.

I looked at her, my body stiff. I wished Ian wasn't in charge so I could sit next to him and ask my questions as they popped up. I had Liza, but she wasn't the same as Ian. But a complete stranger? N.O.T.H.A.N.K.Y.O.U.

"I don't know," I finally said.

"Oh." She was silent for a moment. "Well, trust me when I say Liza always brings the best cookies. Literally to die for."

Liza giggled beside me. "Thank my mom. She's the one who bakes them."

I nodded at both of them trying to keep a smile. I didn't know what else to say. Ian reached me, passing me a paper with a black, gray, white, and purple background. He kept his eyes on me for a moment before he moved on to Claire.

"What is his problem?" I whispered to Liza.

Ian was acting weird. Or was it just me?

"Who knows?" She laughed.

"Before I have Claire share her story, I thought I would give some key information about the ace community. Ace, of course, being short for asexual," Ian began once everyone had a paper.

It felt like I was in a class, handed a note that I likely wouldn't bother reading. And yet there was something mesmerizing about how Ian conducted things. He sat on the edge of the table where the snacks were.

"First off, the definition of asexual is, according to Google—without sexual feelings or associations."

My stomach dropped. *What?* I looked over to Claire, whose eyes were fixed on Ian. I looked around the room. No one reacted. It was like this was normal information. Like this was common sense. I looked at Ian, who glanced my way for a moment before back down at the papers in his hands. *How can everyone be so calm?*

"It's a myth that asexuals are cold, loveless, and hate sex. They have the capacity to form happy, healthy relationships based on romantic orientation. Romantic orientation is what determines the kind of person they're attracted to *romantically* or *emotionally* rather than *sexually*. There's heteromantic: romantic attraction to opposite sex. Homoromantic: romantic attraction to the same sex. Biromantic: romantic attraction to men and women. And Panromantic: romantic attraction to all genders. There's also aromantic, which means you don't have any interest in forming romantic relationships with anyone."

I couldn't believe what I was hearing. It was as if Ian was

taking all my thoughts and feelings and explaining them—helping me understand them. It was like getting glasses for the first time, finally able to see what was once a blurry world through clear lenses. I must have had my mouth gaped open because Ian gave me a sly smile. Did he know? Did he have a hunch all this time? Is that why he invited me here?

"Although asexuals don't experience sexual attraction, they can see and appreciate the aesthetic attractiveness of someone else, the same as how you can appreciate the beauty of flowers or Christmas lights. It's also untrue that the lack of sexual attraction is due to hormonal, libido issues or any mental health concern or the result of any possible past sexual abuse. No one should ever assume there are *reasons* behind someone's sexual orientation."

I rubbed my nose, trying to catch the tears spilling out of my eyes before anyone noticed.

Holy shit.

"I'll let Claire take things from here." Ian gestured to her.

Claire stood and took Ian's spot in the middle of the room while Ian sat where she had been.

"You okay?" Ian asked when he was beside me.

I just looked at him wide-eyed. "Do you—do you think—I'm?"

Ian smiled and placed a hand on my shoulder. "That is ultimately up to you to figure out. But I'm here for you."

I laughed and shook my head. I felt pathetic for crying so much lately. But I was overcome with joy. Joy over the possibility of finally knowing who I was, finally understanding myself. Despite finally feeling like I could breathe, my chest felt tight. My foot tapping, I crossed my arms across my chest to stop from shaking. Anything to keep me in my seat. It was like I was going up a rollercoaster anticipating the fall. I wanted—no, I needed to get out of here. I needed the internet to find more, learn more, drown myself in it.

Glancing up at the clock on the wall, there were only twenty minutes left of the meeting. But Claire was also asexual, so I could learn from her too. I wanted to hear what she had to say. I could always ask her questions. It was like my eureka moment, like in this moment my whole life came together.

"Hey, where's Connor?" Liza asked.

It wasn't until Liza asked that I realized Connor wasn't even here. I hadn't seen him around lately either. I knew I was taking Ian away from him, but Connor could hang out with us too.

"Oh that." Ian shifted in his seat. "Yeah, we broke up."

"What? When did this happen? Why didn't you tell me?" I asked.

Ian shrugged with a smile. "You were going through a lot. I didn't want to make a big deal about it or make you feel bad about anything. It wasn't your fault we broke up. Connor was kind of an ass."

"Wait, what? He seemed nice," I said.

"Well, he would always hang out with his ex and give him rides and stuff, and he didn't care that it made me uncomfortable."

"It felt like he never cared about your feelings," Liza commented. "Are you alright though?"

I watched his expression, wondering how he was doing. Wondering how the hell I deserved such an amazing friend, wishing I had asked him about it myself. Liza was actually active in his life. She knew what was going on, while I took advantage of Ian being involved in mine.

"I'm sorry," I offered softly.

"It's okay, really." We were silent for a moment, and I wondered if I should say more. Should I ask him what exactly happened? When exactly it happened? If he needed to talk about it? Or should I let it be and hope he'd tell me if he wanted or needed to? I sat there trying to decide what else to say, but our attention was brought back to Claire.

"I didn't know I was asexual at first," Claire began to tell the group. "After all, I liked sex. Not all asexuals are repulsed by sex. There are asexuals who are fine talking about sex but aren't willing to have it themselves. There are asexuals who like sex in theory but not in practice. There are asexuals who don't really care for it, but they are happy to do it with someone they love. There are asexuals who enjoy or even love the stimulation of sex but have no actual need or craving for it; it's just like any other activity to do with someone and can be easily replaced with anything else. There are asexuals who do have a sex drive, but it's only triggered by a strong emotional attachment rather than physical factors.

"Being asexual is much more than just saying you don't like sex. So it was really confusing for me at the start. Because I knew I enjoyed sex, but I just never thought about it. It wasn't until I was in my first real relationship where my partner expected me to engage in it all the time that it became an issue. I just didn't understand why they always thought about sex, and I didn't. We argued about it a lot. I would say I thought we should stop, and it would make him mad." Claire sighed, like recalling the memory was painful. "Sexual attraction and sex drive are two separate things. Sexual attraction is *this person* makes you feel horny. Sex drive is *you are* horny."

I could tell she was holding back some information, but I still admired her bravery for sharing something so personal in front of strangers. Her story reminded me of Quinn. My heart sank. Quinn got mad at me for not wanting sex. She seemed to think about sex all the time—or at least more than me. Except I also knew there was nothing wrong with that. There was nothing wrong with liking sex and having a lot of it. But I did think there was something wrong with me for not wanting it.

A smile tugged at the corners of my lips. My side was right too. Claire had gone through the same thing I had. I chuckled quietly to myself at the feeling of not being incredibly alone with my feelings.

"Anyway, we ended up breaking up over it. I think that, despite the common definition of 'doesn't experience sexual attraction,' there is a lot of evidence to suggest that asexuality is more supposed to be a term for people who feel some kind of disconnect from sex or sexuality, not specifically sexual attraction, but including it. I really think that was my problem. I had heard of the term asexual before; I knew the definition Ian provided us today. But it was so much more complex than that, that I didn't think I fit into it.

"See, I knew I *could* enjoy sex. I do have enough of a libido to crave it every now and then. But to have sex is more like satisfying an itch, and then that makes me feel guilty. Because I'm just 'scratching an itch' without actually being attracted to the person. It made me feel like I used them, and I *should* have been sexually attracted to them in order to enjoy sex with them. Or I'd have sex I didn't particularly want at the moment to make them happy, and it'd make *me* feel used. It's a mess."

I wanted to scream yes. To stand and applaud her. *Yes. Yes. Yes.* Everything she was saying felt so true, so real, so ... me.

"So it took a lot of self-reflection, research, and time before I felt comfortable with using asexuality to describe myself. But now I know who I am and am in a new and healthy relationship with my beautiful girlfriend, Sarah." Claire gestured to the girl who had been sitting on the other side of her.

A tanned-skin brunette with a forest of freckles laughed, covering her face as everyone applauded her. Claire then sat back down beside her.

"Thank you, Claire, for sharing that with us," Ian said, returning to the middle of the room while Claire went back to her seat. "Now, there's also gray ace. Which is a part of the spectrum of asexuality. Like all sexualities, it is up to the individual to know where they rest on this spectrum. Gray ace people don't normally experience sexual attraction but sometimes do. They can experience sexual attraction but have a low sex drive. There are people who are technically sexual but feel it's not an important part of their lives and don't identify with the standard sexual culture. And just as Claire informed us, asexuals can have sexual feelings but don't engage in them, enjoy sex but only under very specific circumstances, or don't want to have sex altogether."

"You might want to close your mouth," Liza said to me.

I pressed my lips together, not even realizing I had my mouth gaped open—literally. But how could I not? How was no one else in shock? Where had this information been all my life? I wanted to tell Quinn. I wanted to run after her and tell her everything. I finally had an answer. I was normal. I wasn't broken. There was a reason for how I felt. Why I didn't think about sex. Why I didn't care to have sex. It all made sense. There was no other explanation. This was it. This was my answer.

After Ian went over the paper he handed out, he switched the topic to organizing an LGBT+ mixer in April before we broke off into smaller groups to play giant Jenga.

While everyone was cleaning up the garbage and Jenga pieces, preparing to leave for the day, I decided to approach Claire. She was tossing toothpicks from the fruit tray across the room into the trash can while calling out a basketball player's name with each throw.

I had so many things I wanted to ask her. When did she first come across the word asexual? How was she positive she knew? How could she tell the difference between sexual attraction and a sex drive? How did she figure out her romantic attraction? Before my brain finished thinking one question, it was already on to the next. There was just so much I wanted to know. I wanted to keep hearing her story. Hear someone else have the same feelings I'd had.

"Hey." I smiled as I approached.

"Hey! So how'd you like it? Great snacks or what?" She paused her free-throwing to face me.

"I will literally die if I do not come every week just for these snacks," I faked worry.

"Didn't I tell ya?!" She grinned.

"So about your story today ..." I trailed off, trying to collect my thoughts. I could feel the sweat begin to surface on my palms.

"Yeah?" She seemed so nonchalant and comfortable. Like whatever I asked her wouldn't be serious.

I swallowed. Was it too personal to ask Claire all these questions? I literally just met her. But she seemed okay sharing her story with a group of people today. I took a deep breath, my nerves consuming me.

"I just wanted to say thank you." I tried to smile, despite wanting to say more. I thought I should get to know Claire better before grilling her. Do my own research. Then go to her with any questions I can't solve through the internet.

"Oh," she paused as if she expected me to say more, then she smiled. "No problem."

I smiled with a nod before I went to join Ian, who was finishing up collecting garbage.

The rest was a blur. I don't remember leaving school. I don't remember the drive home. All I could think about was the black, gray, white, purple paper tucked into my jeans.

When I opened the door to my house, my dad was in his usual spot in the living room, a *Game Of Thrones* book in hand.

"Hey, how was school?" he asked, looking up for a split second.

"Hey, uh," I opened and closed my mouth, searching for more

words. I wanted to tell him about the LGBT+ group. I wanted to scream that I finally felt like I knew who I was.

My dad let silence fill the room, waiting for me to answer him. But—I needed more. I needed to know more.

"Good. I, uh, I'm going to go do homework now." I darted out of the living room and upstairs to my bedroom.

Shrugging my backpack off, I let it fall beside my door before plopping onto my bed and pulling open my laptop. Tapping my hands against the side of my laptop while I waited for it to start up, I couldn't stop smiling. I craved knowing more, finding more information. I wanted to seek out other asexuals, hear their stories, their views. My night consisted of Google searches of blogs and videos, laughter, and happy tears.

Finally. Finally, somewhere I belonged.

QUINN

"No idea, I don't live with him." I laughed, semi-listening to the story Garrett had started at my locker.

I stopped suddenly at the sound of Julian's laugh. Where was he? Who was he with?

Garrett was still talking. Whatever he was saying wasn't nearly as important as catching a glimpse of Julian. I felt a squeeze on my arm before Garrett left my side, but I continued walking toward Julian's voice.

I had managed to not cross paths with him in about two weeks. I don't know what changed. Maybe I was focusing too heavily on Garrett? Or maybe just enough? Garrett and I weren't dating. We were friends with benefits, *very* casual on the friend aspect. He was funny, and I gave him the space to be funny. That's how I liked to explain it in my head. We didn't talk about anything serious, mainly just about stupid shit our classmates would do. The main focus was that the two of us were great in bed together. Once I got over the fact that Garrett couldn't be Julian—not that I wanted him to be—we fell into a rhythm, to the point it was almost becoming routine.

For example, today was a Thursday, and he was expecting me

back at his place in half an hour because it's what we did. We'd fool around, laugh a bit, fuck, and then I'd go home for dinner. The same routine happened on Tuesdays and Saturdays too.

I was bored.

I was lonely.

I wanted ...

I jumped inside a classroom, peeking my head out into the hallway.

What the fuck, Quinn?

Julian walked out of the drama room, smiling. Ian followed behind—he was carrying the conversation, and Liza walked out after Ian.

Liza?

Liza?!

I slammed the classroom door. Sliding down to the floor, I looked out at the dark empty room.

What was going on? He was hanging out with Liza behind my back? They were now all friends? He looked so happy. His shoulders weren't hunched. His head was high.

I'd be lying if I said I hadn't seen his downfall. The worst part of me found pride in it. While I didn't understand what was going on with him, at least I knew he had cared for me. One thing I hadn't been able to get out of my brain was the way he said, *"Quinn, I'm falling for you."* But it was always immediately followed by, *"I think we should break up."*

"Julian, what the hell was going on with you?" I groaned, gripping my loose curls between my fingers.

When I thought the coast might be clear, I slipped out of the classroom. The hallway was completely empty now aside from the janitors coming out to start cleaning. I walked the direction Julian went, peeking my head inside the drama room.

The walls were covered in various paintings advertising the plays the school had done in the past, but also in the mix were

LGBT+ posters with facts about the community and also different inspirational quotes.

I stepped in further, examining one of the posters.

"LGBT+ community group. Every Thursday, 9th period," the poster read.

Was he ...

Did he think ...

Fuck.

I backed out of the classroom and found myself walking toward my car.

What did this mean? That was where he was, right? Was he gay? Is that why he didn't want to have sex? Was that why he treated me well? He wasn't all about sex because he didn't want it with me—he wanted it with someone else?

Fucking hell, Julian.

But that meant ... Did I not make him comfortable? Could he not come out to me? Was he nervous?

I wanted to find him. I wanted to talk to him and tell him that it was okay, tell him I forgave him.

When I got to my car, I noticed there were only a few cars left in the parking lot. Narrowing my eyes to focus on the figures at the back of the lot, I recognized Julian. I didn't see Ian until his face appeared on Julian's shoulder when Ian pulled him into a hug.

Are they ...?

Ian held him for a second longer than necessary before he squeezed Julian's shoulder and walked a few cars away. Before Ian climbed in, he glanced back at Julian and smiled.

Were they ... shit.

Fuck.

In record time, I climbed into my car and sped out of the parking lot before Ian sat in his car.

JULIAN

It was almost ten at night when I made my way to the theater, the late show being the only time the film was playing. Liza, Ian, and I were seeing *Harry Potter and the Deathly Hallows Part 2* together after having marathoned every film last weekend in preparation. The theater did throwback movies every Friday, and for some reason seeing a movie we could easily watch at home on a bigger screen was so much more appealing.

Ever since yesterday, I had spent most of my free time on the internet reading threads, blogs and articles, research upon research. I just couldn't get enough of it. I wanted to engulf myself in the community, to find others like me. I made a Tumblr account to ask other asexuals anonymous questions. Questions like the difference between sex-repulsed and asexuality. Asking how other people have managed to have healthy relationships even if sex isn't involved. People suggested focusing on the stimulation of sex to enjoy themselves. Others expressed their concerns on whether they should have sex for their partner or not have sex for themselves. It was like a whole world I had never known about, and it made me excited to be a part of it. I watched coming out videos on YouTube of other asexuals, anything I could find, all the while sitting in my room happy crying, learning myself bit by bit.

Just as I was reaching the doors to the theater, I could see Liza in a Hufflepuff scarf walking through the entrance to meet up with Ian, who was leaning up against the wall. They greeted each other and turned to head toward the concession stand.

"Hey. Wait up!" I called out to them. When they didn't stop, I added, "I'm *Sirius*."

Ian turned around, giving me a disgusted and frustrated face. Terrible pun = success. Liza put her hand to her mouth, trying to hold in her laughter.

"Get out," Ian said.

"I'm punny and you know it," I joked while Ian rolled his eyes with a smile.

We went together to grab popcorn and drinks before entering the movie. I found myself smiling the whole time. For once I felt happy with no lingering pain. For once I didn't have the weight of others judging me on my shoulders. And for once I didn't think about Quinn.

QUINN

It had been a long time since I let myself not give a shit. Since I've drunk without caring what could happen. I had only done this once, actually. It was over the summer. During the last big party before eleventh grade began, we all got shit-faced. So much so, no drama could happen because we barely remembered it. That's exactly what I was hoping for tonight.

Tonight was the birthday party Garrett desperately wanted me to go to. I didn't care for it. But I wasn't against it either. After yesterday, my mind took a negative spin on everything. Ian and Julian had been getting closer when we started dating. Could it be that something was going on before Julian broke up with me? A reason for such an abrupt breakup? Possibly even a reason why our sex life wasn't up to par?

When I woke up this morning, I made the decision to just take care of myself again. I didn't need Julian. I didn't need the group. I didn't need Marie or Liza. I didn't need anyone but my family to be happy. Why bring in any other drama?

So when Garrett greeted me in the morning with his gorgeous smile, I decided to fall right in. I'd go to this party; I'd have the time of my life, and if anyone started shit at school on Monday, I'd stand up to them.

Quinn Kennedy was back. Quinn Kennedy was strong. Quinn Kennedy didn't care about any of the stupid, petty high school games.

So I let Garrett pour me a cup of the punch that was being served. They had a full bar, but why have one liquor when you could have a cocktail of them?

I had lost him soon after we got drinks. I mean, we weren't dating. We didn't need to spend the entire time together. So as he went off to go flirt with a girl he was interested in, I went and found my own fun.

But truth be told, seniors weren't more fun. Their title meant shit. This was just a fancy house party with more people than Emerald's. But more people meant it was easier to blend in. And blend in I did.

For a while, I found myself scoping out the room, trying to figure out where I wanted to plant myself.

"Hey, Quinn," came an unusually soft voice.

I turned my head slightly to the left, and Adrian gave me a gentle smile. His hair was styled back; he was in a fresh dark blue button-up, and he wasn't carrying any beverage. His eyes seemed lighter as they crinkled further into a smile.

"Hi, Adrian, you look nice." His face softened, and he looked down at his shirt.

It wasn't that Adrian never dressed nicely; he did have good style. But there was something different about his demeanor tonight. Something authentic.

"I know you're probably busy; I mean, you had to be invited here with someone, but could I talk to you for a second?"

"We are talking." I crossed my arms subconsciously and immediately regretted throwing up the wall.

"I deserve that." He nodded in the direction of the living room.

He led the way as we brushed past people and found two seats on the couch. Luckily, it was more deserted in here; we wouldn't have to shout.

"Look," he sighed, "I just want to ... I miss you at Emerald's. Well, in my life in general. And I know I haven't been the greatest lately."

I hadn't heard this tone from him in years—even when he was trying to manipulate me, he couldn't replicate it. His eyes remained soft and focused on mine, not his malicious eye contact he seemed so keen on using lately.

"People love Asshole Adrian. And it's so easy to feed into it. I was so nervous about starting high school and about being this great football player like my father expected that when I found a way in, I couldn't stop myself."

Was he apologizing? Apologizing for flipping a switch when I told him I wasn't ready to have sex when I broke up with him because he pressured me? For deciding my entire high school reputation would be created because of his anger for not losing his virginity before ninth grade?

I understood the pressure. I witnessed it time and time again when I was dating Adrian. His father pressured him. He was expected to be scouted and get a full ride to a great university. He was also expected to be a straight-A student and a model son inside their home. The difference in our upbringing was that while we were both going out for full rides to college, I made that goal for myself, and Adrian's goal was made by his father.

I used to feel bad for him and always had to help get him out of his head when we were younger. It wasn't fair for him to not live the life he wanted and instead live his father's dream. But it still wasn't an excuse for the way he treated me.

"So you chose to ruin my life in order for yours to thrive?"

He grew rigid, shifting his body away. I watched as his Adam's apple bobbed before he cleared his throat. His eyes focused down on the carpet.

I hated that I felt for him, that pieces of the old Adrian were shining through. All I wanted to do was forgive him and give him a hug. Tell him everything would be okay.

But it wouldn't be because I couldn't trust him. It wasn't the first time he'd played this sympathy card with me, and I've fallen for it too many times.

"You know I'm not a jackass, Q. That's not really me."

A laugh escaped my lips involuntarily, and I stood up, creating space between us. There was a nervous energy that soared through my bloodstream. I couldn't stay here a moment longer.

I swallowed, backing up further out of the room. His eyes connected with mine, and disappointment contorted his face. The new Adrian was returning.

"It might not be who you were, but it's who you are now. Wake up, Adrian. You thrive on making my life a living hell. And that stops now. You no longer control me. If you don't like who you are, then fucking change it. But I refuse to play by your games anymore."

I left the room before he had a chance to speak. I didn't need his bullshit excuses for why he treated me the way he did. What I wanted was an apology, but I sure as hell didn't need it.

Each step I took shed weight off my shoulders. Instead of feeling fear as I walked away from Adrian, I felt like I could take on the world. I knew I was safe here—he wouldn't pull any bull-shit. And if he did, I was confident Garrett would step in.

My smile grew as I sauntered into the kitchen to pour myself a drink. The twins looked up at me when I entered. They were pouring a few shots.

"Happy birthday, guys! Can I join you two?"

They shared a glance before identical smirks consumed their faces. They filled two shot glasses and pushed them my way.

"Drink up, sexy."

I couldn't tell them apart; I barely even knew their names. But they were both wildly attractive in their white t-shirts, James Dean style. The brother with the disheveled longer dark-brown hair eyed me as I lifted a shot glass and tipped it back, swallowing the awful burn of the vodka.

He mimicked my actions, never breaking eye contact. His t-shirt clung to his body between sweat and specks of liquor as he haphazardly poured more shots for others. With the slightest nod, he motioned away from the group. I lifted my other shot glass, clinked it with his, and before we could even swallow the liquid in our mouths, he was directing me away from the crowd.

We found ourselves behind closed doors; he was pressed up against the wall.

"What would you like for your birthday?" I whispered in his ear. I leaned into him on my tippy toes, and his arms enveloped me.

"Come with me." His words were thick with liquor, tickling my neck. He picked me up effortlessly before laying me down across the room on the bed.

HOLY FUCK, he was no comparison to Garrett *or* Julian. But the best part about party sex? You have it, you get dressed, and you move on. Which is how I found myself stumbling over to the punch bowl.

"Quinn," I heard Garrett's laugh behind me. I finished pouring the punch before turning to him.

"You rang?" I giggled.

"I think you should probably slow down. Have you ever had that much alcohol before?"

Garrett seemed to be drinking only beer—claiming the punch was awful. But I thought his taste buds were awful.

"You aren't my boyfriend." I smirked, walking into his arms. "So you have no say." I placed a kiss on his cheek, and his arms tightened around me.

Sliding my hands into his back pockets, he exhaled, dropping his head next to mine.

"Quickie in the bathroom?" I whispered, placing a kiss on his neck.

I cupped his cheeks and directed his lips to mine. Smirking into the kiss, he walked us backward. My only indication that we were in a different room was the change in the brightness of the lights. With a flip of the switch, I turned them off and pushed him against the wall, unbuttoning his pants.

"You're going down, Quinn Kennedy!" I looked across the table, laughing.

The birthday twins stood at the other side of the table. They challenged me to a beer pong match against them and a friend of theirs. On my team was Garrett and his friend. They had argued, wanting to play against just me, but Garrett claimed I couldn't drink all the beer, despite my badass pong skills.

I had already gotten the ping pong ball in four of their cups. They had yet to get any in ours.

"So, boys," I crossed my arms while I watched them struggle to eye the cups, "what happens if I win?"

"You get the other twin."

I don't know who suggested it, but the people watching grew loud—suddenly far more interested than they were seconds ago. For the first time in a long time, their interest didn't leave me unsettled.

Instead, I put on my game face. "Deal."

I never said no to a good challenge. So there is no way in hell I'd let myself lose.

After another cup of punch, I found myself lying back on a bed, collecting my reward, the other twin between my legs. I hadn't anticipated anything further than fooling around, but when his brother knocked on the door and offered me a three-some and another drink, I found myself throwing back the drink and happily agreeing.

"WE'LL MEET you out there? Another round of beer pong?" one of the twins asked.

I was massaging my forehead as they got dressed in front of me. I closed my eyes, trying to focus on the words in my head.

"Y-yeah," my voice was thick, my smile heavy, "lemme get," I couldn't fathom finishing the word "dressed."

My vision was splotchy and had been most of the time spent in this room. The door closing behind them caused me to flinch as a pain shot through my head.

The sex didn't last long, both of them too turned on and neither one caring for foreplay.

I had said yes. I had wanted it. But that didn't stop me from feeling my skin crawl with the memory of their touch, their lips, or their words.

It wasn't bad.

It wasn't angry. Or rough. Or disrespectful, by any means.

But I hated it.

It wasn't ...

It wasn't ... *fucking hell*. It wasn't Julian.

I rolled over, curling myself into a ball before I let out a scream into the pillow.

I WOKE WITH A START. Something crashed, and there was laughter outside the bedroom. I shivered and wrapped myself underneath the blankets. I couldn't be bothered to find my clothes. Honestly, I wasn't sure my body could handle the movement. The act of simply moving underneath the sheets was enough to disrupt my stomach.

What the hell was I doing here? Alone in a stranger's bedroom? Too drunk to leave. Too drunk to find my phone, and too drunk to call someone.

Call someone ....

Who the hell would I even call? I let out a pathetic laugh.

I had no one. No friends, no boyfriend, no supportive family.

I had a sister who was too busy with her new job to help pay for her new apartment. I had parents who would be too eager to ground me again. I had an ex who apparently was gay and was probably fucking his best friend—would he get hard for him?

How did I end up here? How had I pushed every single person away from me?

I let the tears fall as I squinted my eyes shut.

"DUDE, SHE'S HOT."

"Hell, yeah, she is. I bet she's still in there if you wanted to get some."

Adrian? Who was he talking to? Offering my goddamn body to?

I bolted out of the bed, locking the bedroom door. Covering my mouth and swallowing my vomit, I leaned up against the door. I felt the tears brimming again at the pressure consuming my head. I shouldn't have moved.

"Nah, man, not when she's wasted."

"Believe me, it's better if she is." Adrian chuckled.

"Dude, no. That's messed up."

I heard a slap—probably a slap on the back, and footsteps left.

What was his goddamn problem? Was his stupid pride hurt? Was it all a goddamn ploy earlier? The nice guy was just a new act?

Why was he trying to get people to sleep with me when I was drunk? Why did it even fucking matter?

I had been hopeful a year ago after I had slept with him that he'd finally give it all up. Mind his own damn business. I was almost certain he had it out for me specifically because I wouldn't give him my virginity when we were dating. So he was offended when I started having sex in high school. I became an easy target for him when he needed to impress his buddies.

But then we did sleep together—on my own damn account— so why hadn't he moved on yet?

There was a jiggle of the handle and a knock. Someone was back. I crawled across the floor, searching for my clothes as I started to shake. I had to get out of here.

"Oh, Quinn, open up! I have someone here who wants to rock your world."

I found my phone in my jeans and fumbled to unlock the screen. The bright lights blinded me. I could barely keep my hands still enough to sort of make out the words through my own blurred vision.

The phone was ringing as I placed it up to my ear without even knowing who I called.

JULIAN

WE WERE AT THE PART IN THE FILM WHERE VOLDEMORT announces Harry Potter is dead when my phone started vibrating. My first thought was my dad was calling. He wasn't home when I left for the movies and might have been wondering where I was. But it wasn't worth leaving the movie over.

As I reached in my pocket to decline the call, I got a glimpse of the number. *Quinn.* My heart stopped. That was random. Why was she calling me? We haven't talked in a month, and she even stopped seeking me out. Something didn't feel right.

"I'll be right back," I whispered to Ian and Liza as I got up and left the theater. Once I found myself out the doors, I picked up my phone.

"Hello?" I said, but there was nothing on the other end but shuffling.

A pocket dial, I guess. My finger lingered on the hang-up button when I heard something. Bringing the phone back to my ear, I listened. More shuffling. Crying.

"Quinn?" I said into the phone. "Hello?"

"J-Julian? Julian, is that you?" Her words into the phone sounded muffled.

"Yes, Quinn, you called me." I pursed my lips. She sounded drunk. I shouldn't have bothered picking up.

"Fuck, thank god. Okay." She took a deep breath, and her exhale was shaky. "God, I really hate you, Julian." My body stiffened. "But I don't. I fucking love you. I really fucking love you," she choked in the background. There was so much commotion. Where was she? "And I'm sorry. I'm sorry for everything, but you fucked me over too."

My fingers pinched my nose as I took a breath in. "Quinn. You're drunk—"

"I'm not apologizing for being honest!" she yelled.

There was a bang in the background that caused her voice to hitch. She was silent aside from her erratic breathing.

"Did you call me just to yell at me?" I was ready to hang up. I finally felt like I was moving on. I was finally starting to feel better. I wanted to get back to the movie.

"No." Her voice was now a whisper.

I struggled to hear her, but faint music started to come through. A party. Was it Emerald's? I didn't know she still went to those. I hated that I even cared.

"I need a ride; can you get me?" She hiccupped into the phone.

The banging continued. What the hell was going on?

"What? Why me? Can't you call your sister or something?"

"Please, p-please, you're the only person I have." Her words shook before an almost inaudible "please" came through as she started to sob.

I looked at the entrance of the theater and back at my phone. I sighed. "Fine. Where are you?"

"T-the t-twins."

My hand tightened around my phone. Twins? The only twins I knew who went to our school were seniors on the football team. Why the hell was she there? You know what, it didn't even matter. I shouldn't care. It shouldn't bother me.

"Okay, I'm coming."

"T-thank y-you," she mumbled. The banging now came with someone muffling her name. "Please hurry," she sobbed into the phone.

"What's the addre—" But before I finished my sentence the line went dead.

Fuck. What was that banging? Is she okay?

I scrunched my eyes shut before taking a deep breath. I had to tell Ian and Liza I was leaving so they wouldn't worry.

I texted Ian as I ran.

Had to go. Talk to you tomorrow.

I hoped it was enough to have him not worry until tomorrow at least. I jumped in my car, slamming the door behind me, and pulled my gear into reverse, speeding out of the parking lot.

It wasn't until I was down the street that I remembered I had no idea where the fuck the twins lived. I tapped my hands against my steering wheel while I was thinking. I knew she had her location setting turned off on her Snapchat so I couldn't use the map option to see where she was. I scrolled through my contacts on my phone. *Who would know? Who would know? Fuck.* My finger stopped on Emerald's number. He was the only one from the group I felt comfortable speaking to, and he played football with the twins. He was my only hope. I hit call.

"Yo," Emerald said when he answered, music blaring in the background.

Right, it was Friday.

"Hey, man."

"Julian? Hey. What's up?"

Think, Julian. What could you say to Emerald to make it

convincing that you need the twins' address without drawing too much attention? Hell, I don't even know their names.

"Um, listen, there's a party at the twins' tonight, and I totally forgot their address. Do you know it?" God, please don't ask me any questions. Just fucking give me their address.

"Like Kyle and Andrew?"

"Yes," I said hoping to god that's what their names were.

"Uh, yeah, sure, man."

I was already slamming my foot on the accelerator before Emerald finished his sentence.

I said thanks and hung up without any other information.

Their house was only fifteen minutes from where I was, but it felt like an eternity before I finally reached it. I kept my eyes on the numbers of the houses. My car slowed. My heart sped up. I jumped out of my car but didn't turn it off. I didn't even close my door. All I could think about was getting to Quinn.

QUINN

I jolted awake. My eyes weren't even focused before a sharp pain pierced through my head. It felt like someone was coming down on me with an ax.

What happened?

It was dark. My eyes couldn't focus on anything, but something hovering over me. It was suffocating.

Take a deep breath, Quinn.

I wasn't home. This wasn't my bed. It smelled familiar—but I couldn't pinpoint the scent. I wanted to move. I wanted to remove whatever was on top of me. A comforter?

My heart started to beat faster.

My body was paralyzed.

I wasn't alone. Someone or something shuffled near me. Who was it? Despite the heavy layer, I was freezing.

Think, Quinn.

I was dressed in someone else's clothes. They were loose, but I still couldn't breathe. In a panic, my hand lifted, and I was able to pull down the comforter. But the small action was enough to send my body into turmoil. My stomach churned; I could feel my temperature drop through my veins, and my throat pulsed.

Oh fuck.

I didn't have a moment to look around before I bolted up and leaned forward, hurling all over the comforter. The smell hit me instantly, grasping on to the little bit of air there seemed to be, sending me into another fit of vomiting.

I grew lightheaded as I started to gag. There couldn't possibly be anything left in me. I felt like my stomach was twisting itself dry. Eventually, when I felt like I could catch my breath again, I fell back against the pillows. I felt like I ran a goddamn marathon.

I needed to do something about this. I couldn't lay in a pile of vomit.

"Jesus, Quinn, what did you drink last night?"

I remained still, keeping my head on the pillow, but glanced around the room. The walls were painted a light gray—one wall covered in records. On the wall in front of the bed was a black painted dresser with paint chipping at the edges. On top was a small T.V. with a Pop Funko of Darth Vader beside it. Beside the bed was a bookshelf filled with comics and other character figurines. Empty chip bags and coffee cups sat on top of it. The opposing wall had a wide bifold door that I assumed was the closet.

Julian stood up from across the room, where it seemed he had been sitting on the floor.

Wait, Julian? How the hell did I get here?

His steps were slow but stopped fully as his nose scrunched at the smell. He looked like he hadn't slept, bags deep under his bloodshot eyes. His face was hollow despite the small smile he was trying to give me.

"I, uh—" Julian started to say, "we're in my room. We're at my house. I just didn't think you'd want to go hom—" His voice cracked.

I sat up slowly and looked over at him. I shook my head, furrowing my brows at the motion. I wanted to say something. I wanted to ...

thank him? I wanted ... I didn't know what I wanted. No words would come to the surface. I felt like I could barely focus on any thoughts to even make a sentence. What do I ask? Where do I begin? Where the hell did he come from? He couldn't have been at the party.

"Can I get you anything? Water?"

I knew I needed water, but the idea made me want to get sick again. But there couldn't be anything left in me.

I shook my head. He grew blurry; the tears refused to disappear. I had wanted a moment to talk to him all month. I had thought about what I'd say. Where we'd be. How we could get back together or be friends. Whatever it took for him to be in my life still.

I laid myself back down on the bed, but I faced him. A part of me feared that if I took my eyes off him, he would disappear.

"I'll clean that up. Then we can talk?"

I nodded, slowly climbing out of the bed. My body grew hot, and I gripped the bookshelf for balance before lowering myself to his carpet.

"I, uh, I can't help."

He didn't make eye contact with me, but he nodded. I watched as he stripped his bed of my own vomit and I just sat there, a pathetic mess. Why was he still here, after everything?

He left the room in silence. I wished I could take the opportunity to explore his room. It still baffles me out of the four months we were together that I never stepped foot in here. And now, I do. What gives? What is he hiding?

It took Julian a few minutes before he came back in his room with fresh sheets.

"I—" I croaked. My mouth desperately needed water. But I couldn't risk getting sick again. "Kn-know," I started.

He froze, leaning over the bed as he tried to put the fitted sheet on. "Know what?" He narrowed his brows.

"About you."

He finished the sheet and came to sit in front of me. "Quinn," he sighed, "what are you talking about?"

I tried my hardest to find any saliva in my mouth to continue speaking to him. I didn't want to ask for help, not even for a glass of water.

"You could have told me you were gay. I would have supported you, you know. I *do* support you."

"Wait, what? I'm not gay." Julian massaged his eyelids. "Where is this even coming from?"

"I saw you leaving a meeting. And you and Ian hugging. I know Connor isn't around." I started to cough and hugged my knees to my chest.

"What?" Julian paused. "Quinn, I'm telling you, I'm not gay. Ian and I are just friends. Why are we even talking about this right now?"

Something flipped inside of me, and my frustration bubbled over. Not only was I frustrated with myself for how I felt currently but frustrated by this entire goddamn situation. What the hell didn't I know? And why wouldn't he fucking talk about it?

"What would you rather talk about? Why you broke up with me? How you broke up with me? You probably have so many questions and judgments about last night." My voice rose despite it getting raw. "How much I drank? Who did I sleep with?" I choked, trying to swallow the tears, but they fell anyway. "What a slut I am?"

Julian placed his hand on my arm. "First off, please don't use words like that to describe yourself. 'Cause you're not. Secondly, breathe."

I pulled the sweatshirt—Julian's goddamn sweatshirt—over my face.

"W-why ..." I swallowed the tears and only pulled the sweat-shirt down to expose my eyes. "D-did you change me?"

"Yes, you were complaining about your clothes the whole drive back here, practically stripped them off when you got into my room."

"I'm sorry." I looked down at the top of my knees, picking away at his sweatpants. "How did you ..."

"You called me, and I came and picked you up."

Fucking hell, Drunk Quinn. Have you no shame?

How pathetic was I that the only person I could call for help was my ex-boyfriend?

"Did ..." I looked away from Julian. "I don't remember a lot. I need to. But I'm ..." I stopped talking. What was I even doing? How could I have been so stupid to bring Julian into this?

"Nothing happened. You had yourself locked in a bedroom when I got there, and it was only after I convinced you multiple times that it was me and only me, did you open the door. You were actually pretty smart for how drunk you were."

I remained silent for a while. I excused myself to climb back into the bed. He finished making the bed, tucking me in, and told me he had to run out for a few things, but that his dad wasn't home, so I'd be alone.

"Quinn." Julian's voice filtered through my dream as his hand shook me awake. "It's time to get up."

I could already smell the grease before I opened my eyes. He was sitting next to me as I turned toward him; there were a few bags at the foot of the bed.

"I got us some lunch and thought we could get some fresh air afterward."

Sitting up, I saw there was a Target bag and a Five Guys bag.

"How about you go shower quick, change into this, and then

we can have some lunch?" He tossed the Target bag over to me. "The shower is to the right, the next door after mine. Towels are in the closet."

"Thank you." I gave him a small smile before doing as he asked.

I FOUND him downstairs in his kitchen when I was done showering. He had plated our burgers and fries. We ate together silently, and I forced the grease down my throat. I forced the water in too. I needed something. *This* was that something. But it didn't keep me from feeling a dead weight in the pit of my stomach afterward.

"My parents are going to kill me," I said once I ate the last fry. I could feel the fog starting to lift.

"Your mom thinks you slept at Marie's. I texted her last night and again this morning from your phone to make sure she didn't worry."

"Julian." I sighed.

Why was he taking care of me?

"Let's get some fresh air and go for a walk. I think it's time we talked."

The two of us walked slowly down the street through his neighborhood until we came to a small playground. Luckily, there was only one little girl and her mother on the jungle gym. I didn't think I could handle the sounds of squealing children at the moment.

We made our way to the swing set, each taking a swing before either of us attempted to speak.

"Julian, I miss you," I started. He was about to say something, but I shook my head. "No, no. Please." I sighed, looking over at the mother and daughter as I tried to comprehend my thoughts.

I criticized him for not being honest with me; the least I could do was be honest with him.

"I don't know what happened last night when you arrived. I don't even remember calling you. I won't apologize for anything that was said, though, because I'm told I'm an honest drunk. And honestly, right now, you don't need to tell me what's going on with you. But I miss our friendship. I miss who we were before sex was involved. You're the first person in a long while I've trusted and wanted to tell everything to, and now that it's gone, I don't know what to do."

I gripped my curls in my hand, haphazardly trying to put them in a ponytail. "This isn't a pity party, I promise. If you don't want to be friends with me, that's okay. I mean, you broke up with me for a reason."

I let out a groan as Julian continued to let me talk myself into a goddamn corner. If I wasn't mistaken, there was a small smile on his face.

"Did you know there are people with a disorder called Boanthropy, which makes them act like and believe they are a cow? Just picture a farmer going to check on his cows, and there's a freaking person grazing on the grass. And when the farmer asks the person what they're doing, they just go 'moo I'm a cow?'" Julian shook his head as I started laughing. "I have way too much free time on my hands without you."

I continued to laugh, wiping tears from my eyes.

"God, I've missed those random facts. You've made me smarter, you know." I nudged my body into his, and he swayed on his swing.

"I don't know if *smarter* would be the right word." He laughed. "I don't know when any of this information would ever be useful in real life."

"For times when someone needs to break the awkward tension and remember why they became friends?"

"I mean, that's why I know them," he said, winking.

"So, um," I ran my hands over my head, tightening my pony-tail, "how are you?"

"I'm okay." His voice was soft as if he was uncertain of his answer. "You?"

I nodded. "Same. Well, you know, in general. Right now, I feel like shit." I let out an awkward laugh.

"Because you're hungover?" he teased.

I stuck my tongue out, digging my shoe down into the mulch. "I never, ever want to drink again. I don't think I've ever gotten so sick. I'm sorry."

"I forgive you. It was quite entertaining trying to tame a drunk Quinn if I'm being honest."

I covered my face with my hands. "I don't even want to know. But seriously," I separated my fingers, looking over at him, "thank you. I owe you, big time."

He shrugged. "No problem."

The two of us sat in silence for a few minutes, swinging back and forth gently, looking out at the empty field in front of us.

"Julian, I have no friends." My laugh was dry as I turned slightly toward him.

"That's a pretty bold statement. What makes you say that?"

"Well, I called my ex when I needed help. Pretty sure that sums up my life at the moment." I looked down at my pants, picking at the leggings Julian had gotten me.

"Ah. You raise an excellent point. But what about Marie? Aren't you two friends?"

"No. We, uh, we had a falling out around the same time as the two of us."

"Oh?"

I dug my fingers into my leg. *If you want to be friends, Quinn, you need to start off fresh.*

"We had a bet, and I lost, and I told her I was sick of the petty games."

"A bet?"

I swallowed, took a deep breath and then made eye contact with him. His brows were knit.

"The morning before our first date, Marie and Emerald bet that I couldn't last four months in a relationship. I bet six. And well, you ended things six days shy of four months."

"You were counting?" His voice was soft, his feet digging into the mulch to stop the swing.

"Mainly, I counted how many months we were together, kind of having my own celebration for each month mark. It wasn't until things ended that I remembered the bet was, in fact, still on."

Julian was silent for a moment. "James and Tyler had a bet going on between themselves for how long it'd take for you, and I quote, *beg* me for sex. But I just ignored their stupid bet."

"To beg you?" I leaned my head back, rubbing my face. "God, people really have an awful opinion of me, don't they?"

"Not everyone. I think you're pretty great."

"If that's the case, may I ask you a question? That you must be honest about?" I looked over at him. The tension in his body didn't go unnoticed.

"That's scary. What?"

Looking ahead of me, I narrowed in on the mulch surrounding the jungle gym. There was no way he'd have an answer for me, but I had to let my frustrations out on someone.

"Why can't a girl love sex and a guy not love it? Did you know Adrian was trying to get people to sleep with me at the party? Claiming it'd be fine, and I'd love it, all because I'm fucking Quinn Kennedy? Why am I not allowed to sleep with whom I want, when I want?" My tone grew flat as I spoke. It felt like I had exhausted this concern in my head so many times over the past few years.

All I wanted was space and freedom to not be judged for who I chose to be.

"Society has made women out to be these docile creatures who can't express their needs. Meanwhile, men are taught that our masculinity is based on how much sex we have."

"Well, I think it's fucking bullshit." My tone came out harsher than intended, but I didn't have the energy to soften my words.

"I second that."

I stopped my swing and looked over at him. He's agreeing with me? A guy who has had James and Tyler as his friends for years, is agreeing that the world is fucked up?

A hint of a smile on his face relaxed my body slightly, and I exhaled, looking back out at the jungle gym.

"I like sex, I do, but god has it made my life a living hell."

"We should all be free to enjoy what we want without any shame."

I nodded. I wanted to lean my head on his shoulder or take his hand in mine and feel that comfort of his. It was hard knowing we could so easily fall back into being friends and having these honest conversations—knowing we were on the same wavelength for so many things—yet knowing we weren't together.

It only had me questioning even more, what the hell happened between us?

JULIAN

It felt like I hadn't slept all weekend. Or all week for that matter. Between the night with Quinn and my obsessive need to find the asexual community online, I sort of put sleep on the back burner. At school, life seemed to go on normally. Which, to be honest, felt incredibly weird. I thought it'd bring me some comfort to have the normal routine of my life to keep me sane. But I felt off. Like I was supposed to be seen differently somehow now.

I guess that's the strange thing about coming out. You don't just come out once. You have to come out again and again. The initial coming out doesn't suddenly let the whole world know. But I also didn't feel the need to come out. Sure, I wanted to tell Quinn eventually. But Ian and Liza knowing was enough for me for now. Besides, on the outside, I looked the same and acted the same. It wasn't the same as being gay, where it would become obvious when someone was involved with someone of their same gender. Hell, it really only affected my sex life. So what did it even matter? At the end of the day, it was my business and mine alone. I didn't owe coming out to anyone.

Emerald never questioned why I asked for the twins' address.

Other than our phone call, I hadn't spoken to him since the night Adrian beat me up. I did, however, overhear him talking to the twins in the hallway asking about the party. I stood with my back to them, eavesdropping. But I never came up. Nor did Quinn. Not that I expected us to. I did feel like I crashed the party when I got there, and no one knew who the hell I was or why I was asking profusely for Quinn. But whatever. It's over. No sense in overthinking it.

Trying to explain to Ian and Liza why I left the movies so suddenly was a challenge. They exchanged a confused look when I told them Quinn was drunk and desperate for a ride home. Though, they didn't ask me why it had to be me to pick her up or why it was so urgent to ditch them for her. I really didn't know what I'd say if they did question me on it.

"Hey," I said, entering Quinn's room Thursday evening. "Ready to end our friendship over a game of Monopoly?" I held up the game box, shaking it for emphasis.

"I'm the champion in this household," she challenged, looking up from her textbook. "You're later than I expected." She closed her book, tossing it on the ground.

"I would have been here sooner, but I, uh, go to the LGBT+ group with Ian and Liza on Thursdays now."

"You go even though you're not gay?" She furrowed her brows. "How long have you been going?"

"Um, today was only my second time going." I sat on her floor, opening up the Monopoly box.

I knew this conversation would come. I braced myself for it. It's not that I didn't want to talk to Quinn about it. Hell, I had been wanting to tell her since last Thursday. But telling her meant telling her everything else too. Namely that I'm human garbage.

"Why?" She shuffled, moving to the edge of the bed, but she didn't join me on the floor. "Sorry, I mean, what do you do there?"

"Um, Ian runs it, so he often does a discussion on different topics. Then we basically just play games and hang out."

She nodded and pulled her comforter up over her lap.

"I know it's not my business, but I'm glad you hang out with him more. Something happened between you, James, and Tyler, right?"

"You could say that." I focused on dividing up the Monopoly money, unable to meet her eyes. I sighed, finally looking up at her. "James got pissed that I wasn't 'being a real friend' to them." I made the air quotes while I rolled my eyes. The whole thing with James was just dumb. "He basically abandoned me as a friend because I care about you and didn't use you for sex."

She leaned back against her headboard, bringing her blanket to her chin, but she didn't respond.

"So, are we going to play or what?" I motioned to the game board that I finally finished setting up.

She shook her head. "I'm confused. Why do you go to the group? If Ian has always been running them, why the sudden interest?"

"Um. Uh," I stumbled on my words as my body began to shake.

I didn't expect to be so nervous about this. I had imagined this conversation in my head over and over again. I thought up different ways it could go and how Quinn would react differently depending what I said.

"Uh ... well." I fiddled with my hands.

Where did I start? Did I just flat out say it? That I'm asexual? But could I really be sure ... or did I tell her about Tyler? Or at least that I thought I was gay at first?

I sucked in a breath. "I think. I think I'm asexual." I tried to hold it back, but a giggle escaped from my mouth. "Sorry. I'm sorry. I just haven't said that out loud before."

"Asexual?" Quinn said slowly. "I'm sorry, but I don't understand."

I shrugged. "Basically, put simply, I'm not sexually attracted to anyone."

"Okay, um. Can you come here and explain further? I don't want to talk about this above you."

I got up and sat beside her on the bed. I told her about the discussion Ian had about asexuality. I told her Claire's story, being mindful to keep Claire's anonymity. I even told her about all the things I learned while perusing the internet. All the while, she sat there listening, nodding occasionally, and asking questions when they came up.

"You told me I never pressured you, but if you didn't like it or even think about it, were you lying to make me feel better?"

"I wanted to want it for you. I wanted to make you happy."

"But you weren't happy, right?"

"I don't know if I would say I was unhappy." I pressed my lips tightly together, trying to decide on my wording. "I more felt confused. Like something was wrong with me. That if I kept trying, I would get over it and the 'problem' would miraculously go away."

"I'm sorry," she whispered. "I wish I would have known. I had no idea someone could feel like that."

"I'm sorry I didn't tell you."

"Does this ... please don't hate me, but," she sighed, "does this have anything to do with us breaking up?"

"I don't hate you," I whispered. "But you might hate me."

She looked directly at me, raising her brow. "How could I possibly hate you? I never even hated you when you were a jackass about the whole thing." There was a hint of a smile on her lips, but it didn't last.

My lip twitched. "I'm sorry ... I'm sorry about everything." I sighed. "After we had sex, and I still wasn't into it, I only got more and more confused. At first, I thought maybe I was gay." I fell silent, knowing the next thing I was about to say could ruin everything. It could make Quinn hate me. It could make her walk out of my life forever. "I ... I got drunk one night ... and uh ... I slept with Tyler."

Quinn jumped out of her bed and began pacing in circles around the monopoly pieces.

"The day of our fight. That's why I couldn't find you." She stopped walking, turning toward me. "Because you were cheating on me?"

I didn't get the chance to stop it. The tears just started spilling out against my will.

"I'm sorry," I choked out between sobs. She started pacing again. "I'm so sorry. I—I have no excuse. I shouldn't have done it." I sniffed, trying to lessen my tears but they wouldn't stop coming. "The first thing I did afterward was to come here ... I knew after that night I wasn't gay, but I still didn't understand myself. I didn't know what was wrong with me." My tears grew louder, my words hardly coherent.

Quinn stopped pacing and sat down across the room, pulling her knees up to her.

"I couldn't bring you down with me. I loved you too much. But I couldn't love you that way. I couldn't give you what you needed. I don't deserve you."

"What do you think I need? Who are you to judge that?"

"You told me yourself that you needed sex ..." I mumbled, staring at my lap, tears still rolling off my cheeks. Quinn didn't say anything.

We sat there in silence as my tears finally subsided. I rubbed the back of my hand against my damp cheeks.

"Julian?" she whispered.

"Yeah?"

"When were you going to tell me? Would you have even?"

"I wanted to. I had planned to." I let my body sink into her pillows. "I just didn't know how to bring it up."

I heard her walk across the room. She sat on the edge of the bed and looked down at me.

"I don't hate you." She sighed. "Am I disappointed? Yes. Was I worried sick that day when I couldn't get ahold of you? Yes. But I also can't fathom what you were, and I guess, still are, going through. I'm just sorry I was such an ass to you. I imagine I only made your confusion worse."

I sat up. "You? I'm the one who should be sorry. I fucked up. I fucked everything up."

"Hey," she placed her hand on my arm, "stop. We both fucked up, okay? But guess what, here we are, talking it through. I don't think that means you fucked *everything* up."

I let my head fall onto her shoulder, desperate for her comfort. Her chin rested on my hair. "Thank you," I whispered.

QUINN

As soon as Julian left last Thursday, I consumed my night with researching the internet. I needed to learn everything I possibly could about asexuality. I lost myself in a vortex of YouTube videos of people coming out and Reddit threads. I even found people similar to me who had relationships with people who identified as asexual. Reading their concerns just placed me back in my memories of all the times I probably made Julian feel awful.

I know I didn't understand, and I couldn't have possibly understood. But to get so mad at someone who couldn't get hard? What does that say about me?

I was shitty at being a girlfriend, that's for sure.

But learning the truth, researching more, hanging out with Julian over the weekend and discussing it further, and even not discussing it at all, had my heart begging for things to be okay with us.

I never stopped loving him, so how could I possibly stop myself now when Julian was finally handing me all the pieces? Before, even without knowing, I was only loving a part of him.

I wouldn't press it though. I couldn't. Even though I didn't want to believe it, I knew that I needed to be patient.

We were still figuring out what the hell friends with each other meant. If I couldn't keep friendships in general, how was I supposed to have a boyfriend?

ALL WEEK, I contemplated going to the LGBT+ meeting after school. Technically allies were invited too, and, well, I was one, right?

I kept talking myself out of it. One, I feared Julian really wouldn't want me there; he'd still want his own space, but he wouldn't want to tell me no. Two, well, there was Liza, and I still hadn't spoken to her. Nor had I asked Julian about his newfound friendship with her. Three, was it necessary?

I mean, I thought I had a pretty decent understanding of what asexual meant between the internet and Julian, and while I still couldn't fathom not having sexual attraction, I did try.

By the end of the day on Thursday, instead of giving my brain any more time to debate, I beelined it to the drama room.

"Quinn!" My scattered brain halted for a moment. But just as quickly as it stopped, my brain went into overdrive, quickening my steps. "Quinn, please stop!"

A few heads turned, but I couldn't be distracted. I needed to get to the group. And I most definitely didn't need to be distracted by *him*.

I could hear his panting before his hand gripped my arm, pulling me backward.

"Let go of me," I grunted, making eye contact with Adrian's pathetic eyes.

"Please, can we talk?" His hand left my arm, and he retreated a few steps, giving me space.

"No, and I hope we never do again."

"I'm sorry, Quinn. I'm really sorry."

I ran down the hallway, ignoring his words and the attention he was calling to us. I didn't stop until I made it through the doorway of the drama room.

"Quinn?" I froze. Lifting my eyes to meet hers across the room, I saw her head was tilted, and the girl next to her looked over confused.

I pathetically lifted my hand in a greeting. All words were lost as my mouth grew dry.

"What are you doing here?"

"Liza," I heard the girl next to her say, placing her hand on her arm. "This is a safe space. Let her be."

Liza took a breath before giving me a slight nod. I forced myself to cross the room. I couldn't let Liza ruin this for me. This wasn't about what happened between the two of us; this was about supporting Julian.

I saw her swallow and shift uncomfortably before she patted the metal folding chair next to her.

"Here, sit. Are you, uh, here for Julian?" I nodded and slowly sat down. "Does he know?" I shook my head, glancing around the room.

It looked exactly the same as it had a couple weeks ago when I first saw Julian leave here. It didn't seem possible that just a short time ago I was hiding in a classroom hoping Julian didn't see me and thinking he was dating Ian, to now, sitting here, being friends with Julian again.

Maybe this was all a mistake. Were we forcing something too fast? Should we even be doing this?

"Quinn," I jumped at her words, "it'll mean a lot to him that you're here."

"I hope." I let out a breath with the first words I spoke.

Relax, Quinn. Your friendship with Julian is real.

I looked over at Liza; she was about ready to start talking to the other girl again.

"I'm sorry," I blurted. Both of them looked at me, but Liza's posture straightened. "I know this isn't the time and place, and there's nothing I can say to make it better. But I'm sorry. About *everything*. I just, I want you to know that I'm changing and that doesn't excuse me being a bitch, but I do hope we can work things out."

She remained silent as the empty chairs started to fill. I couldn't look anywhere else but her direction.

"Claire," she spoke, and the girl beside her looked over at me, "this is Quinn. Quinn, this is Claire Hannon."

We exchanged hellos but then fell silent as that was all Liza offered.

The bell rang, signaling the start of the after-school period. Ian and Julian walked in last, laughing about something. Ian placed some papers over on a table in the front of the room. Julian was halfway through the middle of the circle before he stopped in his steps.

"Quinn?" It was only then that I realized someone else was sitting next to me. I had taken his seat next to Liza.

"Hi?" I gave him an awkward smile.

Way to fucking go, Quinn. That's real confident and supportive.

Ian looked from me to Julian and back again with a smile. "I'm glad you could join us today, Quinn," he said, sounding professional. No wonder he was the one who organized these meetings.

Julian just stood there—the biggest smile plastered on his face.

"Wow," he finally said, shaking his head, still smiling before he sat down in a seat across from me.

Within seconds, Ian took to the middle of the circle and began talking about organizing a queer craft show at the end of the school year. People amongst the group raised their hand to sign up and spoke about what art they would contribute. Claire said she was going to have a booth of LGBT+ merchandise—pins, bags, and shirts that had witty puns about sexuality on them. Even Liza raised her hand, offering to bake rainbow-colored cupcakes for the event. Julian never raised his hand. The whole meeting, he sat back in his chair, arms crossed, holding his chin smiling. And he was flat out staring at me.

"Okay, I think that's all for today. Next week we'll talk about dates and locations for the event," Ian said, backing away from the group and going up to Liza and Claire to talk. The moment Ian was out of the circle, Julian got up and came over to me.

"Fancy seeing you here." He smiled.

"Well, you know," I shrugged, "I happened to be in the neighborhood."

Julian laughed. "Seriously though, what are you doing here?"

"Well, I figured if I came, I might be able to learn and understand you a little better. But I hope I didn't intrude?" I looked down at my lap, only seeing him through my lashes.

"Oh." He blushed, turning his head to try and hide it. "You came here for me? Uh—no, no you didn't intrude." His smile returned. "I'm just surprised is all."

I smiled, standing up in front of him. "I honestly didn't know I was coming here until well, I ended up here. Sorry I didn't tell you."

"So you just stumbled in here with no idea where you were? Like the wardrobe to Narnia or something?" he teased.

I playfully pushed his shoulder and laughed. "No, you nerd. I had been debating it all day but was afraid you may not want me here. I didn't want to make it seem like I was forcing myself back into your life. But after all the research I've been doing, I wanted to kind of learn on a more personal level." I crossed my arms, suddenly feeling awkward.

"Ah. So how about Professor Quinn tells me what she has discovered through her research over some milkshakes?"

I nodded, letting out a light laugh. "Yeah, yeah that sounds perfect."

THE MOMENT we got into his car Julian asked, "So, tell me. What is this *research* you have done?"

"Oh you know, watching coming out videos on YouTube, finding, learning, and confusing myself more on Reddit."

"Ah, the rabbit hole that is Reddit. Yes, I've been there. I love reading those threads, though. It makes me feel less alone, you know?" Julian said as he pulled out of the student parking lot.

"I can imagine so. I found myself reading a lot of threads by people similar to me who had relationships with asexuals. The honesty and support of it all were amazing."

"The only thing I've seen like that is people saying the only way they can make their relationship work with an asexual is to have an open relationship. So they have meaningless sex with random people to satisfy their sex drive. But that whole concept makes me so uncomfortable. Is it selfish of me to want someone committed to me even if I can't offer them that aspect of the relationship?" Julian fell silent for a moment, his eyes on the road. "Sorry, I rambled there. Don't mind me. I'm just worried I'll never find love."

I waited for him to find a parking space as we pulled up to the cafe. It broke my heart that he was even thinking that in order to have a relationship with someone, he may have to sacrifice that commitment. No one should ever have to feel like they aren't worthy of someone's full attention.

Once the car was in park, I placed my hand on his arm, giving it a squeeze.

"Julian, it's never selfish for you to want someone who is committed to you. You shouldn't ever have to settle for anything less than you deserve. And if someone makes you feel like that, then they aren't worth your time."

"Wow. Okay, you sound like one of those inspirational posters." He smiled before getting out of the car. But as his head turned, I could see his smile falter.

I climbed out of the car and made my way over to him. He juggled his keys in his hands. As he was about to walk toward the door, I stood in front of him, stopping him in place. Before he had a chance to question me, I wrapped my arms around him.

He didn't reciprocate, so I pulled away quickly.

"Uh Qui—" he started.

"I'm sorry," I shook my head, letting out an awkward laugh, "I uh, I just, I want you to know that I'm sorry your first time had to be with me. I really don't like the idea of you thinking the only relationship you can have is one where you let your partner sleep with other people. And with your only experience being me ... well, I get how that can make it feel even more true. And well," I shuffled on my feet, looking down at the pavement, "that's really shitty."

Julian looked down at me, straight-faced. What was going through his head?

"Thanks, I guess?"

Fuck, Quinn. Get your thoughts together.

"Let's go inside," he said.

The two of us walked into the cafe, ordered our usual and sat in the booth we had deemed ours, all like the past month and a half never happened.

What were we even doing? I liked being back in his life, but these small moments, which seemed almost insignificant at the time, kept reminding me of how good it once was.

"Julian." I looked across the table at him. He had been examining the advertisement for their newest milkshake.

"Yeah?" His eyes shifted to me.

"I know we've avoided talking about the party, but can I tell you why I called you? Or well, subconsciously did, at least?

"Sure."

"First, please don't judge me, okay?"

"No promises," he teased.

I could feel my face warm as the pit of nerves erupted in my stomach. This was a stupid idea.

"Well, okay. Uh. Hmm," I started.

Our milkshakes were delivered at that moment, giving me a chance to take a few sips before I continued.

"Let's just say, I had fun at the party."

"So you had sex." He smirked. "Don't worry, Drunk Quinn enlightened me on the way home how good Garrett and *both* twins were."

My mouth dropped open. *Holy fucking shit. Fuck you, Drunk Quinn.*

"But then you started crying. I couldn't make out what you were saying, though. Something about how things were different now." Julian shook his head. "I don't know. I didn't really understand." He paused. "You're going to catch flies in your mouth if you keep it open like that." He laughed, and I snapped my jaw shut.

"Do you know how many times I talked myself out of having this conversation with you? And you fucking already knew?" I placed my elbows on the table as my head dropped into my palms. "Jesus, Julian."

He shrugged with a laugh.

"Well," I lifted my head slightly, dragging my hands across

my face, "that didn't start out as well as I hoped. I bet that only proved to you that someone like me could never be with someone like you." He didn't say anything, his eyes focused on the window.

"But I don't believe that. I don't think it's true. The moral of this awkward and embarrassing story is, I felt really empty afterward. Yes, I still enjoyed it while it was happening, and I did want it, but it wasn't you."

He raised his eyebrows. "What do you mean?"

"I mean, there was so much more to us than just sex. And I didn't know it at the time. I was always against relationships. I didn't understand people tying themselves down in high school. I like sex, so why wouldn't I just do something casual if I could? But then I got to know you, and despite everything, you can't deny that we get along really well." I took a moment to collect my thoughts, taking a few sips of my milkshake.

"Yes, sex was on my mind often, but I was happy pleasuring myself. It wasn't until we had sex that things started to get twisted and awkward and my mind went crazy. Sex never used to change things for me. It was always casual, no feelings at all. But with you, it changed everything. It was different this time around. Because I was in love with you. Sex had a different meaning. And I wasn't used to that. And because I didn't know what was going on in your life, I was taking it all personally. I convinced myself that your lack of interest in bed was in direct relation to me."

"If it's any consolation, I forgive you."

I gave him a small smile and nodded.

"But while I was at the party, in that room, all I could think about was how I wanted what we had. Even despite the hiccups, each time we were intimate, it meant a hell of a lot more than any other person." I rubbed my eyes and let out a sigh.

"Hey, Quinn ..."

"Yeah?"

"I'm sorry. I'm sorry for not at least trying to talk to you about what was going on in my life. Instead, I went behind your back. Cheated on you. Fucked up my friendships. And temporarily made my life a living hell. I know I told you that already. But—I can't seem to forgive myself for the way I treated you."

"Julian?" I reached out for his hand and gave it a squeeze. "I forgive you."

JULIAN

IT WAS THE LAST DAY OF SPRING BREAK. WE SAT ON HER bedroom floor together. Quinn against her bed—me against the wall across from her in the midst of an intense game of Battleship. Intense for me anyway. I only had one ship left afloat, but I had yet to sink any of hers.

"A7," I said.

"Nope."

"Okay, how? You have to be cheating."

She laughed. "Maybe you just suck?"

"Wow. Ouch."

"All is fair in love and war." She smiled. "Hmm, let's see. I believe I'll hit your boat at G5?" She winked.

"Fuck you. Hit."

She giggled.

We continued to play, and each time it was her turn, she hit my boat.

"I win!" she screamed, getting up and doing a happy dance.

"Cheater!"

She stuck her tongue out, playfully giving me the finger as she laughed. I rolled my eyes but couldn't keep the amusement off my face. When she sat back down, her face suddenly grew serious. Just a goddamn flip of the switch.

"Can I ask you a question?" she asked, and I nodded.

"Are you afraid of being in a relationship?"

I went silent. It's not that I didn't want to be in a relationship. The problem was I *did* want one. But I just wanted someone I could kiss and cuddle without the fear of things leading to sex. I didn't think a relationship like that existed. Not only that, but there was this fear of getting involved with someone. Actually really liking them and then having to come out to them, and them running away.

"Yeah, duh. We already had this conversation. Who wants to date someone who doesn't want sex?"

"Julian, look at me."

I looked up, meeting her eyes.

"You're really amazing, okay? Not everyone thinks sex needs to be a major part of a relationship."

"You're starting to sound like Ian." I smiled.

"I sound like him because we are speaking the truth. I imagine there are others like me, who would realize love doesn't equal sex. I mean, it's not like you're repulsed by sex, right?"

"I just don't know how to find a compromise, I guess, when it comes to sex. Do I do it for them or not do it for me?"

That was the whole reason we broke up, right? Sex. It was an issue in our relationship. Despite her telling me she didn't want to pressure me, there was still a pressure to do it. To please my partner and make her happy.

"I didn't understand, Julian. I didn't know there were people who didn't experience sexual attraction. All I knew was my experience. And to be fair, I was really selfish for a long time. Even Marie mentioned to me once that not everyone thinks about sex the way I do, and that I should try and make you more comfortable." She sighed, crossing her legs and moving away from the game. "But now? I don't know what it would look like. But I do feel like I'd be able to respect others more."

"Okay. Well, I'm glad you at least grew from this."

I almost made that last part a question. Because what the hell was I supposed to say? *Yay, our failed relationship helped you grow as a person, but I still feel shitty and alone?* Sure, she learned that not everyone loves sex as much as she does. But what about me? Was there really a love out there where sex wasn't an obligation? Where I could be happy with someone without sex being a big part of the relationship? Everyone seemed to want sex. And from my knowledge, asexuals were a rare breed of sexuality, making meeting one, let alone forming a relationship with one, a very unlikely scenario.

"I'm sorry." She shook her head, running her hands through her curls. "This is about you. I just want you to be happy, Julian. But you never answered the question; you're not repulsed by sex, right? So, is there any way for a decent compromise? Did you find any happiness in it?"

I tapped my fingers against the sides of the Battleship board. "I'm not repulsed by sex. I just don't ever think about it." I shrugged. "Sex doesn't gross me out or anything, but I'd rather not do it. It's kind of like a chore. Boring even. I don't know about your last question."

"Well, from what I've learned, which I'm sure you've seen, it seems like people can be turned on by different things. Not necessarily sexual attraction, but by having an emotional connection or seeing their partner in a certain way."

I leaned forward. "What you're describing is demisexual." I smiled.

I had learned a lot about what different sexualities and identities were from Ian at the meetings and outside them. Sure, I didn't know everything, but I definitely felt more knowledgeable now.

"But, yeah, I get what you're saying. I've also read that it helps asexuals to focus on the actual stimulation of sex rather than the person or what is happening, if that makes sense? Which, I mean, I haven't had the opportunity to really try that out, other than with masturbation."

"And does it work with masturbation? Like do you actually find joy or relief or whatnot? Or is it a waste of time?"

"Wow. I never thought I'd have a conversation with a girl about my masturbating habits." I looked at her straight-faced while making the joke. "But, yeah. Relief is a good word to use."

"Do you ever feel the need to masturbate? Or is it like, I'm bored, let me do this?" She covered her face while she laughed. "Sorry if this is weird."

"It's very fucking weird." I laughed. "Uh, no. It kind of just helps me sleep or relieve stress."

"Well, then, there you go! You aren't so different from me."

My breath caught in my throat. *What?* She feels the same way when it comes to masturbation? I could hear my heart in my ears. *Whoa. Okay, so I'm not as abnormal as I thought.*

"Stress relief masturbation is the best. But no one ever has these conversations. Honestly, I do it more for that than anything else."

"Wow." I smiled. "Wait. Girls masturbate? Since when?" I had never even thought about that before. Not that I really thought about sex, period, but the media made me believe masturbating was something only guys did.

"Since forever! Have you never heard of the 'hysteria' period? We've been masturbating for as long as humans have been around. It's just society has shamed women for it."

"Huh. You learn something new every day."

"That you do, Julian. But focus," she said, furrowing her brows before letting out a laugh. "Masturbating is great. The fact that you do it has to mean something, right?"

"I think it means that I sometimes touch myself. But sure," I teased.

She groaned, rolling her eyes.

"Well, okay. Wait. Whenever I tried to have sex with you, you'd take to just pleasuring me. Does that make you uncomfortable?"

"No. It was easier to pleasure you than have things done to me. Having things done to me requires a lot of focus on my end." I laughed. "Seriously, though, I would never have this conversation with anyone else."

"I'm one of a kind, Julian." She winked. "And I hate to break it to you, but I'm not going anywhere."

"That's a bummer." I smiled.

She leaned over and pushed me in the shoulder. "You're a jerk. But seriously, did you find any pleasure in doing things for me, or was it just to keep me from having sex with you?"

"I guess seeing you enjoy it made me happy. So yeah, I'd say I liked it."

"Then, surely that's a decent compromise?"

"But that isn't actual sex. Would there really be someone who'd be okay with only fooling around the majority of the time? And even then, I'd hope we could have time together where there isn't any sex involved at all."

I didn't know why I was telling her all this. It didn't make any sort of difference. Finding love seemed hard for the normal heterosexual male, but to throw asexuality into this mix? Yeah, good luck. But Quinn seemed so positive there was someone out there for me. It gave me a small ping of hope. A flicker of a candle flame that I wasn't about to let burn out.

She looked down for a few moments. I didn't know what was running through her mind, but when she lifted her head, she had a small smile on her face. Even slightly sad?

"Any girl who is lucky enough to be loved by you would be

okay with whatever compromise made you happiest." She glanced down again before looking back up. "What you have to offer, Julian, is so much more than just sex. Any girl would be a fool to walk away from that."

"Thank you," I whispered.

Where was this coming from? The girl sitting in front of me, she wasn't the same Quinn who sat across from me in the spin the bottle game at Emerald's. Before, everything had been about sex. Not just with Quinn, but even with my friends. Except now ... that wasn't the case at all.

I had thought I was falling for her. I could have sworn I was in love with her. This, though, this friendship we had was something entirely new. It was more than what our relationship ever was. Stronger. This ... I met her eyes. She was smiling at me, a smile I never saw when we were dating. No, I was wrong before. I wasn't falling in love with her. I was falling in love with this idea of her I created. However, the Quinn sitting in front of me now was someone new. And fuck, I was in love with her.

EPILOGUE

Julian

"I'm going to propose to Quinn."

"Wait, what?" Ian asked as we sat down for lunch in the cafeteria that May.

I laughed. "To prom, I mean."

"Why don't you guys just date already?" Ian rolled his eyes.

I shrugged. It hadn't really come up. And I wasn't sure how to exactly bring it up. We were such good friends now that I couldn't even tell if she had lingering feelings for me like I did for her. Either way, I wanted to take her to prom, even if it ended up just being as friends.

Besides, there was the whole asexuality thing. I mean, Quinn really seemed to accept it, so I couldn't see it being a problem. But I still had that fear it might be. I still go to the LGBT+ group, and I've even shared my story with the group. At the end of the day, it's just another part of me. And I'm more than happy with it.

It was the last week we could buy tickets for our junior prom. It was now or never.

"So how do you plan to ask her?" Ian asked, taking a bite of his sandwich.

"I saw this idea on Pinterest." Ian raised a brow. "Yes, I Pinterested promposal ideas. I'm not that creative. And I saw one with candy and chocolate, and I thought perfect! Quinn loves eating after all. So I filled a box of her favorite kinds. Then on the box, I'm going to write a little poem thing."

I had gone and bought all the chocolate and candy last night, decorated the box, and stashed it in my locker this morning. The plan was to bring them with me to the LGBT+ group. Quinn said she was coming this week, so I thought it'd be the perfect unexpected moment.

"I can't tell if that's adorable or dorky."

"Probably both." I smiled.

Quinn

I HAD BEEN PLANNING this moment for a few weeks. There was no doubt in my mind that I wanted to go to junior prom with Julian. We weren't dating, but we spoke of it every once in a while. I wanted to be able to call him my boyfriend again. But that meant everything had to be perfect.

So naturally, I recruited a few members from the LGBT+ group with Liza's help. I had gone to two LGBT+ meetings so far. It was Julian's thing to do for himself, and I never wanted to encroach on that, but it was nice to also be able to share that vulnerable side with him too.

"Are you nervous?" Liza asked, putting up the last of the posters.

"A little, but I'm pretty sure he'll love this." I smiled.

I glanced around the drama room. Today was Thursday, so there was supposed to be an LGBT+ group meeting happening today—and there might still be, but I wanted to surprise Julian before the meeting. I knew he'd arrive here naturally, and it would be best to catch him off-guard instead of asking him to meet me someplace strange. A few members and I came during lunch to decorate the drama room, and now we were just putting up finishing touches.

There were posters hanging on the walls with asexual puns like "My sexual preference is nope," "Netflix and actually chilling," "Asexuals don't fuck around," and "Only an actual milkshake can bring me to the yard." We had a massive asexual flag broadcasting their colors: black, gray, white, and purple, hanging on the wall right behind where I was to stand. We had blown up balloons in those colors as well. Everyone helping me was also either dressed in a single color of the flag or had gray and purple shirts on. For myself, I had found an asexual pun shirt that felt like an ally could actually wear. But it was also a part of my skit.

I made last minute finishing touches to my poster board with a majority of what I wanted to say on it. Liza had helped me all week to make it look presentable. Art was not my forte.

I got the warning that Ian and Julian were walking down the hall. I picked up my poster, fixed my shirt, and got into position. The lights dimmed.

Julian and Quinn

"A long time ago in a galaxy far,
far away, she found the one she
was looking for," Liza spoke.

"What is going on?"
I whispered to Ian as
we stood in the doorway
to the drama room, my
box of candy in hand.
Ian shrugged.

The lights brightened.
Liza stood in front of
Quinn. "Yoda one for her."
She smiled, stepping away.

I stood there grinning,
holding my poster up,
watching as Julian's
smile grew.

I don't fucking believe
it. I looked over to Ian,
who looked like he
was smiling just as
much as I was.

"I don't give a fuck

That you don't like
to fuck. So embrace
the ace, and let's
close this space.
So, whattaya say?
Me + You at prom?"

I burst out into a
fit of laughter.
"Oh my god. Oh
my god. I love it."
I couldn't stop the
laughter from
erupting out of
me. "Okay. Yes.
Yes, I will. But first
I have something
for you."

I opened the box
of candy. "Roses
are red. Candy
is sweet. It has
been said that I'm
a real treat. So
come with
me to prom?"

*Holy shit. Holy
fucking shit. He
didn't just do
that, did he?*

My cheeks warmed
as I held my laughter
in for just a few more
moments. I had one
last surprise before
I could respond. I
dropped my poster to
reveal the caption on
my shirt: "Aced it."

I handed the box of
candy to Ian, my
cheeks hurting,
my eyes glued
on Quinn.

Julian strode across
the room, meeting
Quinn in the middle.
Their lips collided.

RESOURCES

Websites:
https://www.reddit.com/r/Asexual/
https://www.tumblr.com
http://www.whatisasexuality.com

Michael Paramo:
https://twitter.com/AsexualJournal
https://www.asexuality.org/

Books We Also Love:

Autoboyography by Christina Lauren
Holding Up The Universe by Jennifer Niven
More Happy Than Not by Adam Silvera
Running with Lions by Julian Winters
Simon vs. the Homosapiens Agenda by Becky Albertalli
They Both Die At The End by Adam Silvera
The Princess Saves Herself In This One by Amanda Lovelace
Will Grayson, Will Grayson by John Green

ACKNOWLEDGMENTS

To our Beta readers: Ari, Cass, Christie, Paul, and Sam—you helped us make our book the best it can be. Your criticism and guidance was beyond helpful and appreciated. We needed honest and diverse readership and we are so grateful all of you delivered. Thank you!

Winter Neverland crew: Sam, Paul, J.D., and Krystle, thank you guys for being you. We started this project right in the middle of *Winter Neverland: An Anthology* edits and somehow still managed to pull everything together. Thank you guys for the constant support and the far—too—long Twitter GIF vortexes that left us all unproductive.

Tom: Thank you for introducing me (Chelsea) to the Red Bull's and having soccer become a constant fixture in my life. So much so, that Brittany and I ended up with main characters who play soccer. Thank you for answering every and all texts—even the repetitive ones about the intricacies of soccer.

Riley: Thank you for always being there to talk to me (Brittany) about the topics in our book. For passing down your knowledge on the problematic topics our book discusses. Your advice and wisdom has helped make our book stronger and shine light on how to properly approach certain subjects. Not to mention being one of my best friends who always has my back and encourages me with everything I do. I love you!

Chelsea: I cannot express the gratitude I feel for you agreeing to write this book with me. When the idea first struck me at work, you were the first person who came to mind to write this with. This wasn't a story I could tackle alone and felt in my heart it was just as much my story as it was yours. It's been a roller coaster. Our friendship grew from it and we grew as individuals. It was a book that my heart needed to write. And I couldn't have asked for a better co-writer to join me for the journey.

Brittany: I always said that I would never co-write with someone because I can be a control freak when it comes to my writing. But when you reached out with a story as important as Julian's and Quinn's, I couldn't say no. Never in a million years would I have expected a friendship like ours. The vulnerability, honesty, and support that needs to be shared is not something that everyone can have. I am beyond grateful that we were able to seamlessly work together. You're forever my brain twin. Here's to many, many more stories in the future!

LGBT+ community: You are human, you are loved, you are not abnormal. There is absolutely nothing wrong with you. You deserve to be loved and to find happiness even in the crazy messed up world we live in. Don't ever let anyone say you aren't good enough. You deserve to be your true self. We will continue to fight for you. Promise us, you'll continue to fight for you too.

Love will always conquer hate.

ABOUT THE AUTHORS

Photo credit: Mackenzie Dockery

Brittany was a lonely girl living in the middle of nowhere, some-where in Canada. One day a mutual friend of theirs, (hi Paul), retweeted an ad for Chelsea's book *Underneath the Whiskey*. Fangirling, Brittany bought a signed copy of the book and thus started a beautiful friendship.

From there the two ended up talking everyday through Twitter about everything and anything. While writing short stories for *Winter Neverland: An Anthology*, Brittany approached Chelsea to write *Simply An Enigma*. A year after first encountering online, the two were finally able to meet in person when Brittany visited Chelsea in New York—Chelsea's home state—even though she's trying her hardest to become a Canadian citizen.

After *Simply An Enigma*, the two plan to tackle future projects together while both still maintaining solo careers.

Follow on social media:

Joint Twitter: @evansandlauren

Brittany:
Instagram and Twitter: @imbrittanyevans
Youtube: brittanyyyye

Chelsea:
Instagram: @chelsealauren92
Twitter: @chelslauren92

Represent Publishing
Instagram: @representpublishing
Twitter: @representpub